FROZEN SUN

SUN

Stan Jones

SOHO CRIME

Copyright © 2007 by Stanley E. Jones

Published by
Soho Press, Inc.
853 Broadway
New York, NY 10003

Library of Congress Cataloging-in-Publication Data is available.

ISBN 978-1-64129-006-7
eISBN 978-1-56947-839-4

Interior design by Janine Agro, Soho Press, Inc.

Printed in the United States of America

10 9 8 7 6 5 4 3 2 1

This book is dedicated to my father, Rufus E. Jones

One day, as our ship rounded the top of the great circle, I noticed a string of strange bare mountains rising out of the sea along the northern horizon. They resembled heaps of smoking slag; the sun, striking their sides, gave them a greenish cast like verdigris on copper. I asked a fellow passenger what they were. "Illusions," I thought he said, but now I realize he said they were the Aleutians.

—**Corey Ford**, *Where the Sea Breaks Its Back*

A NOTE ON LANGUAGE

"Eskimo" is the best-known term for the Native Americans described in this book, but in their own language they call themselves Inupiat, meaning the People. "Eskimo," a term brought into Alaska by white men, is what certain Indian tribes in eastern Canada called their neighbors to the north; it probably meant "eaters of raw flesh."

Nonetheless "Eskimo" and "Inupiat" are used more or less interchangeably in northwest Alaska today, at least when English is spoken, and that is the usage followed in this book.

The Inupiat call their language Inupiaq. A few words in it—those commonly mixed with English in Northwest Alaska—appear in the book. They are listed below, along with pronunciations and meanings. As the spellings vary among Inupiaq-English dictionaries, I have used spellings that seemed to me most likely to induce the proper pronunciation by non-Inupiaq readers.

NORTHWEST ALASKA GLOSSARY

aaka **(AH-kuh):** mother

aana **(AH-nuh):** grandmother; old lady

Arii! **(ah-DEE):** I hurt!

atiqluk **(AH-tee-cluck):** a woman's hooded overshirt, often of flowered fabric, with a large front pocket

Inupiaq (IN-you-pack): the Eskimo language of northern Alaska; an individual Eskimo of northern Alaska

Inupiat (IN-you-pat): more than one Inupiaq; the Eskimo people of northern Alaska

kunnichuk **(KUH-knee-chuck):** storm shed

muktuk **(MUCK-tuck):** whale skin with a thin layer of fat adhering; a great delicacy in Inupiat country

naluaqmiiyaaq **(nuh-LOCK-me-ock):** almost white; a half-breed

naluaqmiut **(nuh-LOCK-me):** more than one white person; white people

nanuq **(NA-NOOK):** polar bear

PART I
CHUKCHI

CHAPTER ONE

"Beautiful, wasn't she?"

Nathan Active studied the mural-sized photograph on the wall outside the principal's office at Chukchi High School. A girl, half Eskimo and half white, stood on a bluff overlooking the lagoon behind Chukchi on a summer day. She held a bouquet of roses and wore an evening gown, a tiara, and a sash that said "Miss North World." A small brass plate underneath read GRACE SIKINGIK PALMER.

"She was beautiful from the day she was born." Jason Palmer was in his early fifties, Active guessed. Tall, swept-back silver hair, jeans, hands pushed into the hip pockets. A good-looking face, with a slightly fox-like cast to the eyes and the bridge of the nose. "That's why I named her Grace. But I doubt she looks like that now."

Active pulled a notebook from his pocket. "How long since you've heard from her?"

"It'll be ten years this Christmas," Palmer said. "She started at the university in Anchorage the fall after this picture was made, came home for Christmas, and we never saw her again."

"She didn't call? Or write? How about her mother? Did anybody else in the family hear from her?"

"No, but my son Roy crossed her trail when he was in Anchorage for a basketball tournament three years ago this past winter. She was hanging around that bar down there. The Junction."

Active grimaced. "Whew."

"You know the Junction."

"Everybody in Anchorage knows the Junction, sir. It's a behavior sink."

"A what?"

"Behavior sink. It means . . . ah, never mind. It's social worker talk for hell on earth." He turned back to the picture. "Did Roy just hear about this or did he actually see it with his own eyes?"

Palmer nodded. "He saw her, all right. She . . . She . . ."

His voice broke and he turned away. He pulled a handkerchief from a hip pocket and blew his nose. He walked across the hall to a fountain, bent and drank, then crossed back again.

"She was coming out of the Junction and she was drunh-hunh-hunk—" Palmer pulled out the handkerchief and turned away once more, his shoulders shaking.

The misery here was too deep to touch with words. Active waited silently, studying the girl in the black-and-white mural.

The principal of Chukchi High School was right. His daughter was, or had been, a looker. A fine straight nose, high cheekbones, dark almond eyes with a slight tilt and an odd silver gleam at the corners, full lips. Long dark hair and clear dark skin aglow in the summer sun of the photograph. She had inherited some of her father's looks, especially around the eyes.

Finally the sobs stopped, and Palmer blew his nose again. His face took on an expression of stony resolve and he spoke in a monotone, like the robot voice on an answering machine.

"Roy saw her coming out of the Junction drunk. She was

with two men, Roy thought they were soldiers from their haircuts. They were holding her up between them. A black one and a white one."

Palmer paused, pressed his lips together and swallowed twice, blinking rapidly. Active wanted to say something, but sensed that a word would bring on another collapse. He nodded encouragingly.

"Roy—did I tell you Roy is my son?"

Active nodded again.

"Roy tried to get her to come with him. He said, 'Come home, Sikingik.' You know what that means, Nathan?"

"'Sun,' I think?"

"That's right, 'Sun.' She was grace and sunlight. Like a gift from God." Palmer paused and pressed his lips together again for a moment. "Anyway, Roy says 'Come home, Sikingik.' And Grace just says . . . it's hard for me to use words like this, I'm an educator. And she's my daughter. You understand?"

Active nodded.

"She says, 'Fuck you, Roy.' And the white soldier says, 'What did you call her, there, Nanook?'"

"'Sikingik,' Roy says. 'That's her Eskimo name.'"

"'She told us her name was Amazing Grace,' the black one says. 'And now she's gonna amaze us.' After that, they put her in a cab and drove off. Roy saw some Eskimos hanging around the bar, so he talked to them a little. They said she was just living on, what do they call it? Four Street?"

Active nodded. "Technically, it's the bars along Fourth Avenue. But really it just means you're homeless in Anchorage."

Now Palmer nodded. "Well, they said she was living on Four Street and . . . doing whatever she had to for drinks."

Just then a buzzer sounded in the quiet, empty hall. Classroom doors banged open all around and a flood of students surged out, mostly Inupiat but with an occasional white or Korean face mixed in. They stared curiously at their principal standing in the hallway with a trooper. Palmer took the opportunity to use his handkerchief again, and Active resumed his study of the picture of Grace Palmer.

There was a kind of angry remoteness about the eyes and the lips. Enough steel there, he would have thought, to save her from whatever it was about Four Street that sucked down so many village girls.

He shook his head and wondered how she would look today. Like Palmer had said, probably not much like the picture taken on the bluff ten years ago. He imagined the flawless skin coarsened by drink and weather. Perhaps it would be pebbled with the acne that seemed to come with life in the bars and shelters and Visqueen camps where the street people of Anchorage made their homes. He pictured a couple of teeth missing and a brush-stroke of dried blood below one nostril.

As suddenly as it had come, the tide of students ebbed and the hallway was quiet again. Active turned back to the principal. "Why did you wait so long?"

"It's hard to admit your child has rejected you." Palmer looked at the mural. "You keep hoping she'll turn up, call, something. If you talk to the authorities, it seems like you're giving up, making it official that she's gone."

Palmer cleared his throat and put the handkerchief back into his pocket. "I did try once before, though. My wife asked me to go look after Roy saw her at the Junction. You know the Bible, Nathan?"

Active shook his head. "Not much."

"Me either. But my wife does. 'My daughter, shall I not seek rest for thee, that it may be well with thee?' That's what Ida said. She told me it came from the Book of Ruth." He paused, a distant look in his eyes. "But in the end I couldn't go. I couldn't face . . . I couldn't face it."

"And now? Have you heard something?"

"No, it's my wife again. She's got liver cancer from what they call Silent Hepatitis. She had to have a lot of blood when Roy was born and I guess she got it from the transfusion. " He turned from the mural and faced Active. "Anyway, she wants to say goodbye to her daughter. I don't see much hope of finding Grace after all this time, but you know how a woman is, a mother. She wanted me to ask you to go look."

Active frowned. "Your wife knows me? I don't think we've ever met."

"All the Eskimos know you, Nathan. The Chukchi boy that got adopted out as a baby and came back as a trooper? You bet. Ida said, 'You ask that Eskimo trooper, he'll do it.'"

Active spoke as gently as he knew how. "I'm sorry to have to ask this in your time of trouble, but are you sure she's still alive? Ten years is a long time, especially on Four Street, and nobody's seen her in three years."

Palmer flinched and gazed at the mural. "I tried to talk to Ida about that but . . . well, she's a mother."

"I can file a missing person report with the city police in Anchorage." Active wondered if Palmer knew how little effort the report would generate. Homeless Natives drifted on and off the city's streets like the shadows of passing clouds. They went back to their villages for a while, they got temporary jobs out of town, they moved in with boyfriends or girlfriends. Generally, the overworked city cops took an interest only when one of them turned up beaten to death in an alley, drowned in Ship Creek, or frozen solid under a bridge. "Maybe the cops down there can visit some of the shelters, hit some of the bars, that kind of thing."

"How hard will they work it? Ida needs some kind of hope she can cling to." Palmer looked more in control of himself now. Perhaps it was because they were easing away from what he saw as the womanish stuff of emotion, getting back into the man's world of practical action, talking about what to do.

Active sighed. "They won't work it very hard, I'm afraid. Unless they have reason to think something's happened to her."

"Unless something's happened to her! My Lord, she was sleeping with soldiers and—" Palmer stopped and shook his head. "But you can't go, Nathan? Ida made me promise to ask."

"Tell your wife I'm sorry, but the troopers won't pay for travel on a missing person report like this."

Palmer turned back to the mural and studied it silently. Then he sighed. "I told her it would probably be that way. At least we tried."

"Does Ida have any other family with her?"

"We're trying to find the money to have Cowboy Decker bring her sister Aggie down from Isignaq in a few days. That'll help some, I guess."

"I can't go, but I'll see what I can do. I have a buddy on the city force down there." Active motioned at the mural behind him. "Do you have a normal-size picture of her? I'll send it down with the report."

Palmer reached into his windbreaker and pulled out a tattered photo-finisher's envelope with a blue rubber band around it.

"Ida found this around the house somewhere." Palmer handed him the envelope. "I don't know what's in there, I just couldn't look. I probably should have this mural taken off our wall here, but . . ."

Active looked at it once more. "But you can't quite give up on her."

Palmer shook his head.

"I understand."

CHAPTER TWO

Martha Active Johnson was considering Leonora Oneok's request for muskrat leave when Nathan stuck his head into her office.

"I can come back," he said.

"No, no, Sweetie." Martha shook her head. "You just wait outside a minute. Leonora and I are almost done. Ah, Leonora?"

Leonora twisted in her chair to see who Martha was talking to, then quickly turned back and nodded yes, they were almost done.

Leonora's lips were pressed primly together and her eyes, uncharacteristically, were on her hands. Was she blushing? Martha studied the girl, her newest teacher aide. Leonora, like most women in Chukchi with twenty-twenty vision, must have noticed how Nathan looked in his Alaska state trooper uniform.

As always when Martha saw her son unexpectedly like this, her heart was stirred, too, but of course in a different way. It was not just that he was so young and handsome with his buzz-cut black hair and clear brown skin. It was the wary, deep-set eyes and the boyish, vulnerable lips. They told someone who knew Nathan as well as she did that deep inside he was still the child who did not fully believe he was loved, or would ever be.

She shook off the regrets and turned her attention back to

Leonora Oneok. Leonora was from Ebrulik, a village on the Isignaq River eighty miles inland. The surrounding tundra was dotted with lakes, all teeming with muskrat. Now that spring was coming over the Arctic, the Oneok family was heading out to trap muskrat, and Leonora wanted two weeks' leave to go along.

Martha approved of girls staying in touch with their families, and of Eskimo girls keeping up the old hunting and gathering traditions. It seemed like girls who did this actually coped better with the white man's world than girls who turned their backs on the old ways and tried to be completely modern. The Chukchi Region School District saw things the same way, maintaining an official policy of honoring leave requests like Leonora's.

But Martha, as head of the teacher-aide program at Chukchi High, had to survive the remaining month until the end of school. With daylight already perpetual as the Arctic sun climbed toward its summer zenith, with the rivers inland breaking up and the sea ice in front of town starting to rot, keeping a high school full of restless adolescents in their seats would take everything the aides and teachers could do, and then some. She decided to throw a scare into Leonora.

"I need you here," she told the girl. "You know how these kids are. And you're a new employee, so you haven't built up much leave time yet."

Leonora wrinkled her nose in the Inupiat squint of negation and dismay. "*Arii!* I promised my mom. She worry about me, over here in big city like Chukchi."

Martha smiled. Chukchi had all of twenty-five hundred people, but that was still five or six times bigger than Ebrulik. She recalibrated her expression to a frown, and tried to look like she was wracking her brain for a solution.

Leonora was just a village girl. But she was smart, she spoke Inupiaq fluently, and she worked hard. With a little coaching and a few nudges in the right direction, Leonora might go off to the University of Alaska in Fairbanks or Anchorage, and come back a real teacher some day.

"How about you take one week off, then you come back for the rest of the school year?"

Leonora's face lit up in a big smile, and she raised her eyebrows in the Inupiat sign of assent. "Thank you. I'll tell my family you're good person." She rose to go.

"How's your father's boat, anyway?"

Leonora stopped with a confused look on her face. "It's good, I guess."

"It never breaks down?"

"Sometimes, maybe."

Now Leonora looked wary, probably scenting the trap. Martha closed the girl's folder and dropped it into a wire basket on her desk. "I sure hope it doesn't break down when it's time for you to come in from camp at the end of next week."

Leonora sighed. "I'll tell Dad to check it real good before we go."

Martha raised her eyebrows in assent and Leonora hurried out.

It was still more likely than not, Martha calculated, that Mr. Oneok's outboard would suddenly and inexplicably malfunction when the time came to bring Leonora back to Ebrulik to catch the plane for Chukchi and her job at the high school. But Martha decided she would manage somehow if boat troubles kept the girl in muskrat camp. She could use the unapproved week's absence to gain some kind of leverage. Maybe she would make Leonora start work early in the fall, to help get things organized for the next school year.

Martha smiled as Nathan came in and took the seat vacated by Leonora. "So nice to see you, Sweetie! How long since you came over to the house? Almost a week?"

Martha studied her son closely as he squirmed for a defense to the implied accusation. His color was good, he looked well-fed and well-rested. Martha didn't fully approve of Nathan's girlfriend, Lucy Generous, but at least she appeared to be taking good care of him.

"I've been going to the Rec Center at night," he said finally. "I put on a little weight over the winter."

"Maybe it's somebody's cooking making you fat. I could give that Lucy some of my diet recipes. Bean sprouts, yogurt, tofu, brown rice, I got a recipe for whatever you want."

Nathan grimaced, then at last came up with the smile she had been fishing for. "I think I'd rather spend a year working out than five minutes eating that stuff. Anyway, I didn't come to talk about food. Or Lucy."

She smiled back. "You mean it's official business? I didn't know you troopers would arrest a mother just for trying to do her job."

Nathan pulled a notebook from a back pocket and a pen from his shirt. "Actually, it is official business. Do you remember Grace Palmer?"

"Of course I remember her. Prettiest girl in school. Smartest one, too. Valedictorian, Miss North World, then next thing you know, she's on Four Street. So sad, ah?"

"What happened to her?"

"That Anchorage is a bad place for Eskimo girls. Boys, too. Couple times when I went to Anchorage before I met your step-father, I went on Four Street, all right, and I almost thought about staying there, it's so—anyway, that's why I always . . ." She stopped, realizing the conversation was heading for the place where she always started fighting with her son. Well, he was on duty, maybe he would let it pass. No, he had that look on his face.

"That's why you always worried about me when I was growing up down there? You should have thought about that when you adopted me out to white people."

When the troopers had posted her son to Chukchi two years earlier and they had begun having this argument, Martha would always start crying at this point, and she felt her eyes misting up now. But, from long practice, she was learning to hold back the tears and just get through this ordeal they seemed to have to repeat every few months.

"But you know how it was, Nathan. I was only fifteen when I had you. All I wanted to do was drink and party. I knew I couldn't take care of any baby." She heard the pleading in her voice and was ashamed to realize once more that if she could just convince Nathan she had done right to adopt him out to two teachers at Chukchi High, then she would be able to believe it herself. "I knew Ed and Carmen would take good care of you, even if they move to Anchorage. Didn't they?"

"Yes, but like babysitters. Not like real parents."

"That's not true. I talk to Carmen every couple weeks when you're growing up down there. She loves you very much. Ed, too, I think. And you always seem pretty happy when you're little boy and they bring you up for visit."

Nathan sat silently, thinking this over. At first he looked sulky, his eyes and lips pinched, then his face opened up in that honest way he had. "I guess I know that. I'm just saying how it felt to me when I would think about you sending me away."

"Well, I'm sorry. l did the best I could, even if it was wrong."

"I know you did, *aaka*. Up here I know it, anyway." He tapped his right temple, then dropped his hand to his heart. "Down here, I just can't seem to learn it."

She had to wait a moment before she could say anything. "Well, I'm just glad the troopers sent you up here for your first assignment, even if you didn't want to come."

She waited, hoping he would say he had changed his mind about Chukchi, about being near her again. Or at least something polite and vague enough to allow her to believe what she wanted.

But not Nathan, not with his painful honesty.

"*Aaka*, I'm still putting in papers every time there's an opening in Anchorage," he said gently. "I've told you that."

"I know, Sweetie, I know." She misted up again and this time Nathan reached for his handkerchief. She shook her head to stop him. "Don't mind me."

She opened a drawer in her desk, found a Kleenex, and dabbed her eyes. "Anyway, why you interested in Gracie Palmer?"

"Jason Palmer asked me to find her just now. He said her mother has cancer and wants to say goodbye."

"Oh, so much trouble in that family. Jeanie die huffing snowgo gas, then Gracie end up on Four Street. And now Ida is sick."

"Jeanie? Who's Jeanie?"

"That's Gracie's little sister. Couple years after Gracie go off to college, they find Jeanie slumped over the gas tank of her snowgo with her parka over her head, she's already dead."

"Jason didn't say anything about that."

Martha looked at him, marveling at how little this smart son of hers knew about people. "Maybe it's not an easy thing for a father to talk about."

"I suppose not," Nathan said with a depressed look. "We've had three huffing deaths just since I got stationed here. It's like an epidemic all over the Bush, from what I see in the trooper reports from the other villages."

Martha nodded, still pondering the bad luck of the Palmer family. "You could go to our library, see the yearbooks from when Gracie's here. She's on every other page, seem like. She's perfect girl till she get to Anchorage. That happen sometimes."

"Lots of times, I guess." Nathan shook his head and wrote something in his notebook, then put it away. "These kids, huffing, Four Street . . . Anchorage, the villages. What happens to them?"

"Nobody know, Sweetie. I'm just glad it never happen to you." She looked at Nathan, and gave a little prayer of thanks that her own bad behavior as a young girl hadn't killed both of them. "You want to come over for dinner Sunday? I'm cooking *muktuk*. Point Hope people already caught four whales this spring and one of my old students said he will send some down tomorrow."

She knew that Nathan, despite his efforts not to like anything about Chukchi, had developed a great fondness for the succulent strips of whale hide with the blubber still on, especially when it was freshly boiled. "Lucy can come, too."

"I'll ask her. She's still scared of you. You've got to stop asking about her grades at the community college."

"Well, I don't want you marrying somebody dumb."

"She's not dumb and we're not getting married. We're just . . . going out."

Martha stifled the impulse to say they were staying in a lot, from what she heard. She was finally learning to avoid fights she couldn't win, sometimes. "Ah, hah. Well, you tell her I won't talk about grades if she comes over for *muktuk*."

"I'll tell her. Goodbye, *aaka*."

"Bye, Sweetie. You call me about Sunday, ah?" She watched as he crossed the hall to the library. In a few minutes, he came out with four Chukchi High yearbooks under his arm and started down the hall.

He was overdue for a haircut, she noticed as he put on his trooper hat. She wondered if that Lucy girl had said anything to him about it.

CHAPTER THREE

Active stopped on the deck outside the school to savor the spring weather now gracing Chukchi. Blue sky, his face chilled by a breeze off the sea and simultaneously warmed by a sun that would stay above the horizon until August.

Across Beach Street and fifty yards offshore, Chukchi Bay was a sheet of light too bright for the eye, pools of blue meltwater rippling on top of the ice.

Between the ice and the shore, spring runoff from the Katonak and Isignaq rivers rushed along the narrow tongue of beach gravel and tundra where the village stood. He spotted the sleek black heads of two seals moving against the current. Did their instincts tell them there would be food upstream now, or were they just restless and curious, like humans at this season?

A red Honda four-wheeler buzzed north along the gravel of Beach Street, carrying an Eskimo woman with a little girl riding in front of her. The woman's parka had a hump in the back, and a baby's head poking out at the neck.

Active descended the steps and walked to the trooper Suburban nosed up to the side of the school. He unlocked the door, tossed the Chukchi High yearbooks onto the seat and climbed in. He turned the key and the old rig rumbled to life. The Suburban, he had found in his time in Chukchi, would always run, but never completely right. Lately, the left-turn signal didn't work unless the headlights were on. So he switched them on as he pulled away from the school, even though the day was so bright they would surely be invisible to other drivers.

Chukchi was beautiful enough this time of year, he had to give it that. Unless you pulled your vision in from the glories of nature and looked at the town itself, with its square, unpainted wooden houses and straggling dirt streets. The vanishing snowdrifts were disclosing a winter's worth of dog droppings, caribou bones, discarded trash bags, lost mittens, cigarette packs, and crumpled beer cans. He passed two ravens at work on the rear half of a tortoiseshell cat, the head and forelegs still frozen into a rotting snowbank.

And all too soon, the sea ice would go out and take the good weather with it. Weeks, maybe months, of fog and wind would ensue, with a day or two of blue sky and sunlight thrown in here and there for torment. Well, if he kept putting in for jobs in Anchorage, he was bound to get one eventually.

He parked in front of the Chukchi Public Safety Building and went in, the yearbooks under his arm. He stopped at the dispatcher's station, where Lucy Generous sat speaking into a headset.

"Uh-huh . . . uh-huh . . . uh-huh," she said, rolling her eyes with each "uh-huh." She held up a finger to indicate "one minute" and silently mouthed "Elmer."

Active nodded with a sympathetic grimace. Elmer Newsome for twenty-seven years had tended the oil furnace at the government hospital in Chukchi, then retired and unexpectedly remained in town. Everyone agreed he was one of those unhappy white men who stay too long in the Bush and find themselves unsuited for life anywhere else. Now he spent most of his time drinking in his cabin on Lagoon Street and calling Lucy and the other dispatchers to demand the arrest of one or another of his neighbors for letting their dogs do their business in his yard.

Active waited, but the "uh-huhs" didn't stop. Finally, Lucy shrugged and threw up her hands, still saying "uh-huh" every few seconds.

He gave up and hauled the Chukchi High yearbooks up the two flights of stairs to the trooper offices on the third floor. In the reception area, Evelyn O'Brien, the red-haired trooper secretary, had a headset on and was transcribing a tape into her computer. She glanced up, nodded, and looked back at the computer screen without slowing the faint rattle of the keyboard.

One other trooper, Dickie Nelson, was present, just visible through the window in his office door. A telephone receiver was crunched between his shoulder and ear, and he was scribbling notes on a yellow pad, saying "yeah . . . yeah . . . yeah" as he wrote.

Active walked into his own office, dropped the yearbooks onto a chair, then went out and stood by Evelyn's desk. After a moment, she stopped typing, turned off the transcriber, pulled off the headset, and extended it his way. "You volunteering to finish this transcription for me? That would explain the interruption."

Active raised his hands in supplication. "Sorry. I was just wondering if you knew Grace Palmer."

"What, Lucy's not keeping you busy enough, you're interested in Gracie Palmer now?"

"No, this is business." He told the secretary about Jason Palmer's request.

Evelyn laid the headset on her keyboard and leaned back in her chair. "It was Jason this time? Usually it's Ida begging us to find Gracie."

"I guess she's getting pretty sick."

"Yeah, I heard that." The secretary was quiet for a moment. "Sure, I remember Gracie. Who wouldn't? Smart, beautiful, and a basketball star. An unbeatable combination, at least in Chukchi."

"You didn't like her?"

Evelyn looked at him pityingly. "This isn't dislike, you moron, it's envy. No one deserves that much youth, brains, and beauty. It's not fair."

"Did you feel better when she hit Four Street?"

Evelyn blushed a little and looked at her keyboard, which he took as an admission of guilt. But she said, "Of course not. No one deserves that much pain, either."

"So what was she like?"

"She was perfect, like everybody says. She used to babysit for us when our kids were little. Matt and Lisa loved her—she used to tell them Eskimo stories, even did the dishes and vacuumed the house, which is something that no other babysitter I ever had, white, Eskimo, or Korean, ever did."

Active returned to his desk and opened the first of the annuals, from Grace Palmer's freshman year. As Martha had suggested, she was everywhere and in everything—girl's basketball, orchestra, the yearbook staff, Honor Society, Inupiat Heritage Club, even Math Club. She was gawky and hadn't gotten her hair right yet, but the beauty she was about to become already showed. So did the defiance that stared out of the Miss North World mural at the high school.

The other three annuals were the same, except that activities came and went. Math Club and the yearbook work vanished, to be replaced by cross-country skiing and the school newspaper. And she had matured into the Grace Palmer of the mural.

Next, he opened the photofinisher's envelope Jason Palmer had given him, expecting to find a few shots of Grace in the last couple of years before she left for Anchorage.

Instead, he saw what amounted to her life in pictures—shots from infancy through high school. He arranged them in his best guess at chronological order and flipped through the stack.

Pictures of the baby Grace alone, Grace with an Eskimo woman he took to be Ida, the mother, and Grace with a girl he took to be Jeanie, the younger sister. A picture of toddler Grace strapped into the right seat of a Cessna Bush plane with a young Jason Palmer at the controls in the left seat.

He stopped at a picture of Grace at a birthday party, maybe her fifth or sixth. She stood in the middle of the room in a frilly white dress and shiny black patent shoes and a little gold tiara. Fancy clothes for the Chukchi of that day, even for a teacher's daughter, Active thought. Her hands were clapped together, her eyes wide, her mouth open in delight. She was looking at something, probably someone with a gift, off camera to the photographer's left.

He stopped again at a small version of the mural shot—the beauty with the inaccessible eyes, in her Miss North World regalia.

Active sighed, put the photographs back in the envelope, and replaced the rubber band. It was his impression all girls became angry when they hit puberty. It had happened to Kelly, his own little sister— his adoptive sister, really, the natural child Ed and Carmen had produced three years after adopting him.

In a single year, Kelly had turned from a sweet gawky twelve-year-old soccer fanatic into a screaming demon who didn't like anything about her life. Not her parents, especially not her mother, not her adoptive brother, not their house in Muldoon, not the school she went to, not soccer, not anything. It all sucked.

Yet Kelly, like the sisters of Nathan's friends, had gotten through it somehow, had steadied up and turned human again when she was about seventeen. Now she was happily married to a federal wildlife biologist in Ketchikan and expecting her first child around Thanksgiving.

No such luck for the Palmer sisters, apparently. Whatever it was that hit girls at puberty, it had killed Jeanie and never let go of Grace Palmer, had dragged her onto Four Street in Anchorage and left her there. Maybe it was because she was from the Bush, or because she was half Inupiaq and half white, but she was probably beyond redemption, if she was still alive.

In any event, her redeemer would not be Nathan Active.

He picked up his phone and punched the speed dial code for the Anchorage Police Department. "Hi, it's the troopers in Chukchi," he said when a dispatcher answered. "Is Dennis Johnson in?"

"Hang on, I'll check," the dispatcher said. She sounded like her vocal cords had been tanned into shoe leather by whiskey and smoke.

Active had known Dennis Johnson since they had both turned out for Youth Hockey at the outdoor rink at Muldoon Elementary School at age ten. He had been the only Eskimo on the team, Dennis the only black.

Actually, as he had discovered the first time he went to Dennis's house, his new friend was only half-black, the son of a black father and a white mother. And Dennis, like his father, had married a white woman.

The dispatcher came back on the line. "He's out on patrol. You want me to patch you through?"

"No, just put me on his voicemail, will you?" There was a click and he listened to Dennis's voice ask him to leave a message or press zero to talk to a dispatcher right away.

"Hey, Slick," he said after the beep. "How'd you like to track down a beauty queen? Look for a package in the mail." That should get Dennis interested enough to at least scan the pictures and the report when they reached Anchorage.

He hung up, typed up what he knew of Grace Palmer, and sent it to the office laser printer. He put three of the most recent pictures of the girl into a manila envelope, added the report, then sealed the package and addressed it to Dennis.

He stacked the annuals on a table by the door, figuring he could take them to the high school the next time he left the office. But what about the rest of Jason Palmer's pictures? Palmer hadn't said anything about returning them. Active tossed them into a desk drawer.

CHAPTER FOUR

At noon, right on time, Lucy Generous looked up from her console to see Nathan come out of the stairwell and walk toward her dispatch station, that smile on his lips.

"What's for lunch?"

"Tuna sandwiches, just like your *naluaqmiut* mother in Anchorage used to make," she said with a smile of her own. "I won't tell Martha if you won't."

Nathan, she knew, was well aware of what they were having for lunch. She had been making the sandwiches that morning when he stopped to pick her up for work. He had watched as she sealed them in ziplocks and dropped them into a shopping bag with two Diet Pepsis and a big package of tortilla chips. It was a running joke between them, how Martha was trying to lure Nathan into the Chukchi lifestyle while Nathan clung stubbornly to his Anchorage habits, including the tuna sandwiches—with mayonnaise and a touch of mustard—they had for lunch at least once a week.

As she pulled off her headset and lifted her coat from the back of her chair, she wondered if Nathan knew how serious this particular joke was. Every time she made him a tuna sandwich, she wasn't just giving him food he liked—she was doing something for him that Martha wouldn't do.

She came out of the dispatcher's booth and they left the Public Safety Building together. She wanted to take Nathan's arm, but she knew he didn't like that when he was in uniform. So she put her hands in the pockets of her coat until they reached his Suburban.

She waited by the big side mirror while Nathan pulled out his keys and opened the passenger door. As usual, he had locked up the trooper rig like a bank vault, even though it was within easy view of herself and several other public safety employees who worked on the ground floor.

"Someday I'm going to catch you leaving something to chance."

Nathan looked at her and put on his most serious expression. "I could arrange that. What day would you like it to be?"

She laughed, climbed in and reached across to unlock his door, thinking how much she loved their lunches. Especially on days like today, when they weren't going to a restaurant, but would park on Beach Street in the spring sun and look out over Chukchi Bay as they ate their sandwiches and listened to the radio. At times like these, she could imagine that whatever it was they had would go on forever.

Nathan climbed in, started the engine and pulled away from the Public Safety Building. He turned on the radio so they could catch *Mukluk Messenger*, the most popular program on KCHK.

For the past few days, much of Chukchi had been avidly following a saga of love and betrayal threaded among the messages about grocery shipments, public hearings, church meetings, and flight schedules for the swarm of Bush planes that linked Chukchi to the surrounding villages.

It seemed that one Harvey Salmon had left Chukchi and

traveled up the Isignaq River by snow machine for a spring ptarmigan hunt. But when the hunt was over, the ice of the river and of Chukchi Bay were too soft for a safe return.

So Harvey had informed Margaret Salmon over *Mukluk Messenger* that he would leave the snow machine with his cousin Charlie in Ebrulik for the summer and return to Chukchi by air charter the next day.

But Harvey had slept in and missed his plane, according to his message on the second day, and would have to stay in Ebrulik another night or two until the next plane arrived.

That had provoked a message from Margaret Salmon, inquiring in the most insinuating of terms why Harvey would be so tired as to oversleep, reminding him the same thing had happened the preceding spring, and ordering him not to miss the next plane. A second message from Margaret had suggested that someone identified only as "Shirley in Ebrulik" go to church and talk with God about what she had been doing in her "spare time."

But Harvey had indeed missed the next plane, this time explaining by message that he had to help his cousin work on a four-wheeler.

Now, five days into the saga, came the latest message from Margaret: "To Harvey at Ebrulik: Coming down with Cowboy Decker this afternoon. You better be at the airport and Shirley hadn't."

"I wouldn't want to be Harvey," Nathan said as he stopped at a little pullout on Beach Street. The ice in front was so bright, it made her squint.

"Or Shirley." She opened the shopping bag and handed him a sandwich, then a Diet Pepsi. "That Margaret is real fat and she's real mean. Before you came, she went to jail once for setting Harvey's hair on fire with a Bic lighter."

"Did you see this with your own eyes?"

She slugged him lightly in the side. "You always say that. Of course I didn't see it myself. But everybody knows it's true."

Nathan chuckled and shook his head, then took his sandwich out of the ziplock and bit into it. A thoughtful look came over his face while she opened the tortilla chips and put the bag on the seat between them. "Did you ever know Grace Palmer?"

"Grace Palmer?" She reached to switch off the radio, then changed her mind and pulled her hand back, hoping she didn't look or sound as alarmed as she felt. "What about her? Did she come back?"

Nathan gave her an odd look. "No, but her father asked if I . . . if the troopers could find her. Her mother has cancer."

"Oh, yes, I heard that." She was embarrassed by the relief she felt. She hoped he didn't pick that up in her voice, either. "That poor family, so many troubles."

"I gather. So, did you ever know her?"

"Gracie? Not really. She was a lot older than me, you know. She left high school before I went in. I just remember she was really pretty and the older girls all hated her. They called her bossy."

"Bossy?"

"You know." She tilted her nose into the air and tapped her chin from below with two fingers. "Always had to have her own way. Stuck-up."

"Stuck-up, huh?" Nathan sounded amused.

"Yep, stuck-up." She nodded, then stuck her nose into the air again and pushed out her lower lip and giggled. "Bossy."

"Well, did Miss Bossy Stuck-Up have a boyfriend who might know what happened to her?"

She twisted in the seat to face him. "I don't think so. I heard Jason Palmer never let his girls date much."

She reached across the seat and punched his shoulder. "Aren't you glad some fathers aren't like that?"

"I should say!" He smiled, glanced around, and gave her a fast kiss on the lips. They both chuckled, and bit into their sandwiches.

She was feeling good, now, feeling like the situation was under control. She was about to open her Diet Pepsi when the stupid question she had been trying to choke back came blurting out.

"What if you met her before me?"

"What?" He said it with a guilty little start, she thought. "What do you mean?"

"She's so pretty. Smart, too. What if you met her first?"

"You're pretty and smart." He lowered his voice in mock secrecy, as if someone might be listening outside the door. "Good in bed, too."

She knew he was trying to tease her out of it. Which was exactly what he should be doing, because she was being silly. Unless he was really doing it because he was guilty. She smiled a little.

"So nothing would happen if I met her first."

She smiled again, took a sip of Diet Pepsi, and looked out the passenger window, away from Nathan.

"Anyway, she's probably not pretty or smart now, not after all that time on Four Street," he said from behind her. "And I doubt she could make a tuna sandwich like you."

She could feel herself getting furious, so she kept looking out the window to keep Nathan from seeing. The knot of unease that lay like a stone in her stomach lately felt heavier now, tighter and harder to keep down. Now the sun on the ice seemed cold and harsh, a blue flame that burned the eye without warming the heart.

It was all the questions she couldn't ask him that were balled up into that knot in her stomach. Questions like, I know you're a lot smarter than me, but how much does that matter to you? Like, if you get a job in Anchorage, am I coming, too? Or am I just a way to pass the time while you're in Chukchi?

It scared her to think about it, but their relationship had reached the point where all these questions could be answered only one way. That would be if Nathan asked a question of his own: Will you marry me?

But she knew that wasn't about to happen, no matter how many times she wrote "Mrs. Lucy Active" on napkins and the backs of envelopes, then felt stupid and ripped them up before anyone saw.

"You're too handsome," she said finally. She knew it was unsatisfactory, but everything else that was trying to bubble out of her at that moment was even worse.

Dimly, in the passenger window, she saw Nathan's reflection throw up its hands and look out the driver's window. Then it turned toward her and switched off the radio and spoke. "I'm sorry," it said. "What did I do?"

"Nothing." She knew she was being ridiculous, so she turned and looked at him with what she hoped was a neutral expression. "I guess I'm not feeling too good, is all. Can you take me home? I think I'll call in sick for the afternoon."

When Nathan tried to ask her why, she just repeated it and he didn't say anything after that. He drove her to the little cabin she shared with her grandmother, Pauline Generous, when she wasn't staying at his place.

He started to get out to walk her to the door, but she said "Don't!" and jumped out and hurried into the cabin before he could say anything else.

It was quiet and dark inside. Her grandmother must be at the Senior Center with the other *aanas*, probably playing snerts and gossiping. She went into the cabin's one tiny bedroom, threw herself onto her bed, and, finally, let out the sobs.

As Nathan Active watched Lucy vanish into her grandmother's cabin, he marveled again at the intuition or ESP or whatever it was she used to read his mind before he knew what was in it himself. The moment Lucy had asked, "What if you met her first?" he had realized the truth and begun to dissemble.

And now he was ashamed. He should have been honest with her: All right, Grace Palmer is, or was, very attractive and of course I would have been interested if I didn't know you. But I do know you so it doesn't matter. Besides which, I'm not going to meet her. And if I did, she probably doesn't look like that now . . .

He shook his head. No, this was one of those conversations that could take any one of a thousand paths but would always end up in the same place. Lucy would be hurt and angry and he would realize once more how little he understood women. Or any other variety of human being, for that matter. He switched KCHK back on and pulled away from Pauline Generous's cabin.

"I gave you the account number yesterday!" Evelyn O'Brien was snarling into the phone as Active, still preoccupied with the Lucy situation, opened the door to the trooper offices. "Now where's our damned toner?"

She looked up, caught his eye, covered the mouthpiece with her hand, and glared at him. "Fucking Anchorage, a lot those idiots care if our copier runs out of toner."

He didn't know if this meant the problem was his fault, perhaps because he was from Anchorage, or if he was just supposed to sympathize. After some thought, he shrugged ambiguously, then shook his head with what he hoped was an expression of collegial dismay at the incompetence of whichever idiot in Anchorage had lost the toner shipment.

The secretary shook her head, too, and seemed satisfied. "Oh, yeah. The boss wants to see you."

She jerked her head toward Captain Patrick Carnaby's office, then uncovered the mouthpiece again. "Two weeks? What am I supposed to make copies with for two weeks?"

Active stepped into the detachment commander's office and closed the door just as O'Brien was demanding to talk to the Anchorage idiot's supervisor.

"I see Evelyn's on the rampage again." Active dropped into one of the two green plastic chairs in front of Carnaby's desk.

Carnaby looked up from a stack of spreadsheets on his blotter and glanced out at the secretary. "Yeah, she needs to vent once in a while or she starts to take it out on us. Having this toner thing to give her was a godsend."

Active had never thought of it before, but Carnaby was right about how to manage their combustible but highly competent secretary. Yet another example, he supposed, of the combination of insight, intuition, and intellect for which Carnaby had become known as the Super Trooper.

That, and the fact that he *looked* like a super trooper: six-two, square-featured and devoid of fat, his hair and mustache just starting to fleck with gray.

"Yep, better Anchorage should taste Evelyn's wrath than us," Active agreed. "She said you wanted to see me?"

"Oh, yeah. Got some good news for you here." Carnaby thumped the spreadsheets in front of him and began thumbing through the stack. "This is the quarterly budget revision. They can't seem to get us our toner and they cut ten thousand bucks out of our undercover operations against the bootleggers, but they can buy us new computers. Let's see, here we are."

Active studied the sheet Carnaby pushed across the desk and whistled. "We're dumping the Macintosh and getting Windows? I thought that was some kind of religious issue with our computer guys."

"I think it has something to do with the fact that our new public safety director likes Windows. He apparently doesn't think the Apple Macintosh is manly enough for people who carry guns and arrest crooks."

Active, who felt the same way, chuckled.

"And he got hold of some study saying the Apple company is turning into a music service and we'll be stranded on Macintosh Island if we don't switch," Carnaby said. "So I believe a vision of a burning resume appeared unto our systems people and they had a conversion experience. Now they're all Windows believers. Who cares, as long as the darn things can do email and run these spreadsheets?"

Carnaby took the page back and pointed to a line about halfway down. "Anyway, that's you."

"Me?" Active looked and saw that the line said "Windows Training (P.I.T. Anchorage)—$1,000."

Carnaby nodded.

"I don't need any Windows class. I have a Windows machine at home." Active looked again at the line. "What's 'P.I.T.' anyway?"

"The latest thing. 'Peer Instruction Training.'"

Active struggled to parse the chain of nouns, then gave up. "Okay, so what does it mean?"

"It means they're too cheap to send all of us down to Anchorage for training, or even bring people up here to train us." Carnaby shook his head, presumably at the dimwitted parsimony of the department's budgeteers. "So we're supposed to send one person down there to learn how to teach the rest of us. That's why they're giving us the thousand dollars—a round-trip ticket to Anchorage, plus room and board for one person."

"I'll be trained to instruct my peers, is that it?"

"You got it."

"But why me?"

"Two reasons. One, you minored in computer science, according to your file. So you're the logical one to come back and teach the rest of us." Carnaby stopped, as if awaiting Active's reaction.

"And the second reason?"

"Well, that's kind of where the silver lining comes in." Carnaby dropped his eyes to the spreadsheet and looked embarrassed.

"What silver lining?"

"Seeing as how you're from down there, I figured you might stay with your folks and save us a little expense money. A hundred here, five hundred there, we might be able to scrape up enough for a little undercover operation one of these days."

"What? Why should I . . ."

Carnaby held up his hand, dug through some mail in his in-basket and pulled out an Alaska Airlines envelope. "And, I've got some frequent-flyer coupons here. You can travel free, on me."

He rocked back in his chair, put his hands behind his head, and raised his eyebrows in the white expression of inquiry.

Active was trapped and he knew it. The City of Chukchi had banned liquor a couple of years earlier, producing an immediate reduction in murder, wife-beating, child abuse, and other indicators of social malaise.

But the improvement had proven temporary. Chukchi's little cadre of drug dealers had quickly branched into liquor, the most lucrative and dangerous drug of all, and now crime rates were creeping back toward their old levels. It was up to the troopers, allied with Chukchi's city police, to enforce the increasingly leaky alcohol ban.

The problem was money. It took money to bring in undercover agents and maintain them in Chukchi long enough to get the confidence of the bootleggers and make the buys needed to make a case. Traveling on Carnaby's frequent-flyer coupons and staying with Ed and Carmen would leave a thousand dollars lying around loose, and the Super Trooper had no doubt already figured a way to slide it into undercover operations without attracting the notice of the bean counters at headquarters in Anchorage.

"All right, I'll go. When is it?" Active pulled his notebook from a hip pocket.

"Next week. The eleventh through the fifteenth. You can have Evelyn make the arrangements." Carnaby looked out at the secretary again. "And God help anybody who screws them up."

Active wrote the dates in the notebook. "Okay, anything else?"

"Now I'm feeling guilty, beating you out of your per diem." Carnaby stuck the computer training spreadsheet back in its place, then squared up the stack. "You could take some leave after the class if you want. Spend a little time with your family down there, catch up with some of your old pals, decompress a little from Chukchi. You'll be surprised how much you need it after—how long you been here?"

"Two years, about."

"And when was the last time you were out?"

"Last summer, I guess."

"Yeah, but that was to testify in that cocaine trial that got moved to Anchorage, right? That wasn't a real vacation."

Active shook his head. "I don't enjoy relaxing all that much."

"Well, you should learn. You'll burn out, you don't kick back once in a while. We're at full strength now, so this is a good time to be gone."

"I'll let you know." Active left Carnaby's office and walked back to his own, turning it over in his head. What if he invited Lucy to come too? That should please her. If she could be pleased by anything he did these days.

CHAPTER FIVE

He called her at midafternoon, and gave up after ten rings. If she was there, she wasn't interested in talking.

He drove to Pauline's cabin after work and knocked on the door. No answer there either.

He turned on the stoop and looked up and down Beach Street for a moment, as if the answer might be caught in the afternoon sunlight bouncing off the sea ice. Nothing in sight but some high-school boys in a pickup basketball game on a vacant lot that had dried out early, and two girls too young to drive tearing past on a Honda four-wheeler. Finally he shook his head and returned to the Suburban.

He realized where she was when he pulled up at the tiny, ply-wood-sided house the troopers rented for him and saw that the *kunnichuk* door was ajar, as was the door beyond it into the house proper.

On spring days, she liked to open up the bachelor cabin, as everyone at the trooper offices called the place, and let in the sun and the breeze off the ice. It cleared out that lived-in-too-long smell a place got from being sealed up all winter. Through the open kitchen window he caught a side view of her, working at the sink.

He supposed coming over to make dinner was her way of apologizing without having to bend her pride and say the words. But, as always after one of their fights, he wasn't quite sure what he should say. He still didn't know by the time he had parked and walked inside, so he sniffed loudly and said, "What smells so good?"

She turned from the makings of a salad in a big bowl on the drainboard and said, "That's sheefish. Martha brought it over."

"I thought so." The sweet white meat of the big bottom-feeder that people caught through holes in the ice had become one of his favorites during his time in Chukchi.

She bent and looked through the window in the oven door, then straightened. "I guess your stepfather was out this past weekend. It'll be ready in about fifteen minutes, maybe twenty."

The afternoon sun caught her through the kitchen window and he was amazed again at her loveliness. She was dressed in white jeans and a short-sleeved white T-shirt that contrasted dazzlingly with her brown skin and the thick black ponytail hanging down her back.

And her face, that impossible study in reflected diagonals: mouth curving up at the corners, upturned almond eyes, slanting brown cheekbones. He had often tried to memorize Lucy's face, but he could never call it up at will. Instead, it would come to mind of its own volition, especially when he was out in the country, admiring some white fold in the winter mountains or a thunderhead mushrooming up from the inland hills on a summer day.

"What is it?" she said and he realized he was staring in silence.

"Twenty minutes?"

She cocked her head and smiled and put her hands on the edge of the sink behind her, pulling the T-shirt tight across her front. "Why, are you too hungry to wait?"

Obviously, she had caught his drift. Or maybe he had caught hers. With Lucy, he never knew if he was one step ahead or three steps behind, but he suspected it was usually the latter. Now it didn't matter because he saw they both had the same idea about how to make up.

He walked over and slid his arms back through hers and cupped her buttocks, pulling her against him as hard as he could. She gave a little moan that was not so much the voice of passion, he thought, as of relief or welcome or homecoming. Then he covered her mouth with his own, feeling at that moment that he wanted to inhale her and keep her safe inside him for a while.

He felt her arms come off the sink and wrap around his neck, so tight it hurt a little. Then her feet came off the floor and her legs wrapped around his waist and he walked her into the bedroom exactly that way.

"My God," she said from beside him a few minutes later. "I never, like that . . ."

"Yeah, I know." He was studying her belly now, running his fingers over the smooth mound of flesh just below her navel.

"I would have taken them off, you didn't have to . . ."

It had been the white cotton covering that little hillock, that and the glimpse of pubic curls through the fabric, that had caused him to rip her panties off.

Not that he had planned it that way. He had intended a more gradual unveiling, sliding the panties slowly past the swell of her hips, over first one knee and then the other, then down the slender brown calves until she was free.

But watching her pull the T-shirt over her head, then free her breasts from the bra, then tug off her jeans, had been all he could handle. When he saw the panties and put his hand inside and felt her hot, slick, inner flesh grip his fingers, that had been it—without conscious thought, he had grabbed the waistband and yanked and then they were just a wisp of cloud in his hand.

"They were so white against your skin, I'm sorry . . ."

"Don't be. I'm not. It was like, it was like . . . I don't know what it was like."

"I'll buy you some new ones."

"Never mind, I just won't wear any when I come over."

And somehow that set them off again and suddenly he was on top of her again and in her again, her so female and smelly and slippery from the first time that he was screaming out loud before the second time was over and she was laughing or crying, he wasn't sure.

They fell apart gasping. She threw her arm over her eyes and he watched her breasts heave as her breathing slowed.

"Mmmm," she said finally. She rolled to face him, and nipped his bare shoulder. "That was a ten."

"A twenty. Two tens."

She giggled and said "Mmmm" again and snuggled up against him, her body wet and warm and utterly relaxed now. He worked his arm under her head, so that her cheek was on his chest.

"I have to go to Anchorage for a while."

"Mmmm" she said. Then he felt her stiffen. "When? Why?"

"Monday," he said, and explained about Peer Instruction Training and how he'd be staying with Ed and Carmen to build up the Chukchi detachment's budget for undercover work against the bootleggers.

"So you'll be back Friday?" He felt her relax again. "You want me to stay here and watch your place? And make sure you feel welcome when you get home?"

"Actually, I was thinking I might stay down there and take some leave. You want to come down and spend a few days in Anchorage together?"

"And stay with Ed and Carmen?" He could hear the unease in her voice. She had never met his adoptive parents.

"Well, you'd be in the guest bedroom." He pulled his arm from beneath her head and rolled on his side to face her. "But it's right next to my room and it has a queen-size bed and the springs don't squeak and neither do the floorboards in the hall and I'll oil the hinges on the doors."

She smiled. "Well, maybe I could . . . no, I can't. I have finals coming up. How long will you stay?"

"A week, I suppose. Carnaby says I'll burn out if I don't take a vacation."

"A week isn't much of a vacation."

"Well, I'm not much for vacations."

"What will you do?"

"I don't know. Visit Dennis Johnson, I guess. Maybe play some hockey if he's still on a team. Hang around headquarters a little, see what's posted on the job-announcements board."

She pushed herself up onto an elbow and gazed down at him with a serious expression. "Will you look for Gracie Palmer?"

"Not really. It's a case for the city cops down there. I'll probably nudge Dennis to poke around a little so I'll have something to report to her father when I get back, that's about all. Except . . ."

"Except what?"

"It is odd nobody's seen her in three years. You'd think somebody would have run into her and it would have gotten back to the Palmers."

"Maybe she died."

"Maybe. But then the Palmers would have heard from the cops for sure. Unless she was a Jane Doe. They get two or three bodies they can't identify every year in Anchorage."

"That's sad." She rolled off her elbow and onto her back. "You die and nobody knows you and your people never hear what happened."

"Yeah, maybe I'll check with the Jane Doe guys down there, show them Grace's picture."

Lucy was silent for a long time. The only sound in the house was the trickle of his leaky toilet. "So you will look for her."

"Only a little."

She was silent again, so he poked her in the ribs with his elbow. "You think I shouldn't? Jason Palmer sure seemed torn up about it."

"Do what you feel is right."

"I don't know." He locked his hands behind his head. "Maybe I'll ask Martha if I should. She knows the family, she knew Grace when she was in high school."

She sat up with a lurch, her eyes blazing. "Of course Martha will tell you to look for her!"

"What?"

"That Martha . . . oh, never mind!"

Now her eyes were squeezed shut, with tears trickling out. Two crying spells in one day was a lot, even for the new state of their relationship. "Are you having . . ."

"No, it's not PMS!"

"You're not . . ."

"No, I'm not pregnant!" She rolled off the bed, gathered her clothes from the floor, and stamped out of the bedroom. A moment later, he heard the bathroom door slam and the water come on.

He pulled on his pants and walked to the bathroom door as he buttoned his shirt. "What is it? Look, tell me the problem."

Silence.

"Look, the sheefish is going to burn."

"Turn it off. Even a man should be able to do that."

He walked into the cramped kitchen and shut off the oven. As he turned back to the bathroom, Lucy emerged, fully dressed and wearing the coldest face he had ever seen on her. She grabbed her jacket off his sofa and went out through the *kunnichuk* without a word.

He hurried to the *kunnichuk* door and shouted at her back. "Let me drive you home." She didn't stop or turn, so he hopped after her in his bare feet.

He caught up to her and pulled at her arm. "Well, at least let me put on some shoes so I can walk you home."

"No!" She jerked her arm away and kept walking.

He stood there until she was thirty feet away, then, lacking a better idea, started to follow her.

She turned, picked up two rocks, heaved one with an awkward throw, and missed him by ten feet. "Stop following me or I'll call the police." She threw the second rock, missed again, and picked up a third.

This was ridiculous. If he kept following, she'd keep throwing rocks and eventually hit him. She might even flag down a cop if the Chukchi Police Department happened by on patrol.

At a minimum, he'd take a merciless kidding for becoming part of Chukchi's street theater. At worst, the police might actually investigate him in connection with a domestic disturbance. It would be on the police blotter on KCHK, his mother would hear, Patrick Carnaby, Evelyn O'Brien . . . He turned and started toward his house.

When he reached the *kunnichuk*, he stopped and looked once more at the stiff little figure in white hurrying up the sunlit street, paced by a long afternoon shadow. So much pain in the world, and so little he could do about it, especially the part he caused himself.

PART II

ANCHORAGE

CHAPTER SIX

After the starkness of the Arctic, springtime in Anchorage was like a splash of the tropics when Active landed there three days later. His eyes fed on the luxuriance as he drove in from the airport in a tiny rented Neon, the cheapest car Avis offered, in honor of Carnaby's scheme to pilfer travel money from the Peer Instruction Training budget for use against the Chukchi bootleggers.

Even Spenard Road, a meandering track through Anchorage's tenderloin, was ablaze in green. Birch, spruce, aspen, mountain ash bursting out in bud and leaf, yellow dandelions popping up along the shore of Lake Spenard, long new grass springing up from the shoulders and medians and any other unpaved patch where soil, sun, and rain could combine.

It all seemed to bespeak a kind of chlorophyll-drenched tumescence, which perhaps explained the two hookers in hot pants loitering at a bus stop in the morning sun outside a strip club called Illusions.

Their eyes flicked over his car and apparently recognized it as a rental. One gave a "pull on over" wave while the other turned sideways and threw back her shoulders to show off her profile. He wondered about hookers who could get themselves out on the street so early on a Monday and also who the clients would be at that time of day. How many commuters wanted to start the work week with oral sex in a Spenard parking lot?

He thought of pulling over, listening to their pitch, and then showing them his badge. But he couldn't think of a good punch line to cap the stunt and they probably knew the troopers didn't work Spenard anyway, so he just waved and drove on.

Peer Instruction Training was not at the rambling old plywood trooper headquarters on the east side of town but rather in a fancy downtown hotel owned by a Native corporation from the southwest part of the state. He supposed the choice of venue was connected with the fact that the current governor was a Democrat who had slid into office by under a thousand votes statewide, thanks to his margins of up to ninety percent in the Native villages of the Bush.

No doubt the Democrats would lose control someday, and then classes like this would move to a more Republican venue, such as the hotel a few blocks west owned by a former Republican governor.

He parked the Neon and walked into the hotel and climbed a jade staircase to the mezzanine. There a sign told him the class was in the Sheenjek Room. The Sheenjek, he seemed to remember, was a river that ran south out of the Brooks Range somewhere east of Chukchi.

He found the Sheenjek, collected a blueberry muffin and a black coffee from a table at the back, and took a seat just as the instructors introduced themselves to the class.

At first he had some hope that the day would be entertaining, if not instructive. Something was obviously going on between the two instructors, identified by their badges as Neil and Christie, from Microsoft's customer-training division. But what?

They exchanged meaningful glances as Neil started the laptop hooked to a projector. There was a balletic avoidance of contact as Neil started the PowerPoint program and laid out his notes beside the mouse and Christie dug the Peer Instruction Training handouts from a big, black travel case and distributed them to Active and the other students.

Then Neil touched Christie's arm, pointed at something on the screen, and began to explain it to her. Christie bent toward him, bared her teeth, and hissed something in his ear. He shut up and looked straight ahead and Active thought the tips of Neil's ears were turning red as Christie walked to the door and dimmed the lights.

She waited a moment, frowned, waited a little more.

"Neil, if we could have the first slide now?" The disgust in her voice was undisguised.

Neil jumped and did something to his laptop. The PowerPoint logo vanished from the big screen at the front of the room and the first Peer Instruction Training slide replaced it. It consisted of the words themselves and a cartoon of a young black executive showing a young white executive how to do something on a computer—how to use PowerPoint, it appeared.

Active sighed and settled back into his chair. PowerPoint presentations were the most potent soporific that human ingenuity had ever devised, in his experience, and he resigned himself to the probability of getting little more than nap time out of the classes unless Neil and Christie actually came to blows.

Well, he could study the handouts later for the gist of Peer Instruction Training, and wing the rest when he returned to Chukchi and actually had to use it on Patrick Carnaby, Evelyn O'Brien, and the rest of the trooper staff.

Christie was welcoming them to the class now, Neil dutifully clicking through the introductory slides.

The Nerd and the Cheerleader, Active finally decided, that was the problem between Neil and Christie. Christie was a creamy-skinned blonde, not gorgeous, not cover-girl material, but certainly more attractive than one might expect for a teacher of computer classes.

Neil, meantime, appeared to have long ago given up the battle to disguise his nerdiness. His lank brown hair was combed, but just that—combed. Not brushed or blown, just combed. No adhesive tape holding the glasses together, but the frames were thick and black. No acne to speak of, but a world-class Adam's apple that bobbed in agitation every time Christie looked his way. No plastic sheath to protect the shirt pocket, but Active did count three pens standing at attention.

Active wondered how Neil had gotten himself teamed with Christie. Had he hacked the company scheduling software to make sure Christie never left Redmond without him?

Active smiled, closed his eyes, and tried to drift off as Christie chirped away, now moving from the overview of Peer Instruction Training to an introduction to the Windows operating system for those who had used only Macintosh before.

Active had used both extensively, so he was in agony as Christie said, "The biggest difference from the Mac is this little task bar that pops up at the bottom of the screen whenever . . ." agony so intense he found himself unable to go to sleep.

He sat up, dug into his briefcase, and pulled out the photo-finisher's envelope Jason Palmer had given him back in Chukchi. He flipped through the pictures, found the two he wanted, and placed them on the shiny folder Christie had passed out.

As Christie burbled away, he peered through the dim light at the two bookends of Grace Palmer's life in Chukchi. On the left, Grace on her sixth birthday, mouth open in joy at the gift held by someone off camera, soul open to joy in general. On the right, the stone-eyed beauty, soul open to nothing.

Class ended a little after six, Christie snapping her binder shut and heading for the door the moment she had said, "Thanks, you guys have been great, see you tomorrow at eight," obviously trying to get out of the room while Neil was still turning off the projector and shutting down the computer, before he could ask if she wanted to grab some dinner, maybe see a movie.

The late finish meant Active didn't have much time for dinner himself if he was to make his seven o'clock meeting with Dennis Johnson at Anchorage police headquarters. Fast food, obviously, but not a cheeseburger or taco from one of the plastic and neon grease pits along Northern Lights Boulevard or East Fifth Avenue if he could avoid it. He galloped down the hotel's jade staircase and into the Neon and drove to the west end of Fifth Avenue, then south on the mysteriously named Minnesota Bypass to a Carrs supermarket and rushed inside.

The last time he had been in Anchorage, the deli section had offered—yes, it was still there, the bin of crushed ice covered with plastic foam trays of sushi. He grabbed one with eight pieces, a combination tray with eel, octopus, crab and tuna, got himself a Diet Pepsi at the do-it-yourself soda fountain, sat down at a table where somebody had abandoned a copy of that day's *Anchorage Daily News*, and began to eat.

It was his first sushi since being posted to Chukchi nearly two years ago and his first thought was how good the first piece tasted, this cool, meatless, fatless dish the Japanese had dreamed up. His second thought was, it tasted familiar, and he realized that except for the rice stuffing, the sushi tasted like some of the Inupiat dishes Martha was always trying to get him to sample up in Chukchi if he wanted to be a real Eskimo.

Well, the Japanese and the Inupiat were both Asian and they both lived on cold northern seas. So it wasn't surprising they both ended up liking raw fish, he thought as he flipped open his peer instruction folder to review what he had been unable to absorb during the day, stupefied as he was by the PowerPoint slides. There, one peeking out of each pocket, were the two pictures of Grace Palmer. He put them in his shirt, face-to-face to protect the images, and began to scan Christie's handouts as he wolfed down the other seven pieces of sushi.

The clock on the dash of the Neon showed 7:02 when he nosed up to the curb at police department headquarters on the east edge of Midtown. The headquarters was on the edge of a big park, and so was surrounded by birch, aspen, and cottonwood, all leafing out in the spring shower that pattered down as he locked the car.

He dashed inside, paused in the foyer to shake the rain from his clothes and hair, then asked for Dennis Johnson at the window at the rear of the lobby. Active was out of uniform and he saw the watch officer's caution flags go up at the sight of this casually dressed civilian, a Native to boot, even if he didn't look or smell particularly drunk, here after hours and asking to see a cop.

"Your name?" She was frowning and her voice was cold and robotic.

"Nathan Active. I have an appointment."

"That's the guy Dennis told us about," said a voice from out of sight to one side. "See there?" An arm appeared and pointed at something on the desk in front of the dispatcher.

Her frown melted into a smile. "Sure, Dennis will be right out," she said.

While he waited, Active studied the Wall of Death, a gallery of photographs of Anchorage police officers killed in the line of duty. He had seen this wall before, and a similar one at trooper head-quarters in Juneau, and he was wondering again if the pictures were a good idea when Dennis Johnson boomed out a loud, "Hey, Nathan!" from behind him. He turned and shook Dennis's hand, punched him in the shoulder.

Then Active waved at the Wall of Death. "You really think these guys are a suitable role model for impressionable young officers like ourselves?"

Dennis glanced at the wall and grimaced. "You gonna start that again?"

"These guys messed up, right? Otherwise they wouldn't be up there, right? I'm just saying, is all."

"Will you shut up? What if one of the other guys hears you?"

Active shrugged. "I just think they should put up shots of all the guys who made it through to retirement and now they're running fish charters down in Homer or doing security consulting on the pipeline. Give us pups something to shoot for."

"You oughta see some of the older guys out here looking at this sometimes," Dennis said. "These are people they knew, they get all misted up . . ."

"Yeah, there's nothing a real cop likes more than a good cry," Active said.

"Christ, still the same old smart-ass." Dennis motioned him toward the door that led to the offices where the work of the

Anchorage Police Department got done. "I thought maybe a couple years up there in that deep freeze would straighten you out."

"Guess not," Active said. "Chukchi is my hometown, after all."

The watch officer buzzed the door open and Dennis led them into a long hallway, offices opening out to either side. "Hometown, huh? I thought you wanted out of there as fast as possible."

"I do," Active said. "Of course I do. It's just a figure of speech."

"Sure you do." Dennis was grinning broadly. "I'm just saying, is all."

"Saying what?"

"Nothing."

"Yeah, right. What is it?"

"It's just that anybody who would disrespect the Wall"—Dennis jerked a thumb back the way they had come—"has the makings of a serious Bush rat. You're going feral, is what I think."

"Oh, fuck you." Active realized he sounded more like he meant it than he had intended, but couldn't think of a way to ease the moment.

"You get the files?" he asked after a few seconds of strained silence.

"Right here." Dennis opened a door into an interview room: No windows except for a mirror on the back wall that was presumably a window from the other side, three metal chairs, a fluorescent fixture on the ceiling giving off a harsh institutional light that made it feel like three A.M., and a beat-up wooden table with a stack of file folders on it.

Dennis thumped the folders. "This is everything I could find so far. Some of it's our paper files, some of it's stuff that's only on computer now, so I made printouts for you."

"Nothing from your guys on Four Street, huh?"

"Nada. I had the foot cops show people her picture, ask around over the weekend."

"And?"

"You know how it is. Couple people thought they remembered seeing her, couldn't remember when except it was way back, couldn't remember if they heard anything about her lately." Dennis shrugged. "Four Street."

"And you checked for a death certificate?

Dennis nodded. "Nada again. If she died, either she didn't do it in Alaska or she was a Jane Doe."

Active hefted the stack of paper. "That's a lot of work. Thanks."

Dennis shrugged. "It was nothing."

"You don't have to babysit me. I can let myself out when I'm done."

"What if you want to make copies?"

"I'll find a copier and make them."

"You'll need an account code."

"So give me yours."

"We're not supposed to give 'em out. Department policy."

Active turned in his chair for a better look. Dennis wouldn't meet his eyes. "You interested?"

"Well, I kind of got into it, you know. That picture . . ." Dennis shook his head and opened the top folder to show the Miss North World photograph Active had sent down a few days ago. "She's something, huh?"

"She was, anyway."

"You know, they called her Amazing Grace on Four Street."

"Yeah, I heard." Active pulled his chair into a better position, then saw that Dennis was still standing awkwardly.

Active turned back to the folders and said over his shoulder,

"Come on, sit down, then. I'll probably need an interpreter for this APD gobbledygook anyway."

Active squared up the stack of folders and studied the index tabs. All bore Grace Palmer's name and a case number. Each number included a two-digit year code, but the numbers were obviously generated by different systems. One kind of case number he recognized as originating from the Alaska Court System's criminal files; the other had to be case numbers assigned by the Anchorage Police Department before the suspect was turned over to the courts.

He verified his guess with Dennis, used the year codes to arrange the files in chronological order, and opened the first one.

"Officers Jarvis and Tedrow responded to a reported obstruction of a highway on East Fifth Avenue in front of Anchorage Radiator Service," it began.

Jarvis and Tedrow had, it appeared, located and contacted an intoxicated Native female subject who appeared to be intentionally blocking the outside eastbound lane of East Fifth Avenue, creating a danger to herself and to motorists "engaged in lawful use of said eastbound lane" during an evening rush hour in late January.

Despite repeated requests from the two officers, the subject had refused to cease and desist and had, in fact, advised Jarvis and Tedrow to "give each other blow jobs in the back seat of their patrol car" after which she had picked up "an unknown object, possibly an ice chunk" from the snow berm by the eastbound lane and thrown it at the two men. That, according to the report, had put Officer Tedrow "in fear of immediate physical harm," whereupon the subject—subsequently identified as Grace S. Palmer—was subdued, restrained with handcuffs, and charged with obstructing a highway, resisting arrest, and assault. There was a mug shot of Grace Palmer, looking bleary-eyed and belligerent but otherwise pretty much like the Grace Palmer of the mural at Chukchi High.

The police file ended with a court system case number and a note saying the matter had been referred to the Anchorage district attorney's office.

Active found the court system file with the right number on it and flipped it open. It contained a single sheet, a computer printout that made no mention of assault or resisting arrest, reporting that Grace Sikingik Palmer had pleaded guilty to obstructing traffic and been sentenced to thirty days in jail, twenty suspended.

"Ten days," said Dennis, who had been reading along over Active's shoulder. "That's a lot for a piddly case like this. Usually it's just a fine, fifty dollars maybe."

"What do you make of it?"

Dennis frowned in concentration, flipped through the first file again. "Well, she would have gotten the other charges dismissed in return for the guilty plea on the traffic charge, that part makes sense. But I don't know where the judge was coming from with the jail time." He shook his head.

"Maybe said subject advised said judge to give said public defender a blow job," Active suggested. "Behind said bench."

Dennis chuckled. "I wouldn't put it past her."

The next case was dated fourteen months later. Officer Terrence Wilson, working plain clothes in the Junction Bar, had been approached by a Native female subject who had offered to have oral sex with him for a thousand dollars. He had attempted to take her into custody, she had resisted, he had subdued her, she had been charged with resisting arrest and soliciting prostitution.

The mug shot showed Grace Palmer with a black eye, a cut and swollen lower lip, and a bottom tooth missing in front. Active studied the uninjured parts of her face. They were bloated, roughened, her looks not gone yet but being sucked out of her by Four Street.

Active glanced back over Wilson's summary of the arrest, which was much shorter than Jarvis and Tedrow's agonizingly detailed account of their encounter with Grace Palmer on East Fifth the preceding year.

He turned to Dennis Johnson, who seemed mesmerized by the mug shot. "A thousand bucks for a blow job," Active said. "Isn't that a little steep for Four Street?"

"Out of the question. Twenty dollars is more like it. Fifteen if the girl really needs a drink or a fix."

Active found the court file on the prostitution case, and opened it. Again a single sheet, reporting only that the case had been dismissed in the interest of justice.

"What about the arresting officer, this Terrence Wilson?"

Dennis frowned, shook his head. "Don't think I know him at all." He flipped to the first page of the file and pointed to the date of the incident at the Junction. "See, that was a couple years before I started with the department. Maybe Wilson left before I got hired."

"Maybe," Active said.

"But our girl does seem to have some issues about oral sex, huh?"

"I guess." Active opened the next file, noted idly that the date would have been around the same time Roy Palmer had spotted his sister coming out of the Junction with two soldiers looking forward to an evening of amazement. Active wondered briefly if soldiers could afford thousand-dollar blow jobs, decided not, dismissed the train of thought, and began to read the file.

This time there were no ambiguities, no dismissals in the interest of justice or anything else.

An intoxicated Native female subject had been apprehended

at three o'clock on a summer morning smashing the windows of a Fourth Avenue dive called the Sunrise. Further investigation had revealed that the windows of every bar between the Junction and the Sunrise had been similarly smashed, presumably with the same two-by-four the subject was wielding when contacted by officers Lucas and Tedrow. Tedrow again. No wonder the prose sounded familiar.

Subject, who identified herself as Amazing Grace but was known to Officer Tedrow as Grace S. Palmer, had readily admitted smashing all the windows, had stated it was the bars' fault for closing "too fucking early," and had advised the two officers to go into the alley behind the Sunrise and give each other blow jobs if they didn't like it.

Whereupon Officers Lucas and Tedrow had placed the subject under arrest, during which action she had dropped the two-by-four on Officer Lucas's foot, possibly injuring two of his toes. However, upon subject's claiming the dropping was accidental and apologizing to Officer Lucas, it was decided to charge her with criminal mischief for the windows only, the two-by-four incident being noted only in the event a subsequent disability claim by Officer Lucas should be necessary.

The mug shot showed a face that was pure Four Street. Red, bloated, the fine Miss North World features disappearing as if they were sinking into a bowl of fat, the lower tooth still missing. Active winced and closed the file and glanced up to see Dennis covering the Miss North World photograph with the corner of a file folder. Active looked at him questioningly and Dennis said, "I don't want to see this anymore. You need coffee?"

Active nodded and opened the court file on the window-smashing incident as Dennis went out the door of the interview room.

Ninety days in jail, sixty suspended, restitution totaling nine thousand dollars to be paid to assorted bar owners along Fourth Avenue, Grace S. Palmer's Alaska Oil Dividends, if any, to be paid into the restitution account until the bar owners had been made whole.

He opened the last file—it was a police file, he noticed, without a corresponding file from the court system—just as Dennis came back with the coffee in two Styrofoam cups.

Once again, fate had thrown Amazing Grace and Officer Tedrow together. This time, Tedrow was partnered with a female officer, one Teri Amundsen, causing Active to attend closely to see what sexual advice Grace Palmer might have for two officers of opposite gender.

Tedrow's prose, while turgid, had been at least intelligible in the other files, but Active could barely follow the thread of events the winter night Tedrow had once again contacted his favorite intoxicated Native female subject, this time at Aurora Bingo on Northern Lights Boulevard.

It appeared subject had repeatedly been thrown out of, and finally banned from, Aurora Bingo for memorizing too many cards. On the night in question, she had "infiltrated" the premises despite the ban, and had been detected by Aurora Bingo runner Edward Noyuk. In the ensuing altercation, Noyuk had been jabbed in the eye with something called a dauber, whereupon Officers Amundsen and Tedrow had been dispatched to the scene.

Upon arrival, they had found the subject being detained in a back office by an Aurora Bingo security guard and Edward Noyuk, whose right eye appeared to be bruised and/or bleeding. Noyuk said he would not press charges if the officers would remove the subject, whom Noyuk identified as Amazing Grace but who was known to Officer Tedrow as Grace S. Palmer.

Whereupon Officers Tedrow and Amundsen advised subject to leave Aurora Bingo or be arrested for trespass and for assaulting Noyuk with the dauber. In response to which subject had—with a fine impartiality, Active thought—advised Tedrow and Amundsen to go out behind Aurora Bingo and give each other blow jobs, but had, in fact, left the premises and was last seen proceeding north along C Street.

No mug shot and no arrest, which explained why there was no court system file on the dauber-jabbing.

"Can you make any sense out of this?" Active pushed the file over to Dennis, who scanned it quickly, already having caught most of it over Active's shoulder. Dennis scratched his cheek and frowned. "I don't know why you'd get banned for memorizing bingo cards."

"Maybe you can cheat that way?"

Dennis shook his head. "I don't see how. The little balls just pop out of the cage at random. Memorizing the cards wouldn't change anything."

"Well, what's a dauber, then?"

"You don't know what a dauber is? Don't they have bingo in Chukchi?"

"Of course. It's a religion in the Bush, like basketball. But I never go, except to drop Lucy's grandmother off once in a while."

Dennis's eyes lit up and Active knew instantly he had made a tactical blunder by mentioning Lucy Generous to Dennis, to whom he had previously said nothing about his social life in village. It was too late now, and Dennis dragged the story out of him, not every detail but enough for Dennis to fill in the blanks and eventually demand, with an air of triumph, "So you're saying this Lucy does keep, like, a hair dryer and a couple of bras at your place?"

Active nodded, feeling obscurely embarrassed by something he knew shouldn't embarrass him at all, something perfectly normal and natural. Well, at least Dennis hadn't coaxed out anything about the fight over Grace Palmer, Active was thinking when Dennis asked, "Got a picture of her?"

He pulled out his wallet and showed Dennis the little snapshot Lucy had given him the day she asked for one of himself. He had been reluctant to take hers or give his own, it was another step down some road he didn't know or trust, but he had gone along because . . . why did he go along? He didn't know.

"Nice," Dennis said. "Very nice."

Active took the picture and studied it. Lucy did look very nice. Bundled up in a parka, big wolf ruff like a sunburst thrown back on her shoulders, soft winter daylight bathing her face, smiling eyes, smiling lips.

"Yep, I'd hang onto her," Dennis said. "She looks much better than Grace Palmer does now."

He knew Dennis was referring to the last mug shot, the shot of the bloated, gap-toothed Grace Palmer, but his eyes involuntarily fell to the Miss North World Shot, uncovered again as they had worked through the files.

"Mind your own business," he said as lightly as he could. "Just tell me what the hell a dauber is."

"It's this kind of felt-tip thingie they mark their bingo cards with." Dennis made dotting motions with an imaginary dauber. "You know, I-twenty-seven, O-sixty-nine. When the daubs line up right, a diamond or an X or whatever you have to make for that game, you got yourself a bingo."

"Sounds challenging."

"Oh, yeah, very. Why do you think drunks and street people can play it?"

"A dauber doesn't sound like much of a weapon, though."

"Maybe that's why the bingo runner let her off the hook."

Active checked the date of the bingo file, the last trace of Amazing Grace Palmer in the records of the Anchorage Police Department. "Pretty cold trail. This file's over three years old."

"Yep, but there's always Ludovic," Dennis said.

"Who's Ludovic?"

Dennis stood. "Follow me. The files will be okay here for a while."

He led the way down the hall to an open area with a half dozen computers in it. Women in civilian clothes—records clerks, Active guessed—were hunched over two of them.

"All right if we use one of your terminals, Karla?" Dennis asked the older of the women.

Karla didn't look up from her screen. She just put a Kleenex to her nose and sneezed. "Fuckig hay fever. I hate it when trees fuck."

Then she waved a hand vaguely at one of the vacant machines. "Go ahead," she muttered. "They're all workig todight."

Dennis sat at one of the terminals and logged on. "You don't have Ludovic in Chukchi?"

"Never heard of him," Active peered over Dennis's shoulder as a dense text menu came up. "Or it. I guess the troopers are too cheap, or too broke. What is it?"

Dennis typed something at the bottom of the screen, and another screen came up with fields for last name, first name, middle name. "Ludovic is this nerd downtown who buys tapes of every public record the state creates. Somehow he merges it all into one huge database. Driver's license, hunting license, court cases, Oil Dividend applications, if it's not confidential by law, Ludovic's got it."

Active whistled softly. "Big Brother, huh?"

"Absolutely. We tried to compile something like this, the ACLU would be all over us. But Ludovic's the private sector, so he can get away with it, which means we can get at it by paying his fee, and the good old ACLU can't do a damned thing about it." Dennis as he talked had typed in "PALMER, GRACE."

"That oughta do it." Dennis pressed ENTER and the screen blanked for a few seconds, then blinked and scrolled out several lines of data.

Now it was Dennis's turn to whistle. "She doesn't leave much of a trail. Never had a driver's license apparently, never hunted or fished, just the court cases we already looked at and Oil Dividend applications up till four years ago."

"None after that?"

"She probably stopped applying when her dividends were seized to pay for the windows she smashed."

"Of course. Can we pull up the last application?"

Dennis nodded, pressed a key, and a summary came up with Grace Palmer's name on it, followed by an address and room number on East 16th Avenue. "Whoa."

"Yeah, rough neighborhood, all right."

"Especially that address, " Dennis said. "The Creekview Apartment. It's a flophouse the street people use when they get a few bucks or the weather gets real cold. Even if they don't live there, the owner will let 'em get their dividend check there and then cash it for them, minus a hundred bucks for his trouble."

"Maybe we ought to have a talk with him."

"Yeah, probably." Dennis pressed a key and the printer beside the terminal whirred to life. "I could pay him a visit while I'm on patrol tomorrow, show him the picture, see if he's heard from her lately."

Active pulled the Oil Dividend information from the printer. He nudged Dennis. "See this? Looks like she had a couple roommates that applied at the same time."

Dennis nodded. "Maybe. Or maybe they were all just paying the hundred bucks to get their dividends there. They may not even have known each other."

Active studied the names. "Shaneesha Prather, Angelina Ramos. Ever run across them?"

Dennis took the paper and sounded the names to himself. "Don't think so."

"Should we look them up?"

"We could, but they're not gonna be any easier to find than your beauty queen. You know how it is with these people off Four Street."

Active shrugged. "Yeah. I'll just throw it in the file, I guess."

They walked back to the interview room and Active squared the files into a neat stack, then slipped the Oil Dividend printout into the last folder, the one from Grace Palmer's visits to Aurora Bingo. "All right if I keep these a few days?"

"Sure, just don't lose 'em. I had to sign for them."

They went back down the hall and out past the watch window, where Active smiled his thanks to the dispatch officer and surrendered his visitor badge. Then they stepped into the spring sun, still just above the snow peaks across Cook Inlet to the west of Anchorage.

"You want to come by the house?" Dennis asked. "Francie would love to see you. And the girls, you wouldn't believe how big they are now. I remember when I could . . ."

He held out one big dark hand and cupped it as if cradling a kitten, then shook his head.

"Thanks, but I better get over to the folks' place. I don't check in pretty soon, Carmen will be calling your people out to look for me."

They were stopped now at Active's rental car.

"How about tomorrow night? Come over for a quick dinner, then play some hockey? We've got a game at six and somebody's sure to turn up missing or get a busted lip or something. Anchorage's Finest can always use another player."

"I'll pass," Active said. "I think I'll drop in at Aurora Bingo and see if I can find Edward Noyuk. According to your files, he was the last person we know of to see Grace Palmer, ah, ah, to see her."

Dennis looked at him oddly, and Active guessed he had noticed the hesitation. He wondered if Dennis had figured out that what he had almost said was, "last person to see Grace Palmer alive."

CHAPTER SEVEN

Aurora Bingo took up a long, low storefront on the north side of Northern Lights Boulevard. The windows glinted in the slanting evening sun as Active pulled in a little after seven the next day. That no doubt explained the plastic blackout curtains over the glass, that and the fear of reminding players they were whiling away the precious summer daylight on bingo and rippies.

As he parked and locked the rental, Active tried to remember what had been in the building before Aurora Bingo. Some kind of weird Alaskan department store. Muskeg Outfitters, that was it. The Muskeg had sold a little of everything, from ladies' underwear to the big white inflatable bunny boots men would buy when they hired on for the winter with a North Slope seismic crew. The Muskeg had been the official dealer for Cub Scout merchandise, so young Nathan Active had been marched in once a year by his adoptive mother to be fitted out with a new uniform.

The Muskeg was long gone, now, wiped out as Anchorage fattened up on oil money and the big stores—Fred Meyer, Wal-Mart, Costco—heard the news and moved in. But what was the Muskeg slogan that had been on the radio a hundred times a day when he was a kid? He shook his head, unable to remember it.

He went in and paused just inside the door to survey the big room. Off to his left was a small stage with the caller's booth where bingo balls churned around in a Plexiglas cage. Whenever one whooshed out the top, the number would pop up on television monitors scattered around the big room and then a scrawny little long-haired Native guy, an Eskimo, Active thought, would call it out over the public-address system.

The players sat at long tables on the floor in front of the stage, daubing away at paper sheets with—Active looked over the shoulder of the nearest player to count—with six bingo cards printed on each sheet. Occasionally, one would raise a hand to draw a runner over to sell them more sheets.

The faces were mostly dark like his own, or darker—Native, Asian, Hispanic or black. And the players had another thing in common: working-class clothes. Aurora Bingo was a sea of jeans, khakis, sweatshirts, T-shirts, and sweatpants; baseball caps and cowboy boots and sneakers; tattoos on the men, big hair on a lot of the women, and here and there an *aana* in the traditional calico summer parka called an *atiqluk*.

A Plexiglas partition divided the big room into two parts. The section Active was in, nearest the door, took up about two-thirds of the space. He studied the layout for a few moments before he understood the purpose: His section was filled with smoke and smokers; a sign on the partition declared the other a SMOKE-FREE BINGO ZONE."

The back wall was taken up by a concession stand where pretzels and hot dogs baked under heat lamps, and by a counter where two women sold bingo sheets. In between were the restrooms, and a little booth where two more women sold rippies, the little cardboard strips that peeled apart to show slot-machine symbols and paid off accordingly. The rippie business looked pretty slow at the moment, though, what with the players all hunched over their bingo sheets in fierce concentration as the balls rolled out of the cage and the caller sounded the numbers.

He walked to the counter at the back of the room and waited until one of the women was free. She was Asian, maybe Filipino, he thought. "Is that by any chance Edward Noyuk up there?" He pointed at the caller in the booth.

The Filipina laughed. "Yeah, but around here we call him Special Ed."

"Special Ed? Why's that?"

She shrugged. "I dunno. That's just what he goes by."

"How long till the intermission?

She looked at her watch. "Maybe ten, fifteen minutes."

"How much for a sheet?"

"Just one sheet? Fifty cents."

He nodded and pushed a dollar bill across the counter. She pushed back two quarters in change.

"What color you want?" She pointed at the stacks of sheets on the counter. Each stack was printed in a different background color: brown, red, green and several others he couldn't name, probably mauve and puce and teal and other indeterminate hues understood only by interior decorators.

"Well, what do you recommend?"

She stared at him and shook her head, looking irritated. "Each game is a different color. See?" She handed him a printed list of the games for the current session. "They're on number five now. That's the olive game. Then number six is the Red Game and then there's intermission."

"All right, red, then."

She peeled a sheet off the red stack, placed it in front of him, and put the list of games on top of it. "You need a dauber?" She held up a green bottle about the thickness of a garden hose. "It's a dollar fifty."

He pulled out another bill and added it to the quarters still lying on the counter. She put the dauber on the list of games and raked in the dollar fifty.

Active nodded, thanked her, collected his bingo gear and walked towards the booth, planning to watch Special Ed in action. But as he got close, he realized the smoke rising from the players like a valley of fumaroles was too thick. He walked around the end of the partition into the smoke-free zone and found a seat near one of the calico-clad *aanas* just as someone in the smoking section cried "Bingo!" A runner left the booth to check the winner's card against the display screens around the room.

The old lady was round-shouldered with age, gray hair sticking out in all directions. She sat next to an obese young Native woman in Anchorage clothes, probably a granddaughter, Active judged, and it was clear from the *aana*'s calico and their features that they were Eskimo. But they didn't look Inupiat and the language the old lady spoke to the granddaughter as they readied their sheets for the Red Game didn't sound like Inupiaq. He decided they must be Yup'ik, the branch of the Eskimo family tree that occupied the deltas of the Yukon and Kuskokwim rivers, south of Chukchi and the other Inupiat parts of Alaska. They had four sheets apiece, he noticed, making him feel rather inadequate about his single sheet.

He uncapped his dauber and tested it on the back of his red sheet. It left a nickel-sized blob of green, and he figured he was ready for his first bingo game as the first ball popped out of the cage and Special Ed called out "O-seventy-four, O-seventy-four."

Only one of the six cards on his sheet had an O-seventy-four, in the upper right corner, so he put a green blob there and waited for the next number. The old lady growled something in Yup'ik to the granddaughter and he looked up to see the *aana* glaring at him.

The granddaughter shook her head, shrank down inside a hooded white sweatshirt, and stared at her bingo sheets. The old lady spat tobacco juice into a Styrofoam cup sitting near her own sheets and repeated the growl. This time she apparently elbowed the girl, because the granddaughter jumped and said, "Ouch" and leaned toward Active, face aflame.

"My grandmother told me to tell you, you don't mark the corners and don't you know anything?" The girl returned her eyes to her bingo sheets. "I'm sorry, but my grandmother is very old-fashioned."

Active studied his own sheet, and the nearest TV monitor, which clearly displayed O-seventy-four as the first number of the game. "But that's what he called, O-seventy-four," Active said. He pointed to the green blob he had made.

"This is the Big Diamond game." The girl pointed to the Number Six game on his list, which indeed had the words "Big Diamond" beside it, along with a diagram showing that you had to get enough daubs to make a big diamond in the middle of the card to win.

"See, the corners of the card are outside the diamond," she said. "So you don't mark anything there, even if it gets called."

He started to say "Well, why on earth does it matter?" but looked up into the old lady's glare again and thought better of it. "Tell your grandmother I'm very grateful for her help," he said instead.

The girl nodded and spoke to her grandmother in Yup'ik just

as Special Ed called out G-fifty-four, the second number of the Red Game, the Big Diamond game.

G-fifty-four was inside the big diamond area on two of Active's cards, so he daubed them in. It was outside the diamond on a third card and he almost daubed that one in, too, before remembering his bingo manners. He looked up and nodded to the old *aana*, who returned an approving smile and shot another jet of tobacco juice into her cup.

The Red Game ended with somebody in the smoking section calling out "Bingo!" The *aana* crumpled up her red sheets and growled something to the granddaughter, then they stood and moved towards the back of room. The girl stopped at the concession stand, but the *aana* continued on to the rippies booth.

Active walked around the partition into the smoking section and up to the booth where Special Ed was putting the bingo balls back into their cage and getting things organized for Game Seven, which, if Active remembered correctly, was the Blue Game. Up close, Special Ed looked even scrawnier than he had from a distance, with long hair, droopy Pancho Villa mustache and an Aurora Bingo T-shirt. One skinny forearm bore a tattoo of the Harley-Davidson wings.

"Nah, I don't remember anybody by that name," he said after Active introduced himself and asked if Special Ed had seen Grace Palmer lately. "How come you want to know? You her husband?"

Active realized he was out of uniform. "No, I'm a state trooper from her hometown. Her father asked me to find her. She hasn't been back in a while."

He handed Special Ed the two pictures, one of Grace in the mural, the other the battered, bloated Grace in the final mug shot. "Sometimes they call her Amazing Grace on Four Street, I guess."

Special Ed took the pictures, studied them briefly, then handed them back. "Amazing Grace? Of course I remember her." He shook his head. "She poke me in the eye with a dauber! Boy, she was mean!" He took a drag on his cigarette and blew the smoke towards Active, who sidestepped the plume.

"Yeah, I heard about that. I guess you had to ban her?"

"Oh, yeah. She always make the other players mad, especially the women. They say she's too bossy."

Active groped for the word and finally remembered. Lucy Generous had also applied it to Grace Palmer. "You banned her for being stuck-up?"

"Yeah, she never mark her sheets."

"What?"

"She just remember them." Special Ed grabbed a discarded bingo sheet from a table near the caller's stand and showed it to Active.

"She never do this." The caller pointed to the dauber blobs spotting the six cards on the sheet. "She leave her sheets blank. She just look at them couple minutes, then read a book and listen to the numbers. Somehow she know when she got a bingo and she yell it out. She daub them in her mind, I guess. When we check our machine against her card number, she's always right, even though there's no marks on it. Even if she's drunk."

Active took the sheet from Special Ed and studied it. Six cards on the sheet, each card with twenty-five numbers. "There's a hundred and fifty numbers on here." He looked at Special Ed. "You mean she memorized this and played the game mentally?"

"No, she play four sheets, maybe eight sometimes, remember them all."

Active did some more math, then whistled. "Eight sheets would be twelve hundred numbers. You saw this with your own eyes?"

Special Ed nodded, looking indignant at the memory. "Sure

I see it my own self. She sit there and read that book while them other ladies are flipping through all their sheets and using their daubers, getting ink all over their fingers—they don't like it. That's why they call her bossy."

"So you banned her."

"Yep, unless she use a dauber. That one time, she's in here and reading her book with them sheets spread out in front of her. I go over and give her a dauber and say she have to use it like that friend of hers always do. She say, 'All right, then, I will.' And she jump up and turn the table over, poke me in the eye."

Active studied Special Ed's eyes. They both looked normal. "Did it hurt much?"

"Nah, my eye look like it's bleeding from the red ink in that dauber, but I don't hardly feel it. Still it mess up the game and then everybody's really mad. So the boss call the cops, only they never arrest her because I won't sign the complaint." Special Ed shook his head with a disgusted look. "Not from getting poked in the eye by a girl!"

Active pulled out his notebook. "You say she had a friend with her that night?"

Special Ed nodded. "Just about every time she come in they're together."

"You ever catch the friend's name? I don't think it was in the police report."

"Nah, the police never talk to her," Special Ed said. "She take off when the fight start. I guess that Angie girl know Amazing Grace pretty good, know she's trouble."

"Angie, that was the friend's name?"

Special Ed nodded and Active wrote it in his notebook, frowning because it seemed slightly familiar. "What about Angie's last name?"

Special Ed thought about it for a moment, then shook his head. "Don't think I ever hear that."

The players were finishing their rippies and snacks now, and Special Ed began organizing his stand for the next game. Active realized the intermission was about over.

"What did Angie look like? Was she Native?"

"Don't think so," Special Ed said. "Kind of short, dark hair, dark skin, darker than mine. Not Native but Mexican maybe."

Active wrote it in his notebook. "How about Amazing Grace?"

"Yeah, she's Native, all right. Inupiaq like me, I think." Special Ed squinted at Active. "You, too, ah?"

"No, I mean, how did she look?"

"She look like Amazing Grace, I dunno."

Active laid the two pictures on Special Ed's counter and touched each in turn. "More like this, or like this?"

Special Ed bent over the photographs in concentration, then touched the Miss North World shot. "More like this, I guess."

Active looked at the picture, then at Special Ed. "You sure?"

Special Ed shrugged. "I guess."

Active scooped up the pictures and put them in a shirt pocket. "That was, what, about three years ago when she poked you? She ever come back?"

Special Ed laughed. "Not that I ever hear about. She know the boss will call the cops again."

"You ever hear what happened to her?"

"Nah, I never—wait a minute, seem like somebody say she's working at Illusions."

Active wrote it down. "Illusions? The strip club over in Spenard?"

"I guess." Special Ed turned to the microphone in the booth. "Game Seven, the Blue Game, is starting now."

The players hurried to the tables, plunking down their bingo sheets and foil-wrapped orders of fried chicken or fish and chips in plastic baskets.

Active went to the pay phone at the back of the room, between the doors to the men's and women's rooms, dropped in a quarter, and dialed Dennis Johnson's home. "I have to go to Illusions and check out a tip," he said when Dennis answered. "You know who to talk to there?"

"She's working at Illusions?"

"Maybe. Or she might have in the past."

"I'll meet you there in fifteen minutes."

"I thought you had a hockey game."

"I did. We won."

"Well, you don't have to come with me. Just tell me who—." There was a click, then silence on the line, and Active realized Dennis had hung up. He sighed and hung up, too.

"All right, boys and girls, this game is Double Hollywood, the Double Hollywood," Special Ed was saying over the public-address system as Active stepped through the doors of Aurora Bingo into the sun. It had swung towards the west now, but was still as bright as when he had come in an hour before. As he unlocked the rental, he noticed that, with the sun hitting the front of the building from a different angle, it was possible to make out the faded lettering of the old "Muskeg Outfitters" sign beneath the newer paint that said "Aurora Bingo."

He could even make out the famous Muskeg slogan that he had been unable to recall on the way in: "We cheat the other guy and pass the savings on to you."

CHAPTER EIGHT

It took him only eight minutes to reach Illusions, a rundown one-story building with brown T1-11 siding and a flat roof on a curve in Spenard Road. A plastic sign over the door spelled out "Illusions" and "Topless-Bottomless" in stick-on black letters.

Active considered waiting in the Neon for Dennis. Then it occurred to him that Grace Palmer might, at this moment, be dancing on the stage not fifty yards from where he sat. He locked the car and walked across the asphalt parking lot, paced by a long shadow that gave him an uneasy feeling of being followed by a spirit. He hurried through the door and stepped into the gloom of the strip club.

A huge bouncer, a Samoan, Active thought, gave him the once-over and waved him in, apparently concluding he was not too young for Illusions, or too dangerous.

The club was split into two levels. The one nearest the door, where he stood, had a bar, some video games, and a few tables where near-naked dancers drank with men who looked a little too casual about the expanses of bare flesh surrounding them. Without a break in the chatter, several sets of eyes flicked over him and were gone, leaving him with the feeling he had just been measured for a suit, or for a girl.

He moved past the tables of cash-register eyes and down two steps into the club proper. A stage took up the back wall. Perhaps a quarter of the tables and chairs facing the stage were filled with men who definitely looked like customers, their eyes fixed on a heavy-bodied, thick-featured blonde who was dancing naked to throbbing rock music he didn't recognize. A few of the customers sat on chairs pulled up to the edge of the stage.

Active took a table a few rows back and watched idly as the blonde worked the crowd. Her act incorporated a hula hoop, which she occasionally straddled as if it were a horse or a bicycle. One of the men at the edge of the stage laid down a bill. The blonde undulated over, turned her backside toward him, bent forward, and peered at him between her knees.

If the customer liked what he saw, he didn't show it except to lay a second bill on the first. The blonde reached between her ankles, grabbed the two bills, straightened, and danced away, folding the money around her fingers like expensive silk.

"Hi, I'm Gina. Can I get you something?"

Active turned to see a skinny, pallid brunette in high heels, a G-string and bikini top leaning over the table. Ordinarily, he would have been happy to look down her front, as she apparently intended, but she seemed so wasted, so nearly used up with her dead-white complexion, he couldn't bring himself to do it. Instead, he found himself checking the stick-like forearms for needle tracks and, finding none, wondering if she had AIDS, a meth habit, or just an eating disorder.

"Can I get you something?" She said it louder this time, almost shouting to be heard over the music pounding from the boom box on the stage behind the blonde.

"A Diet Pepsi, I guess."

She looked so disappointed that he said, "I'm waiting for someone. Bring him one, too."

Her expression didn't change, and he decided that what he had taken for disappointment might just be numbness, or perhaps she was high.

"Okay? Two Diet Pepsis?"

"Two Diet Pepsis, right." She wobbled away on the high heels. As he followed her with his eyes, unable to stop himself from checking the backs of her knees for needle tracks, he saw Dennis Johnson near the bar, peering toward the stage. He stood and waved and his friend hurried over.

"Nathan!" he said. "She here?" Dennis peeled off a windbreaker, dropped it on the next table and slid into a chair beside Active.

Active shook his head. "Haven't seen her if she is. Who do we ask without setting off a dumb grenade?"

Dennis chuckled. "Yeah, the hear-no-evil, see-no-evil, speak-no-evil, at-least-to-cops, syndrome."

Active looked toward the tables on the riser by the door, where the skinny brunette was now talking to a young guy in a leather jacket and absolutely no one was looking at Nathan Active or Dennis Johnson

"You think they know we're cops?

"Of course they do," Dennis said.

"But we're not in uniform."

"They've got their own radar. Look."

Active looked and saw that Leather Jacket was headed their way.

"Evening, officers," he said tightly when he reached the table. "I'm Ian, the manager. Anything I should know about? Do we have a problem tonight?"

Dennis smiled a huge smile, his teeth fluorescing in the black light around the stage. "Nope, no problem. Just dropped in for a visit with Feather. She around?"

Ian looked relieved. "She's back there." He pointed at a door beside the stage. "Go on back if you want."

Dennis looked at Active. "Nathan?"

Active didn't know who Feather was, but he was sure he didn't want to ask her about Grace Palmer with a bunch of half-naked strippers hanging around, maybe a few bouncers and boyfriends too. "Can she come to the table?"

"I'm sure she can." Ian started away, then turned back to them with a thin smile. "The Diet Pepsis are on the house, by the way. Tell your waitress I said so."

"Who's Feather?" Active asked as Ian disappeared through the door beside the stage.

"You never heard of Feather? She's the head stripper here. Famous bodybuilder, too. Won a bunch of national awards— Geez, look at that." Dennis pointed at the stage, where Gina had replaced the fat blonde. Some sort of angry-girl piece had replaced the rock and Gina was drifting about the stage like a zombie. "Pathetic, huh?"

"She said her name's Gina. You know her?"

Dennis shrugged. "No, but I knew a couple dozen like her when I worked vice."

He paused as the fat blonde, now clad in a tube top and a miniskirt, set down two Diet Pepsis. "It's five bucks," she said.

Dennis nodded toward the door leading behind the stage. "Ian said it was on the house."

"Yeah, right."

Dennis shrugged, gave her a ten and she padded away in her bare feet. "What about the change?" he shouted.

"Yeah, right," she shouted back.

He laughed. "That one'll probably make it. But the girl on the stage there? Look at her, practically a ghost already. Some of them seem to eat this up, they support a couple of kids or put themselves through college on it, get on with life. Others, they just get eaten. Come back in a month, that one up on the stage there will be gone, nobody will know where."

Active worried over this for a moment. "Even Feather doesn't keep track of them? I thought Feather would know—"

"Feather would know what?" said a feminine voice from behind him. He felt a hand on his shoulder and the same voice said, "And who's asking, anyway?"

He turned to see a honey-blonde with muscles like gilded marble slide into the chair next to Dennis and give him a quick peck on the cheek. She set down a glass teacup filled with an amber liquid, a slice of lemon impaled on the brim. She was barefoot, wearing blue satin bikini briefs and a policeman's blue tunic, all of the buttons open.

"Feather! Its been too long!" Dennis cried.

"I been right here, honey. Where you been?"

Dennis looked down, looked sideways, took a swallow from his Diet Pepsi, looked embarrassed.

"Home with the little woman, huh?" Feather winked at Active and turned back to Dennis. "Well, that's right where you should be. You keep it up." She patted the back of his hand and looked at Active. "Who's your friend here? Another lonely cop?"

"Nathan, meet Feather. Feather, Nathan Active, of the Alaska state troopers in Chukchi."

Active put out a hand and Feather took it. Hers was dry, warm, and small. "Welcome to Illusions, Nathan."

"Pleasure," he said.

"Those new?" Dennis pointed at the tunic. "They look bigger."

Feather opened the tunic and eyed her breasts critically, as did Active and Dennis. They were large, round, and totally sag-free.

"Whatta ya think?" Feather asked. "Too much?"

Dennis narrowed his eyes appraisingly. "Well, I always thought of you as the itty-bitty-pretty-ones type, Feather. You're not a large woman. These are a little out of proportion."

She sighed and covered herself. "I know. A girl's gotta keep up, though. And they got this hot new plastic surgeon who just hit town. He was doing introductory specials so five, no, six of us here got new ones."

She sipped amber liquid from the cup and studied Active. "So what brings you two in?"

"Nathan here is looking for a girl."

Active started to object to this characterization of the situation, but Feather spoke first, with a mock frown.

"Now, Dennis, you know we don't provide that kind of service here at Illusions." She grinned and Dennis grinned. "But if we did, what kind of girl would he be—"

She stopped as Active shook his head and raised a hand.

"Please, Ms. Fea . . . er, Feather. Don't listen to this idiot. I'm trying to track down a girl from Chukchi as a favor to her father."

Feather sipped again and raised her eyebrows. "Native girl?"

"Yes, half Eskimo, half white."

He pulled out his two pictures of Grace Palmer and laid them on the table. "I heard she might be working here, or may have in the past. Her name's Grace Palmer."

Feather picked up the mural shot, looked at it, and whistled.

"Miss North World?" Then she picked up the final police mug shot, looked at it, and winced. "How does she look now?"

Active and Dennis shook their heads simultaneously, then Active spoke. "I'm not sure. Nobody's seen her in about three years. The last guy to see her said she was looking more like this." He touched the mural shot.

"Well, I can tell you nobody here looks like that. And even Illusions wouldn't hire someone who looked like this." She tapped the mug shot.

She glanced at the back of the room where Gina the Stick Girl was finishing her routine and gliding offstage. Feather shook her head and picked up the mural shot.

"We don't hire many Native ladies in here," she said. "They tend to be a little short in the leg and flat in the hip, to be perfectly frank. But I can tell you, if this girl had come in, I'd have hired her in a minute, and I'd remember her. Sorry, Nathan."

Active took the mural shot from her and studied it. Feather stood and picked up her tea cup. "I'm on."

"What is that stuff, anyway?" Active pointed at the cup.

"Ginseng and honey." She curled her arm and popped up a biceps. "You don't get a body like this from Diet Pepsi, Nathan."

She winked and disappeared through the door that led backstage and reappeared in a moment on stage, the police tunic now buttoned all the way up. She was wearing a police cap, too, the brim pulled low over her eyes, and pointing a Colt .45 straight at the audience. Something loud, pulsating, and jazzy boomed out, and Feather began to move.

She was much more choreographed than the other two, and much more athletic, prowling the stage like a tiger, blowing a police whistle, mime-firing the prop automatic at imaginary crooks. After each shot, she would blow imaginary smoke away from the muzzle of the gun, then work it into the folds of the tunic and unsnap another button.

Active had ample time for a close inspection of her breasts only a few minutes earlier, but he still found it mesmerizing to watch her uncover herself with the gun.

"Hell of a show, huh?" Dennis shouted over Feather's theme. "The rest of 'em, they just come out and peel and jump around naked. But Feather, she makes you wait."

"Hell of a show," Active said. He picked up the two pictures of Grace Palmer, studied them briefly, put them in his shirt pocket, and stood.

"Yeah, and it's not over," Dennis complained as he too rose and turned to leave the club.

Instead, Active headed for the back corner of the bar and pushed through the men's room door. He turned the cold water tap on full strength and splashed it into his eyes and ears and hair, rubbing it into his face as hard as he could.

When he finally turned off the water, Dennis spoke from behind him. "What next, pal? Haven't we kind of run out the string here? Maybe it's time to go see the John Doe guy."

Dennis ripped a length of paper towel from a roll sitting on the toilet tank and handed it to Active. Then he put down the lid and sat on the toilet.

Active dried his face, then pressed the towel hard into his eyes. It was damp and cool, and felt good. He stared at himself in the grimy mirror over the sink. Who was that red-eyed stranger staring back, and what the hell was he up to?

"You get anything from the manager at that flophouse where she was living?"

"Nah, he was out." Dennis shook his head. "I left my card."

Dennis sounded sympathetic, which irritated Active. He turned and looked at his friend, tried and failed to think of a way to tell Dennis to drop the sympathy, and finally shrugged.

"See if you can set up something with the John Doe guy at lunch tomorrow, okay?"

Dennis nodded.

CHAPTER NINE

At Peer Instruction Training the next morning, Neil of the frenetic Adam's apple had mysteriously been replaced by someone new from Redmond, a dark-haired woman named Rita who was in her forties and all business as she helped Christie with the presentation.

Active wondered idly how Christie had pulled this off. Maybe she was tight with someone in the training office at Microsoft, had called down there and asked this person if there wasn't some assignment somewhere that only Neil could handle, promising some favor in return, maybe that she, Christie, would take the next class in Fargo or Gary or Newark without whining, and suddenly Neil was on his way back to Redmond and Christie wasn't being hassled anymore.

Active sighed and tried to pay attention to the class but all he could think of was what was coming up at noon. At the first coffee break of the morning, the good-looking female Tlingit trooper from Sitka he'd been bantering with all week asked him what he was doing about lunch, but even then he didn't consider, not even for a moment, calling off his appointment with Walter Cullars, the Anchorage Police Department's John Doe man.

• • •

Cullars worked out of a basement office at Anchorage police headquarters, down two flights of stairs, along a hallway lined with white cardboard file boxes marked for shipment to the department's archives offsite. Cullars's was the second door to the left, labeled MISSING PERSONS.

"Walt Cullars, Nathan Active," Dennis said as they went in.

Active took the hand Cullars extended and studied him in some surprise. Not at all the file-clerk type he had expected, but someone who looked like a senior cop, a detective lieutenant perhaps. Trim, medium height and build, fifty-something, neatly clipped salt-and-pepper mustache, graying hair just long enough to show a little natural curl, a firm quick handshake. Cullars didn't look the part of someone who would end up working Missing Persons in the basement, and Active wondered what his story was. Well, maybe Dennis would know. He'd ask later, if he remembered.

"Dennis has told me a little about your project, Nathan," Cullars said as the two visitors dropped into yellow plastic chairs before his dented gray Steelcase desk. "But why don't you sketch it for me, while I get us some coffee. With, without?" He raised his eyebrows in the white expression of inquiry.

"Black," Active said. "Brown, no sugar," Dennis said. Cullars nodded and busied himself at a Mister Coffee on a file cabinet behind his desk.

Active tried and failed to imagine how Grace Palmer's story could be compressed into a sketch, so he just told the back of Cullars's head her name and the date of her last known contact with officialdom, the encounter with Special Ed at Aurora Bingo three winters ago.

Cullars returned to the desk, set down two Styrofoam cups of coffee and one ceramic mug that said, "Life's a Bitch, Then You Marry One." He scrawled the Aurora Bingo date on his desk blotter and frowned at it. Absently, he opened a desk drawer and came up with five paper packets of sugar. He clamped them in the crook of a thumb and forefinger, ripped off the tops, and emptied them simultaneously into the Life's a Bitch mug, stirred the result with a ballpoint, and took a long swallow.

Nathan picked up one of the Styrofoam cups and took a sip, looking over the rim at Dennis with his eyebrows raised. Dennis rolled his eyes and gave his head a tiny shake of mystification.

"We've had two since then that might work," Cullars said finally. He pushed back from the desk and stood. "Hang on a second, let me get them."

He pulled out a drawer under the Mister Coffee and came back with two folders, one red and one blue, neither very fat. "Never got far on either one of these. Maybe we can close one of them today."

He opened the blue folder and laid it in front of them. Active started to read the report on top of the stack, but Cullars waved his hand and Active sat back to listen.

"Some kids found this one the spring after your bingo date, leaning up against a birch tree in a little park near East High School. She was wearing winter clothes and pretty decomposed, so it seemed like she had been there a while."

He moved the report aside to uncover a small manila envelope of photographs, closed with a metal clasp. "Weird deal," he said as he opened the envelope. "No sign of foul play, no I.D. on the body, no one ever reported her missing, nothing with her but an old Bible and an empty vodka bottle. I figure she took shelter under the birch one winter night and just never woke up. Nobody noticed she was gone, I guess."

Active waited uneasily as Cullars opened the envelope and spread the five-by-sevens across the desk, some from the scene, others from the autopsy.

The pictures from the autopsy showed nothing Active could recognize. Those from the scene showed a decaying mummy slumped under a tree in a ragged gray parka, dark sweatpants, and a pair of worn purple snow machine boots. The woman had dark straight hair, no trace of gray, and Native features, but the face was too far gone to tell anything more.

Active winced and looked away. "How old was she?"

Cullars pawed through the file and read from an autopsy report. "Twenty-two to twenty-seven years of age at time of death, an old break in the left tibia, well-healed, probably no pregnancies, smoked heavily. No gross evidence of trauma or disease except for a probable enlarged liver, probably due to alcohol abuse, but no guarantees on any of the soft-tissue stuff because of the condition of the body. Think this is your Grace Tucker?" He looked up at Active.

"It's Palmer. Grace Palmer."

"Right, Palmer." Cullars shook his head ruefully. "Anyway, you think it's her?"

Suddenly the mug shot from the prostitution arrest flashed into Active's mind. "Any teeth missing?"

Cullars flipped to the second page of the autopsy report, then back to the first. "Molar, upper right," he said. "That's it."

"The one we're looking for has a tooth missing here." Active touched his lower jaw in front to show the spot. "Unless the pathologist overlooked something pretty obvious, this isn't her."

Cullars looked at the signature on the autopsy. "Nope, this was Dr. Kenders. He never misses anything."

He sighed and scooped the reports and pictures back into the blue folder. "I guess the file on Birch Tree Doe stays open."

"What kind of tree?" Active said. "Let me see the pictures again."

Cullars handed him the envelope from the file and he looked through the photographs till he found one with a clear view of the woman's tree. He nodded to himself, then looked at Cullars.

"This isn't a birch, it's a spruce." Active pointed to the tree in the picture. "See?"

Cullars glanced at it briefly. "Looks like a birch to me."

"No, a birch has regular leaves and smooth, white bark." Active pointed again. "This one has needles and rough, black bark. It's a spruce."

Cullars took the five-by-seven and studied it. "Really? Guess I got them mixed up. I always thought the dark ones were birch."

Active glanced at Dennis as Cullars put the pictures back in the envelope and slipped it into the blue folder. Dennis was grimacing and tapping his temple with an index finger. Apparently Cullars was a little daft, that must be why APD kept him in the basement, Active decided.

Cullars slid the blue folder under the red one, which he touched with a forefinger. "That leaves Heavenly Doe, but I gotta warn you, there's not much to work with."

He flipped open the red folder and pulled out a manila envelope of photographs. He worked the flap loose and removed the pictures, eight-by-tens this time, then spread them across his desk blotter. Active looked, had a brief impression of a collection of bloody red body parts that didn't add up to complete human being, and looked away. So did Dennis.

"One of the city's rotary snowplows hit her out at the east end of Four Street," Cullars said. "This was in February, around midnight, about six weeks after the contact at Aurora Bingo. Blizzard conditions, the kind of night when there isn't a soul in Anchorage doesn't wonder how the hell they ended up here and why they stay."

Cullars, apparently noticing their discomfort, swept the photographs into a single stack and faced them down. "Rotary operator sees this figure come out of the snow and darkness waving its arms, hears a thunk, and she's in the screw before he can touch a brake."

He tapped the stack of inverted photographs. "These pieces here came out of the blower and ended up in the snow trailer behind the rotary. We spent two days raking through the load and this was all we found. But the rig jack-knifed when the driver did hit the brakes and we figure the rest of her got sprayed into the berms along Four Street there and just never turned up."

Active stared at the stack. "No I.D. on her?"

Cullars shook his head. "Nothing. Of course we never found most of her clothes, so you don't know."

"Any witnesses other than the snowplow driver?"

"Not that we could find. Couple minutes later, the driver thought he saw somebody, maybe another homeless woman, come out of the blizzard, take one look at everything, and hightail it, but he was too shook up to be sure. If somebody else was there that night, we never found her. Or him."

While Active was thinking dejectedly that he wasn't too surprised Cullars couldn't find the blizzard woman, Dennis picked the on-scene report out of Cullars's folder and thumbed through it. "Homicide ever open a file on this? You know, if somebody else was there and they took off, that would raise questions, right?"

"That's kind of the way I figured it, maybe she was pushed, but I couldn't get Homicide interested. They were sorting out some kind of gang war up in Mountain View at the time, a Filipino dead on Pine Street, couple of Vietnamese kids hit, and there was nothing to go on here, really. Some homeless person running from the scene of an accident, what does that mean? They're not gonna hang around and talk to cops even if they're innocent. And I'm just a guy in the basement, you know? Homicide's not gonna listen to me."

Dennis shrugged. "They're like that sometimes."

"All the time," Cullars said.

"Autopsy turn up anything?" Active said.

"Not much." Cullars ran his finger down the report and read off the main points. "Twenty-six plus or minus two years, at least one pregnancy, heavy smoker. Pretty drunk and suffering from a fairly severe chest cold when she got hit."

"Get anywhere with the fingerprints?"

"Didn't get any," Cullars said. "Never found the left hand, right hand only had two fingers and they were too mangled to take impressions."

"How about the tooth?" Active touched his lower jaw again.

Cullars shook his head. "Most of the head was missing, just a piece of scalp with the left ear and about two inches of upper jawbone attached was all we found. No teeth at all."

"And you think she was Native?" Active said. "Why is that?"

"Maybe Native," Cullars said. "The skin and hair were dark. Maybe Asian, Filipino, Hispanic, South Pacific Islander, American Indian, you know. Wanna look at these?" He tapped the photographs.

"I guess not, if all you have is an ear and some scalp," Active said. "Nothing there to go on. I never saw Grace Palmer's left ear."

He rose to go, depressed that he was no closer to any answers than when he came in.

"Guess not," Cullars said. "I guess Heavenly Doe stays open, too."

Active sat down again, an alarm bell tinkling in a distant corner of his mind. "I meant to ask, why do you call her that? Heavenly Doe?"

Dennis, who had also risen, sat down, too.

"The tattoo, of course." Cullars gazed at them idly. "I mentioned the tattoo, right? You saw the pictures of the tattoo?"

They stared back uncomprehendingly. Cullars suddenly looked embarrassed and said, "Fuck, I'm sorry, I thought I told you. She had a jailhouse special."

While Dennis tapped his temple and grimaced again, Cullars turned the photographs face up, flipped through them, and slid two of the color eight-by-tens, one above the other, across the desk.

In the top one, the frame was filled by a headless, mutilated female corpse, left arm severed in mid-biceps, right arm complete but mangled, left leg intact, right leg gone below the knee, a gaping diagonal slash across the abdomen. She had had a pretty nice figure once, though she had developed a little pot belly, probably from drinking.

Cullars tapped the corpse's left breast, where an image of some kind was visible on the skin, then slid out the bottom photograph. "This is why I call her Heavenly Doe."

Active studied the close-up of the image just above the areola—a pensive, androgynous angel hovering over the dead woman's heart. It was done in a fine, if unschooled, black stroke that captured a kind of yearning or loneliness in the face. "This was done in jail, you said?"

Cullars nodded. "Most likely. Apparently they'll take some

toothpaste, mix in some cigarette ashes or melt down a plastic checker, tattoo each other with a sharpened guitar string and the motor out of a cassette player, whatever they can find. Some of 'em get pretty good, when they get out they actually go into legitimate tattooing, if there is such a thing."

Active pushed the photograph away, feeling at a loss. An angel tattoo, that street name— Amazing Grace. It could be. Or it couldn't. "You check around with the tattoo parlors, see if anybody recognized the work?"

"Yeah, I hit a couple." Cullars shook his head. "They don't like to talk to cops any more than street people do, but they claimed not to recognize the hand. They're the ones told me it looked like jailhouse work."

Dennis bent his head over the angel for a closer look. Cullars stood and refilled his cup from the Mister Coffee and was just ripping the tops off five more sugar packets when Dennis said, "Hey, what's this?" He was pointing at a dot between the angel's feet.

Cullars bent for a closer look, then waved a hand dismissively. "Oh, that. A mole maybe. Or maybe the needle slipped." He dumped the sugar into his coffee.

Active bent over and studied the dot, wondering how he had missed it earlier. Dennis's head came down to hover beside his own.

The dot didn't look like a mole, or like a solid blob of ink. Was there some lifework inside it? "You got a magnifier?" he and Dennis said together.

Cullars fished one of out the same drawer where he kept his sugar and passed it over. Dennis held it over the dot while he and Active squinted at the fuzzy little image. Definitely something in there, Active thought, but hard to make out. The details of the dot were just at the limits of resolution of the lens used to take the picture.

"Looks like letters," Dennis said finally. "One inside the other. O-R, maybe."

Active looked at Cullars. "These jailhouse artists ever sign their work? Ever hear of one named O.R.? Maybe we can find him or her, ask who this was."

"I never heard of one of 'em signing a tattoo." Cullars took a long, savoring pull at the coffee cup, sucked wind through his side teeth. "Sometimes they'll name the picture, though."

"Name the picture? Shit." Active grabbed the magnifier from Dennis and bent over the dot again. "G.P. That's what it says. Not O.R., but a G with a P inside it. Shit."

Active felt his stomach heat up, conviction growing inside him. He threw down the magnifier, took a last look at the other eight-by-ten, the shot of Grace Palmer's mutilated torso with its weirdly nice breasts and its sad little boozer's paunch, stood and went to the door, breathing rapidly to fight down the nausea.

Dennis, who had picked up the magnifier and was now studying the initials again, nodded. "Yeah, I think you're right, Nathan. Definitely a P inside a G." He sighed, a big whooshing sigh, and laid down the magnifier.

"You think it's her?" Cullars was looking at the initials himself with the glass.

Active already had the door open, was halfway out when he heard Dennis answer Cullars's question. "Yeah, Walt, I think you can close your file on Heavenly Doe now."

"But that's a P," Cullars was saying as Dennis came through the door. "I thought you said her name was Grace Tucker. This says G.P."

CHAPTER TEN

"Sorry, man," Dennis said from behind him. "I forgot Cullars was such a doofus. I guess he rolled his unit in a high-speed chase about five years back and got some kind of head injury. That's why he's in the basement."

Active, elbows on a stack of archive boxes, face to the wall, said nothing.

"At least we know now, huh?"

"You think he was right about her being pushed?" Active turned to look at his friend.

Dennis rubbed his chin. "Hard to say. I heard his instincts were pretty sharp before his accident, but now . . . well, you see how he is."

"Yeah, but he does seem to pick up on stuff, like the woman hanging around in the blizzard that night. Think it was that Angie girl?"

"Who?"

Active recounted his conversation at Aurora Bingo with Special Ed.

Dennis frowned when Active was done, concentrated for a moment. "Who knows? Pretty cold trail if it was this Angie. But I can hook you up with Homicide if you want."

"You think they'll do anything?"

"Let's see, this was, what, almost three and a half years ago, victim and suspect both street people, no witnesses, no evidence, no leads. Yeah, I think they'll do something. They'll take your information down and file it, just like they did with Cullars."

"No thanks, I guess."

Dennis shrugged. "Anyway, I gotta get back on duty now. You gonna be all right?"

"I'll be fine. Another afternoon of Peer Instruction Training is just what I need."

They started down the hall together. "Wanna do something tonight?" Dennis was a little too casual. "Movie, maybe?"

Active cut him a sideways glance. "You babysitting me now? I said I'll be fine."

Dennis shrugged.

"Anyway, I need to spend some time with Ed and Carmen or they'll kick me out," Active said. "The price of free rent is, you have to spend time with your parents. Remember?"

Dennis chuckled. "How about Friday, then? The Finest have another hockey game and I think we're going to need a defenseman. One of our regular guys is pulling some night shifts." He looked at Active. "This is no bullshit. Really."

Active thought the idea of all that whacking and banging and colliding sounded pretty good. No brains required, just speed, reflexes and a manly indifference to pain. "Yeah, sure. What time?"

"Eight o'clock, Fire Lake Rec Center," Dennis said.

"Way out there in Eagle River? Still hard to get ice time, huh?"

"Yep, same as always. When we play downtown at the Ben Boeke, we have to start at five or six in the morning.

Active grimaced. "I guess I can make it out to Fire Lake."

"We got some extra gear if you can't find your old stuff," Dennis said.

With Christie and Rita in charge, Peer Instruction Training was devoid of tension, drama, or conflict that afternoon, leaving Active's mind free to prowl back over the past few days.

What? This was only Wednesday? Was it really only five days since Jason Palmer had called him to Chukchi High to look at the mural of Grace Palmer, five days since Lucy Generous sensed what was in the back of his mind before he did and they got into that huge fight?

Now it seemed like Grace Palmer had been in his head for years, not days, seemed like he had known her, had actually seen her smashing windows along Four Street, advising cops and maybe even a judge to give each other blow jobs, had watched her disrespect the *aanas* at Aurora Bingo and jab Special Ed in the eye with the red dauber. And now she was gone.

No, that was stupid. In fact, it was nuts. She had never been there, had tangled with a snowplow three years before he ever heard her name, before he ever saw the silver gleam from the foxlike eyes on the wall at Chukchi High.

He imagined Grace Palmer windmilling into the path of the rotary snowplow, rolled the image around in his mind to see how much it hurt. Not that much, actually. It wasn't so hard to let her go, really, and he felt Lucy Generous around him again in a way he hadn't since . . . since when? Since the night he went through Grace Palmer's police files with Dennis Johnson.

But now Lucy was back in his mind, warm and smiling. Had he ever known anyone so emotionally open? He remembered their makeup sex after the big fight last Friday . . . no, between the two big fights really, felt himself stirring there in the Peer Instruction Training classroom and had to cross his legs so as not to embarrass himself.

He'd get Lucy something nice before he went back up to Chukchi, apologize again if she seemed to need it, he could imagine the homecoming now. Maybe he'd call her tonight, say something a little suggestive, see how she reacted, maybe they'd try phone sex, they'd never done it that way. He shook his head, took a sip from the Diet Pepsi under his chair, and put the thought away for later.

So what had it been about, this Grace Palmer thing? Panic, probably. Panic about Lucy Generous, he supposed, though he couldn't remember exactly why she scared him.

Marriage? Was that it? Maybe he was scared because he was starting to be able to imagine himself popping the question, not that there was any real doubt about Lucy's answer.

Maybe he had fixated on Grace Palmer—beautiful, mysterious, lost and, most important, unattainable—because of his panic at the thought a marriage proposal might be building up inside him like the aurora just starting to flicker in the winter sky. Distracting himself from what he was afraid of by focusing on something he couldn't have and probably wouldn't want if he found it, that's all he had been doing.

Whatever it had been about, just knowing that Grace Palmer was gone seemed to have ended it. That was why it didn't hurt as much as he had expected when he thought about how she died. A sad story, sure, a tough thing to tell Jason Palmer when he got back, but not an unusual story on Four Street.

• • •

Carmen Wilhite was on the back deck barbecuing halibut and baking potatoes on the new gas grill when she heard the sliding door open behind her. She turned to see her adoptive son stick his head out.

"It's after five," Nathan said. "You want a beer?"

She looked at her watch. "So it is, and what was I thinking?"

He grinned, disappeared, and returned in a moment with a Heineken and a frozen mug for her, a Diet Pepsi and a glass of ice for himself. He poured, they drank, he looked at the grill. "Halibut, huh? Nature's most nearly perfect food."

"Isn't that milk?"

"Only because no cow ever ate a halibut."

She chuckled and studied him as she sipped the icy Heineken. It was the first joke he'd cracked all week. The tension that had closed him up like a fist was gone now, thank goodness.

She wondered what the blues had been about. Was it the job, maybe, a problem in this computer class that brought him down to Anchorage? A fight with the girlfriend in Chukchi, this Lucy Generous, that Martha had phoned her about but Nathan had not mentioned? Or did it have something to do with this project he and Dennis Johnson had been working on in the evenings, trying to run down Grace Palmer, the lost beauty queen, as a favor to her father up in Chukchi?

After a certain point in adolescence, sons didn't talk about anything important to their mothers, especially anything that was bothering them. She knew that. But she had always thought Nathan was reserved beyond what you'd expect of a normal kid, even what you'd expect of an adopted Eskimo kid raised by white parents six hundred miles from Eskimo country. He certainly hadn't opened up about anything so far this week. Maybe he would now.

"Good day?" she said, lightly and after considerable thought.

He sighed. "Yes and no."

"Kind of a zen day, was it?"

He laughed, but only a little. "We found out Grace Palmer is dead, is all."

Carmen probed a halibut filet with the barbecue fork and saw that it was done, though she knew the potatoes had a few minutes to go yet. She transferred the filets to a plate, covered them with foil and set them on the barbecue's upper grill, where they would stay hot but not cook any more. "That's too bad. How'd she die?"

He told her about Grace Palmer's rendezvous with the municipal snowplow on Four Street three winters ago, how Dennis's sharp eye had noticed the little dot that was Grace Palmer's initials, and how he and Dennis had speculated that she was pushed into the snowplow by the hazy figure the driver had seen loom out of the blizzard.

"Really? She was murdered?"

He frowned. "I don't know. Maybe. But it's so long ago and that person in the blizzard might as well be dead, too, for all the chance there is of finding her now. Or him. Anyway, it's APD's problem, not mine. I know what I need to tell her father, which is all I wanted."

He walked over to the grill, lifted the foil off the halibut, and pinched off a bite, then held it between his teeth and blew air in and out of his mouth to cool it off. "Mmmm, iss is guh. You err know err?"

"What? Don't talk with your mouth full, especially of hot halibut."

He tried again a few moments later, the halibut safely swallowed. "Mmmm, that was good. You ever know her?"

"Grace Palmer? No, if I'm doing the math right, she would have still been a baby when we moved down here." She folded down the flap of foil that Nathan had left up. "I think I remember a new school teacher coming to town while we were there. Might have been her dad, all right. And I definitely remember reading about it when a Chukchi girl won the Miss North World contest, but the name didn't mean anything to me. What a hard, sad little story."

"Yeah." He shook his head and frowned again. "It'll be a tough thing to tell her father but it's good to get to the end of it."

She poked the barbecue fork into a potato and pulled it out again. It slid easily, no resistance to speak of, and the stuff that came back on the tines looked about right. "I think it's done. You want to slice up some bread while I do the salad?"

Nathan picked up the platter of halibut as she transferred the potatoes to a platter of their own. "What about Ed? He's not eating tonight?"

"He's got a field trip to a fire station with his fifth graders tomorrow. He had a sandwich and then he went back in to get things organized."

They went in and busied themselves over the bread and salad, and she decided to push her luck a little. "Martha tells me you're seeing someone? A Lucy Generous?"

He shrugged. "I guess."

"And she, ah, is she nice?"

"No, I prefer the meaner ones."

Carmen felt herself blush slightly. "Sorry, didn't mean to pry, but you know how mothers are."

"Yep," he said. "Both of you."

"You're kind of outnumbered, huh?"

"Yeah, I guess." Then he surprised her by leaning over and kissing her cheek. "But in a good way."

She smiled at that, and then he surprised her even more. "Don't worry," he said. "I think I might have some news for you two in that department pretty soon."

She turned and stared at him. "What news? What department? Are we talking wedding bells here?"

"Well," he said with one of his grins, "if I told you now it wouldn't be news, would it?" And with that he walked over to the table, sat down, and began piling halibut onto his plate.

She hurried after him with the salad, probed a little more over dinner, got nothing but the grin.

So she switched gears and they talked about the halibut trip they would take to Homer that weekend. They would replenish the family freezer, she said, maybe even send some back to Chukchi with him.

He expressed polite enthusiasm, but confessed he was beginning to entertain some doubt that even Homer halibut could compete with Chukchi sheefish, and promised to bring some down the next time he came.

As he gave her another of his grins, she was thinking she would call Chukchi soon and see if Martha had any idea what this news was. Maybe Nathan had told his birth mother something he wouldn't tell her.

After dinner, Active helped Carmen load the dishwasher, then went up to his old room. He checked and was happy to discover his old phone line—the "Teen Line," as it had been listed in the Anchorage phone book—was still connected.

That was lucky, he thought. If he got up the nerve to attempt a seduction of Lucy by long distance, Carmen or Ed couldn't pick up an extension somewhere and accidentally plug into what had equal chances of being the sexiest, or the stupidest, telephone conversation ever conducted under their roof.

Could he do it? He tried to imagine himself saying, "What are you wearing?" to Lucy but the scene wouldn't come into focus. He'd either freeze at the crucial moment, or giggle. Or Lucy would laugh out loud at his male foolishness.

No, it would be safer to call and have a normal conversation, limit it to telling her about Grace Palmer being dead. He would indicate somehow that the Grace Palmer thing had been a crisis point for him and he had now passed it, let that serve in lieu of the apology he felt in a vague way he owed Lucy, but couldn't think how to frame.

At least it would be an improvement over their other two conversations since he had come to Anchorage. Those had consisted principally of Lucy saying, "Did you find her?" followed by him saying "No," followed by Lucy saying "You still looking? Well, good luck," and hanging up.

He sat down at his old desk and saw beside the phone the stack of police files on Grace Palmer that Dennis Johnson had dug up. He had dropped them there two nights earlier, after the records crawl at APD, and now the folders were scattered all over the desk, except for two that had slid onto the floor. He scooped them back into a stack and secured it with a big rubber band he found in a desk drawer. Then he put it on top of his briefcase, next to the bed.

The desk finally clear, he picked up the phone and dialed Lucy's grandmother's number in Chukchi. It wasn't Lucy who answered, but Pauline Generous, which certainly put an end to any thoughts of phone sex with Lucy.

Before he could ask to speak to her, the old lady said exactly the same thing her granddaughter had been saying all week.

"You find that Gracie Palmer yet?"

He debated telling Pauline what he had learned, but decided against it. He didn't want Jason or Ida Palmer hearing of their daughter's death through the river of gossip that coursed constantly through Chukchi's streets. Lucy could probably keep the secret, at least for a few days, but Pauline wouldn't be able to stay quiet about it more than ten minutes once she sat down with the other *aanas* at the Chukchi Senior Center for her daily session of snerts, the incomprehensible card game that didn't seem to be played anywhere but Chukchi and the villages around it.

"No, I didn't find her," he said. "But I gave up. I'm all done."

The old lady harrumphed. "Good thing, too. You looking for Lucy? She's over your place, defrosting your refrigerator, I think."

He thanked her and hung up, thinking to himself he might have a chance at the phone-sex thing, after all. What was it Lucy had said when he ripped her panties off during the makeup sex a week earlier? That she wouldn't wear any the next time she came over?

Could he ring her up at the bachelor cabin and say, "Are you wearing what you're supposed to be wearing when you come over to my place?" Yeah, he thought maybe he could do that. He'd get the words out, see if she got on the same wavelength, and let nature take its course. Or not.

He walked over and locked the door to his room, walked back to the desk and was reaching for the phone when it rang. He stared at it in surprise, trying to think as he picked it up why somebody would be calling Ed and Carmen's modem line.

"Hey, buddy, the old Teen Line still works, huh?"

"Geez, Dennis, you must be the only person on earth who still knows the number."

"Yep, flypaper for a brain, that's me. You got a minute?"

"I guess." Active hoped against hope it really would be only a minute, so he could reinitiate his seduction plot on the unsuspecting Lucy.

"I was thinking I might drop over and get those files from you, take them back in tomorrow."

"Now? You want to come over tonight? Why don't I run them over at lunch tomorrow? Or you can come get them at the hotel."

"Um, well, I, ah . . ."

"What?"

There was a long silence on the line. "You sure you want to hear about this?"

"What?

Dennis sighed. "You remember I was supposed to talk to the guy at the Creekview?"

Active searched his memory for a moment. "Oh, yeah, the flophouse where Grace Palmer was getting her Oil Dividend."

"Right. Well, I missed the manager the other day but he called me this afternoon. And he remembered her. She actually did live there for a while, it wasn't just a mail drop."

Why was Dennis bothering him with this? Either way, the late Grace Palmer was just a file about to be closed in Walt Cullars's basement office. "So?"

"So you remember the two women who supposedly lived there with her? One of 'em actually did, according to the manager."

Active was getting an uneasy feeling now, something about the roommates tugging at his mind. Shaneesha Prather, that was one, but the other one—

"Angelina Ramos," Dennis said.

"Angie," Active said. "That Angie girl Special Ed told me about."

"That's my guess," Dennis said.

"So what is Ramos, Mexican?"

"Nope, Filipino. It's a real common name with them."

"So did the Creekview guy know where she is?" Active said it casually, forcing it past a tightening throat.

"Not a clue." He was starting to relax a little when Dennis added triumphantly, "But the computer did."

Active sighed. "Go ahead."

Dennis explained that he had found Angelina Ramos in the Oil Dividend records. She had skipped the dividend for a year after Grace Palmer's death, then applied from Dutch Harbor. Her most recent application, filed only three months earlier, listed her in care of Elizabeth Cove Seafoods in the Aleutian fishing port. A call to the Alaska Department of Labor, Dennis said, had confirmed that unemployment insurance premiums were being deducted from the paychecks of one Angelina Ramos at Elizabeth Cove Seafoods in Dutch Harbor.

"And it was Cullars who knew to call the labor department," Dennis concluded. "I guess he's got something on the ball, even if it's not much. Maybe it's all the sugar."

Active thought it over. "So where does this leave us?"

"I'm turning it over to Homicide," Dennis said. "Ramos drops out of sight after Grace Palmer dies, turns up in Dutch Harbor. Why would she skip the Oil Dividend for a year unless she was trying to lie low? Nobody in their right mind gives up free money from the state of Alaska."

"I still don't see why you have to get the files now. Why can't it wait'll tomorrow?"

"I want to go over them again tonight, see if she pops up anywhere but the Creekview," Dennis said. "Then I'll write up some kind of report and give it to Homicide in the morning, try to get 'em interested no matter how busy they are. And then I can go back to my real job and forget about this beauty queen of yours."

"Yeah, right," Active said.

"Yeah, right."

"Okay, come on over. I already bundled it all up for you, anyway."

They hung up and Active got the files from atop the briefcase, figuring he'd go downstairs and wait on the steps for Dennis, enjoy the evening sun and try not to think about anything.

It didn't work. He put his head back on the steps and closed his eyes and there was Grace Palmer's face from the mural. The fox eyes veiled, no flash of silver there now. Dead eyes.

He trudged back upstairs with the files, flopped onto his bed, pulled off the rubber band, and opened the first folder.

Fifteen minutes later, just as the doorbell rang downstairs, he closed the last file and looked at the three sheets of paper he had extracted during his search. One was the Oil Dividend printout, showing Grace and Angie living together at the Creekview. Another was from the file on Grace Palmer's arrest for obstructing traffic. Someone named "A. Ramos" had bailed her out for fifty dollars. The third sheet was from the file on the window-smashing spree on Fourth Avenue. Officer Tedrow had diligently recorded the names of everyone at the scene, including an "Angie Ramoth," who admitted knowing Grace Palmer but denied any knowledge of the window smashing.

So what, he told himself. Whether Angie Ramos did or didn't serve time for killing Grace Palmer, the dead eyes would stay dead. So what? Not his jurisdiction, not his case, not his problem.

He heard Carmen go to the door and let Dennis in, heard his friend clumping up the stairs, and had the files shaped back into a neat stack, the rubber band in place, by the time Dennis filled the doorway to his room.

"That them?" he said.

"That's them," Active said. "But I need to keep them for a while."

Dennis frowned, looked like he was trying to figure out what the joke was. "Yeah, for your scrapbook, right?"

"No, for Dutch Harbor."

"Dutch Harbor?"

"I'm going down there."

"You are? When?"

"Friday night after my class ends, Saturday morning, whenever I can get a seat."

"I don't know . . ."

"Come on, you said yourself Homicide might not be interested. How soon are they going to send somebody down there?"

Dennis looked thoughtful, tugged at his lower lip. "Look, man, a couple of street people get into a drunken squabble over a bottle and one of them ends up sucked into a snowplow—how much does it matter? It's more of an accident than a murder if you think about it. Let it go, let our Homicide unit handle it. It's their job."

Active shrugged.

"You know, you're getting pretty close to the edge here."

Active shrugged again.

"Yeah, okay." Dennis rolled his eyes and pulled a sheaf of papers from inside his jacket. "You better take these, too, then. I got a copy of Cullars's Heavenly Doe file when I saw him today."

Active took the papers. "Even the pictures?"

"Even the pictures."

Active tossed the sheaf on top of the other files. "Thanks, Dennis. I . . . well, thanks."

Dennis rolled his eyes and clumped down the stairs.

PART III
DUTCH HARBOR

CHAPTER ELEVEN

No seats to Dutch Harbor were open after noon on Friday, so it was Saturday morning when Active handed the Aleutian Air agent his driver's license and a credit card, and heaved his bag onto the scales beneath the counter. His head throbbed from even this mild exertion, a consequence of the previous night's service on Dennis's hockey team, when two players from the opposition had checked him into the side board so hard he lost consciousness for a few seconds.

The agent, a prim-looking man in a white shirt, blue tie, and steel-rimmed glasses, eyed the bag, then Active. "That it?"

"That's it, except for my briefcase here." Active held it up for inspection by Mr. Jenkins, as a name tag identified the ticket agent.

"That bag would fit in the overhead," Jenkins said. "You might want to carry it on, too."

Active shook his head and said he'd rather not have to bother with it.

Jenkins looked at him and raised his eyebrows significantly. "You still might want to carry it on."

Active asked him why and Jenkins leaned over the counter with a confidential air.

"We're not supposed to say this, but . . ." He paused, looked at Active, and waited expectantly.

"Oh," Active said, realizing what Mr. Jenkins expected. "I won't tell. Your secret is safe with me."

Jenkins nodded and continued with the same confidential, even conspiratorial, air. "Once, one of our planes was trapped on the ground in Dutch Harbor three days by a storm. Ever since, our crews have tended to expedite the turnaround there whenever the weather is inclement."

Active's lack of comprehension must have shown, for Mr. Jenkins elaborated. "And today the weather is very inclement."

He paused, looked at Active, and apparently detected no sign of enlightenment. "There may not be time to unload the baggage," he whispered.

He straightened and watched approvingly as Active pulled his bag off the scales and said "Thank you very much" and asked himself how any woman, however dead or beautiful, could take him where the weather could ground a jetliner for three days.

The flight to Dutch Harbor was two hours long. That's what the ticket from Aleutian Air said, but it might as well have been twenty minutes. That's how long it took Active to fall asleep after he got two aspirins from the cabin attendant and opened the Peer Instruction Training Manual on his lap. It was his usual response to the noise, the smell, and, especially, the helpless immobility of air travel.

He awoke as the cabin attendant launched into her lecture on the need to raise his seat back to the full upright and locked position. The moment she finished, a deep confident male voice clicked on.

"This is Captain Ross," the voice said. "Dutch Harbor is experiencing a little weather just now, so we're in a holding pattern north of the island. We've got enough fuel to do this, oh, maybe forty-five minutes, then we'll have to head back to Anchorage."

But, Captain Ross went on to explain, the "weather" consisted of a series of squalls moving through, with pretty decent breaks in between, so they would probably—

Suddenly, the deep voice clicked off, then came back on, tense now, no sign of the lazy verbal grin that had been in it before.

"Ladies and gentlemen, Dutch Harbor has opened up and we're cleared to land," said the now all-business Captain Ross. "Please check to see that your seat belts are securely fastened. Cabin attendants, prepare for landing."

He clicked off and the 737 rolled into a bank steeper than Active had ever experienced in anything larger than a Super Cub. Equipment groaned somewhere out of sight, the flaps on the wing dropped, and deceleration pushed him forward in his seat.

He pulled his eyes from the gray murk outside as Captain Ross rode the bucking 737 down through several thousand feet of cloud that Active hoped was rock-free. They never actually broke into the clear, but he became able to see waves below, then a few seconds of brown crags and gravel slopes, then more water. Then there was a flash of beach and runway lights and the screech of tires on pavement.

The engines roared as the pilot kicked in the thrust reversers and the plane slowed as if it had rolled into a lake of molasses.

Finally the noise and deceleration abated, and the cabin attendant clicked the public-address system back on. "Welcome to Dutch Harbor," she said, "the shortest runway in the world certified for a Boeing 737."

The plane taxied to a halt and Active lined up with the rest of the passengers at the door near the cockpit. They filed down the ramp into a razoring wind and horizontal rain that evidently qualified as "between squalls" in Dutch Harbor. He was nearly to the terminal door, the carried-on bag bumping safely against his leg, when the soundness of Mr. Jenkins's advice was demonstrated. Captain Ross hurried past with long strides and bounded up the steps into the terminal.

By the time Active got inside, Captain Ross was up on a chair addressing a crowd in front of the Aleutian Air ticket counter. "That's what I'm saying," Ross was telling a long-haired young white man who had evidently just asked a question. "We don't have time to load the baggage. We haven't even unloaded the bags we brought with us. Another squall will be here in ten minutes, and I'm taking that plane out ahead of it. If you want to get out of Dutch Harbor, you need to come with me right now."

Captain Ross jumped off the chair and rushed out of the terminal with the same purposeful, long-legged stride that had brought him in.

The crowd of travelers at the counter looked at each other uneasily, then at the woman behind the counter. "We don't even have our seats assigned yet," said the man Captain Ross had spoken to.

The ticket agent shrugged and said, "That'll take at least twenty minutes." With that the crowd stampeded after the pilot. For a moment, Active felt the same panicky need to get out of Dutch Harbor and had to fight down the urge to run after them. Well, at least he had his bag, thanks to Mr. Jenkins.

Inside the terminal, he rented a Topaz, barely flinching at the tab of eighty dollars a day, even without the extra collision insurance.

The clerk, a bored teenage girl, gave him a map and swept a

forefinger from the airport south to a dimple on the east shore of a body of water called Captain's Bay when he told her he had a reservation at the Royal Islander.

"Right there at the back of Elizabeth Cove." She tapped the dimple. "You can't miss it."

He bent over and studied the dimple. Sure enough, tiny letters identified it as Elizabeth Cove. He straightened and looked at the girl. "Is Elizabeth Cove Seafoods along there, too, by any chance?"

"Sure." She touched a pen to the mouth of the cove, just where the shoreline turned south again to run down Captain's Bay. "If you miss the hotel, that's what you'll hit next. Elizabeth Cove Seafoods."

The girl—Dora, according to her name tag—slipped her headphones back on and picked up a magazine called *6TeeN*. Dora was plump and Native, Aleut presumably, as Dutch Harbor was in the Aleutians. The girl on the cover of *6TeeN* was white and looked to be about five pounds from anorexia.

He walked outside, found the Topaz, and tossed his bag into the rear seat just as Captain Ross's 737 roared past the terminal, raised its nose and lifted off, wings rocking in the wind pouring over the island from the west.

Active climbed behind the wheel and studied the map as rain pelted against the windshield and the little car rocked occasionally in the gusts. It appeared Dutch Harbor was really two islands. A little one called Amaknak, with the airport and a web of roads at its south tip. To the east, a big one called Unalaska, with a narrow strait separating it from Amaknak.

In fact, the whole place seemed to be called Unalaska. Unalaska Island, City of Unalaska, even Unalaska Lake. Why, then, did they call it—ah, there it was, an inlet north of the airport side that bore the label "Dutch Harbor."

Well, Dutch Harbor was good enough for him. Any place with weather so bad people abandoned their luggage to get out should certainly not be called "Unalaska." It was very Alaska, in his opinion. Perhaps the quintessential Alaska.

He ran his finger along the route from the airport to Elizabeth Cove and started the Topaz. Elizabeth Cove was on the Unalaska side, a mile or so south of the strait between the two islands. He glanced at the bridge spanning the strait, then held the map up to the window for more light. Yes, the tiny letters really did say, "Bridge to the Otherside."

He smiled and put the car in gear, thinking this was very Alaska, indeed, and that Dutch Harbor might be likable enough, the panicky stampede out of the terminal notwithstanding.

Dora's prediction was accurate. It was impossible to miss the Royal Islander, a sprawling new structure with a four-story English manor in the center and less grandiose three-story wings to either side.

This, he realized with a sinking feeling, was not going to be cheap. Just as he was wishing he had put a little more effort into shopping around for a better deal before leaving Anchorage, he noticed a cluster of buildings two hundred yards down the beach, with a sign identifying it as Elizabeth Cove Seafoods. Easy walking distance, meaning his eighty-dollar-a-day Topaz was pretty much superfluous. Maybe he should just cancel the room and sleep in the Topaz?

He pushed away the thought, took his bag inside, through a lobby with a huge stone fireplace, and up to a counter where the clerk confirmed his worst fears. The room was one-seventy-five a night.

Well, at least there's the fifty-seven channels of satellite television and the Jacuzzi, he consoled himself a few minutes later as he started the Topaz for the two-hundred-yard trip to Elizabeth Cove Seafoods.

He probably wouldn't be around long anyway. Maybe Angie Ramos would be gone now, or maybe she would somehow be another Angie Ramos. Surely mistakes were possible, even likely, in something like this.

Maybe she would be the right Angie Ramos, but would say she hadn't seen Grace Palmer for a month before the snowplow accident and would have a plausible explanation for moving to Dutch Harbor. Then it really would be over and he could let Jason Palmer's daughter rest in peace.

Or maybe some word, some look, would tell him Angie Ramos had pushed Grace Palmer in the way of the snowplow. And then what? Unless she actually confessed and put out her wrists to be cuffed, he would be stuck with a three-year-old murder case, no evidence to speak of, and the agency with jurisdiction—the Anchorage Police Department—not likely to put much effort into it. One homeless person kills another, leaves town, somehow puts herself back together, and lives quietly in the northern version of Dodge City—why should any cop shop care?

Why, in fact, should he? He was tempted to switch off the Topaz, go back to the Islander, and watch the fifty-seven channels of satellite TV until the next flight out of Dutch Harbor.

Go back to Chukchi, patch things up with Lucy, and either marry her or do the honorable thing and break it off. What the hell was he looking for anyway? If it wasn't Lucy, he had no business dragging her around by the hair until he found it, which he might never do, anyway.

Until he knew how Grace Palmer had died. He leaned his

head on the steering wheel and sighed. This was like a cup of coffee with one more swallow left. He had to drain it and look into the dregs. He put the Topaz in gear and pointed it at Elizabeth Cove Seafoods.

At first, the two women at the counter at Elizabeth Cove Seafoods told him they had all the hands they needed, what with the yellowfin sole starting to thin out now and the rockfish not in yet.

Then, when he said he was not a job applicant but an Alaska state trooper and he needed to talk to one of their workers, a woman named Angie Ramos, they looked skeptical. One moved over and put her hand on a phone and he realized he was not only in civilian clothes, but also somewhat rumpled after the flight from Anchorage.

They relaxed when he pulled out his badge and told them his bag was at the hotel and he hadn't thought to unpack and put on his uniform before coming over. The older of the two picked up a clipboard and ran her finger down the page, stopping a few lines from the bottom.

"Yep, she's here today. She's on the slime line." The woman pointed at a door leading back into the depths of the building. "Down that way, second set of double doors on your left. Ask for Mr. Phan, he'll find her."

The other woman said, "She do something?" as he turned for the door. He pretended not to hear.

He walked down a long hallway with coat hooks on the walls, some of them hung with fish-smelling orange overalls and rubber gum boots underneath. At the end, he pushed open the double metal doors and stepped into the factory.

It smelled of the sea and of spoiled fish, so strongly that he had to pause to let his breathing adjust. The room was alive with

activity, but such a blur of activity that he couldn't detect the organizing principle underneath.

His main impression was of many people in pale mesh hair
nets and the orange overalls working with a stream of white filets
that poured out of a machine at one end of the room and flowed
across it on a network of conveyor belts, like a river breaking into
meandering channels upon reaching its delta. Why the channels
of filets separated as they did, what the workers—the slime liners,
he assumed—did to the filets at various points along the channels,
and what happened when the channels converged at the far end
of the room, these were all mysteries to him amid the maddening
throb and clang of the machinery that drove the process.

He studied the slime liners who were close enough to make
out. Five were women, two of whom, he judged, could be Filipino.
Or Korean, Vietnamese, or Thai—the question was, was one of
them Angie Ramos?

At the side of one of the conveyor belts, an Asian man sat at a
small table, flipping through a carton of filets. He nodded to himself, heaved it onto the conveyor belt, and pulled another carton
from the belt onto his table. He was halfway through it when Active
walked over, showed his badge and, shouting to be heard over the
din of the machinery, asked, "Are you Mr. Phan?"

The Asian looked up from the filets and studied the badge, then
nodded without speaking, mistrust in his eyes. Active supposed
life had taught Mr. Phan that no policeman ever brought anything
good.

Active started to ask which of the women on the line was Angie
Ramos, and was surprised to find his voice didn't want to work. He
swallowed twice and finally got out the name.

Mr. Phan pointed at a woman working the second table from

the front, and facing away from them. She wore a purple base-ball cap over her hair net and the same orange overalls as her neighbors.

"I need to talk to her." Active shouted.

Mr. Phan frowned. "No good. Nobody to replace her. You wait for lunch break." His voice was high-pitched, querulous, even in a shout.

Active looked at his watch. "How long?"

Mr. Phan looked at his own watch. "Five minutes. Lunchroom out there." He pointed back through the double doors. "I tell her you looking for her."

Active turned to leave, then glanced back at the slime line, something about Angie Ramos plucking at the edge of his consciousness.

Just then she turned to the slime liner on her left and he caught a glimpse of her profile as she spoke, just a glimpse, but enough to disclose something fox-like about the brows and the bridge of the nose, an odd silver gleam from the corner of the eye. He put a hand on the edge of Mr. Phan's table to steady himself and studied the profile until—yes, there was no mistaking it—until Grace Palmer turned her attention back to the slime line.

"You gonna be all right?" Mr. Phan said.

Active waved a hand. "Yes, yes, it's just the smell."

"You not puke in here, you go in john." Mr. Phan stood and put a hand on Active's elbow, making to walk him to the doors.

Active shook him off and hurried out and leaned against the wall until the dizziness passed. Then he started back up the hallway that had brought him to the slime line, searching numbly for the lunch room.

Only three rooms opened off the passage. Two were marked

"Men" and "Women" and the third had swinging double doors with a window at the top. He peered in and saw dining tables with orange plastic chairs, a bank of vending machines, and a semicircle of the plastic chairs and a stained brown sofa, all focused on a TV on a wheeled cart. At the back of the room was a cafeteria-style tray line with food steaming in big stainless steel tubs. Whatever was for lunch had plenty of fat in it, he thought as he pushed in. The room smelled like roast turkey or pork.

A Perry Mason rerun played soundlessly on the TV. He found the remote, turned up the volume, and, still numb, watched from the sofa as the TV lawyer buffaloed another killer into standing up and blurting out a confession from the spectator seats.

How could she be alive? If she wasn't Heavenly Doe, who was? Angie Ramos? Probably, almost certainly, but how had Grace Palmer . . . ?

CHAPTER TWELVE

He shook his head and was starting back over the whole thing, one step at a time, trying to line up the dates and remember everything in the files Dennis Johnson had dug up and everything Cullars had told him about Heavenly Doe, when he heard footsteps and talk outside, the swish and crackle of the rubber overalls coming off and being hung on the hooks along the hall, doors slamming as, he assumed, the slime liners went into the washrooms off the hall to clean up. In a few minutes, people began coming in, heading for the serving line at the rear. Mostly, they looked burned-out and dirty, ready for the lunch break but not too excited about it.

He had counted seven slime liners when a pair of dark eyes flashed through the window in the lunch room door, barely visible under the bill of a purple cap. They met his for a moment, then vanished.

He jumped up and rushed to the door, vaguely aware of slime liners stepping out of his way and staring, and pushed into the hall just as a female back vanished into the women's room. The door slammed and he stood in the hall staring at the "Women" sign.

What to do? He had found Jason Palmer's daughter and she was apparently well, or at least better than when Roy Palmer had seen her in the company of soldiers outside the Junction, better than when she was smashing windows on Four Street.

But she was passing as Angie Ramos, who had in all probability died three years ago in a blizzard on Four Street. Could Grace Palmer have pushed her into the path of the snowplow, taken her money and identification and—

Through the door of the women's room he heard, faintly, a barking sound. When he leaned closer, he realized Grace Palmer was throwing up.

He should ask her about Angie Ramos, but Heavenly Doe was APD's problem. With some embarrassment, he realized he wanted nothing to do with it now that victim and suspect had traded places. He could clear his conscience by briefing Dennis when he passed through Anchorage, say that Grace Palmer had refused to be interviewed but was using Angie Ramos's identity, and that Heavenly Doe was almost certainly Angie Ramos. She definitely wasn't Grace Palmer.

Dennis could sic Homicide on the case, if he wanted to, while he, Nathan Active, went back to Chukchi and told Jason Palmer that his daughter was alive and well in the Aleutians, or at least alive. And then maybe he could get those damned fox eyes out of his head and get on with life.

But he hadn't told her of her mother's illness before she vanished. He decided to write her a note and leave it with Mr. Phan. He returned to the lunchroom and found a chair in a corner and opened his notebook to a blank page. He wrote "Dear Grace" and stopped. He had been thinking of her as "Grace" for days, he knew her so well from his crawl through the police records and his talk with Special Ed. But she didn't know him at all.

Miss Palmer? Not for someone who smashed windows on Four

Street, memorized forty-eight bingo cards at a glance, jabbed Special Ed in the eye with a dauber, and dropped out of sight with a dead girl's name.

He wrote "Dear Ms. Palmer," at the top of the page and studied it. It looked ridiculous, but it was the best he could come up with.

"Your father asked me . . ." He stopped as his cop genes finally kicked in and told him he should stand outside the women's room in case murder suspect Grace Palmer made a break for it after she finished barfing. Go back to Anchorage without talking to her, perhaps taking her into custody? What had he been thinking?

He shook his head, started to rise, then froze as a pair of legs stopped across the table from him and a voice said "You're Inupiat."

He looked up into the face from the mural. It was older, but—intact. That was the word that came to mind. Intact again. The missing tooth replaced, the street bloat gone, the skin slightly weathered perhaps, but still flawless except for a small, pale scar, three-quarters of an inch long, running horizontally along the right cheekbone. The eyes had regained the extraordinary luminosity, the silver gleam, they possessed in the mural, and the resentment too.

No, not resentment. It was something else, now. Self-knowledge, perhaps, or resignation—it was hard to be sure.

But just now they were impatient eyes. "You're Inupiat," she said again.

It wasn't a question, but he nodded and started to rise. "I'm Na . . ."

"You're from Chukchi?"

He nodded again and put out his hand. "I'm Nathan Active."

Her own hands stayed at her sides while her eyes roamed over him, then returned to his own, narrowed for a moment, then relaxed as if she had reached a decision. "I can't talk now. Come to the Triangle tonight at seven. Bring cigarettes." She turned and walked away. He had a vague impression of rust-colored bib overalls, Carhartts, he thought, and a red plaid shirt, then she was gone.

"Wait—what's the Triangle? What kind of cigarettes?" He was shouting and the slime liners were staring again, this time grinning and raising their eyebrows knowingly at each other. He hurried after her, but she pushed through the lunchroom door and was out of sight before he reached the hallway.

His cop genes told him to go after her, until he remembered that the next flight off the island wasn't until ten o'clock, at least according to the Air Aleutian schedule he had inadvertently committed to memory while trying to book his trip to the island. Well, if she didn't show up at the Triangle on schedule, he could talk to the city cops, if Dutch Harbor had any, or the local troopers, or even stake out the ten o'clock flight himself if he had to.

Driving back to the Royal Islander, he went over the conversation. Twenty words, maybe. The voice low, warm and . . . and what? Amused, he guessed. She had seen him, thrown up, spoken twenty words to him, x-rayed him with her eyes—and been amused by it all. And now she would talk to him at seven o'clock if he brought cigarettes to the Triangle, wherever and whatever that was.

"A bunk house," said the clerk in the Royal Islander gift shop. She was very wide, approximately square, in fact. Her name tag said Stella, and her hair was blonde except at the roots.

"A lot of the slime line workers stay there?"

She nodded, and he handed her the map from the rented Topaz.

She studied it a moment, then jabbed a spot south of the dimple representing Elizabeth Cove. "Down the beach about two miles. Triangle Seafoods. The bunkhouse is in back. Just look for the eagles."

"Eagles? On the sign, you mean?"

Stella snorted. "On the dumpster. Triangle doesn't take care of its trash right and there's always a flock of bald eagles at the dumpster by the bunkhouse. At the outfall of the processing plant, too, when it's running."

"You mean our national symbol eats garbage?"

"Yep, flying rats, we call 'em. Welcome to Illusions, pal."

The phrase rolled around his head for a moment. "What did you say?"

"Flying rats. That's what we call eagles around here."

"No, the other. Welcome to what?"

"Oh, welcome to Illusions. That's what we call the Aleutians around here."

He shook his head, marveling at the Four Street grapevine that had somehow learned Grace Palmer had gone to Illusions—the islands in the North Pacific, not the strip club in Spenard—and communicated it to Special Ed, who was able to retain it, if not interpret it correctly, until he, Nathan Active, came along three years later.

"So what do they charge at the Triangle?" he asked.

She folded the map and handed it back to him. "Fifty bucks a night, no questions asked and none answered." She gave a wheezy chortle, and pulled a cigarette from a pack somewhere behind the cash register.

"Which brand is most popular with your women customers?" He pointed at the shelves of cigarettes behind her as she lit up.

"These right here." She pulled out her own pack and showed him. "Marlboro 100s."

"Marlboros, huh? I thought they were for cowboys."

"Oh, we gals just lie awake nights dreaming the Marlboro man will gallop up and carry us off on that great big horse of his." She wheezed out another laugh in a cloud of smoke.

"Me too," Active said after a pause.

This time the wheeze was a genuine guffaw.

"I'll take a pack."

She pushed it across the counter, along with a book of matches with the Royal Islander's burgundy logo on the cover. He pushed some money back and she rang up the sale.

"But you'll need more than a pack of Marlboros if you want to get lucky in Dutch," she said as he turned away. "Women around here can afford to be picky."

She was still wheezing as he opened the directory at a pay phone just off the lobby and looked up the Triangle Bunkhouse. Yes, they had a vacancy, a Hispanic woman told him, but they didn't take reservations so he'd better get over there if he wanted a bunk.

He went to his room, packed, checked out and drove the Topaz down the shore of Captain's Bay in the same drizzle that had been falling when he landed. The Triangle was a big complex—offices, warehouses, something that looked like a larger version of the factory at Elizabeth Cove Seafoods. He pulled between two of the buildings fronting on the bay and there behind them, just where Stella's forefinger had indicated, was a long single-story building with a "Triangle Bunkhouse" sign on the front.

Also as Stella had predicted, three bald eagles were at work on a dumpster at the far end of the building. One, it appeared, had a strip of toilet paper caught on its talons. Another, he saw as he walked up for a closer look, had something black—it looked like chocolate frosting, or perhaps syrup—smeared along its bill and part way up the white patch on its head.

When he was about twenty feet away, the eagles noticed him and two flew off. The third, the one with the toilet paper dangling from its claws, hopped down from the dumpster, turned sideways on the gravel, aimed a fierce glare at him, and let loose a long and, even from where Active stood, smelly stream of white excrement.

He walked back up the side of the building and went in the door under the sign, into an office with nobody in sight. But a door to his left was open and he heard a television tuned to a shopping channel and someone making kitchen sounds. He was about to put his head through the door when he saw a bell on the counter, so he gave it a couple of slaps.

Soon a dark-haired woman in an apron hurried out, and checked him into Room Thirteen in the same Hispanic accent he had heard on the phone. "You want the meal plan?" she said as he pulled out his credit card. "It's seventy-nine dollars with the meal plan."

Since the room itself was fifty a day, that was twenty-four dollars for three meals. One meal, a very basic one, was around twenty-five at the Royal Islander. "Sure, sign me up," he said.

She gave him a blue card that said "Meal Plan" and pointed to a door next to her counter. "Number Thirteen is down the hall on your left, the cafeteria is down at the end. Breakfast six to seven, lunch noon to one, dinner six to seven." With that, she hurried back into the living quarters, closing the door behind her.

Number thirteen had three beds—a two-tiered bunk and a free-standing cot occupied by a shaving kit and a green duffel bag. He tossed his own bag and briefcase on the bottom bunk and sat down to think.

It was two-thirty now. Four and a half hours until Grace Palmer would talk to him. There was the Topaz. Now that he had found her, he wouldn't be doing much driving. So he could return that and save himself eighty dollars a day.

Then what? There was dinner. He had paid for the Triangle's meal plan, but dinner was at six o'clock. That meant Grace Palmer was planning to talk to him after she ate. Now that he thought of it, what would happen if she came in after her shift on the slime line and saw him eating there, too? The sight of him had made her throw up at lunch.

He ended up driving the five miles to the airport to return the car, catching the shuttle van back to the Royal Islander, where he paid out most of thirty dollars, counting the tip, for a blackened salmon salad and a Diet Pepsi in the dining room, all for the privilege of not eating the dinner for which he had already paid some fraction of twenty-four dollars at the Triangle. And then there was a fifteen-dollar cab ride back to the Triangle.

At five minutes before seven, he was back in Number 13, digging into his briefcase for the Marlboro 100s and the burgundy matchbook from the Royal Islander, sliding them into a pocket of his windbreaker and walking down the windowless tunnel-like hallway to the cafeteria.

When he pushed through the swinging doors, three tables were still occupied, one by two bearded young men in blue coveralls that said "Aleutian Seafoods," one by a stocky, short-haired woman in jeans and sweatshirt who was reading a John Grisham paperback, and one, in a corner, by Grace Palmer, who was staring at a plate of untouched meat loaf and mashed potatoes. She glanced up, met his eyes briefly, and returned her gaze to the plate.

He walked over, sat down across from her, and put out his hand.

"Nathan Active." She was still in the Carhartts and purple cap, and smelled slightly of the slime line.

She kept her hands in her lap. "I'm Angie Ramos."

That stopped him for several seconds. Why, after accusing him of being an Inupiaq from Chukchi, would she pretend to be Filipino? She certainly didn't look Filipino. "No, you're Grace Palmer."

Now it was her turn for a long silence. Finally, "Did you bring the cigarettes?"

He pulled the cigarettes and matchbook from his windbreaker and pushed them across the table. "Hope you like Marlboros."

"It doesn't matter." She glanced up with what he thought was a mixture of contempt and irritation, then picked open the cigarette pack. She lit up and took a long, deep drag, eyes closed, cheeks going concave. "She's dead. Maybe she should stay that way."

It took him another long silence to realize she was responding, finally, to his challenge on the subject of her identity. "She looks very much alive to me, even if she doesn't have much of an appetite."

Her lips curved slightly in what could have been a suppressed smile. She said "Ah-hmmmph" and dropped a little cylinder of ash onto the shiny skin forming on the gravy over the mashed potatoes. "You're a cop."

"I'm an Alaska state trooper."

Her eyes flicked over him, then back to her plate. "You're not in uniform."

"I'm here on my own time."

"Why?"

"Your father asked me to find you and give you a message. Your mother's ill and she wants to see you again before . . . well, she's not expected to recover. It's cancer."

"What kind?"

"Liver. Apparently she got hepatitis from a transfusion when your brother was born and it led to this."

She smoked and studied him. "Why didn't she ask you to come herself?"

"I gather she wasn't well enough. Your father said your aunt was coming down from Isignaq to be with her."

"Aggie?"

Active nodded. "I think that's what he said, yes."

"Is she bringing Nita?" She smoked and studied him.

"Who's Nita?"

"Aggie's little girl." She paused and smoked again. "My cousin. She must be nine or ten by now. Not so little anymore, I guess. I lost track of a few years."

"Your father didn't mention anyone by that name. I don't know if she's coming or not."

She looked at her plate, then at him. "But you're doing all this on your own?"

He looked away, wondering that she didn't ask more about her mother, and embarrassed by the question she had aimed at him. "I came down here to ask Angie what happened to you."

"All this way?" Her eyes were still on his face.

"I had to know." He shrugged.

"A round trip from Chukchi must be over a thousand dollars."

"I was in Anchorage anyway. It's only about nine-fifty from there."

She smoked again and appeared to think this over. "Where are you staying?"

"I was at the Royal Islander. Now I'm staying here." She flinched slightly, then was silent, so he added, "I could move, though."

"It doesn't matter."

He was silent for a while. She had agreed to see him and knew why he was here, so perhaps she had a story to tell. But she just smoked the Marlboro and stared at her plate.

Active slid his chair along the table a few inches, hoping to avoid the air current bringing smoke to his eyes and nose.

She noticed, and extended her arm so that the cigarette was downwind from him. "Sorry."

"It's all right," he said. "It's just that I don't smoke."

She drew on the Marlboro and looked at her plate and mumbled "Filthy habit," or so he thought. When she didn't say anything else, he picked up the conversation.

"Can I ask you some questions?"

"You can try."

"I was wondering how you turned into Angie Ramos and what happened to the real one?"

"We were roommates, if you could call it that." Her voice was flat and so low he found himself straining to hear.

"How'd she die?"

"Snowplow hit her one night while she was directing traffic on Four Street." The Marlboro was down to the filter now. She snuffed it out in the mashed potatoes. "Tell me when five minutes are up and I'll smoke another one."

Active looked at his watch to note the time, but what he saw was Cullars's photographs of what was left of Heavenly Doe. "Did she have an angel on her breast?"

Grace Palmer looked up, surprise on her face. "You knew her? That well?"

"I didn't know her at all. The Anchorage police showed me her autopsy pictures. They never identified her. They called her Heavenly Doe because of the angel. I thought she was you."

Grace winced and looked down at the mashed potatoes again. He caught the flash of silver and studied her eyes until he realized what it was. The whites weren't really white, not a normal flat white. They were reflective, like mercury, quicksilver literally, producing the gleam when she was not looking directly at him. "Why?"

"We found what looked like your initials on the tattoo."

"I was just signing my work."

"You did the tattoo?"

She nodded. "I learned how in jail."

He thought of asking when and where, but decided it was probably a pointless detour.

CHAPTER THIRTEEN

"Why didn't you report Angie's death? Maybe her people would like to know what became of her."

"Fat fucking chance. Her father kicked her out when she was fourteen because she got pregnant." She gave a sharp, harsh bark of a laugh. "Fucking Catholics. How long?"

"How long?"

"Till the five minutes are up."

He looked at his watch. "Its been about ninety seconds."

She shrugged. "Anyway, how could I have borrowed her name if I told the police she was dead? They would have wanted all her papers and stuff. Besides, street people never talk to the cops. Nothing but trouble."

"You said she was directing traffic?"

"Yeah, she had a cold that night." Grace Palmer fiddled with the Marlboro butt in the mashed potatoes and stopped talking as if that cleared up Angie Ramos's death and everything connected with it. The kitchen doors banged open and she watched as a Native teenager came out with a bucket and mop and set to work on the cafeteria floor.

Active shook his head and tried again. "Why would she be

directing traffic on Four Street in the middle of the night, cold or no cold?"

She gave him a pitying look. "You direct traffic when you want to get arrested. Some motorist calls the cops on a cell phone, a blue-and-white shows up in about five minutes and you spend the night in a nice warm cell. Angie had a cold that night and decided she needed to sleep inside for a while, so we went out to direct traffic."

"You were with her?"

"Not when it mattered." A look of pain crossed her face and she dropped her eyes to her plate. "I took her up there and kind of showed her what to do, since it was her first time. Sure enough, some John Q. stops to yell at us for blocking the street. We tell him to go fuck himself, he threatens to call the cops, we say he can go fuck them, too, and then he's driving away with his cell phone to his ear." She did a remarkably effective pantomime of a man steering with his elbows as he held a cellular telephone in one hand and punched its buttons with the other. Then she chuckled miserably.

"I'm cold, I'm out of Bacardi, I don't want to get busted again, and I figure Angie's all set, so I head back up Four Street to the bars." She lifted her eyes, glistening now. "I heard a noise, kind of a scream on the wind and then a thunk and I went back and looked and I, I, I . . . fuck, I knew I should have stayed with her. She was sweet, God, she was sweet, but she was simple. You know?"

She looked down again as he thought it over. If the driver had called 9-1-1, the Anchorage police should have a record of it. If there was a driver. Cullars hadn't mentioned any call from a motorist, just the snowplow driver's report of a hazy figure in the blizzard. Should he give her a Miranda warning? Ask something else to keep her talking? If his head were clear about this woman, would he have any basis for suspecting her? She gave no sign of suspecting him of anything but a genuine interest in her story, which now seemed to have taken on a momentum of its own.

"You were sleeping out in the winter?" He said this gently, sympathetically, not sure if he was being sincere or manipulative, but definitely putting off the question of the cell-phone call that didn't show up in the police records. "What about the shelters?"

"They won't take you if you're drunk, which Angie and I always tried to be at night. Anyway, we were both at that phase of our recovery where we couldn't sleep indoors. We always slept out."

"Your recovery?"

She nodded, but looked annoyed and didn't elaborate. He changed the subject.

"So you had a camp somewhere? A tent or a lean-to or something?"

She picked the Marlboro out of the mashed potatoes and studied it. "How much longer?"

"What?" Then he understood and looked at his watch. "About a minute."

"Hmpph." She pushed the cigarette back into the potatoes.

"You want it now? You don't have to wait."

"No, I don't want to cheat. Under cars."

By now, he thought, he should be used to the hairpin turns in her conversation, but he couldn't sort it out. "Under cars?"

"There was no camp. We slept under cars."

"Not in them?"

"Under. That was as close to inside as we could stand at that phase of our recovery."

"And that was warmer than sleeping under a tree or a picnic table?"

"A little. We'd hang around the condos downtown until

somebody drove up in a nice wide car like a Suburban or something. Then we'd crawl under it and lie close together. There'd still be some heat from the exhaust pipe and the engine. And that frost that falls out of the air on a cold night? It wouldn't get on our faces. So it was a little warmer, yes."

She looked thoughtful, for a moment, then chuckled.

"One real cold morning the woman who owned the car started it up and backed out while we were still asleep. We open our eyes and there she is yelling and honking at us. Then she comes running over and feels our throats to see if we've got pulses. 'Don't move. I'll call an ambulance,' she says, and she goes running back into her house."

He smiled and gave a noncommittal "Hmmph," not ready for any more of the dismal street yarn she seemed to find so cheering. But he saw there was no stopping her, and resigned himself to hearing it all.

"We certainly didn't want to go anywhere in an ambulance," she continued, "so we had to get away. But we always slept with our arms folded on our chests for that little extra warmth and this morning they were too cold to move, so we couldn't push ourselves up. So we rolled around till we got up on our butts and we rolled around on our butts till we could get ourselves on our feet and then we tried to run away."

Now she stood beside the table, still talking. "But our ankles and knees were frozen, too, so we looked like two little homeless Frankensteins making our escape." She demonstrated, tottering stiff-kneed across the cafeteria, arms crossed on her chest. The short-haired woman looked up from her paperback, followed Grace with her eyes, looked at him briefly without expression, and returned to her novel.

Grace returned to the table and sat down. "All the way down the street, we're working our fingers, working our wrists, and pretty soon I can get my cigarettes out and I light up and I take a drag and I give Angie a drag. And Angie, she gets where she can pull the Bacardi out of her jacket and she unscrews the cap and she gives me a pull and she takes a pull and we're ready for another day on Four Street."

She laughed, saw his expression, then looked into herself and fell quiet, muttering something he didn't catch as silver flashed again.

"What?"

"That angel. You know who that angel was?"

He shook his head.

"Angie's baby. She got an abortion after her dad kicked her out and the boy ran off, and it drove her crazy." Grace stopped and shook her head at the memory. "Whenever she got drunk, she'd start crying about that baby, how it was an angel up in heaven now and how much she missed it. So one night I told her I could put the baby next to her heart and that's how it got there."

Active nodded, said nothing.

"She didn't even know the sex, so I had to make it a little hermaphrodite."

She chuckled again and he nodded absently, thinking of how Cullars had called the androgynous angel a jailhouse special.

"I did it one night after the Oil Dividends came out," Grace went on. "We were at some motel, one of those three-day parties the street people throw when they get a little sudden money, and I did it in the bathroom after everybody else was passed out. Never got infected, either."

"Did it help?

"The party?"

"The tattoo."

She paused before answering. "I thought so at first. But then Angie started talking about the baby again and how much she missed it and it was worse than before. She even tried slashing her wrists, but she screwed it up. She did it like this." Grace drew a finger across her the base of her hand. "The ER doctor said you have to do it along the veins or the bleeding stops by itself."

She shrugged. "So I think maybe Angie jumped in front of that snowplow to be with the baby. Who knows?"

When Active didn't answer, she glanced at his watch, then at the cigarette in the mashed potatoes. "Time yet?"

"Yep, five minutes is up."

She pulled another Marlboro from the pack and lit it with a match from the Royal Islander book.

"If you smoke, why did you ask me to bring cigarettes?"

"I don't smoke."

He was still thinking that one over when she seemed to realize it needed explaining. "I quit smoking and drinking at the same time. But I knew I was going to have to do one or the other again the first time I talked to somebody about this, and I decided a long time ago I'd smoke. I can stop smoking again, but I don't know about drinking."

"You threw up when you saw me today."

She shrugged.

"But you're talking to me anyway."

"I knew I'd eventually have to talk to somebody about this to complete my recovery. I figured if you came all this way, it might as well be you."

She lifted her eyes to his and for the first time he had the impression she wanted him to explain himself. And for the first time, it was he who looked away.

"I don't know why I came. I mean, I thought you were dead when I saw your initials on that tattoo, and I thought Angie Ramos could tell me how you died. And then I caught a glimpse of you on the slime line today and it was like seeing a ghost. Mr. Phan told me to go to the washroom if I wanted to throw up." He stopped, realizing he was babbling like a suspect who confesses helplessly at the first question.

She drew in on the cigarette, then spoke through a cloud of smoke. "One glimpse and you knew it was me?"

He nodded, feeling a great need to change the subject. "You keep referring to your recovery."

She looked annoyed again, but answered this time. "Yes, I was in denial the first few years I was in Anchorage. I've been recovering ever since."

"Even when you were drinking and sleeping under cars?"

"Especially then. I read some books and realized I was self-medicating with alcohol and that made me think I might be able to cure myself. So I started."

"This was around the time Angie died?"

"I was thinking about it before. I saw my brother Roy outside the Junction one night. He said, 'Come home, Sikingik.' That's my Eskimo name."

She must have caught something in his face, he thought, because she stopped and raised her eyebrows. "Yes?"

"Your father told me about that."

"Then he probably told you I was drunk and in the company of two men with dishonorable intentions. This was in my Amazing

Grace phase." She grinned defiantly, anticipating, he supposed, his disapproval. He tried to project indifference.

"You want Amazing Grace's story, you'll have to live with the unexpurgated version. It would hinder my recovery if I tried to clean her up."

He nodded. "Roy thought the men looked like soldiers."

She gazed at him with an amused look. "Were they? I can't remember that, or much else about that night, except that what Roy said kept going through my head: 'Come home.' I knew I couldn't do that, not in the sense he meant, but I started to think I was ready to find some kind of home, and not on the streets. That was when my recovery really began. And then Angie died. I got completely drunk for a couple of months because I blamed myself, but somehow it wore off or I got used to it, and then I wanted out even more."

He nodded and noted the time as she snuffed out the second Marlboro in the mashed potatoes.

"And Angie's death gave me a way to do it. At that point, we were keeping our stuff in some bushes behind the junked cars in the rail yards, and Angie left her ID down there because she was hoping to get herself arrested under a fake name and keep her record clean. So I just took it and became Angelina Corazon Ramos."

He shook his head. "It was that easy?"

"That easy." She gave another harsh laugh. "All street people look alike to people who check IDs. Cops, bouncers, Alaska state troopers." She studied his face. "All brown people, too. Even half-brown people like me. You could vanish in no time, Nathan. If you weren't a trooper."

He smiled. "Why would I want to?"

She shook her head. "Never mind. How long?"

He checked his watch. "About three minutes. Why did you need to be Angie Ramos to complete your recovery? Grace, Angie, what's the difference?"

"Angie didn't have a criminal record, which meant she could get jobs." She paused to look into herself for a moment. "She's on the street all those years and never gets arrested. And then the first time she goes out to direct traffic, a snowplow hits her and she still doesn't get arrested." There was another of her harsh laughs, ending in a half-sob.

He offered her his handkerchief. She took it but didn't wipe her eyes or nose. Instead, she looked up and to his right, and he sensed that someone was at the end of the table.

"You okay?" It was the short-haired woman who had been reading the novel. He realized now that subconsciously he had been aware for some time of her watching his conversation with Grace Palmer.

Grace blinked rapidly and smiled up at the woman. "I'm fine, Wendy. Really."

"You sure?"

Grace smiled again. "Really. You go on back to the room. I'll be along soon."

He sensed resentment from Wendy, who stood indecisively for a moment, then bent forward. He tried not to react as he realized she intended to kiss Grace, probably on the lips, but then something happened—he wasn't sure if Wendy changed her mind or Grace tilted her head—but the kiss landed on the crown of the purple baseball cap.

Wendy straightened, hesitated, and looked him in the eye for the first time. She glared for a moment, then nodded with a jerk and walked away before he could nod back.

Grace's head was still down, the bill of the purple cap blocking his view of her eyes. "Wendy is my roommate."

Everything he could think of saying sounded wrong, so he just said, "Uh-huh."

"She takes care of me."

He stifled the impulse to say, "I gathered," and managed to get out what he hoped was a non-judgmental "I see."

"You don't see, but I don't have to explain anything to you."

"Of course not."

She was silent for a moment, wiping her eyes with her fingers but not, for some reason, with his handkerchief. She just sniffed it and passed it back to him. "You smell nice. Safe."

He studied the handkerchief, sniffed it, and smelled only clean linen. He returned it to the pocket.

"Plus Angie could still get Oil Dividends and I couldn't."

Another swerve. Where had they been before Wendy came over? Oh, yes—directing traffic, and Grace's decision to borrow Angie Ramos's identity.

"Yeah, I remember your dividends were seized to pay for the broken windows on Four Street," he said. "It was in the police records."

"Sure. I couldn't get a job, I couldn't get a dividend. There wasn't much way out for Grace Palmer. The dividends were just going into the mail when Angie got hit and all the street people were waiting for them. So I picked hers up at the Creekview and took it to one of those check-cashing places and I had myself a little grubstake."

She glanced at his watch, which was covered by his right hand at the moment. "How long?"

He uncovered the watch and looked at it. "A minute to go."

"So I took Angie's dividend and got myself a room in a

flophouse in Spenard, where people didn't know Amazing Grace, and I started applying for jobs where they can't be choosy—hotel maids, dishwashers, janitors, that kind of thing." She stopped and closed her eyes for a moment. "I didn't have my looks back yet, or maybe I would have hired myself out to adorn some lawyer's front office. But I think this was a better transition. Is it time?"

He nodded and handed her a cigarette. The janitor came up as she lit it and stood silently by the table. "What is it, Joseph?" she asked gently.

"I should lock up sometime." Joseph didn't meet her eyes.

"Oh, God, I'm sorry." She looked at Active, then back at Joseph. "Can we have five more minutes?"

Joseph nodded and shuffled away. "A Yup'ik," she said. "Fetal alcohol syndrome, I think."

Active looked around the cafeteria. The two other diners were gone—how had he not noticed them leave?—and now it was just himself, Joseph and Grace Palmer.

CHAPTER FOURTEEN

"You saw my police file, huh?"

He nodded. "You left quite a trail."

"I wasn't really a prostitute, you know."

"You don't have to explain anything to me."

She went on as if she hadn't heard. "My price was a bottle of Bacardi if the guy seemed right. But that vice cop had mean eyes so I told him I wouldn't give him a blow job if he paid me a thousand bucks." She laughed. "I guess that pissed him off, because he beat the shit out of me. And then he arrested me! But a thousand dollars for a blow job was so ridiculous even the judge didn't buy it, so I got off."

"I know. It was in the file."

She laughed again. "Soon as this cigarette's done, so are we."

He still had questions, more perhaps than when they had begun, such as what about the cell call the police had missed. "Maybe we could go . . . well, go somewhere."

"Nope. I've said about all I can for one night. Five minutes more, that's all you get. You can come back tomorrow night if you want to talk to me again. Same time."

The thought of another empty day in Dutch Harbor burning through his savings made him wince, but he said, "Okay."

"So, I got a job at a 7-Eleven in Spenard. Slurpees, Slim Jims, Unleaded or Premium, Bacardi, Everclear, whatever it takes to get you through the night. My friends, they'd come in and steal food sometimes. I'd let them, those places always have a certain amount of shoplifting. If they took too much, I'd just pay for it myself so the company wouldn't know." She inhaled, held it, blew out a cloud of smoke, and waved the Marlboro at him. "They stole a lot of these things, too. Not good for them, but it makes life on Four Street a lot easier. Maybe even more than liquor."

"You were able to quit drinking just like that?"

"Of course not. I went through the Twelve Steps and everything, I still go to meetings down here. But I did find that I could control it enough right away to hold down my little 7-Eleven job, which was one of the things I wanted to know. Made me realize even more that I was just self-medicating and liquor wasn't my real problem."

"What was it, then?"

She smiled, a tight, joyless grimace. "Not tonight. Maybe tomorrow night if you come back."

The ensuing silence was so gloomy, he felt compelled to lighten things up. "So the Oil Dividend and 7-Eleven saved you?" It didn't sound light at all, just forced.

But she laughed a little, and not the angry bark like before. "Yep. Angie Ramos, young urban professional. When my looks came back a little, I even went into Nordstrom's and got some decent clothes with the last of her Dividend."

"And the tooth?" He was ashamed the moment it was out, but she didn't seem to mind.

"Oh, I had it fixed after I got down here and saved some money. What do you think?" She bared her teeth like a dog snarling.

"Perfect. I can't even tell which one it was."

She tapped a lower front tooth and smiled. "It's an implant. They can screw a new tooth right into your jawbone now."

In his mind he went back to the stack of police reports and tried to sort through the dates, hoping to ease her around to the cell-phone question.

"That business at the bingo parlor when you jabbed the guy in the eye—wasn't that around the time Angie died?"

"Yeah, that was about the last time we ever went out together."

"You could really memorize forty-eight bingo cards at once?"

She laughed again. "Impressed?"

He shrugged.

"Like I said, I was thinking of leaving Four Street, trying to cut back on the drinking, even before Angie got hit. One of the things I wanted to know was, was there anything left of my brain? So I'd go down to Aurora Bingo to see if I still had the photographic memory. Turned out, I did. But I guess some of the other Native ladies thought I was being bossy."

"I gather."

"I have other remarkable talents, too."

"I'm sure, but why are you in Dutch—"

"Got a business card?"

"Business card?"

She nodded, eyes wide and merry and expectant.

He pulled one from his wallet and handed it to her. She studied it for a moment, then looked at him.

"You put your home phone on your business card? Don't the drunks and wackos call you up in the middle of the night?"

"Not as much as you'd think. And besides, as our secretary pointed out, they all know where the trooper cabin is anyway. If I didn't publish my phone number, they'd just come over."

She grinned and began to whistle. It was delicate and airy, anchored by a short musical phrase that sounded vaguely familiar, but not enough so that he could name the song. It lasted about two minutes, he guessed.

"Recognize it?" Her eyes were still wide and merry.

"I don't know, Mozart? I'm not very good about classical music, I'm afraid. And what does it have to do with my business card?"

"It's your song. Nathan's Song."

"What?"

"Look." She pointed to his home phone number on the business card and whistled the anchor phrase again. "See? That's your phone number."

He had to close his eyes and tap the digits out on an imaginary keypad on his palm before he was sure, but, yes, she was right. Her anchor phrase was the sound of his number being punched into a push-button phone. "You can do this with any telephone number?"

"Except 9-1-1."

"Somebody tells you the number and you can make up a song from it?"

"It's a piece, not a song, if it doesn't have any words, but I could hardly call it Nathan's Piece, could I?" She stopped and gave him the merry, expectant grin again. "Anyway, this is a piece and, no, I didn't exactly make it up. First I hear the number in my head, then I listen for a bit more, and then I hear the piece itself. Then I just whistle what I hear in my head. Or I can play it on the piano."

She pulled down the bill of the purple cap and hunched her shoulders and played a little air piano on the dining table, the Marlboro dangling from her lips making her look like a jazz musician. Then she grinned up at him and stubbed the Marlboro out in the mashed potatoes. "One more question and that's it for tonight."

Should he try the cell-phone question? Maybe not, she was pulling away already. Maybe tomorrow. "Why Dutch Harbor?"

The grin vanished and she looked around the cafeteria and out the window at the gray drizzle of what passed for a summer evening in the Aleutians. "Lots of reasons. It was risky doing the Angie thing where so many people knew Amazing Grace. Plus I needed to get farther from Four Street than I could in Anchorage. Plus this pays better than 7-Eleven and there's no place to spend your money. Maybe I'll need a couple more tours on Four Street to get it all out of my system, but right now I think Illusions is where I belong."

He thought of asking again what it was she had to get out of her system, but figured she'd just tell him again to wait until tomorrow night. "What are you saving for?"

"Sorry, you used up all your questions." She smiled and pushed the Marlboros toward him. "You bring these back tomorrow night at seven and I'm your girl." Then she winked and stood and left so quickly that he didn't have time to answer. He just followed her out of the room with his eyes. He picked up the Marlboros and matchbook and pocketed them as Joseph came to the table to clear away her tray.

"Will you hurt her?" the boy said.

"What?"

"Will you hurt her? Too many people hurt her already."

"Not if I can help it." But he thought of Dennis Johnson and the APD Homicide unit and had the feeling it was beyond his control.

He went down the hall to his room, wondering which door Grace Palmer had entered and what he would do if he knew.

There was still no sign of his roommate, except that the duffel bag was now open with underwear spilling out, two white T-shirts and a pair of boxer shorts adorned with red hearts.

He looked at his watch. He felt like the conversation in the lunchroom had gone on for hours, but it was not even eight yet. More than twenty-three hours before he would see Grace Palmer again, more than twenty-three hours to kill in what—garbage-eating eagles aside—was surely the most claustrophobic town in Alaska if you didn't like rain or bars.

He peered out the window. It was still light out and would be for several hours more in the long summer twilight of the North Pacific. Maybe he'd take a walk. The rain had dwindled from a horizontal torrent to an almost-vertical drizzle. He'd walk to a bar or a cafe, maybe even up to the Royal Islander, drink a Diet Pepsi, and watch TV. Maybe a hockey game would be showing.

He pulled a rainproof anorak from his bag and left the room. He was passing the pay phone in the lobby when it hit him, the thing undone that had been tugging at the edge of his conscious-ness. He had not called Lucy Generous.

Not last night, after playing in the hockey game that left him with the headache now starting to throb again, and not the night before, when Dennis Johnson had derailed his scheme—how stupid it seemed now—to seduce Lucy over the phone. Lucy had been chased out of his head by the news that Angie Ramos, Grace Palmer's friend and possibly her killer, had surfaced in Dutch Harbor.

He stopped at the pay phone and started to pull his calling card from his wallet, then thought better of it. How could he tell her he was in Dutch Harbor with Grace Palmer?

No, better to take his walk, think of what to say, perhaps call from a restaurant, from space not occupied by Grace Palmer.

He went back to the room for some aspirin, left the bunkhouse, picked his way between the buildings of the Triangle complex and

out to Captain's Bay Road, the music of his own phone number
now stuck in his head. The drizzle was thinning but the peaks
he had glimpsed as Captain Ross slipped the 737 into the airport
between squalls were still veiled intermittently by shifting curtains
of gray. He pulled up the hood of the anorak and started north
along the road, crunching along the gravel shoulder.

A pair of headlights swam out of the mist. He watched as they
grew into a white stretch limousine throwing up a bow wave of
gravel and water. He realized too late the wave reached to both
shoulders of the road, and so his legs were drenched below the
raincoat as he leapt the ditch. He scrambled up a little bank to a
footpath alongside the road and started walking again. Limo drivers
were the same everywhere, apparently.

The limousine continued south, presumably bound for the
Triangle complex behind him. What resident of the Triangle Bunkhouse would travel by limo?

Ten minutes later, he heard tires on the gravel behind him and
realized even before he turned that it was the white limo headed
back to town. He stepped a few feet off the footpath to avoid another
drenching, but this time the limo crunched to a stop beside him.
"Nanuq" was painted on the fender in black letters. The window on
the passenger side slid down with an electric whir.

"Want a lift?" rasped a female voice that sounded vaguely
familiar.

He leapt the ditch again, leaned in the window, and studied the
driver. "You're from the gift shop at the Royal Islander. What is it?
Sheila?"

"Hey, you're the young fella with the Marlboros." The driver
stuck a ring-encrusted hand across the seat. "It's Stella. Stella Quintano. Get on in."

He shook the hand. "No, thanks, I'm on a budget. Anyway, I need some air."

"Marlboros didn't work, huh? I told you you'd need something stronger." The lock button beside his left hand popped up, Stella wheezing at her own wit. "Anyway, get in, this one's on the house for dousing you back there. Just put that raincoat on the floor of the back seat is all I ask."

He thought it over, then shrugged out of the anorak and tossed it into the back. Then he slid onto the passenger seat across from Stella. The window whirred up, the lock snapped down, and she dropped Nanuq into gear. They sped off in a shower of gravel and mud, Active reflecting that it was far better to make such a shower than to receive one.

The limo was warm and steamy inside and Stella was drinking something from a wide blue plastic insulated mug with a Big Dipper of gold stars printed on the side, like the Alaska flag.

"Want some coffee?" Stella waved the mug at him, then used it to tap the top of a green metal thermos on the seat beside her. "It's on the house, too."

"I could, I suppose." The walk in the rain had cooled him off more than he expected. He opened the thermos and poured coffee into the stainless steel cup that served as the bottle's cap, then drank and studied the driver. She was wearing a baseball cap with "Quintano Enterprises" lettered on the bill.

"You own the Nanuq, do you?"

"Oh, yeah." Stella waved a hand around the interior as though she were taking in an empire, not just a lone limo squelching along a gravel road in the Aleutian drizzle. "The gift shop at the Royal Islander, too, a coupla cabs, and a B&B."

He whistled. "You're a busy girl."

"Ah, you gotta have three or four things going to stay afloat in Dutch."

He studied her again, something tugging at a corner of his mind. "Quintano. Why is that name familiar?"

She gave one of her wheeze-laughs, then turned and studied him. "You from Nome? You look like a Nome Eskimo to me."

"My father was. My mother's from Chukchi."

"Ah." She turned her attention back to the road. "Is that where you're from? Chukchi?"

Was it? He liked to think he was from Anchorage, but he was well into his second year in the Arctic now. "At the moment, yeah, I'm from Chukchi. But how would you know what a Nome Eskimo looks like?"

Stella wheezed again. "I'm proud to say I was run out of Nome by the city council and the League of Arctic Churches."

"That's it." He stared at his benefactress with new appreciation. "You made the news even on public radio in Chukchi. Something about prostitution from a limo?" He stopped and looked around the interior, thinking that any number of lewd puns could be made from the name Nanuq. "This limo?"

"This limo, but no prostitution. The police chief's brother owned a cab company and he didn't want any competition from old Nanuq here, so he started those rumors about me." A telephone clipped to the dash trilled. Stella picked it up and rasped "Quintano's," then listened silently. "You bet, Sweetie, I'll be there in a jiffy."

She hung up and turned his way. "Some fish guys going out on Alaska Airlines. We gotta pick 'em up at the East Wind. What was I saying?"

"I think you were telling me how nobody ever turned a trick in your limo."

"Right, right. Well, when the rumors didn't work, this guy gets his brother the police chief to make it official. Next thing I know, there's ads in the paper and posters around town signed by the police chief and the church council saying Stella's Limo Service is engaged in—what the hell did they call it?—'illicit commerce.' The city council yanked my permit without a hearing and there I was!" She shook her head and wheezed out a laugh.

"So what did you do?"

"What could I do? I loaded Nanuq here,"—she patted the white leather of the limo's dash—"on the first Herc out of Nome. Stopped in Anchorage to get my lawyer after the Nome city council and he told me Dutch didn't have a limo and here I am, fat and happy. There's nothing a fisherman hates more than having a big wad of money in his pocket."

"Well, I'm glad you landed on your feet."

"Better 'n that. My lawyer nicked the city of Nome half a mill for slander, business interference, I forget what all." She patted the dash again. "Old Nanuq here turned out to be my ride to Fat City. We turned a trick, all right, but it was on the city of Nome."

She wheezed again, so violently this time that Active reached over and put a hand on the steering wheel to steady Nanuq.

"You got half a million and you're here, working like this?" he said when she had regained control of her breathing and the limo.

She gazed around at the drizzle falling into the gray water of Captain's Bay and got a surprised look on her face, though whether at his question or her whereabouts, he couldn't tell.

"I guess I missed too many planes," she said.

"What does that mean?"

"That's what they say in Nome about white people who stay around too long." She shook her head, the dyed blonde hair bouncing. "You miss too many planes out and the next thing you know, you're not fit to live in a normal place anymore. If you leave one Bush town, you'll just end up in another one."

They rolled along in silence few moments, until he realized he had distracted her from the story of her arrival in Dutch Harbor. He apologized and asked if her reputation had not beaten her to Illusions.

"What's that, Nathan?"

"Your reputation. The Dutch Harbor city council didn't mind giving you a permit after the unpleasantness up in Nome?"

Stella guffawed. "Nah, they were happy to see me. The women on the council believed me and the men hoped I was lying was the impression I got." She hoisted her mug and drank, then waved it between them. "Anyway, here's to the Nome City Council. You believe me, don't you, Nathan?"

"Oh, absolutely." He hoisted his steel cup and drank and they crunched along in companionable silence for a while.

"So this Marlboro girl. You came all the way to Dutch to find her?" Stella swerved Nanuq around a pothole and gravel sprayed sideways as the car fishtailed. Stella caught the skid and got Nanuq pointed up the road again, all without spilling her coffee. "She must be something."

Active, who had not been as lucky, fished out his handkerchief and dabbed at the wet spot on his right knee. At least the coffee had cooled off in the metal cup, so he wasn't burned much. "Yeah, she's something, all right."

CHAPTER FIFTEEN

"Hurts to talk about it huh?" Stella made a tsk-tsk sound that he took to be sympathetic, giving him hope she would shut up about the Marlboro girl.

False hope, as it turned out. "What's her name?"

"Grace." He looked out the passenger window. Maybe if he avoided eye contact.

"Whew. You got it bad."

"Mind your own business." Maybe the direct approach would work.

"I'm just saying, is all."

"Saying what?" He was sucked in despite himself.

"The way you say her name. You got it bad." She shook her head. "Bad. I wish some man would say my name that way just one more time."

"Your sweetie doesn't?"

"My sweetie?"

He reminded her about the call to pick up the fishermen.

"Oh, Eddie. He runs the East Wind. Yeah, he's my sweetie, all right." She smiled to herself.

"But he doesn't say your name the way you like?"

"Oh, Eddie'll do, but he's just a bedwarmer." She pointed the coffee mug at him. "How about you and this Grace?"

"I'm a state trooper. She's just another case."

"Yeah? What'd she do?"

He was silent for a long time, looking out the passenger window.

"Uh-huh!" Stella's tone was filled with triumph and accusation. "You're out of uniform, you're on a budget, and Grace is a non-suspect in just another case. Right?" She glanced over at him then returned her attention to the road, a knowing smirk on her face. "Uh-huh."

The gravel turned to pavement and what passed for downtown Dutch Harbor came into view. He saw a big restaurant named The Captain's. "Let me out up there," he said. "You can pick up your fishermen and I'll make a phone call and walk back to the Triangle."

Stella waved the ring-encrusted hand again. "Nah, it's too far to walk. Stay where you are. We'll take the fish guys to the airport and then I'll drop you back at the Triangle."

She reached between her legs and pulled a "Quintano Enterprises" hat from under the seat. "Here, put this on, they'll think you're my copilot."

He studied the hat, shrugged, and put it on. It wouldn't hurt to stake out the flight, in case Grace Palmer made a run for it, though that seemed even unlikely after their talk at the Triangle.

He sank back into the cushions, sipped the now-tepid coffee, and studied the rain-blurred landscape until Stella stopped Nanuq in front of a big Quonset hut with a neon "Eddie's East Wind" sign on the front.

She honked her horn, waited about a minute, then honked again.

"Damn fishermen." She switched off Nanuq and looked at him "Guess I'm gonna have to go in after them. Come on, you can be my muscle."

"Muscle? Do I look like muscle?" He sank into the cushions again and closed his eyes. "You're on your own."

He heard Stella say "Shit!" Her door opened and closed and her feet crunched on the gravel. Then his door opened, letting in a gust of rainy wind. "Look at those windows."

He pulled himself out of Nanuq's cushions and looked where Stella was pointing. "They're kind of milky-looking, I guess."

"That's because they're Plexiglas instead of the real thing." Stella looked at him, apparently expecting him to grasp the significance of this information without further assistance.

"Plastic windows in Dutch Harbor? Seems right to me." He reached for the door, but Stella planted a broad hip against it and held it open.

"Don't you want to know why?"

"Not if I can avoid it."

"It's because Eddie was going broke replacing the glass all the time." She gave him another expectant look.

He sighed and surrendered to the inevitable. "All right, why does Eddie have to replace his windows all the time?"

Now Stella looked triumphant again. "From drunk fishermen throwing each other through them. In fact, I'm surprised my clients aren't lying under one of 'em right now."

Active took a closer look. The ground under the windows did seem to be pretty well covered with shards of real glass. "Great. Now can we close the door?"

"You mean the state troopers would send a girl into a place like that by herself?"

"What girl?"

Stella said "Fuck you, Nathan" and slammed Nanuq's door in his face and stomped off toward the East Wind.

He laughed to himself, got out and caught her at the door. "All right, I'm your muscle." He tugged the bill of his Quintano Enterprises cap low over his brow, put on what he hoped was a menacing expression, and followed Stella's wide back through the doors at the front end of the long, half cylinder of corrugated sheet metal. It was like entering a giant culvert.

She paused just inside, looking over the crowd of fishermen in Carhartts, sweatshirts, and beards. At the far end of the bar, country music blasted from a jukebox, its red and blue lights half-lost in the cigarette smoke. "We got winners, we got losers," the singer was rasping in a voice that sounded like it had been pickled in whiskey and testosterone. "We got hustlers, we got fighters, early birds and all-nighters."

Active looked around the entry and saw a sign on the wall that said, "Absolutely No Photography" in big red letters. Underneath, small black letters said: "Film and videotape will be confiscated and destroyed. Not responsible for damage to cameras. Eddie."

He nudged Stella's back. "What's this?"

She saw where he was pointing and laughed. "One time Eddie let a National Geographic film crew in here and they accidentally got some tape of a famous bank robber from Tennessee who was up here working the slime line till things cooled down. When the program ran, some cop back in Tennessee recognized the guy and flew up here and arrested him. If there's anything Eddie hates, its losing a good customer, so up went the sign."

Active was thinking that was pretty nice work by the cop in

Tennessee—probably an FBI agent if the fugitive was a bank robber—when Stella pointed down the bar.

"The guy was sitting right there at that table drinking St. Pauli
Girl when they taped him, and you know what?"

Active thought he probably did know what, but shook his head
anyway, as long as Stella was on a roll.

"He was sitting at the same table, drinking St. Pauli Girl, when
the Tennessee cop showed up to arrest him four months later."

"Missed too many planes, huh?"

Stella stared at him for a moment, then grinned and broke
into one of her wheezy guffaws. "I guess he did, Nathan, I guess
he did." She clapped him on the shoulder and shook her head.
"Missed too many planes. That's good."

She turned her attention back to the bar. "Now where's that
little rat Eddie?"

Finally, a tiny, wizened Asian—another Vietnamese, Active
guessed—materialized out of the murk at the far end of the bar.
He hurried up and dropped a tray of empties on the counter, then
spotted Stella at the entrance.

"'Bout time you get here. Your clients causing lotta trouble."

Active tried to picture the diminutive Eddie warming the bed of
leviathan Stella, but could not. Just then Eddie noticed him behind
Stella. The bartender's eyes narrowed, "Who this? He not a cop, is he?"

"No, no." Stella put a big hand on Eddie's spindly arm. "He's
just here to take care of any problems that come up. This is Nathan.
Nathan, Eddie."

Eddie put out a hand, then snatched it back after the briefest of
shakes. "Won't be any problem if you get your clients out of here."

Stella surveyed the bar again. "All right, Sweetie, which ones
are they?"

"Dance floor," Eddie said.

Stella frowned. "Horizontal or vertical?"

"Horizontal." Eddie shook his head, then hurried behind the counter and began unloading the empties into a sink.

"Not good, not good." Stella frowned again and looked at Active. "Well come on, let's find 'em." She started down the bar and he followed.

As they approached the dance floor, it became clear the crowd was gathered in a circle, yelling and gesticulating. Stella pushed through the perimeter, Active following in the wake she opened up in the sea of bodies. The country singer from the jukebox now rasping something about dancing girls and hookers, as best Active could make out.

They were still three rings out from the center when he realized the crowd was cheering, not a pair of hot dancers or even a couple coupling, but two men on the floor in the final stages of a drunken fight. One had given up altogether, lying on the concrete with his face covered as the other rained half-hearted punches onto his forearms.

The upper combatant, apparently sensing the time had come to finish the fight, drew his fist back to his ear and said, "I'm 'na rip off your head 'n' puke down y'r throat." He let fly, missed, and rammed his fist into the concrete, then collapsed onto the floor beside his opponent, holding the injured wrist and moaning "Oh, fuck me dead."

Active looked at Stella as the crowd broke up. "That them?"

"Must be." Stella nudged the wrist holder with the toe of a gum boot. "You call for a limo?"

"Oh, fuck," the man said.

Stella shook her head. "Any ideas, muscle?"

Active squatted between the two heads on the floor and spoke softly into their ears. "Flight's leaving in thirty minutes. You don't want to miss too many planes out of Dutch, from what I hear."

The head ripper said "Oh, fuck" again, but he sat up. He was white, wearing jeans and basketball shoes and a nylon East Wind jacket. A patch over the pocket said "Dale." He struggled to his feet and stood there, swaying slightly, a thread of bloody saliva dangling from the corner of his mouth. "Less go. Dough wanna miss 'at plane."

"What about your buddy here?" Stella nudged the still-horizontal one with her toe, drawing no response.

"Gotta help Lonnie," Dale said. He bent over, put his hands under his buddy's shoulders, and fell on top of him.

Stella shook her head and yanked Dale upright again "You follow us," she told him. Then she looked at Active. "You get his feet." Active did, Stella got his shoulders, and they lurched out of the bar with Lonnie between them and Dale trailing along behind.

"Let's throw him on the hood," Stella said when they reached Nanuq. Active complied.

Stella turned on Dale, who had stopped beside Nanuq and was staring up into the gray sky, his mouth open to the Aleutian rain. "You gonna puke on my white leather?"

"Nah me," Dale said. "Never puke. C'n hold my liquor."

Stella snorted, reached into Nanuq, and did something that made the trunk lid rise with a whoosh. She grabbed Dale by the collar and shoved him into the back seat. Then she reached into the trunk and came up with a plastic pail. She stuffed it between Dale's knees and shook him by the collar. "You gotta barf, you do it in this. You miss and my security man here will shoot you. Right, Muscle?"

"Not g'nna barf," Dale said.

Active made a pistol out of his right hand and pointed it at Dale. He jerked his thumb like a hammer falling and said, "I hope not."

Dale raised his hand, like a first grader needing to go to the bathroom. Active nudged Stella with an elbow. "I think he wants to speak."

"What is it, Dale?" Stella said.

"Wha'bout Lonnie?" Dale pointed at his buddy, still supine in the rain on Nanuq's hood.

"Is he gonna barf on my white leather?" Stella said.

"He jus' might. Can' hole his liquor like me." Then a worried frown came over Dale's face. "Will Muscle shoot him? Maybe we better just leave him. I think he's better off here than shot."

Dale paused and looked out at the East Wind and the rain. "Prolly better off here."

"Nah, I got a special compartment for guys that can't hold their liquor." Stella moved to the trunk, pulled out a wad of Visqueen, and unfolded it to cover the floor of the compartment. Then she went to the hood and put her hands under Lonnie's shoulders again and motioned with her head for Active to take the feet. Active obeyed and followed Stella to the back of the car, where she said, "Drop him in."

Active lowered the feet into Nanuq's big trunk, then they worked Lonnie's hips over the rim and finally his head and shoulders and laid him on his back on the Visqueen.

Stella studied their work for a moment, then grunted approvingly. "Good. If he barfs, the Visqueen will catch it."

Then she frowned. "Nah, he might choke on it, though." She rolled Lonnie onto his side and pulled his arms and knees out in front of him for stability, then grunted again in satisfaction.

"That oughta hold him." She slammed the trunk lid and walked back to the front of the car.

Dale, who had swiveled around to watch, now un-swiveled and stared at Stella. "He'll suff'cate back 'ere!"

Stella frowned. "You're probably right. You better ride back there and look after him." She grabbed Dale's collar and Dale said, "I guess's not that far to the airport."

Stella let him go and climbed behind the wheel. Active got into the passenger seat. "Where's your stuff?" Stella was looking at Dale in the rearview mirror.

"Our stuff? Oh, yeah, our stuff. The company van took it over 'iss af'rnoon."

Stella dropped Nanuq into gear, backed around to face the road, and they were off in another spray of gravel.

"So, whattaya think, Nathan? Want a full-time job as my muscle? You seem to have the look down and I guess if you got the look you don't need the moves." She wheezed out a laugh and lit a Marlboro.

"Yeah, Dutch Harbor's the place for me all right." He gazed through the rain at the mix of World War II Quonset huts like the East Wind and the newer, plywood office buildings and steel warehouses, presumably thrown up after the Bering Sea fishery got hot. "The pearl of the Aleutians."

"Ah, these little Bush pissholes." Stella waved her Marlboro at the wet, gray town outside Nanuq's windows. "You walk down the street, you know the stories of everybody you meet and they know yours. Who had a good season in the fishery, who struck out. Whose old lady was good while he was out on the boat and whose wasn't. Who's hitting the bars and whose kid got into Harvard. It's like the houses are transparent."

"Fuck, listen to me go on." She shook her head. "These places get their hooks into you and they just never let loose, is all."

"Only if you miss too many planes."

Stella wheezed and stuck the Marlboro back between her teeth. "Yup, too many planes."

Stella was silent for a while then, "What about this Marlboro girl?"

"What about her?"

"She miss too many planes?"

"I don't know yet."

He looked at his watch. After nine already. By the time they got the two drunks unloaded at the airport and he staked out the departure lounge and Stella drove him back to the Triangle, it would be ten o'clock or later. Too late to call Lucy Generous—her workday started at seven. She'd be in bed already. His bed, probably, looking after his place while he was in Dutch, looking for . . . what? He sighed, closed his eyes, and sank again into Nanuq's white leather, ignoring the sour stench of used booze from Dale in the rear seat and listening just enough to drop in an "Uh-huh" or a "Really!" at the right spots in Stella's account of how the hill looming into view back of the Dutch Harbor Airport came to be called Mt. Ballyhoo.

CHAPTER SIXTEEN

The main course at the Triangle cafeteria had been fried chicken, judging from the smell of the place and the remains on the Marlboro girl's plate when Active showed up at seven the next night.

Judging also from the remains, the Marlboro girl still didn't have much of an appetite. A chicken breast had maybe two bites out of it, as did a green salad, and that was it. A biscuit, a puddle of creamed corn, some kind of reddish purple cobbler dessert, all were untouched.

But one thing was different, he noticed as he looked around the cafeteria. There was no sign of Wendy. He noticed something else as he said hello and slid into the chair across from Grace. She was done up.

Lipstick, something on the cheeks, something around the eyes, not a lot of makeup but with her skin she didn't need a lot. No smell of the slime line tonight, just the hint of some perfume he couldn't name, something floral, he thought.

And the hair was not under the purple cap but free, looking glossy and brushed, if somewhat short.

Very short, in fact, barely longer than his own. It reminded him of . . . what? Otter fur, that was it. The trappers around Chukchi caught river otters and the women used the fur to trim parka ruffs. Dense, sleek brown-black fur that looked exactly like Grace Palmer's hair. He wanted to brush his palm over it until he realized it was about the same length as Wendy's hair.

She looked up and smiled for a moment, her eyes widening, the whites briefly flashing silver. Then she was serious again. "You bring the cigarettes?"

He pushed them across the table to her, then pulled off his windbreaker and laid it on the chair beside him as she lit a Marlboro. She inhaled, closed her eyes, opened them, and spoke through a cloud of smoke. "What did you do?"

The first swerve of the evening and the conversation not even started. He thought about the question, but came up dry. "About what?"

"About the day."

He thought some more and still didn't get it. "Sorry, what day?"

"This day. If I'm the reason you're in Dutch Harbor, what did you do all day today?"

"Oh, I see. Not much really. Slept in, read, watched CNN, made some calls." He shrugged.

"What?"

He started to repeat his answer, then decided she didn't mean she hadn't heard. "What . . . what?"

"What did you read?"

He smiled. "A computer manual, believe it or not. I have to go back to Chukchi and teach the other people in the office how to use Windows."

"I hate Windows." She had been twirling a fork in the creamed corn. Now she jabbed it into the chicken breast and mopped that through the corn. "Fucking Bill Gates."

"Yeah, a lot of people in the troopers prefer Macintosh, too, but . . ."

"Macintosh is worse. I like Linux."

He had to stop and think things over again. Linux was an operating system for geeks in computer labs and server farms. Based on his few encounters with it, he was of the opinion it had been written by martians and would never be successfully adapted for use by earthlings. Was Grace Palmer saying she—

"You actually understand Linux?"

She dragged on the Marlboro and gave him her cool gaze, the one that seemed to say he didn't measure up. "Whom?"

He was about to say, "You—do you really understand Linux?" when he realized this was another swerve and now she wasn't talking about computers. He threw up his hands in surrender. "Whom what?" Then he smiled because it sounded so ridiculous, and shook his head. "What are you asking?"

Again the cool gaze. "Whom did you call?"

He looked away from the gaze. "Oh, just some people up in Chukchi. You know, checking in."

"A woman?"

"She was out. I left a message." Telling himself, naturally she's going to be out if you call Dispatch on her lunch hour, you know that.

And thinking farther into Grace Palmer's question, was Lucy Generous a woman? He thought of her as a girl, he realized that now. Here he was, within sight of thirty and dating—no, sleeping with, there was far more sleeping with than dating—someone he thought of as a girl.

Maybe a girl was a girl until she had a child, was that what he thought? But what if she never did? He felt depressed at the thought of a sixty-year-old girl. Still, if she was never a mother perhaps she was never a woman.

No, that wasn't right. Not with Grace Palmer there across the table, looking as if she were made of diamond or tungsten, something beautiful and indestructible. Childless but definitely a woman. Would Lucy, could any girl, become this kind of woman without going through what Grace Palmer had gone through on Four Street? How many girls would survive it?

She seemed physically healthy—aglow, actually. She had definitely recovered her looks, and he marveled at the constitution that had not only survived Four Street but seemed to thrive on the slime line while her coworkers looked like the inmates of a homeless shelter.

But what about her mental state? She was smart, had to be smart if she could memorize bingo cards by the dozen, make music from telephone numbers, even understand Linux. But there was that opaque, nervous brightness, the jittery swerves in the conversation, the aura of a shattered psyche held together by the force of an extraordinary intellect and will.

He pushed it all into the back of his mind and looked at her again. Whatever her condition, Grace Palmer was not a girl. Every trace of girlhood had been burned out of her long ago.

"Hey, you over there," she said. "What's her name? Maybe I know her."

He shook his head. Apparently she had already asked the question once, while he was thinking. "It doesn't matter."

Grace Palmer dropped her gaze to her hands with a little smile, eyes flashing again. "Okay. I'm saving for college."

He backed his way through their conversation, trying to connect this latest swerve with anything either of them had said tonight.

She put the cool, appraising gaze on him again, and apparently took pity.

"That was your last question last night, the one I wouldn't answer." Her voice had a hint of laughter behind it. "What was I saving for? Well, the answer is college."

It occurred to him that the swerves were perhaps not evidence of a damaged psyche, but a tactic, a stunt. Like memorizing forty-eight cards at Aurora Bingo.

"You're going back to the university as a dead person?"

"No, I've applied for readmission under my own name. I'll work the summer here, then go back in the fall, pay restitution for the windows I broke, and register as Grace Palmer again."

"What's your major?"

"Pre-law."

"You want to be a lawyer?"

"Or a social worker if I can't hack law school." She drew on the Marlboro, eyes closed.

"You know, the police records in Anchorage don't mention any call from a motorist about you and Angie that night."

She didn't bother opening her eyes. "So?"

"Well, normally the dispatchers log everything."

Now she looked up at him. "Maybe they forgot or they were busy or something. Or maybe the guy couldn't get through. Does it matter?"

He shrugged. If she was lying about it, she was doing a good job. Acting exactly like she would act if she was telling the truth.

She shifted her weight on the chair. "You want to get out of here, walk around or something?"

He glanced out the window. "It's still raining sideways."

She shrugged. "I've got rain gear. Everybody here does. Don't you?"

He nodded. She put out the Marlboro. They stood and he followed her down the hall, noticing for the first time a tiny waist and flaring hips and realizing that he had not previously thought of any part of Grace Palmer except her face. Then, a whiff of the perfume again. Something old-fashioned, he thought—lavender? Had Grace Palmer, the Dutch Harbor slime liner, the one-time window-smashing, eye-jabbing Amazing Grace of Four Street, put on lavender? For him?

She stopped four rooms away from his own, put her key into the lock, and pushed open the door. She entered and pulled a slicker from the back of a chair and turned to face him. "Would you like to stay?"

He started, then told himself she couldn't mean that. "No, I don't mind if we walk. It's all right."

She nodded, came out of the room, and locked the door. "I meant for the night. Which room is yours?"

He said "Number thirteen" before it dawned on him what she had said. He turned and stared at her, but she was watching the numbers on the doors, looking for thirteen.

He stopped and caught her arm. She flinched violently and he released her, but she stopped beside him. "For the night? With you?" His throat was so tight the words came out in a hoarse whisper.

She looked up at him and he caught the scent again. Definitely lavender. "I don't know," she said. "Would you like to?"

"What about . . . what about Wendy?"

"Wendy moved out today. I asked her to. To complete my recovery."

He was having trouble with his breathing, so he broke their gaze and looked away. "I'll have to think about it."

"Me, too," she said. "I know this isn't how normal people do it but I'm not sure I can learn. Here's your door."

He got the anorak and they walked out into the gray spray of the long Aleutian evening. It was gloomy under the overcast, but the late summer sunset and real darkness were still hours away.

He started for Captains Bay Road, but she stopped him and pointed back of the bunkhouse, at the hills burying their heads in the scud. "There's a trail that leads up there. I go that way a lot."

He followed her along the bunkhouse wall to the back of the gravel pad of the Triangle Seafood complex, then on a path through the dripping knee-high grass that made up most of the island's natural ground cover.

The path was narrow, especially after it started up the hillside, so they had to walk single file, making conversation impossible. He was alone, or almost so, with the pattering of rain on his hood, the swishing of their clothing through the brush, and his thoughts. Where was Grace Palmer taking him, or where would she if he went along? What about spending the night?

Unthinkable if he was on a case, but this wasn't quite a case, not even close, really. Yet it still felt unthinkable, but in a different way. It would be like having sex with someone unconscious, or even with a corpse. Someone long past the capacity for informed consent.

As they climbed, the clouds scudding overhead got closer and closer. He began to sweat from the exertion and wondered if she planned to hike right up into the mist. But, no, they came to a kind of shelf where the hillside leveled off for a few yards. She stopped and sat on a lichen-covered bolder at one end of the little ledge and patted the spot beside her. "This is my place."

He took the spot and looked back the way they had come. The

Triangle complex, Captains Bay Road, a few hundred yards of the bay itself, then everything was lost in rain. The wind was blowing uphill, towards them, but their rock was a little distance back from the edge of the bench, so they were shielded from the full force of it.

"You flinched when I touched your arm back there."

She touched the place, suggesting she remembered, but said "Where?"

"In the bunkhouse. Right after you invited me to spend the night." His whole face was wet from the climb in the rain, but only the water in his eyebrows bothered him. He ran a finger along them and flipped the moisture away. She hadn't answered, so he said, "Sort of invited me."

She pulled a branch from a plant beside the boulder and plucked off a leaf, rolling it between thumb and forefinger.

"That's why I'm going to law school." She put the crushed leaf to her nose and sniffed, then tossed it away and pulled up a different kind of plant, this one with tiny green berries.

He was silent, thinking this over, so long that she added, "I can't have a man touch me unless I'm drunk." She looked at him expectantly.

"Law sch—I'm sorry, I just can't connect the dots here. Law school, your fear of intimacy . . ."

"You were looking at my hair before. You know why it's like this?"

He had, he realized guiltily, been thinking perhaps it was because she had been sick with something from Four Street, something she might still have. "No," he said, and shook his head.

"When I quit drinking and turned myself into Angie and some of my looks came back and men, normal men, started hitting on me again, I found I couldn't handle it. I'd either start swearing at them like a crazy person or I'd have a panic attack and freeze up completely. Once I passed out in the Anchorage public library when a guy, a perfectly decent guy, asked for my phone number."

She gave him the expectant look again and he shrugged, feeling stupid and inadequate. "Sorry. I still don't get it."

She studied her berry branch for a moment and finally shrugged. "I got myself a crew cut and stopped wearing makeup and started telling guys I preferred women." She shrugged again. "It was especially helpful down here."

She was watching him closely now, for his reaction, he assumed.

"That would explain Wendy?"

"I warned you this was going to be the unexpurgated version."

"I'm not judging—"

"Well, don't. My point is, I don't fear intimacy. I need it like anyone else. And now that I, I'm bringing Grace back to life, I'm letting my hair grow again and . . . fuck, why do I have to explain anything to you?"

"You don't. I already said that."

Suddenly her face crumpled and the cool, appraising Grace Palmer of the past two days vanished. The nervous ragged brightness, the toughness, were gone, too, replaced by a look of deep, angry exhaustion. "Goddammit, Nathan, every girl deserves a few years to just be a girl! Crushes, pretty things, proms. You should see the girls in little old Chukchi dress up for the prom, it's, it's . . . ahh, no!" She was crying silently now, tears rolling freely down her cheeks without a sound.

She wiped her eyes and shook her head and plowed on. "Shit, you're supposed to grow up and find the right man and be able to enjoy a good fuck, a good back rub, even just a good cuddle, just ordinary goddamn human contact, but I, I, hi, hi." She cried silently again.

He reached to put an arm around her shoulders but she sensed it and flinched, so he withdrew it.

"Look, you don't have to go on with this." He was really asking her to stop for his sake, because now he was picking up what was coming but not wanting to hear it yet, wanting time to prepare himself, feeling stupid for not having seen it before, a textbook case, really, but she wasn't going to stop, not now, he knew that.

"I'm going to law school and become the meanest ball-busting bitch prosecutor in Alaska and I'm gonna take men that do this to girls and I'm gonna put'em away for life."

Now she broke down and sobbed, great, wrenching bottomless sobs in the rain and wind coming up the slope, sobs with something in them that reminded him of Jason Palmer breaking down in front of the mural of Grace Palmer in the hall at Chukchi High.

Jason Palmer breaking down over the lost daughter on Four Street, Jason Palmer not telling him about the daughter who died slumped over a snow machine gas tank, Jason Palmer—.

Suddenly he was hot inside, the heat rising toward his throat like magma and he had just time to swing away so his back was to Grace Palmer and put his head between his knees before his stomach emptied itself onto the gravely soil.

As the attack passed in a series of diminishing heaves, he felt a hand, a very small and tentative hand, patting the back of his raincoat. He composed himself and swung back around, facing the bay again, and spoke gently, acid at the back of his throat. "Your father?"

He was aware of her nodding beside him. "Your sister, too?"

"Yes, of course."

"Her death— was it suicide?"

"Of course not. She thought huffing would induce a miscarriage. All of us little girls thought it back then."

"Miscarriage?" He knew she was about to break down again, but could see no way to avoid the question. "She was . . . Jason was the father?"

"Of course." She spoke rapidly, as if to hurry out the words before she lost the power of speech. "If I hadn't gone away, he would have had me still, he would have left Jeanie alone, I had a secret compartment where I could put it when it wasn't happening. I could handle it, I was stronger, I came home that Christmas and I should have stayed there to protect her, or I should have killed the son of a bitch, but I couldn't, I just couldn't, I, oh, I—" Now she broke down again, more than before, sobbing and shaking and almost howling. He put an arm around her shoulders again and she shook it off again, seeming angry, then curled into a fetal position and continued to sob, but more quietly, and finally was silent.

"What did Jason do when the autopsy report came back that she was pregnant?"

"There wasn't any autopsy."

"No autopsy? Why not?"

"How would I know? Maybe because the cause of death was obvious?"

Active stood and walked a few feet off. Could Jason Palmer be prosecuted now, after all this time? He turned back to the girl—as he now found himself thinking of her, at least for the moment— the girl on the rock. "Does anyone else know?"

"I told my mother." She was a heap of glistening rain gear on the boulder now. It was hard to know where the voice came from.

"She told me I was having nightmares and I should put them out of my mind. I don't hold it against her, though. She's a very traditional woman, very devout. How could she believe it of her own husband?"

He was silent, the question unanswerable.

"Will you tell her that, that I don't hold it against her? If you see her before she dies?"

He nodded. "You sure you don't want to tell her yourself?"

She shuddered. "I'm never going back there. Never."

"Did you tell anyone else?"

"My Aunt Agnes. She taught me about the secret compartment. She had some Inupiaq word for it, I forget what. Her uncle did it to her when she was a girl." The heap of rain gear gave a bitter laugh. "What is it with you men, anyway? You deface the wombs wherein you were bred."

He wondered at the old language, and asked her if it was from the Bible.

Another bark-laugh. "The Bible was written by men. Shakespeare's girlfriend wrote that."

He started to ask about it, but dismissed it as another detour, and shook his head. "Whoever she was, she was wrong. It's not all men."

"It's enough men."

She sat up and stared out into the weather. "You know what his favorite place was? The school. He'd take me with him when he went in to grade papers or work on his lesson plans at night or on the weekends."

She pulled her rain hood forward and shrank inside it. "When I was little, it was so wonderful. The classroom was just his place—his papers, his books, the smell of his aftershave. If it was winter, he'd kick his mukluks off at the door and I'd put them on and clump around while he worked and I'd picture how my husband would be just like him. Little did I know my husband would be him."

She gave one of her short mirthless laughs. "So I stopped going to the school and he had to do the best he could around the house. He would follow me into the bathroom sometimes and I got to where I just wouldn't go if he was home. For four years it was like that. The doctors at the hospital up there treated me for chronic constipation, but I just threw away the medicine and waited for school the next day. But nothing really worked. Love will always find a way, eh?"

Active walked to the rock and sat down again, but said nothing.

"Did you ever hear the story of reflected man, Nathan?"

He shook his head. "I don't think so."

"Aunt Agnes told me the story after it started." Grace dropped her eyes to her hands and spoke softly. "She couldn't do anything really, but she told me this story, and I guess it helped a little."

She looked up at him, eyes glistening but not crying now. He nodded.

"Once there was a man whose friends decided to play a joke on him. So they crept into his house while he was asleep and with charcoal from the fire, they marked his face so it looked like he was tattooed." With two fingers, she traced imaginary vertical lines below her lips. "You know how women would tattoo their chins in the old days?"

"I've seen it in books."

"In books." She paused, then shook her head. "My grandmother had them. Anyway, this man's friends marked him up to look like a woman. The next day he went out hunting and he came to a lake.

Feeling thirsty, he started to put his lips to the water when he saw the face of a beautiful woman in the lake. But when he reached out to touch her, she vanished."

"The next day, and the day after, he told his wife he was going hunting again. By now, she was in on the joke and said nothing, so he returned to the lake, but the beautiful woman always vanished at his touch. Finally, he could stand it no longer, so he jumped in the lake to be with her."

Active digested this for a few seconds. "And then?"

"His friends had been following him around all this time to see the effect of their joke. They all had a good laugh at his foolishness. So did he."

"So he didn't drown."

Grace shook her head with a smile that seemed to say Nathan Active was naive indeed. "Of course not. But if I ever tell a daughter of my own this story, I'm sure going to drown the son of a bitch!" She laughed one of her unpleasant laughs, then was silent for a long time.

"How could you function in school, the straight-A grades, Miss North World, with all that going on at home?"

"I don't know. I guess I thought if I made myself the perfect girl, he'd see how precious that was and leave me alone." She shook her head and shrugged. "Plus, anything to get out of the house, right?"

He grimaced and she picked up the berry branch again, crushed one of the tiny green globes and sniffed it.

"Will you help if we investigate this?"

"You mean make a formal statement, testify in court with him . . . with him sitting there?"

Active nodded.

She shuddered. "No. I've never talked about this since I told

Aunt Aggie and she showed me how to put it in the secret compartment. I don't ever want to talk about it again. I don't know why I talked to you. You seemed so . . . so trustable, I guess. You felt right, somehow."

She tasted one of the green berries, then spat it out with a grimace. "What do you think would happen if I did testify?"

"Well, you're the only witness, although I suppose Aunt Agnes' testimony would help some, and your mother, if she'd say anything about what you told her, unless—is Jeanie buried in Chukchi?"

"No, he had her cremated. Why?" She looked at him. "Oh, you're thinking of DNA testing on the baby?"

He nodded. "Maybe Jason thought of it, too."

"Maybe."

"Well, I guess you're it, then. Could you do it?"

"I don't know. I couldn't before, except to Ida and Aunt Agnes. The thought of challenging him head-on, his power, what he did, you know, it puts a kind of hold over you, a paralysis. You say to yourself, 'If he touches me again, I'll scream,' and then he does touch you again and once again you're helpless. Kind of numb and somewhere else. Gone." She shuddered. "I don't know. What would happen in court?"

He shook his head. "The defense attorney, any decent defense attorney . . ."

"Yeah," she said with another bitter laugh. "I can hear it now. 'On one hand, we have Amazing Grace Palmer of Four Street, favorite of soldiers and anyone else with a bottle of Bacardi, more recently living under the name of a dead person whose Oil Dividends and other assets she has converted to her own use. And on the other hand, I give you my client, Jason Palmer, educator, one-time mayor of Chukchi, board member of the Chukchi

Senior Center and a founder of the Katonak 300 Sled-Dog Race.'
Ah, fuck."

Just then a troubling question occurred to him, so troubling he
decided to let the hypothetical defense attorney ask it. "And I suppose they'd point out it was your father who asked me to come after
you. Why would he, if he . . .?

She nodded. "Good question and I haven't a clue about the
answer, except that he's crazy. Maybe he wants to say he's sorry,
maybe he wants me back again. Evil is opaque, Nathan. You can't
see into it. I can't, anyway."

She shuddered, then closed her eyes. "Or maybe it really is
because Ida is sick and he thinks we can all just pretend it never
happened." She opened her eyes and wiped them and shook her
head firmly. "Whatever it is, I'm not coming back. I never want
to talk about this again or see him again. Or testify in court. No."

He fumbled inside his rain coat and produced a business card.
"Take this. It's got our toll-free number in Chukchi on it. Call me
if you change your mind."

"That's all right, I won't be needing it. " She pushed the card
back to him and looked into his eyes. "And if I do, I memorized it
when I was composing Nathan's Song."

She put a hand on his thigh and even through his clothing the
touch reached him. He stirred, and felt ridiculous.

"That sounded sort of like goodbye," she said. "What about
tonight?"

He put a hand over hers, which was small and cold and wet,
and curled slightly under his own, as if seeking shelter. He put her
hand back in her own lap. "This might become a case, turn from
personal to professional, you know."

"No, I said! No case. No investigation. No nothing!"

She touched his thigh again.

"But if intimacy is so difficult for you . . ." He removed her hand again.

"Sorry." She shrugged and stared straight ahead. "I keep hoping. You know, normal relations with a normal man, to complete my recovery, and there haven't been any relations, of any kind, except with women, which doesn't really count, since I became Angie Ramos, but I think I could become a passionate lover, a soulmate, I believe some capacity for joy is still alive in me if I can just . . . if I can just untwist myself and—well, you came all this way."

She stood and started down the path towards the Triangle. After a few steps she stopped and half-turned to look at him. "Some other time, maybe." A silver flash, and she set off down the path again.

"Maybe," he told the back of her slicker.

CHAPTER SEVENTEEN

Active left Dutch Harbor on an unscheduled flight the ticket agent said had come in with a load of cargo. It lifted off at three A.M. in a period of relative calm, with very little rain, no delay, and no sign of the departure panic that had gripped Captain Ross and his passengers two days earlier.

Dennis Johnson had told Active when he called the night before that the Finest's goalie was working a week of midwatches, so Active took a taxi from the airport straight to the Ben Boeke Ice Arena, where the Finest were playing this time. By six-thirty, he was in his favorite position on the rink, squarely in front of the cage of steel pipe and rope netting that was the entire focus of the opposing team. They were the Slopers, the same team the Finest had played the previous Friday, and made up mostly of oil workers on the two-week break between stints on the North Slope.

Active liked playing goalie for two reasons. One, not much skating was involved, so being rusty wasn't as much of a handicap as it had been on Friday, when he had played defenseman with such a striking lack of distinction that he had ended up unconscious after the Slopers body checked him against the side board.

Second, he didn't have to exhaust himself chasing after the

action. All he had to do was squat in front of the goal and wait, and let the action come to him.

There were periods of inaction when the game was between the blue lines, or at the other goal, but he enjoyed those, too. They gave him time to work over the enormous problem of Grace Palmer. Was there any way to settle the question of whether Angie Ramos had been pushed into the path of the snowplow to launch the identity switch that Grace had conducted so successfully—two of the Slopers broke out of a melee at the far end of the rink and sped in his direction, slapping the puck back and forth between them to keep it away from the pursuing Finest.

It was like watching a train or perhaps a rotary snowplow bear down on him, but he didn't mind. He almost hoped the Sloper with the puck would skate straight into him, but, no, the opposing player fired and veered off. The puck stayed on the ice, and Active caught it with his stick. It bounced feebly out into the melee now building in front of the Finest's goal. A jumble of grunts, slams, sticks whacking together, skates scraping on the ice and finally another Sloper scooped up the puck and fired it back at Active, this time in the air.

Active dropped to his knees and caught it on his chest pad—a satisfying 'thump' that reverberated momentarily in his thorax—and fell on it, protecting it until the referee whistled for a face-off.

The Finest's left wing was a little quicker or luckier with his stick and the action moved downrink again, toward the Slopers' goal.

Active adjusted his gear and returned to the problem of Grace Palmer's identity switch and its connection with the death of Angie Ramos.

Here in Anchorage it was easy not to be distracted by the fact that Grace Palmer had smiled just so, that she had offered sex, that he had noticed the tiny waist and the scent of lavender, that he had longed to brush his palm over the otter-fur hair. Here on the ice at the Boeke, it was easy to tell himself none of these things changed the facts.

And the fact was, if it had been Angie Ramos he found on the slime line in Dutch Harbor, he was pretty sure he would at this moment be pounding on the Anchorage Police Department and Officer Dennis Johnson to open a homicide investigation into the grisly death of Grace Palmer by rotary snowplow.

Yet he knew that—this time it was a single Sloper heading his way, an amazingly fast skater who left both the Finest and his fellow Slopers behind as he raced down the side board and lofted a shot at such speed Active was not conscious of actually seeing it. He merely reacted to a streak coming at him and got some glove on it, but not enough glove. The puck ricocheted off the mitt and struck the rim of the goal and bounced into the net.

The Slopers cheered and whacked their sticks together, while the Finest glared at Active or at his sponsor.

"Told ya he had too fucking many teeth to be a hockey player," one of the Finest said to Dennis. Active didn't see who said it, but it sounded like Taylor, who had also been disgusted by Active's performance as defenseman the week before and whose jaws, top and bottom, were devoid of teeth in the front.

The teams moved out to center rink to face off. The referee dropped the puck and one of the Finest got a stick on it and the action moved to the far end of the rink.

Yet, he reminded himself as he resumed the problem of Grace Palmer and Angie Ramos, he knew that if he were back in the cafeteria at the Triangle Bunkhouse at this moment with Grace Palmer flashing her dark eyes at him and telling him she had nothing to do with Angie Ramos's death, he would believe her completely, just as he had known with blazing, agonizing—but mistaken—certainty that Grace Palmer was dead when he saw the photograph of the angel tattoo on the breast of Heavenly Doe.

Which proved only that he couldn't be certain of anything where Grace Palmer was concerned. But she had said at least one thing that could, in all objectivity, be described as a lead, a checkable lead. Perhaps Dennis Johnson could find out if there was support in the records for Grace's claim that she and Angie had talked to a motorist a few minutes before the rotary snowplow had arrived, a motorist who appeared to be calling the police on a cell phone as he drove off after having been told to go fuck himself and to give the same advice to the police—Active dropped into his squat again as the puck, not clearly in the control of either the Slopers or the Finest, came shooting down the ice towards him, a gaggle of players from both teams racing after it.

After the game, he and Dennis Johnson decided on breakfast at Gwennie's Old Alaska Restaurant, a two-story landmark not far from the airport. Gwennie's was famed for an inexplicable wishing pond complete with wooden bridge, real water and a stuffed grizzly eating a stuffed salmon, for enormous portions, for lack of pretense, and—most comfortingly of all to Active after his costly passage through Dutch Harbor—for low prices.

"So she's alive." Dennis shook his head in amazement as an elderly waitress with violent red hair walked away from their second-floor table, still scribbling down the details of two orders for reindeer sausage and eggs, the mild sausage to go with Active's scrambled, the Cajun Red Hot with Dennis's over easy. "But how can that be after all . . . well, you know, the files."

Active had told him a little about it during the call from Dutch Harbor the day before, a little more this morning when Dennis had picked him up at the airport, a little more on the way to Gwennie's. But it had been sketchy and jumbled. Maybe telling it from beginning to end would help him untangle it, help him distill his feelings out of it enough to see the facts.

So he laid it out for Dennis, arranging it in chronological order as best he could, leaving nothing out, until he came to Grace Palmer's invitation to spend the night. That was personal, so what would be the point of telling Dennis, except to make himself feel foolish, but about what, exactly?

"Yeah, so you're going for a walk in the rain?" Dennis was saying. Active realized he had been silent for several seconds as he tried to argue himself into leaving it out of the story.

"And?" Dennis persisted. Maybe he was being a cop, now, sensing that whatever was behind the silence was more important than the words that had preceded it.

Was it? The invitation, or hint, had come a day after Grace Palmer had told him the snowplow story, a day after he had questioned her about the story, a moment after he had asked about the mysterious cell-phone call that didn't show up in the police files. Had she wrapped him in that lavender-scented cloud of sexual possibility to—?

"She offered to go to bed with me."

Dennis's eyebrows shot up and he leaned back slightly. "Jesus Christ! Did you do it?"

Active shook his head and swallowed some coffee. Just then the elderly redhead returned with their orders, huge steaming plates that gave off maddening aromas of reindeer fat and the grease the eggs were fried in, the sorts of smells that ordinarily revolted him. But now, after flying most of the night and playing hockey for two hours on nothing but a package of macadamia nuts and two cups of Aleutian Air coffee, those same smells were the breath of heaven. He plunged into the food like a fast center driving down-rink with the puck.

"Lemmee fee at fiffer," Dennis said a few minutes later, around a mouthful of over-easy, spraying some towards Active in the process.

Active was grateful to see the yellow globules fall short of his plate, although a suspicious ripple spread across his coffee cup. "What?" he said. "Didn't your mother ever tell you not to talk with your mouth full?"

Dennis chewed and swallowed and tried again. "Let me see that picture."

Active tried to look mystified, but Dennis said, "Come on, you know what I mean."

Active dug into his briefcase and passed Dennis the envelope Jason Palmer had turned over back in Chukchi. Dennis flipped though the pictures, pulled one out, and held it where they could both see it. It was the mural shot—eighteen-year old Grace Palmer on the bluff over Chukchi.

"And she still looks like this?"

Active took the picture and studied it. "Yes, basically. She's older, but the Four Street look is gone, except for a little scar here." He touched his cheekbone. "And she's not a girl any more."

He handed the picture back to Dennis

"And where is Wendy when the most beautiful woman in Alaska makes you this astounding offer?"

"This is the second night, and Wendy is nowhere to be seen. Grace tells me Wendy has moved out."

Dennis turned the picture Active's way. "And you said no to this?"

Active nodded, and shrugged.

"This is not just . . . this is . . ." Dennis trailed off and looked at the picture.

"A gift from God," Active muttered.

"What was that?"

"Just something her father said when he asked me to find her." He shook his head. "Sunlight and grace, a gift from God. That's what he called her."

"I'll say." Dennis's eyes were on the picture. "This is pitch-your-job-and-live-in-a-trailer-if-you-have-to. This is . . ."

"Would you?"

Dennis laid down the picture and looked out the second floor window of Gwennie's. There was a Harley-Davidson shop across Spenard Road. Over its roof the peaks of the Alaska Range were visible a hundred miles to the west, still loaded with snow from the winter past and glittering in the morning light.

"I might."

"But you've got a wife, your girls . . ."

"I still might, if she asked me. Some things, you don't expect to find even once in your life, so you have to make exceptions when it does happen." Dennis raised his cup to his lips and gazed at Active over the brim, brown eyes unreadable. "A man doesn't turn down a gift from God."

Active worked on his reindeer sausage for several bites, thinking how to get this back on track. He had wanted Dennis to look at the case with cop's eyes. Instead, Grace Palmer's face, just a picture of it, had pulled his friend into a haze of romantic fantasy, of yearning for what probably no longer existed, if it ever had, except on the surface. The same haze in which Active himself had spent two days in Illusions.

"The problem is I'm not sure if it was business or pleasure," he said finally.

"What?" Dennis looked startled for a moment, then picked it up and was a cop again. "Oh, I see. You ask her a few questions about Angie Ramos's death, and the next thing you know she's kicked out her girlfriend and you're invited to spend the night—is that it?"

Active nodded.

"Hmm." Now it was Dennis's turn to think it through as he worked over the platter of calories and cholesterol. "And she's using Angie's identity."

Active nodded again.

"But she has a reasonable explanation."

Another nod.

"And there's no evidence, no direct evidence, that Angie had any help getting in the way of that snowplow?"

Active studied his friend. "You know, when you thought it was Grace Palmer dead, you were ready to fry Angie Ramos. Now that Grace is the suspect, you're Perry Mason for the defense."

Dennis looked a little chagrined, but didn't back off. "That doesn't change the fact there's no direct evidence Angie was pushed into that snowplow, right?"

Active shook his head. "Except for the part about the guy who supposedly called the cops on his cell phone because they were blocking traffic. I didn't find anything about that in the files."

"Yeah, that is odd." Dennis pushed back his plate, now empty, and pulled his coffee front and center. "If Dispatch sent a unit when the cell-phone guy called, it should have shown up about the same time as the snowplow, eh?" He raised his eyebrows in inquiry.

"Exactly. But your guys weren't dispatched until the snowplow driver radioed in, according to Cullars's Heavenly Doe file. I went back over it on the plane up from Dutch this morning."

Dennis frowned in concentration. "Well, I suppose if Dispatch got the call from the cell-phone guy and never sent anybody . . ."

"Why wouldn't they?"

"Wasn't there a blizzard that night? They probably had fender-benders all over town. It could take a while to get around to a squabble between a couple of street drunks and a motorist."

Active shook his head. "But the call would show up on the Dispatch log, right?"

"Yeah, it would." Dennis nodded thoughtfully. "I'll check and let you know."

The redheaded waitress came up just then and said, "You guys ready for your check?" Active just nodded, but Dennis engaged in a few seconds of gallantry about his willingness to check her out, or be checked out by her, any time. She went away grinning and shaking her head and Dennis asked Active where they were.

It took him a few seconds to backtrack. "We were about to go for a walk in the rain."

Dennis nodded, and Active picked up the story and carried it all the way through the agonizing scene on the hillside above Captain's Bay.

Dennis frowned. "So, first she invites you to spend the night, then she's telling you all the evil things her father did to her and her sister?"

Active nodded, feeling foolish and slightly dizzy for not having put it together that way himself. "Shit."

Dennis shrugged. "Well, the business about her father could be true, I guess. Just like her story about Angie Ramos."

Active nodded and said, "Sure."

"But a bitch to prove. Especially if she won't help."

Active nodded again. "The statute of limitations might even have run out."

"No, I don't think there is a statute of limitations for kiddy-diddlers," Dennis said as the waitress returned with the tab. They pulled out their wallets and peeled bills onto the table.

Dennis stood and pulled on his cap. "What do you want to do?"

"Write up the interview and send it to you. You can give it to Homicide, let them decide if it's a case or not."

Dennis nodded. "Sure. But I meant about her father."

Active frowned as he dropped Jason Palmer's envelope of pictures back into the briefcase. "I don't know."

"What about this Aunt Aggie? Grace allegedly told her about it at the time?"

Active snapped his fingers. "Good point. And I think she's coming down to Chukchi to be with the mother. Listen, can I borrow your cell?"

Dennis pulled it off his belt and Active went into the men's room to get away from the breakfast clatter in the restaurant. He fished out his notebook and looked up the home phone number for Cowboy Decker, chief pilot at Lienhofer Aviation.

"Listen," he said when Decker came on the line. "Did you bring Ida Palmer's sister down from Isignaq yet?"

"Nah," the Bush pilot said in his smoker's rasp. "We're waiting till we've got a backhaul from Isignaq so we can give the family a break on the tab. I guess the medical bills are eating them up, even with what Indian Health pays."

"I need to talk to her. Think you could take me up there tomorrow?"

"Come to think of it, I might be able to bring her down today," Decker said. "I've got to fly a surveyor up to Ebrulik this morning if our Aztec is behaving itself. Maybe I can talk Delilah into letting me go on up to Isignaq and pick Aggie up, too."

"Just do it. The troopers will pay," Active said.

"That settles it, then," Decker said. "I'll have her in Chukchi this afternoon."

Active returned to the table and walked downstairs with Dennis into the morning of early summer. Anchorage had been receiving a rain shower when his flight from Dutch Harbor had landed. Now the sky had cleared and a fresh breeze had sprung up from the north. Everything in sight, even Spenard, sparkled.

"So what did you get Lucy?" Dennis asked as they climbed into his blue-and-white.

"What do you mean?" Active experienced a moment of terror, and began erecting a defense. "Her birthday was two months ago. I got her a very nice—" He stopped when he saw the pitying look on his friend's face.

"You're gone all this time, half of it on your own nickel in Dutch Harbor, chasing around after the best-looking woman in Alaska, and you don't even bring back a present?" Dennis whistled. "You're toast."

"I ran out of time and, anyway, Lucy's not like that."

"Is she female?"

Active brightened. "Maybe the gift shop at the airport."

Dennis gave him another pitying look. "Yeah, I bet she's dying for a T-shirt with a moose on it. How long before that plane leaves?"

Active looked at his watch "An hour and twenty-nine minutes.

That means I should check in—" His words were drowned out by the howl of Dennis's siren and the screech of tires as the blue-and-white shot up Spenard Road, directly away from the airport.

A very few minutes later, Dennis pulled into a taxi zone and waved expansively at the sign on the brown brick wall of the building beside them. "Welcome to Nordstrom's," he said. "A friend indeed to the man in need."

They hurried inside, deciding en route to try lingerie first. "You can't go wrong with lingerie," Dennis said, "and besides, that's where the best-looking salesgirls work."

Active was on the point of confessing he did owe Lucy Generous some panties—one pair of exceedingly flimsy white cotton panties, to be precise—but decided there were limits to even the closest of friendships.

Instead, he contented himself with reminding Dennis how they used to come in as teenagers and pretend to look for birthday gifts for their mothers, just to see the Nordstrom salesgirls.

"Oh, yeah," Dennis said. "You remember that blonde, Janene?"

Active remembered not only Janene's yellow hair, but her astonishing upholstery. Even then, in the relative innocence of youth, they had suspected that parts of Janene were probably not altogether natural, which only added fuel to their lust and admiration. "That must have been, what, twelve or fifteen years ago? I wonder if even her name was real," Active said as they started up the escalator.

"Nope," Dennis said with the air of one privy to a great secret. "It was Wanda. Wanda Goodwin." Active waited for the rest of the story, but Dennis only gazed idly about with a complacent smirk as the escalator groaned upward.

"All right, I'll ask: How do you know that? You didn't date her!"

"No, I busted her." Dennis now wore a look of complete triumph. "Couple years ago when I was working vice. She was dancing at Illusions and turning tricks on the side."

Active digested this depressing news for a moment. "How'd she look?"

Dennis shook his head grimly. "Oh, Nathan, what gravity and Father Time and Wild Turkey will do to even the Janenes of this world, it . . . well, it doesn't bear thinking about. Or looking at. Just be glad you didn't have to see it."

They reached the third floor and started for the lingerie department. Active saw that it was, in the finest Nordstrom tradition, presided over by a blonde perhaps even better put together than the original Janene.

"Man, look at that," Dennis breathed reverently. "Enough leg there to build two girls."

"I know." Active stopped and pulled at his friend's arm. "I can't do this."

"What!" Dennis looked both astonished and outraged. "Why not?"

"I don't know Lucy's size."

"So?"

"So I'm not going to go up to that woman and do this . . ."—he traced out the shape of an imaginary female in the air—". . . and say, 'About this big.'"

Dennis tried to argue him into it, but Active returned a series of variations on "No way" and "Not a chance."

"All right," Dennis sighed, "how about some perfume? The clerks down there are as old as our mothers, but at least the only sizes are Expensive and More So."

Active nodded and turned toward the escalator before Dennis

could see the expression on his face. He rode down in near-total silence, responding only with grunts and chuckles to Dennis's complaints about missing their opportunity to buy underwear from Janene's successor.

By the time they reached the first floor, Active was reasonably certain nothing showed on his face, and by the time they reached the counter staffed by old ladies, he had reviewed his account to Dennis of the Dutch Harbor trip and decided there had been no mention of Grace Palmer's perfume.

So when he asked the saleslady for it, Dennis didn't seem shocked at all. He just said, "So this Lucy wears lavender, huh? Must be an old-fashioned kind of girl."

PART IV

CHUKCHI

CHAPTER EIGHTEEN

"He's had his breakfast. I can take you in now."

Active put down the *Sports Illustrated* and got to his feet beside the nurses aide, a young Inupiat woman in green scrubs. She led him through the swinging doors into the Intensive Care Unit of the Chukchi Regional Hospital, then into the room housing Cowboy Decker.

Decker had steel-gray hair and normally wore a baseball cap, a leather bomber jacket, steel-framed glasses and plenty of attitude. Today, the Bush pilot lay flat on the bed, his left leg in a cast and a bandage covering his forehead and scalp, which seemed to have bled slightly into the dressing. No jacket, just a hospital gown. A monitor to the left of the bed traced out his vital signs, and an IV bag dangled from a stand on the right.

A red-eyed, exhausted-looking woman in jeans, sneakers and a sweatshirt rose from a green vinyl chair near the bed as Active came in. Active and the Deckers weren't close friends, but he hugged the pilot's wife anyway. "Linda, I'm so sorry. How is he? I couldn't believe it when I heard he crashed."

She broke the hug and sighed. "They say he'll make it. He's got a broken leg, maybe a concussion, probably no permanent brain damage." She picked up her purse. "I'm going to get some sleep. When he wakes up again, tell him I'll be back this afternoon."

Active nodded and turned toward the bed. Decker opened his eyes as the door clicked shut behind his wife. "Hey, Nathan," he said. "Sorry I . . . sorry about Aggie."

Decker's voice was slowed down, though Active couldn't tell if it was from medication or trauma. "Take it easy," he said. "These things happen."

"Not to me they don't, or at least they didn't. I, I, I guess the odds finally— you know much about odds, Nathan?"

Active shrugged. He didn't know exactly how to get into the subject of how the Bush pilot had managed to kill the only witness likely to corroborate any aspect of Grace Palmer's story of paternal rape, so it wouldn't hurt to let Decker ramble a little. If he had a concussion, he'd probably ramble regardless. "Yeah, I had some statistics in college. But we don't much go in for probability theory in law enforcement. You're going to put somebody away, you want certainty."

Decker groaned a little. "Think you can raise me up here? There's this doohickey . . ."

Active saw a thick white cable running under Decker's pillow. "Hang on," he said, easing the controller from beneath it. He found the proper button and the bed whirred until Decker's head was elevated a foot or so.

"Yeah, that's better," Decker said. "Look, suppose you flip a coin nine hundred and ninety-nine times and it always comes up heads. Don't the odds say it should come up tails next time?"

"Not if it's an honest coin."

Decker had to think about that for a while. "Okay, say it's honest," he said finally.

Active nodded. "Then it's fifty-fifty whether you get heads or tails next time. The past doesn't matter. It's random."

"Random."

Active nodded.

"Yeah, that's what I used to think," Decker said. "I never worried about the odds. Other than getting laid, a man's life is about competence, right? The more experience I got, the less chance I'd screw up, that's what I figured. I could outrun the weather, beat the goddamn airplanes and their goddamn tricks, go on forever."

Decker fell quiet and Active used the lull to pull the green chair up to the bed. He seated himself and took out his notebook. "Look, I need to ask you some questions."

Decker looked surprised under the bandages. "Questions? I'll get enough of them from the FAA and the National Transportation Safety Board. You, too?"

Active shrugged. "Somebody I needed to talk to is dead, is all." He paused, decided to dive in. "Did you tell Jason Palmer I asked you to go up and get Aggie Iktillik?"

"Yeah, sure," Decker rasped. "He was going to pick her up at Lienhofer's when I got in. So?"

"Is there any chance what happened up in Isignaq wasn't random?"

"What are you after here, Nathan?"

"Could your Aztec have been sabotaged?"

Now Decker's look was beyond surprise. It was pure disbelief, two hundred proof. "You didn't hear?"

Active shrugged shook his head. "I got in yesterday afternoon and all I heard was that you crashed and Aggie Iktillik was killed. I hung around here all night waiting for you to wake up."

Decker closed his eyes and seemed to drift off for a moment. "I tried to take off on one engine."

"You what?" It did sound like sabotage. "You mean one of your engines quit on takeoff? What—"

Decker shook his head, his eyes still closed. "The left engine wouldn't start. So I tried to take off on the right one."

"You mean you taxied out with a dead engine and, and . . ."

"Uh-huh."

"With Aggie in the plane."

"Uh-huh."

"My God, why?"

"I did it once before. I thought I could do it again."

Active wondered if there was any point in taking the interview farther. Unless Decker was raving, Aggie Iktillik's death had been caused by nothing more sinister than another Bush pilot with big balls and a tiny brain. Plane crashes were a leading cause of death in rural Alaska. This one, however stupid, was apparently just another in a long line of depressing statistics.

Suddenly, all Active wanted was to be out of this room, away from Cowboy Decker and this latest dead end in the search for the truth about Grace Palmer. "Look," he said, rising from the chair. "I know you need your rest. Why don't we—"

"That left engine has always been funny," Decker said, as if to himself, eyes glittering. "You get it hot and shut it down, about one time out of ten, it won't start till it's completely cold again. You can grind the battery right down to nothing, and you can get out and throw the propeller by hand till you get a charley horse, but the left one ain't gonna start again that day."

Was Decker out of his head or not? If he was, Active would have to chase down the witnesses to the crash, if any. Or maybe even wait until the NTSB completed its investigation. And how thorough would that be? A single-fatality crash in the middle of nowhere? He decided he had no choice but to hear Decker out. He sank into the chair again. "And that's what happened yesterday in Isignaq?"

"It was Ebrulik, March a year ago, temperature in the twenties," Decker said.

Decker was obviously raving now. Active was about to give up and start hunting down eyewitnesses when he realized Decker was talking about the first time he had tried a single-engine takeoff in the twin-engine Aztec.

"The left one wouldn't start, no way, no how," Decker continued with the same distant look in his eyes. "I called our office here in Chukchi to get them to send another plane and they put our mechanic on the line. You know Henry Draper?"

"Just barely," Active said, happy to be back in Decker's reality again. He tried to maintain the link. "I think I met him once in your office. So, the left one wouldn't start yesterday in Isignaq?"

"Goddamn disgusting Draper," Decker said. "Never washes his overalls or his hair either, that I can see. Those mechanics, they hate us because we get to fly the airplanes and stay clean instead of working on them and looking like a mud wrestler all the time. Bloody knuckles."

"Bloody knuckles?"

"That's how you can tell a mechanic. Bloody knuckles from having to work on airplanes all the time. That's why they hate us."

"Did you call Draper yesterday from Isignaq?" Active asked. Maybe the mechanic could corroborate some of what Decker was saying.

"He says, he says, 'Fly it home on the good one.'"

"Draper told you to bring it in from Isignaq on one engine?"

"I'm on the phone in the village school at Ebrulik and the line is bad and I think I heard him wrong and I say, 'What? Take off on one engine?' And he says 'Yep' and he tells me he's looking at the manuals there in the office and he says, 'Write this down.' And he says he's figured out that with the weather as cold as it is, and the thirty-two hundred feet of runway they got there in Ebrulik, I can probably make it. He tells me if I can get her up to fifty-eight knots before I use up twenty-two hundred feet of runway, I'll make it off. Otherwise, I shut down and I've got a thousand feet to stop."

"And you did it?"

"So I say, 'Nah, you guys get another plane up here.' And he says, 'Nah, you can do it. You're Cowboy Decker, right?' And even though I know he's working me, I go out and I do it."

Active thought of asking why, of asking how the stakes could possibly justify the risk. But he decided not to bother. He had learned long ago that Bush pilots live by a code of performance incomprehensible to normal men.

Decker put his fingertips to the bandage on his forehead, winced slightly, and continued the story. "So I go out and I pace off twenty-two hundred feet of the runway and I stick two spruce boughs in the snow to mark the spot. Then I crank up the good one and roll down the strip and, by God . . . well, that goddamn Draper knows the Aztec, I'll give him that. I've got sixty knots when I pass the spruce boughs and by the end of the runway she's dancing on her toes and she pulls off easy as you please. Goddamn Draper, fuck him."

"So what did he say when you called him from Isignaq yesterday"?

"So I land at Ebrulik yesterday and let the surveyor off and I don't even shut the left one down. He just climbs down and I'm out of there. But at Isignaq, Aggie's not at the airport, so I catch a ride into the village with this kid in a pickup and I find her and the kid takes us back out to the airport and we climb in. And, goddammit, the left one won't start."

Active perked up a little. "This kid in the pickup. You know his name?"

Decker shifted back into the hospital room for a moment, looked at Active. "Sure, Isaac Boxer. His dad runs the store in Isignaq. Isaac saw me when I circled the village and came out to see if I needed any avgas."

Active made a note of the name. "So the left one wouldn't start and that's when you called Draper?"

"Nah, the airport in Isignaq is on that bluff above the river two-three miles from the village and I don't want to bother Isaac for another ride. So I decide to have a look at the left one myself and I open the cowling." Decker's eyes took on the thousand-yard stare again. "Damn, that engine is hot and so is the weather, too damn hot for the Arctic, eighty, eighty-five maybe. Gotta be this global warming you hear about. And great big hungry springtime mosquitoes buzzing around, one gets in my mouth and I cough it out. Then this mangy old husky comes up and lifts his leg on the Aztec's nose wheel, and there's a couple of goddamn little Eskimo kids hanging around, and one of them says, "Is it bwo-kin?" and then they run off giggling like they do. And I'm trying to get one of the spark plugs out for a look-see when it lets go all of a sudden and I slam my hand into the cooling fins of the number four cylinder and there you are, goddamnit, my knuckles are bleeding!"

Decker showed Active his right hand. It had a fresh scab across the two middle knuckles.

"So that's when I start thinking about Ebrulik March a year ago, and how if I can get the Aztec off the ground with the good one, it'll be cool up there over the river, vents open, air blowing through the cockpit, no mosquitoes, no kids, no huskies, just the Aztec and me and Aggie Iktillik cruising down to Chukchi. So I button her up and I tell Aggie, 'We'll fly back on one engine.' She says, 'Can you do that?' and I say, 'Sure, that's why we have two engines. One's a spare.'"

"So you never called Henry Draper?"

Decker returned to reality for a moment and shook his head. "Nope, I just went down to the end of the runway and walked back a thousand feet and tied my handkerchief to a little spruce tree."

He got the stare again. "Course, it was sixty degrees hotter in Isignaq yesterday than it was in Ebrulik March a year ago, and heat means you need more runway to get off. But I had more runway than I did in Ebrulik— about eight hundred feet more— so I figured I was good. And of course there was a thousand feet to stop if I didn't have the fifty-eight knots when I got to my handkerchief on the spruce tree."

Decker paused and touched the bandage above his eyes again. "Call the nurse, will you, Nathan? I need something for my head."

Active tugged the controller out from under the pillow again, found the call button and pressed it. When he pushed the device back under the pillow, Decker's eyes were closed in what looked like sleep. Active thought it over. Decker was making sense, mostly, though it wasn't completely clear whether he was talking about Ebrulik a year ago March, or Isignaq yesterday. But it did seem likely he had attempted a takeoff on one engine, and maybe this Isaac Boxer could confirm it. And that would be the end of trooper interest in the matter. Active decided to make his escape.

"So there we were," Decker said just as Active reached the door. Active sighed and returned to his chair.

"We're at the end of the runway, ready to roll," Decker said. "The prop on the left one is sticking up above the wing like a broken arm, the right one is humming away, Aggie's in the right seat, some kind of knitting on her lap, you know how these older Eskimo ladies always have some work with them? And I'm looking down four thousand feet of gravel runway, heat monkeys dancing over it, and you know what's there at the far end of the strip? The Isignaq cemetery. You know what Bush pilots say about that, Nathan?"

Active merely raised his eyebrows inquiringly, at last bowing to the futility of trying to deflect the lamentation of a man mourning his own competence.

"We say the villages always put the cemetery at the end of the runway so if you auger in they don't have to dig a grave. They just leave you in the hole you made. Funny, huh?"

"Cowboy, look—"

"So I throw the cobs to her and off we go. Twenty knots, thirty, forty, fifty. The little spruce with my handkerchief is just coming into sight, I've got fifty-three knots, fifty-five, I can see I'm not going to get the fifty-eight so I'm just about to chop the power and stand on the brakes when we hit this little heave in the runway and the Aztec lurches a couple feet in the air and when she comes down her wheels don't quite touch again and I can feel the controls come alive in my hands."

The door creaked open and a nurse came in, a white woman in a white uniform, gray hair, serious face. She thumbed up Decker's eyelids and looked at his pupils. "That head's bothering you a little, huh?"

"Yeah, I guess," the pilot said, his tone suggesting he was ashamed to be asking for pain relief. More of the Bush pilot code, Active supposed.

"We can ratchet up the Demerol," the nurse said. She pushed a button on a little console beside the bed. "But you can do it yourself, you know. Didn't they tell you?"

Decker shook his head, carefully.

"Just push this button yourself and you'll get a dose." She put her finger beside the button and waited until Decker looked. "Except if you do it more than once every fifteen minutes, it doesn't work. There's a timer so you don't get recreational with it."

Decker grunted and nodded, and the nurse left.

"Look," Active said. "You don't have to—"

But Decker was back on the runway at Isignaq. "So I think to myself, 'She's gonna do it, just like at Ebrulik,' and I leave the power on. But she just mushes along in ground effect, never gets flying speed, and I hear this b-r-r-r-p which was probably the prop clipping the headstones in the cemetery and then we're going over the bluff and I see the gravel bar along the river down there, a couple kids tooling along on a four-wheeler, and that's it." Decker looked at Active and Active decided the pilot's mind was back in the hospital room.

"That's it?"

Decker nodded. "I guess I was medevaced back here but that's all I remember until a nurse came in to check on me this morning and I asked her about Aggie."

Active stood up. "I'm sorry for your trouble, Cowboy." He walked to the door. As he pulled it open, Decker cleared his throat.

"I guess I should have called that goddamn Draper."

CHAPTER NINETEEN

Jason Palmer wiped his eyes on a handkerchief and leaned his elbows on the desk in the principal's office at Chukchi High. "You'll have to forgive me, Nathan. I'm not always like this."

He wiped his eyes again and went on. "It's just that learning that Grace has been found so soon after—you heard about Ida's sister?"

Active nodded. "Yes, our secretary told me about the crash when I got into the office yesterday. And then I heard the story on Kay-Chuck as I was driving over here to see you. I'm sorry for your trouble."

"That Cowboy. He was an accident looking for a place to happen. Even back when I was flying, everybody knew it. But what can you do?"

"Maybe the FAA will ground him."

"Maybe. If he ever gets up the nerve to fly again. Sometimes they don't." Palmer sighed and tapped a yellow pad on the desk before him, the top sheet half-filled with longhand. "I was just trying to write up something to say at Aggie's funeral."

"Your daughter mentioned an Aunt Agnes when I saw her in Dutch Harbor. Apparently Grace told her everything when she was a little girl."

Perhaps Palmer flinched slightly. Perhaps not. "How is Grace's mother, by the way?"

"Well, she's still in one of her good spells," Palmer said. "Cross your fingers, but the doctors don't hold out much hope for the long haul. And Aggie's death . . ." He shook his head again. "At least she'll have the news about Grace to cheer her up. Grace is working down there, you said?"

Active nodded. "In a fish-processing plant. They call it the slime line."

Palmer gave a perfunctory chuckle. "How'd she look?"

Active stared. Palmer stared back, looking puzzled. "Did she seem well?"

"Very well, physically. You can hardly tell she was on the street, except for a little scar along here." Active touched the place on his cheekbone. "She seems remarkably resilient. Almost indestructible, really."

"Is she coming home?" Palmer's voice was normal on top, perhaps tight underneath, perhaps not.

"I don't think so."

Palmer opened his mouth as if to ask why, but closed it and picked up a pen. "What's the company? Ida will want to call her."

"Elizabeth Cove Seafoods," Active said. "And she's staying at a place called the Triangle Bunkhouse."

Palmer scratched the information onto his pad.

"You won't make the call?"

"I don't think so," Palmer said. "I think her mother would want to do it."

"That's good." Active pulled out a notebook and a ballpoint. "I doubt Grace would talk to you."

Palmer, looking pained, doodled on his legal pad and silence grew until it packed the room like snow. From a bookshelf behind Palmer, the sound of a clock ticking; from the street outside, the buzz of a passing four-wheeler. Finally Palmer sighed and looked up at Active. "What makes you say that?"

"Because you molested her. That's what she says."

Palmer closed his eyes, shook his head, used the handkerchief. "I was afraid she'd say that again. We tried to get her into counseling when she first started telling those stories, but she wouldn't cooperate. The counselor said sometimes teenage girls project their . . . their . . . fantasies on their fathers. An unresolved Electra complex that progressed into erotomania, something like that, is what the woman said, but I never put much stock in that kind of thing. Maybe it was just from Grace being a child of mixed race. *Naluaqmiiyaaq*, that's what the village kids used to call her at school. Half-breed. I guess I hoped, we hoped, Grace would grow out of it somehow, but . . ." Palmer trailed off into silence, looking lost in the past.

"I should tell you what your legal rights are here."

Palmer jerked his head up in shock, or a good imitation of it. "You mean you believe her? That crazy . . . that poor, lost girl?"

"She didn't seem crazy to me."

Palmer looked sharply at Active, surmise in his eyes. "She's still beautiful, isn't she?"

"You have the right to remain silent," Active began. "Do you want a lawyer?" he asked when the Miranda warning was over.

Palmer looked sorrowful, hurt. Active tried to guess how the performance would play in front of a jury. Probably pretty well.

"Of course I don't want a lawyer," Palmer said. "I'm innocent. I never . . . I wouldn't . . . my own daughter?"

"Daughters, actually. Grace says you were the father of the baby Jeanie was carrying when she huffed herself to death."

"Baby? She wasn't—I wasn't—You really think I need to defend myself against these crazy charges?"

Active nodded. "They have to be investigated."

"But there's no evidence, just the same old talk from my poor lost daughter. She was sick then and she's sick now." He paused in thought for a moment. "And why would I have to exploit my own daughters? If I . . . if my wife . . . well, there's always a lady or two on the staff at school or some student's mother who makes it clear that if there's anything I need, she'd be happy to provide it."

He stopped talking, as if something had just occurred to him. "I thought the troopers only handled village cases. Why are you asking me about this?"

Active shrugged. "I talked it over with the city police. We're taking this one."

"Well, it's my word against Grace's and I say it never happened. Never!" Palmer slapped his yellow pad so hard that his pen bounced onto the floor. "I'm a professional educator. Do you know what talk like this could do? Some people are always ready to believe the worst and this is the kind of thing that sticks to you once it gets out."

"Grace says it did happen. In her bedroom, the bathroom, even your classroom when you were still a teacher."

"I, that's . . . " Palmer was silent for a few moments. "You only believe her because I'm white. A white exploiter, that's what you think I am. That's just an ugly stereotype, Nathan, the same as if I was to look at you and see nothing but a dumb Eskimo or a drunken savage, like a lot of white people do. You ought to be ashamed of yourself."

Active, feeling his face start to get hot, said nothing. He

scribbled in his notebook, as if he were taking down everything Palmer said.

Palmer snapped his fingers. "Look, if I was guilty of this . . . this outrage, why on earth would I ask you to find her? Remember how I called you over and gave you those pictures of her? Does that sound like something a guilty man would do?"

"It sounds like a man who couldn't think of a way out when his wife asked him to do it, and didn't figure anybody could find Grace anyway. You certainly didn't seem very disappointed when I said I couldn't go look for her. And if I did find her, there was always the chance she'd keep quiet because of her mother being sick. Or maybe you're just plain nuts. That's what Grace thinks."

Palmer shuddered. "I don't have to listen to this. You'd better get of my office now."

"She says she talked to her mother about it at the time." Active stood and moved to the office door.

"Yes, she did." Palmer stood, and came out from behind the desk. "And her Aunt Aggie, too. I think maybe Aggie believed her but not my Ida." He paused and a look of appalled comprehension spread over his face. "My god, you're not thinking that Ida and Aggie . . . ah, just Ida, now that Aggie's dead, that Ida could be a witness against me in court? You're not going to go talk to Ida in her condition? You stay away from this family!"

Active was in the hall when he heard a sound and turned to find Palmer glaring at him from the office doorway. "You leave this family alone, Nathan! That's what we need, to be left alone! All of us!"

Active was breathing hard as he came out into the west wind prowling through the summer afternoon. The ice of Chukchi Bay had gone out while he was away and now the view to the west showed open water to the horizon. The fog that came in on a summer west wind hadn't shown up yet today, resulting in an odd combination of cold air and hot sun. It felt good, cleared his head after the showdown with Palmer, as he climbed into the trooper Suburban. Palmer would be far more convincing to a jury than his daughter would. It was even possible he was telling the truth. Maybe he acted innocent because he was.

What about the wife, Ida? Was there any point in dragging her through it? No matter what Grace had told her years ago, it was hearsay and Palmer's line that his daughter was "sick then and she's sick now" was impregnable without direct evidence from someone other than Grace Palmer. It was unlikely any DA would waste time and money on the case.

He started the Suburban and remembered he didn't know where Palmer lived. So he had to radio Dispatch for directions.

Lucy Generous's voice was formal and professional as she told him the Palmer house was on Beach Street and read him the number. He tried unsuccessfully to remember what part of Beach Street that would fall on, and keyed the microphone in frustration. "What's it close to?"

"Its two doors from my Aana Pauline's." Even over the scratchy police channel, the chill in Lucy's voice sounded a little deeper.

He thought of asking her out to dinner, something, anything, right there over the radio, but didn't want to do it in semipublic. So he promised himself to stop at the dispatch booth when he got back to the Public Safety Building, feeling vaguely guilty for having been too embarrassed to do it over the radio and for not having realized that Jason Palmer's house was only two doors away from Lucy's grandmother, Pauline Generous, where God knew, he had dropped Lucy off and picked her up often enough. And spread over it all like morning frost was a layer of irritation with himself for feeling guilty, and with Lucy Generous for being able to make him feel guilty over nothing.

He put the trooper Suburban in gear, made his way to Beach Street and bounced north, the old vehicle producing what sounded like a new "clunk" from the right rear shock absorber whenever he hit a particularly deep pothole. He was momentarily depressed at the thought of having to find Billy Clarkson, the Alaska Airlines freight handler who contracted for the trooper vehicle maintenance on the side. Then he remembered that Evelyn O'Brien was now in charge of dealing with Clarkson, whose lack of enterprise was exceeded only by his prices. Active smiled slightly with pleasure at the thought of Evelyn chewing on Clarkson; he could hear her on the phone now: "What the hell are my troopers supposed to drive for two weeks while you wait for your fucking parts?" That was what she always called them, her troopers.

He passed Pauline's place and there, two doors farther along, was the Palmer house. It was a two-story white clapboard on a lot that, he now saw, shared an alley with Chukchi High.

Palmer's clapboard was old enough to date back to when new houses in Chukchi were built one board at a time, rather than being stapled together from plywood or barged in as factory-made modules, which was how Chukchi houses came into being nowadays. Despite its age, the Palmer house looked to be in good shape. Decent paint and no broken windows or dead snow machines around the place where the young Grace Palmer had been so afraid of her father following her into the bathroom that she had been treated for constipation at the Chukchi Public Health Service Hospital.

For a long time, no one answered his knock. Then he heard tiny noises behind the door and finally it opened about six inches.

A girl—ten or so, he guessed, and vaguely familiar looking—peered into the *kunnichuk* for a moment through big glasses, then said, "My aunt doesn't want to talk to you. She say Uncle Jason already tell you everything she have to say."

Active was left momentarily speechless by the fact that Ida Palmer already knew about his visit with Jason Palmer. Then he realized Jason must have called her while he, Active, was rattling up Beach Street in the Suburban.

As that was dawning on him, he realized what was familiar about the girl. Except for the glasses, she looked a little like the pictures of Grace Palmer at the same age. He puzzled for a moment over who she could be before remembering that she had called Ida Palmer "aunt." Hadn't Grace Palmer spoken of having a cousin in Isignaq? That would explain the resemblance. She must be the daughter of Ida Palmer's sister who had crashed with Cowboy Decker. He thought of offering condolences, but wasn't sure enough of his guess. Then she solved the problem for him.

"My mom was fatally killed," she said.

"I heard that. I'm very sorry."

"Is she in heaven now?"

"I'm sure she is. Will you tell your aunt I have a message from her daughter Grace?"

The girl turned and vanished down a hall. She had left the door ajar, so he stepped from the *kunnichuk* into the living room. Moose antlers, caribou antlers and a Dall sheep head with a full curl of horn occupied two walls, and a grizzly hide covered much of the floor. A blue-eyed, fair-skinned Jesus hung from another wall, along with pictures of the Palmer family. Several were copies of those Jason Palmer had given him at Chukchi High. Some showed a boy he took to be the son, Roy, with the latest one show-ing Roy on a military base in a countryside that looked Middle Eastern.

"You have a message from Gracie?" said a voice from behind him.

He turned to see a middle-aged Inupiat woman in the hall. Ida Palmer was dressed warmly, considering that it was summer. Wool slacks, a sweater, sealskin slippers. She looked a little thin, slightly hollow eyed perhaps, but not close to death.

If her face showed her illness, it also showed something of where her daughter's looks had come from. Though Grace Palmer's eyes had come from her father, Active could now see Ida Palmer in Grace's face, and Grace in Ida's. It was easy to imagine the pretty Inupiat girl she must have been when Jason Palmer married her.

The niece hovered behind Ida, looking shy and uneasy.

"I need to speak with you in private." He nodded at the girl. "Perhaps she could wait in another room."

The woman turned to the girl, touched her shoulder. "Nita, maybe you could make us some tea. You want some, Mr. Active?"

He shook his head and said "No, thanks." The girl disappeared down the hall again and Ida closed the door behind her. Distantly, he heard water running, a rattle of pots and crockery.

Ida Palmer moved to an armchair and lowered herself into it, slowly and with care. "I can't stand up too long anymore. You could sit over there." She motioned at a couch, pale green with large white flowers on it.

Active studied the woman across the room and tried to decide if he could deliver the message Grace Palmer had entrusted to him on the rainy hillside above Captain's Bay.

If Ida Palmer still didn't believe her daughter's story about incest, then the message was undeliverable, or at least unreceivable.

The stress might . . . but Ida Palmer was the last witness who could corroborate any part of Grace's story.

"She asked me to tell you she doesn't hold it against you, that you didn't believe her when she told you what her father did to her."

Ida Palmer's face contracted in a look of pain that swiftly mutated into a stubborn, stony frown. "He's a good man. He wouldn't do that."

"Grace says he got Jeanie pregnant before she died."

"Then she will burn in hell, telling them old stories again. I hope now that I'm so sick, she'll forget all that, come home so we can all be together again, be family once more, but I guess not." Her cheeks were wet; she wiped them with a Kleenex from a pocket of the sweater.

The hallway door opened and Nita came in with a steaming mug of tea and set it on a lamp table beside Ida Palmer's chair. "I put in lot of sugar, the way you like."

The older woman nodded, then signaled with a jerk of her head that Nita should leave again. She disappeared down the hall, the door clicking shut behind her.

"I was sorry to hear about the crash and your sister. Nita was her daughter?"

Ida Palmer nodded. "Seem like nothing but trouble for this family. Grace, Jeanie, now Aggie." She shook her head and her cheeks were wet again; again the handkerchief.

"How's Nita's father taking it?"

Ida Palmer's eyes were closed now, her head resting against the chair back. "She got no father, she's an orphan now. My sister's husband die on the river when Nita's three."

Active digested this in silence, Ida now humming something that sounded like a hymn, or a country song, from Kay-Chuck.

"Will the Circle Be Unbroken?" Was that what the announcer had called it?

"Where will she stay after the funeral?" he said.

"Oh, we'll take her. She always like her Uncle Jason, and she can help him when I . . . while I'm sick."

"And after you're . . . if you don't get well?"

"He'll be real good father to her, I know he will."

"Can I talk to her a little bit?"

The fragile head with its papery skin jerked up and the dark, pained eyes looked hard into his own.

"I don't want you scaring her with them old stories of Grace's, Mr. Active. You leave Nita alone. This family had enough trouble already because of that girl." The head sank back again and the eyes closed. "You just leave us alone, Mr. Active. That's what my family need right now."

He rose to go, wondering if Jason Palmer had coached his wife on what to say, and laid one of his business cards on her lap. "I hope you're right, Mrs. Palmer. But if anything . . . if you change your mind about anything, will you call me at the trooper offices? Or you could call Grace in Dutch Harbor. I wrote the number on the back of my card."

She opened her eyes, picked up the card, and tucked it into the pocket with the handkerchief. "I don't think that will happen, Mr. Active. One of my daughters is dead, one is lost and crazy. I won't let anything happen to Nita, not ever." The tired black eyes flashed silver for a moment, reminding him of the lost and crazy daughter.

CHAPTER TWENTY

When Active called the office at Elizabeth Cove Seafoods, the woman who answered the phone told him, no, she would not pull Angie Ramos off the slime line unless it was an emergency.

It wasn't an emergency, not exactly? Then, no, she definitely would not pull Ms. Ramos off the slime line but she would take a message. "Call Trooper Active in Chukchi? Very well. And she has the number? Very well, we'll give her the message at her next break, no, wait, she's off today, we'll give it to her tomorrow."

The story at the Triangle Bunkhouse was much the same, except it came from a man this time, not the Hispanic woman who had checked him in a few days earlier. "No, we won't go find her, but we'll take a message and leave it in her mail slot. No, we don't know if she's in or out, as long as she pays her rent, it's no questions asked and none answered, heh-heh, heh-heh," causing Active to feel simultaneously irritated and stupid as he gave his name and said he was calling from Chukchi and that Angie Ramos already had his number.

Then, feeling he had done all he could, he pushed the Palmer family into a mental drawer and closed it and walked down to the dispatch booth to invite Lucy Generous over for dinner, or out to dinner, her choice.

"What for?" she said. She was dressed for summer. Jeans, yellow short-sleeve T-shirt, long hair braided and coiled at the back of her head, white hooded sweatshirt draped over the back of her chair.

"Well, we both have to eat. I thought we might as well do it together." He grinned, hoping this sounded like the joke it was intended to be, and waited for her reaction.

There wasn't any, not even one of her "Hmmmphs!" So he pulled the little silver box from behind his back. "I got you this."

She glanced at it, but didn't take it when he held it out, so he set it on the counter of the dispatch window. "It's from Nordstrom's."

"You're gone a week and you barely call me?"

"I was pretty busy."

She picked the box up, opened it, studied the bottle. "Looking for Grace Palmer?"

He watched, mesmerized, as she unscrewed the cap, tapped the little opening, touched the inside of her wrist and sniffed. He had to fight the impulse to close his eyes and inhale deeply as the scent of lavender reached him.

"It's nice," Lucy shrugged. She closed the bottle, put it back in the box, and closed that too. "Did you find her?"

"Can we talk about that at dinner?"

"I don't want to talk about Grace Palmer."

"Okay, we won't. Look, I'm sorry I didn't call you while I was gone. If I go back up to my office and call you, can we go out to dinner then?"

The tiniest hint of a grin tugged at the corners of her mouth. "I'll use the 9-1-1 line. Because I missed lunch and if I don't eat something soon it will be an emergency." She grinned for real.

"Okay, I'll pick you up after work and we'll go . . . would you rather go to my place or the Northern Dragon?" He waited in a fever of self-loathing, lust, anticipation, and dread for her answer, knowing where they'd end up if she came over to his place wearing lavender, feeling even worse, even lower than when he had bought the little bottle at Nordstrom's or when he had given it to her moments ago.

She cut him a sidelong glance, then looked straight ahead, as if her console were the most interesting thing on the entire first floor of the Chukchi Public Safety Building. "You're the hungry one. What do you want to do?"

"Maybe the Dragon," he said after a long silence. He felt honorable, dishonest, and depressed, all at once, and decided he would accidentally break the bottle when he got the chance, hopefully before she put any more on.

Lucy sighed a little and said "Okay." She was quiet for a time and then, eyes still on her console, "How'd she look?"

He tried not to jump when he heard the question, the same question everyone who had ever known Grace Palmer seemed to ask when they learned she'd been found. "I thought you didn't want to talk about her."

"I don't."

"Well, maybe we need to."

She was about to answer, he thought, when her console buzzed and a button lit up and she punched it and said "Chukchi Public Safety."

He said, "See you after work," and started to walk away, but she held up a finger and he heard her say, "He's right here. Who's calling, please?"

And he knew the answer before she looked at him, eyes level

and cool, and said, "It's Angie Ramos. Do you want to take it here?" She pointed at the phone on the dispatch counter, one line blinking.

"No, in my office," he said, and starting up the stairs two at a time before he could think it through and force himself to go up at a more decorous pace.

Her voice was low and warm when he picked up his office phone and punched the blinking button, wondering briefly if Lucy was, could be, listening in from downstairs. "Hi, Nathan."

"Hi. Thanks for calling back. How are you?"

"Pretty well, I guess. I had the day off. I went up on the hillside and smoked the last of those Marlboros you bought me."

"I hope I didn't re-implant any bad habits."

She chuckled a little. "No, I didn't buy any more."

"That's good," he said, then found himself stalled. How to get into it? She solved the problem by speaking first.

"So. You called?"

He cleared his throat. "I talked to your parents today."

"Parents plural? Both of them?"

"Uh-huh."

"Not about . . ."

"I . . ."

"Shit! Nathan, I said I don't want to ever talk about that again. It has to stay in the compartment now."

"I felt I had to."

She sighed. "I told you, I'm not giving any statements, I'm not coming back, and I'm not testifying."

"Well, there's something—"

"No, I said!"

"But—"

"How's Ida?"

"Not too bad," he said. "She looks a little weak and fragile, moves carefully, but she does get around on her own. The house looks pretty well kept."

"Uh-huh. I wish I had a Marlboro."

"Uh-huh." He heard a noise like someone walking past her—the pay phone at the Triangle was in the hall, as he remembered—then rustling and crackling sounds. Perhaps she was switching ears with the phone.

"What did she say about, about . . . ?"

"She still doesn't believe you. She says you'll burn in hell for telling those old stories again." He tried to laugh, to turn it into a joke, then realized it was hopeless and cleared his throat, so loudly he startled himself.

"She's in denial, Nathan."

"Yeah."

"And Jason?"

"Same thing, pretty much, except for the part about burning in hell."

She didn't say anything, but he could hear her breathing—gasping, really, as if fighting for control, trying not to cry. "Jason said they tried to get you into counseling but you wouldn't go."

"Fuck, no." There was no tremor in her voice now, just anger. "There was only one mental health counselor in Chukchi back then and she worked at the school. Probably still does. Regina Watkins."

"Uh-huh. Something about an unresolved Electra complex that progressed into erotomania?"

"Yeah, that's Regina, all right. Fucking psychobabble."

"Uh-huh."

"I wonder if you believe me."

It was clear she needed him to, so he said he did, without knowing if it was true. Over the phone, she wasn't as persuasive.

"There's something else," he said into her silence.

"What?" Her voice was tight, alarmed.

"That's what I was trying to say before. Your Aunt Agnes was killed in a plane crash a few days ago. A pilot named Cowboy Decker tried to take off in a twin-engine plane with only one engine working and they crashed."

Her breath came faster and faster and then he heard muffled sobs. He supposed she had her hand over the mouthpiece, or had pressed it to her chest.

"I'm so sorry," he said, and waited for her to calm down.

"And my cousin Nita? Is she dead, too?" Her voice was shaky and it sounded like her nose was blocked from crying.

"No, Nita wasn't in the plane."

A long silence, then, "Who's got her? Dammit, Nathan, are you there? Who's got her? Nathan!" His name came out as a howl.

"Your parents have her. I think they plan to adopt her, or your father will if your mother passes on first."

"Nathan, you can't let that happen. He'll, he'll—with my mother gone . . ."

"Do you want me to take your story to the D.A.?"

"I . . . oh, God." There was a long silence, then the bitter bark-laugh he remembered from Dutch Harbor. "What for? Who's going to believe me?"

"Well, Jason outlined his defense—you were sick in the head then and you're still sick now. "

She drew a shaky breath, exhaled loudly. "Yeah, yeah, and with Aunt Aggie gone . . . It will just make him stronger if I take a shot at him and miss. Nathan, you've got to talk to Nita, find out what's going on with her."

"I'll try, but it'll be hard. Your mother has already refused permission. I'll talk to my boss, see what we can do in a case like this. Maybe a social worker . . ."

"Fat chance if my father's the target."

"Well, I can at least let Jason know I'm watching."

"I doubt it'll stop him."

"I think I'm out of options."

"Thanks anyway."

"Will you be all right?"

"Of course not."

"What will you do?"

"Right now? I'm going to go out and either get some Marlboros or a ticket on the next flight to Four Street."

"You're not serious, about Four Street?"

There was a click and the line went dead.

He hung up, then tried to make himself call the state offices at the north end of town, see if the Division of Family and Youth Services still had anyone in Chukchi, what with the state budget being cut because the North Slope oil fields were starting to run dry. But he couldn't bring himself to take another step into the swamps of the Palmer family's sexual history. Or Grace Palmer's dementia, whichever it was.

Then he realized he could close the book on another aspect of the Amazing Grace story, or at least write himself out of it.

That was the whole Angie Ramos thing. If he wrote up his interviews with Grace Palmer in Dutch Harbor and sent them to Dennis Johnson, Dennis could turn the files over to Homicide and then he, Nathan Active, could forget about it.

It took him a couple of hours, but when he was done he was reasonably satisfied with the result. True, it had required a little needle threading, a little rapids shooting, to explain how an informal welfare check requested by Grace Palmer's family had blossomed into a confession of Oil Dividend fraud and identity theft—which had to be some kind of crime, even if he wasn't sure what—not to mention the actual homicide case itself, which turned on how Angie Ramos had ended up in the path of a rotary snowplow and, perhaps, on whether APD ever found the dispatch logs from the night of her death.

The worst problem was the fact that he had never quite gotten around to Mirandizing Grace Palmer in two evenings of interviews. He finally decided the less said about that, the better, and didn't mention it at all.

He printed out the report, dropped a copy into an envelope and addressed it to Dennis Johnson.

After a moment's thought, he opened the report on his computer screen, copied the text, and pasted it into an e-mail message, then sent that to Dennis, too. Whatever was going to happen couldn't happen soon enough, that was how he felt. Anything to clear up the swarm of mysteries that followed Amazing Grace Palmer around like a band of avenging angels.

He walked back down to the dispatch booth, were Lucy Generous was once again devoting full attention to her console.

"So," he said. "Are we still on for dinner."

"Do you still want to?"

He nodded. "Of course."

"Do we have to talk about her?"

He nodded again. "I'm afraid we do."

"That was her on the phone, wasn't it?"

"Yes," he said. "I called to let her know about her aunt being killed in the plane crash. She was calling back."

Lucy sighed and her shoulders sagged. "Okay. We can have dinner, I guess."

"Okay," he said. "I'll pick you up at the end of your shift."

Lucy Generous watched miserably as Nathan wolfed down his Szechwan beef like this was just another day, just another dinner at the Northern Dragon after which they would go back to his place and . . . how long had it been?

The last time had been the Friday before Nathan left for Anchorage. Now it was Monday, the second Monday since then. That made ten days since the last time she had experienced that melting bliss, which was the only term she could think of to describe it. Certainly none of the terms for it in women's magazines seemed to fit. They sounded nasty, or mechanical, no hint of . . . well, of melting bliss.

Before Nathan, she had almost no experience. Just one boy right after high school and only twice with him, Jimmy Kalina. A sweet enough boy, going to a trade school in Nome now to become an electrician. But Jimmy Kalina had been inexperienced and clumsy and quick and when after the second time she still felt untouched, deeply untouched, she had told him she didn't want to do it anymore. Jimmy had lost interest and found another girl, Esther DeLong, who by reputation did want to do it, and as often as possible.

And that had been her encounter with sex—not very interesting, although apparently necessary if you wanted to hold a man, but why, exactly, would you want to hold him if something as boring as sex was the only thing that would do it?

"So you won't be alone," Aana Pauline had told her when she posed that question.

After that, she had allowed herself to assume she might someday marry a pleasant man who would be a good provider and not want too much sex, perhaps just enough to give her the two children, a boy and a girl, who seemed always to loom on the horizon when she tried to imagine her life. Someday, but not too soon, she hoped.

And then one day she had noticed Nathan. He had been in Chukchi a year when this happened. She had seen him many times. He stopped by the dispatch booth to joke with her every workday, usually. She had idly wondered if he could be the nice-enough husband who would want just enough sex for two children, but hadn't thought more about it until one day he stopped stopping.

He would just walk past the booth on his way in or out of the Public Safety Building, looking preoccupied and not saying a word, not even a nod, and that was when she noticed him, or noticed that he had quietly grown to be this enormous presence in her life without her being aware of it.

And now Nathan had withdrawn, as casually and with as little explanation as he had come, and she was terrified. She had wanted to ask him what she had done wrong, or to apologize for it without even asking what it was, but that was ridiculous. He obviously felt nothing and didn't attach any more importance to not stopping by dispatch than he had to stopping, and therefore her questions were questions that could not be asked, her apologies were apologies that could not be offered.

"What should I do?" she had asked her Aana Pauline, after explaining the situation.

"Look pretty, smell nice, smile a lot, and wait." Aana Pauline had said.

Aana Pauline was seventy-two and a very traditional old Inupiaq, but Lucy had always found her advice about people, men especially, to be timeless. So she had done as Aana Pauline had advised, though it seemed far too inconsequential to make a difference.

Nonetheless, and for whatever reason, there Nathan was at the dispatch booth again one day, bantering away and smiling—those lips!—as if he had never stopped stopping, which made her wonder if he even realized he had done it.

She began flirting back, blushing sometimes when he glanced at her in a certain way, and felt herself opening up, blooming out like the tiny flowers that carpeted the tundra in brief, wild, profusion every spring when the sun took away the snow.

And instantaneously, from one day to the next, she understood all the fuss about sex, because she wanted Nathan Active, would feel a warm, empty, ache down there that she had not felt, had not even imagined or dreamed of, with Jimmy Kalina, would have to look away from when Nathan came to dispatch to keep her voice from shaking or herself from simply bursting into tears.

But no amount of flirting, hinting, smiling, looking pretty, and smelling nice seemed to move Nathan Active. He was content with a few minutes of chatter at the dispatch booth everyday, and that was that.

So finally, with the help of Aana Pauline, she had lured him over one evening on the pretext that Pauline needed a ride to bingo. As arranged, Pauline was out when Nathan arrived, so she had invited him in to wait and, as if by accident, undone him by letting him see her nude as she brushed out her hair after a shower.

That night was her first experience of the melting bliss and she immediately understood why the women's magazines were always writing about it, how to find it, how to make it better and stronger and longer, even if they did call it by those nasty, mechanical names.

Since then, as she recalled, it had never been more than three days from one time to the next with Nathan, except for the five or six days a month when it was unappealing to both of them, and now she depended on it like food or water. Not the sex itself. She had tried and failed to imagine it with Jimmy Kalina when he stopped in at dispatch one day and hinted around about old times. Sex with Nathan Active was what she needed.

And now it had been ten days, ten days when he had been chasing Grace Palmer the beauty queen all over Alaska, this Grace Palmer he was now saying they had to talk about. Ten days without sex and he was sitting there eating Chinese food like he didn't have a care in the world, not even noticing how she was picking at her own food, just stirring it around on the plate and mixing it up with her chopsticks. Ten days and here they were at this restaurant rather than at his place where she could get dinner going, then they could talk with their bodies while it cooked, say the important things that didn't need words, then eat, then body-talk again, then, if they still needed to, they could talk about Grace Palmer and anything else that required words.

But no, here he was, filling up on Szechwan beef, looking a little subdued perhaps, but not particularly worried or alarmed, certainly not miserable and terrified like she felt.

He was telling her a story she could hardly follow, she was so distracted, something about a woman, a former prostitute or madam possibly, who drove a limousine in Anchorage, no, Dutch

Harbor, she was pretty sure it was Dutch Harbor, because apparently this woman felt she had missed so many planes she could never get back to Anchorage. That made absolutely no sense because there would always be a later flight, but probably it would have made sense if she'd been following Nathan's story instead of thinking about the question she'd finally come up with. A question that she might actually be able to get up the nerve to ask and might actually make him think about their relationship and his feelings for her, perhaps even make him talk about it, an act of which to date he seemed not only reluctant but incapable.

The question was not "Do you love me?" or "Will you marry me?"

No, she could never ask either of those questions, or even, "How do you feel about me?" But she thought she could ask this question she had come up with. Even Aana Pauline thought it might work.

"What do you want?" That was her question, "What do you want?" It seemed like a nonthreatening, open-ended question on the surface, but was deep and dangerous underneath because once Nathan started into it there would be no easy way to get back out. Every turn would just lead deeper and deeper towards his heart and she'd find out what was really in there. Maybe Nathan would, too.

She swallowed some tea, took a breath, wet her lips, and was working up the nerve to say, "Can I ask you something?" when Nathan ended the story about the limousine in Dutch Harbor and pushed back his plate and looked at her—turned those amazing, lonely eyes full on her—and said, "So. About Grace Palmer."

Active watched in pain as Lucy flinched, almost like he had swung at her, and said, "I don't want to talk about her." She looked down at her food, which he had seen her fiddling with but not eating all the time he was downing his Szechwan beef.

"I still think we need to."

"Well I don't want to talk about her here. Can we go to your place?" She looked up at him, flushed slightly, and looked down again.

"How about the pullout?"

She shrugged and nodded as he picked up the bill and checked the math in his head. He paid in cash, not wanting to wait for the credit card verification to go through, and they went out into the west wind snapping across Beach Street. Now, in evening, it was bringing in fog from the sea, and Chukchi felt as cold, clammy, and closed-in as a coffin. Lucy shuddered and pulled up the hood of her sweatshirt as he unlocked the passenger door of the Suburban and helped her in.

He raced around the front of the rig while Lucy unlocked his door from the inside. He jumped in, started the engine, and turned the heat on high. He was gratified to feel a little warmth emerge from the blower, and thankful the big V-8 engine hadn't cooled off completely as they ate.

He drove to the pullout, feeling stupid because, with the fog blanketing everything in wind-ripped gray, there was no reason to sit there on the beach and gaze at Chukchi Bay. Except one, which was his certain knowledge that, if they went to his place, they'd end up in bed, making up for ten days of lost time. Nothing would be said about Grace Palmer, no air would be cleared. So he nosed the Suburban up to the seaward edge of the pullout.

And there, with the engine rumbling and the heater whirring and the wind sighing around the rig and the rig itself creaking occasionally in the heavier gusts and the little waves that passed for surf in Chukchi breaking with a rush on the riprap along the shoreline, he told her the Grace Palmer story.

He started with Jason Palmer saying, "Beautiful, wasn't she?" ten days ago, left out nothing and went right up through that afternoon, when he had e-mailed Dennis Johnson the report suggesting Grace Palmer had killed Angie Ramos.

Lucy was silent for a long time after he finished, sipping the tea she had brought with her from the restaurant and looking thoughtful. "So she pushed this Angie Ramos into the snowplow?"

He nodded. "That's how it looks."

Lucy sipped again. "And she says she was molested by her father?"

He nodded again. "Did you ever hear anything like that? About her or Jeanie?"

Lucy shook her head. "Nothing. And that kind of thing travels pretty fast around here."

He thought about what she had said. Should he believe her? Lucy manifestly considered Grace Palmer a rival, so naturally she would want him to think that Grace was lying about the incest, or was crazy, or both. He was trying to think of another way to ask it when Lucy put in a question of her own.

"And she invited you to sleep with her?"

He nodded, remained silent.

"And you wanted to?"

He nodded again, wanted to break their gaze, decided it would be cowardly, and hung on.

"But you didn't."

He shook his head.

"And why was that?"

He groped for an answer as she sipped tea and studied him.

Somehow she had wound up on top in this conversation, and he felt relieved. He realized that was because she had been on the bottom in their relationship so long that it had come to feel almost abusive to him, even though he didn't know how things had gotten that way and was pretty sure he hadn't wanted it.

"Well?" she said, and he loved it that she had the confidence to sound demanding. Not whiny or complaining, just demanding.

"I thought maybe she was trying to make me forget how Angie Ramos died. And besides that it just didn't feel right somehow."

"Why?"

"I'm not sure exactly. Maybe because she doesn't seem capable of informed consent about sex. She's still too twisted, is how it felt."

"But it wasn't because of me?"

He shook his head.

"And you two might get together after"—here Lucy waved her hand vaguely at the fog in front of the truck, which he thought was a pretty good metaphor for Grace Palmer's situation—"after all this clears up or goes away, or something."

"That's what we said."

Lucy shook her head, pulled the Nordstrom's box out of a sweatshirt pocket. "And you brought me this because you wanted me to smell like her?"

He nodded.

"When we . . . ?"

He nodded again.

"Are you blushing, Nathan?"

"I think so."

"Have you ever blushed before?"

"Not that I can recall."

She was silent a long time, sipping the tea until the Styrofoam cup was empty, then dropping it into the vinyl litter bag hanging from the Suburban's cigarette lighter. She shifted on the seat to face him. "Nathan, what do you want?"

He couldn't get it out, so she said it for him. "Grace Palmer?"

He nodded.

"And me?"

He nodded again, waiting for the explosion.

"You'd like me to come over to your place right now and put on this lavender perfume and smell like Grace Palmer and go to bed with you, is that right?"

He nodded and closed his eyes and waited. Whatever she wanted to do he figured she was within her rights and he planned to offer no resistance. Swear, hit him, anything short of pulling his Smith and Wesson from its holster and shooting him. She wasn't very big; she couldn't possibly punch very hard.

"Okay," she said.

He opened his eyes. "What?"

"Okay, let's go." She leaned over and kissed him, harder than he had ever been kissed before. Then she opened the little bottle, touched her fingers to the mouth, and dabbed the sides of her neck. "Put this thing in reverse and let's go. It's the one right next to park." She pointed at the gearshift lever and giggled.

He obeyed, backed out onto Beach Street and started south, through the fog, toward his place. "I thought you'd be furious. Or depressed. Or something. Anything but this."

She looked at him, a little seriousness rippling over the gaiety in her eyes and lips, but not much seriousness. "This is the first time you ever told me you wanted anything from me, Nathan. At least I'm on the list somewhere, and I'm here and Grace Palmer's down in the Aleutians and maybe she'll be in jail pretty soon and in about an hour you won't even be able to remember her name."

She touched the bottle a second time, pulled out the neck of the yellow T-shirt, and reached inside. Dizzily, he realized she was putting lavender between her breasts. She giggled again and put her hand on his thigh, very high on his thigh, and he thought to himself they were both in the grip of some dementia. Perhaps he had caught it from Grace Palmer and passed it on to Lucy, but probably it couldn't hurt to enjoy it for one night. In fact, it would probably be some kind of crime against nature or destiny or dumb luck not to enjoy it, because he was pretty sure that God or Satan or whoever had cooked this up would never again, not if he lived to be a hundred, send him another night like this, or bring him within view of another face lit up like the face of Lucy Generous.

CHAPTER TWENTY-ONE

Much to his surprise, whatever he had created by opening up to Lucy about Grace Palmer lasted long past that amazing night.

In fact, it went on and on. Without planning it or even realizing it at first, he slid into a pretty good summer with Lucy Generous.

It was sweetened, he thought, by a shared but unvoiced sense that they existed, the relationship existed, in the calm before a storm that might or might not break, depending on how the Grace Palmer thing, the many Grace Palmer things, worked out.

For Grace Palmer was always a spectral presence at the edge of his consciousness, in the shadows of the relationship with Lucy, except at its most intense and intimate moments. He came to think of this as their grace period, his and Lucy's, though he never said the phrase to her. It was a time that might have no greater life expectancy than the white-headed tundra cotton now blowing on the rolling prairie around Chukchi.

Not that he had withdrawn from his official relationship with Grace Palmer. He determined that the state presently had no one in Chukchi who was qualified to interview a possible victim of child sexual abuse. The nearest such person was in the district office of the Division of Family and Youth Services in Nome. The caseworker in question was a kind of circuit rider whose next visit to Chukchi was in three weeks. Active asked them to attempt to schedule a visit with Nita Iktillik, care of Jason Palmer, and left it at that.

One day an e-mail came from Dennis Johnson, saying that Homicide had decided to send two investigators to Dutch Harbor to interview Grace Palmer about the death of Angie Ramos. The two investigators had been mightily unimpressed, Dennis reported, by Active's failure to Mirandize the subject, a procedural lapse redeemed only by Active's equally complete failure to get anything useful out of her, leading the senior of the two APD investigators to summarize Active's efforts in the case with the phrase, "Typical trooper hotshot, his dick got so hard when he looked at this beauty queen, it sucked all the blood out of his brain."

A week later, another e-mail from Dennis reported that the APD investigators hadn't gotten any more out of Grace Palmer than he had but at least it was all useable because they had taken the trouble to Mirandize her.

Homicide still hadn't decided if they had a case, Dennis said, because of the missing dispatch logs from the night of Angie Ramos's death. If the case ever went to trial, the missing logs, coupled with Grace Palmer's claim to have left Angie only after help was on the way, would open a hole in the case from which any decent defense attorney could surely mine a large trove of reasonable doubt. So, on the advice of the district attorney's office, APD was turning itself inside out and upside down to find the missing logs, an effort that had already produced a red-faced screaming match between the police chief and the director of the records section in a heavily trafficked hallway at APD headquarters.

And, oh, yes, Dennis added. Grace Palmer had asked the APD investigators to pass along a message: Fuck you, Nathan.

Active sighed and closed the email. At least Grace Palmer was no longer his problem. The Anchorage cops would or wouldn't charge her with Angie Ramos's murder. Their choice, their problem.

The Division of Family and Youth Services would or wouldn't interview Nita Iktillik, would or wouldn't take her away from Jason Palmer, would or wouldn't send the file back to the troopers and the Chukchi DA for possible prosecution of Jason Palmer. Not Nathan Active's problem, not now, not for a while, maybe not ever.

And so he drifted through the early part of the summer with a relatively clear conscience, a relatively untroubled sense of pleasure and leisure. It was as though he and Lucy Generous were by themselves on a raft on a big lazy river, and the river would go on forever.

One day it all gathered itself together in what he recognized, even as it was unfolding, a perfect day, a singularity that, like the magic night after he told Lucy the Grace Palmer story, would probably not recur if he lived to be a hundred.

They swam up out of sleep late on a Saturday morning, still wrapped around each other from the night before and had sex, or made love as Lucy insisted on calling it, before they were fully awake.

Then she showered while he drowsed off again, then he showered while she made breakfast—poached eggs, muffins and, as it was summer and prices even in Chukchi were not completely impossible, fresh cantaloupe.

They ate together almost wordlessly, then set out in the Suburban to pick Pauline Generous's fishnets. Nowadays it was really Pauline's in name only, Lucy told him, because Pauline was getting too old to handle the skiff and work the net herself. She was even getting too old to help Lucy much, so now Lucy usually did it herself. That really made the skiff and fishnet hers, Lucy told him, but it was not something she needed to discuss with Pauline, or ever planned to.

"So you pick it all by yourself?" he asked as they bounced south through town, heading for the little beach past the airport where Pauline's net was anchored. He was forever being surprised by the things Lucy could do, such as the time he went to pick her up at Pauline's and found her taking apart the old lady's water heater. "The element just burned out," she had said. "I'm putting this new one in." And she had done it all by herself as he watched. She let him help only at the end, having him hold the access panel in place while she reattached it with screws at the four corners.

"Yes, I pick it all by myself." Lucy said with a smug look. "All Inupiat women love to fish, which you'd know if you weren't such a *naluaqmiiyaaq*."

Naluaqmiiyaaq was what Lucy and just about everyone else in Chukchi called him whenever he betrayed his ignorance of the Inupiat culture. Not because he was a half-breed, but because of the other definition—"almost a white man."

"Well, I'm trying to learn," he said.

"Lucky you've got a patient teacher. Now turn here."

She pointed at a rutted, sandy track leading through the Chukchi city dump toward the water's edge.

He followed her directions to a little stretch of beach where a line leading out to the shoreward end of Pauline's net was tied to a steel rod driven into the gravel just above the water line. A few yards out, Pauline's skiff bobbed at anchor, a rope running from the stern to another beach anchor to keep the nose into the waves curling in on the west wind.

Lucy pulled two pairs of hip waders out of the Suburban and tossed one to him. "See that boat out there?" she asked with what he thought was excessive sarcasm. "Put these on and wade out to that boat and climb in and sit still till I get there."

He was looking dubiously from the waders to the skiff when she supplemented her instructions. "Go in over the transom or you'll tip it." He looked blank and she said, "It's the part across the back, where the motor is," and shook her head.

He tried putting on the waders like Lucy did, standing on one leg while pulling the waders over the other, but found he had to sit on a driftwood log to get it done.

Then he waded out to the boat and heaved himself over the stern, collecting only a little cold, salty Chukchi Sea water in his boots in the process. He crawled to the front seat and watched as Lucy pulled from the Suburban the big square white plastic tub they had collected at Pauline's and dropped it where the boat's stern line was anchored to the beach.

She unhitched the line, picked up the tub, and waded out to the boat, somehow coiling the stern line with one hand while she carried the tub with the other. At the boat, she tossed in tub and line, and stood for a moment gauging, as he now saw he should have done, the boat's motion in the chop. Then she gave a little leaping turn and was sitting on the boat's rear seat, legs dangling over the transom without, he was sure, a drop of sea water in her waders.

She tucked the rope under her seat, positioned the tub between the two seats, and checked the fuel level in a red tank beside the tub.

"Looks good," she said, and began pulling on the starter cord of the Johnson outboard. The engine didn't start and she finally ran out of breath and sat panting.

"Maybe you could try," she said.

He moved back and sat beside her and pulled twice on the cord, also without result.

"Shit," she said. It was the first time he had ever heard her say that. Maybe being on a fishing boat brought it out in her. She did something to the side of the engine, had him pull it twice, did something else to the engine, and had him pull once more. This time the Johnson burbled to life, coughing a little at first and sending up blue smoke from the exhaust port below the water-line before it steadied up. "You've got the magic touch," she said.

"What was it?"

She shrugged. "I don't know. It just does that sometimes."

"Really?" he said, suspicion dawning.

"No, it really does that." She grinned at him and winked. "Sometimes. And sometimes it doesn't."

He moved back to the front seat. She dropped the Johnson into gear, twisted the throttle, and moved the skiff forward a few feet so he could pull up the front anchor. Then she steered toward the line of floats that marked the top of Pauline's gill net, hanging like a spider's web across the path of the migrating chum salmon as they made their way along the beach toward the mouth of the Katonak River, a few miles north of Chukchi.

She followed the line of floats out to where its seaward end was anchored and cut the engine. In the sudden silence, the slap of the waves against the aluminum skiff seemed loud as she handed him a gaff hook and told him to work the net up over the nose of the boat, then come sit beside her on the rear seat.

He did as he was told and began to see how this was going to work. She pulled the net back till it was almost in their laps and kicked the tub ahead till it rested against the front seat. The steady west wind began to push the boat toward shore, the net sliding across their knees and over the sides of the boat. The first two wriggling silver chum salmon came up and she showed him how to untangle their gills from the net so they could be tossed into the tub.

And so began a magical hour in the middle of a perfect day. The two of them almost literally on a raft, sliding towards shore on the choppy blue-green water, the slap-slap of the waves on the boat, the shrieks of two hopeful seagulls wheeling overhead, the heat of the sun cutting the chill of the west wind and vice versa, the creak of the net sliding over the boat, the salmon flopping in the tub, the look of joy on Lucy's face that made him think of what she said about Inupiat women loving to fish, her little jokes and cries of mock horror at some of the things the net brought up, especially a hideous, huge-mouthed, goggle-eyed fish she called an Irish Lord.

"Imagine being an Irish lady and waking up next to that," she said with a giggle as she threw it back in.

She went back to work on the net and the chum salmon kept crawling up out of the sea in the mesh of the net until the skiff reached the shoreward end of the line of floats, where the anchor rope started that ran in to the steel rod on the beach.

"Not bad," she said as he slipped the net over the nose of the boat. She stood counting, tapping her finger in the air as the boat drifted toward shore on the chop. "Seventeen, not bad for a *naluaqmiiyaaq* and a dispatcher, ah? About a hundred pounds, maybe."

"Not bad," he said, thinking not so much of the fish as of the day itself, and the last hour.

After that, they dropped off a dozen chum at Pauline's. The old lady grumbled about the salmon being too few and too small, and complained of how Eskimo girls today didn't know anything about fishing.

Lucy just grinned as she laid the chums out on a plywood cutting table beside Pauline's cabin and helped the old lady behead, gut, and split the first salmon, score the two halves, and hang it tail up on the fish rack made of spruce poles.

Before long Pauline was grinning also and the two were chattering in Inupiaq and giggling. Once Pauline asked a question with Active's name in it. Then they looked at him and giggled together and he realized the conversation was more than just a couple of Inupiat women sharing a passion for fish.

He smiled and walked off a little distance so they could gossip safe from male ears. The fog bank that usually came with the west wind was building offshore, a gray-white belt swelling along the horizon as he watched. In a few hours Chukchi would be shrouded in it, but before then he and Lucy would be at his place, one of the chum baking as they did what Lucy liked to do while dinner cooked.

He heard Pauline's gruff old voice from behind him. "I'll cut the rest of them. You and Nathan go now."

So Lucy rinsed her hands under a faucet on the wall of Pauline's cabin and they climbed into the Suburban.

"We've got five chum left back there." He jerked a thumb toward the tub in the rear. "Do I really need that many?"

"You're only getting two. One for dinner and one for your freezer. We're taking the other three to your mom."

"What?" Normally it was his mother who brought food to him. Lucy's plan to take fish to Martha was, he sensed, the latest move or countermove in the incomprehensible rivalry between the two women.

"Not me." He shook his head. "I'm not taking any fish to Martha. Leroy probably already got some."

"Nope," Lucy said with a smug look. "He didn't. I checked his site and he doesn't have his net out yet."

Active didn't say anything, or start the Suburban.

"All right, chicken, you can wait in the car while I take them up to the door." She slapped his knee. "Now let's go!"

He shook his head and started the Suburban and drove down Beach Street toward the side road to Martha and Leroy's place, the still-unrepaired right rear shock absorber adding its "clunk" to the bangs, rattles, and squeaks from the old vehicle as it bounced over the potholes.

When they reached the house, he stayed in his seat and watched as Lucy opened the Suburban's cargo doors, found a piece of rope in the junk on the floor, and threaded it through the gills and jaws of three of the salmon—the three biggest ones, it appeared to him.

Lucy walked to the house with the three fish dangling from one hand, opened the outer door and vanished into the *kunnichuk*.

As he waited for the explosion, he studied the house and was mildly cheered to see there weren't as many vehicles out front as usual. Leroy's Ford Ranger was absent, meaning he was probably at work, or perhaps up the Katonak River with one of his hunting and fishing buddies.

Leroy was a solid guy, in Active's opinion, a good catch for a former wild child like his mother. He delivered stove oil for the local Chevron dealer, spent more time out in the country than a lot of Inupiat, and kept the house so spruced up and painted that it almost looked like a little chunk of Anchorage had been dropped down on Chukchi spit.

Not only was Leroy's truck missing, but only one four-wheeler was parked by the door. The question was, did it belong to Martha or Sonny, the half brother Martha and Leroy had produced two years after they married. If Sonny was there, that was one thing. But, if Martha was home . . . he shuddered and turned on Kay-Chuck, where a hymn was playing.

Lucy emerged in about three minutes, not merely uninjured, but beaming.

"Well?"

Lucy's grin got even bigger. "She wasn't even there. Your step-brother Sonny was the only one home. I just told him to put them in the sink and tell Martha I dropped them off."

The grin became a giggle and even he had to chuckle at the thought of Martha's reaction when she returned home and found food from Lucy Generous in her kitchen. It would be funny, as long as he wasn't around to take any of the shrapnel that would surely fly.

Back at his place, Lucy tossed one of the two remaining chums into the sink and wrapped the other one whole. With a little folding and bending, she crammed it into the freezer compartment of his refrigerator. Then she went to work on the one in the sink. He offered to help, but she glared at him. "No way. No Inupiat woman would ever let a man cut fish."

So he leaned against a counter and watched as she readied the fish for baking, slid it into the oven, and slammed the door with a bang.

"There," she said with an air of triumph. "We've got forty-five minutes. Follow me, you."

She seized his belt and dragged him toward the bedroom.

"Wait a minute," he said. "We smell like salmon. Shouldn't we shower first?"

She muttered something that sounded like *"naluaqmiiyaaq,"* but she swerved toward the bathroom, still dragging him by the belt.

They never made it to the bedroom. The shower took up the whole forty-five minutes until the fish was ready. Then they ate, she let him do the dishes, and they watched "My Best Friend's Wedding" on cable. Finally they made it into the bedroom and an hour later Lucy was asleep, purring her tiny cat snores, her sweaty hair spread across his sweaty chest.

She was so childlike in sleep, so unguarded, he wondered if somehow this perfect day could be made permanent.

He supposed she loved him at least five times as much as he loved her, if he loved her at all, but maybe hers was enough for both of them. Whatever the math, it seemed the relationship was afloat on a sea of joy, so perhaps it was better to do no math at all and just proceed as if this grace period would never end. At a minimum, he could make sure nothing he did caused it to end.

CHAPTER TWENTY-TWO

The numbers on the clock-radio read 1:38 A.M. when Active swam hazily up from sleep. He wondered what had awakened him until he heard Lucy saying "What? Who is this?"

Then he realized it must have been the phone chirping. Probably a wrong number, this time of night. "Who is it?" he said, already starting to drift down into sleep again.

"I don't know," Lucy said. "Some drunk in a bar, I guess. Sounds like they're whistling."

"Mmm . . . well, just hang—" He jerked upright in the bed. "What? Let me have it."

Lucy handed him the phone. She looked mystified in the murky midsummer twilight coming in through the window blinds.

"Grace! Is that you?" He was shouting, trying to make himself heard over the airy little melody he had heard once before, in the dining room at the Triangle Bunkhouse in Dutch Harbor. "Hello? Grace? Stop whistling!"

Lucy got up, pulled on a blue robe, began pacing at the foot of the bed.

The whistling stopped and Grace Palmer said: "You told the police I killed Angie. How could you believe that, Nathan?"

She was slurring her words and he heard bar noises in the background: a jukebox, a muted rush and rumble and clatter of conversation, glasses, bottles.

"Where are you?"

"The Junction, fuck of a lot you care, you—just a minute." He heard a male voice in the background say something about a bottle of Bacardi, then Grace's slurred voice, now muffled by something, perhaps her hand over the mouthpiece, said he could just go out in the parking lot and give himself a blow job if he couldn't wait.

Then her voice came back to normal. "I made up that little song for you, Nathan's Song, and you told them I killed Angie. How could you?" She began to whistle it again.

"You're the logical suspect. I'm sorry."

"Fuck logic! Don't you have a heart?" She was shouting now. "You think I'm lying about my father—."

She covered the mouthpiece again and he heard another muffled shout at whoever was waiting with the Bacardi. "Just a minute I told you, goddamnit!"

She picked up where she had left off, as though there had been no interruption. "—about my father, too, don't you?"

"I don't know."

She gave a low howl, a primal mix of grief and rage. "Nobody who's alive believes me about anything. Angie believed me and my aunt Aggie, but now no one does. I knew I never should have told you." She was silent and he thought he heard her draw on a cigarette, then exhale.

"Look, can I have a friend come get you? He's a cop but he won't arrest you. He'll just take you somewhere where you can sleep it . . . where you can get some sleep."

"Fuck, no, he thinks I killed Angie, too, if he's a friend of yours."

She paused to smoke again. "I have all the friends I need right here on Four Street and they believe me." She covered the mouthpiece and her muffled, drunken voice said, "You believe me, don't you, Jake? Jack? You believe me don't you, Jack?"

She came back on. "See there? Jack believes me. He's not like you."

An operator came on and asked for more money, then coins ka-chinked into the slot.

"Can I talk to Jack?" Active said when the coins stopped dropping.

"What for, so you can tell him I killed Angie and lied about my father? Fuck you, Nathan." She paused again to smoke. "Why didn't you leave me alone?"

He heard her catch herself in mid-sob, and smoke again.

"I came to Dutch Harbor to find Angie. You know that. I didn't know it was you."

"I got away from him and all of it, maybe I wasn't well but I was functional at least. And then you showed up and now the police think I killed Angie and he's got Jeanie, no, I mean Nita—goddammit, just a minute, Jack!—oh, Nathan, how could you goddamn you what the fuck do I oh fuck . . . "

She hung up, or tried to. From the sound of it, she had thrown the phone at its bracket and missed. Now it was dangling on its cord and picking up life at the Junction. He heard Grace Palmer say, "All right, goddammit, let's go," jukebox sounds, someone setting a tray of drinks on a table near the phone, voices crying "Right on!" and "About time!" and "Our angel of mercy." Then the operator came on and asked for more money and he hung up.

He looked up to see Lucy studying him from the foot of the bed, a look of calculation on her face.

"Was that her?"

He nodded.

"Where is she?"

"A bar called the Junction."

"In Dutch Harbor?"

"No, Anchorage. She's back on Four Street."

"Four Street."

He nodded.

"Oh," Lucy said. "That's too bad. I'm sorry to hear it."

The next day was Monday. Once Active had drawn himself a cup of coffee and flipped through the morning's mail, he took a deep breath and dialed Dennis Johnson's number in Anchorage. There was no answer at APD headquarters, just Dennis's voice mail, so Active hung up, turned to his computer, and fished through his inbox until he found Dennis's cell number at the bottom of an email. Dennis answered on the third ring. "Johnson."

Active identified himself and asked how the Angie Ramos case was going.

"I dunno, I haven't talked to 'em about it lately." Active heard traffic noises and the squawk of a police radio in the background, and realized Dennis must be in his blue-and-white.

"Not since they got back from interviewing your beauty queen in Dutch Harbor," Dennis said after the radio quieted down. Apparently the call hadn't been for him. "Why, what's up?"

"Grace Palmer's back in Anchorage."

"No shit!"

"No shit. I thought you might want to pass it along to Homicide."

"You want to do it yourself? There's a Lieutenant Boardman in charge. Let's see, I think I got his card here somewhere, or you can just call Dispatch—"

"No, I'd rather you pass it along. I don't want to be involved in this case in any way if I can possibly avoid it."

Dennis sighed. "Hang on, let me get something to write on, I gotta pull over."

Active heard a few seconds of car noises, then Dennis spoke again. "All right, where is she?"

"She called me from the Junction last night, no, this morning a little after one-thirty. She was pretty drunk and I think she was with some guy named Jack."

"Why's she in Anchorage, you know?"

Active paused, reluctant to go into it. But in a murder case, everything needed to be in the file, even things that seemed irrelevant. "I believe the visit from Homicide pushed her over the edge."

"Yeah, those guys can be pretty rough sometimes."

"Actually, I think it may have been my involvement that did it."

"Your involvement? All you did was pass on what she told you in Dutch Harbor."

"Yep."

"Sorry, man."

"Yep." Active cleared his throat. "Any word on the missing Dispatch logs?"

Dennis chuckled. "Oh, yeah. The DA faked up a search warrant and served it on the chief."

Even through his depression, Active found himself laughing at the picture. "The chief wasn't happy, I imagine?"

"Not at all. He's making noises about how the head of records will be writing parking tickets soon as it starts to snow. The *Anchorage Daily News* even got wind of the search warrant and put it in the Alaska Ear last Sunday."

"Well, I'm sure getting into a gossip column was a learning experience for both of them," Active said.

They said goodbye, and hung up. Evelyn O'Brien had come into Active's office, an evil and triumphant smirk on her face, and dropped a folded note on his desk during his conversation with Dennis. Active flipped it open and groaned when he read the five words scrawled on it: *See Carnaby–animal husbandry–Nimiuk.*

Nimiuk was a village a hundred miles east of Chukchi where a few of the men had developed an inexplicable penchant for gratifying themselves with female dogs. The Chukchi DA and the troopers tried to duck these cases or to let them languish till they winked out or the files got lost. But once in a while an animal husbandry case, as they had become known, turned up that was unduckable and then the law-enforcement apparatus of the great state of Alaska was obliged to rumble forward in its awful majesty. Bestiality was, after all, still on the books as a crime against the peace and dignity of the same great state of Alaska.

Active walked into Carnaby's office and dropped the note onto the desk of the head of the troopers' Chukchi detachment. "Not without a signed complaint from the alleged victim."

Carnaby looked up. "Very funny. Now sit down and shut up."

Active sat, but he didn't shut up. "It's not my turn and anyway these things are unprosecutable because there is no testimony from the victim and then it's just the suspect's word against whatever witness—"

Carnaby held up a large right hand. "This time there's a videotape."

"What? The guy taped himself while he . . ." Active stopped, unable to form words for what must be on the recording.

Carnaby looked down at a page of handwritten notes and nodded. "While he was, ah, involved with a three-year-old malamute female named Jewel. One blue eye, one brown, said by our village public safety officer up there to be a lovely animal. Except he didn't tape himself, Jewel's owner did it with one of those surveillance cameras people use on their babysitters."

Active shook his head. "My God, why? This isn't some kind of, of . . ."

Carnaby grinned. "Love triangle? No, it seems that Jewel belongs to Marcus Ashashik—you know who that is, right?"

"Dog musher? Won the Iditarod a couple years ago?"

Carnaby nodded. "That's him, the pride of Nimiuk. Anyway it seems that Jewel comes from a long line of legendary lead dogs, promises to be one of the finest in that line herself, and Mr. Ashashik is concerned that she might sustain some, ah, injury that would prevent her from perpetuating this famous bloodline."

Active shuddered.

"Precisely," Carnaby said. "The alleged perp, one Willie Piqnaraq, refused Mr. Ashashik's entreaties to cease and desist, including even Marcus's offer of the services of Jewel's litter mate and sister, Alanis by name, said to be equally attractive but sadly devoid of Jewel's abilities as a leader. That, it seems, was the last straw for Marcus, who went down to the school computer lab in Nimiuk and ordered himself the nanny cam on eBay and brought us to the juncture at which we find ourselves today."

Carnaby crossed his arms, leaned back, and beamed at Active. "Open and shut case."

"Why do you need me? Sounds like the VPSO up there has done most of it."

"Not really. His interviewing and note-taking skills are limited, and he doesn't have a tape recorder, and apparently he's got some time off coming and—"

"In other words, it's a family affair?"

"It does happen that the alleged perp is his father-in-law, yes."

Active shook his head in surrender. "All right, what do I have to do? Not watch the videotape, I hope?"

"Yes, I'm afraid you have to see this with your own eyes, Nathan. That, and interview Marcus, and also Willie, if he'll be interviewed after you read him his Miranda rights. You will read him his rights?"

Active flinched inwardly. Had Carnaby heard about the lapse with Grace Palmer in Dutch Harbor? If so, what else had he heard? "Definitely," Active said with a nod.

"Good. Anyway, you can fly up there this afternoon, interview the two of them, or maybe just Marcus, watch the tape, and take Willie into custody. You should be able to wrap it up tomorrow, next day at the latest."

Active looked up from the notebook where he was writing it all down. "What about Jewel? Is she evidence? Do I bring her back?"

"No, I'm sure Marcus will maintain her in satisfactory condition for a court appearance."

Active thought for a moment. "Do we need any, ah, lab work on Jewel? I don't have to take any samples, any swabs, anything like that, do I?" He shuddered again.

Carnaby pursed his lips and shook his head. "I think the

videotape will speak for itself and in any event, Jewel's last encounter with the alleged perp was, let's see here, six days ago, so I'm
sure any lab work would be inconclusive. If Mr. Piqnaraq's defense
wants DNA evidence, let them worry about it."

Active closed his notebook and stood. "But this means I'm off
the hook for a while, right? No more animal husbandry cases for
at least a year?"

Carnaby's eyes narrowed in a judicious squint. "You know,
Nathan, those were really good questions you asked. About bringing in the dog as evidence, the lab work and all? I think you may
have a flair for this kind of case and we've been needing an animal
husbandry specialist—"

Active hurried out and slammed Carnaby's door so he wouldn't
have to hear the rest.

Evelyn O'Brien was waiting outside Carnaby's office, her smirk
more triumphant and evil than ever. She seemed to blame him per-
sonally for the office switchover to Windows computers that had
followed his return from Peer Instruction Training in Anchorage.
She had plastered a sticker on the side of her Apple that said "I'll
give up my Macintosh when they pry my cold dead fingers from the
mouse" and had glared balefully when it was, in fact, taken away
and replaced by a gleaming new Dell.

Since then, she had gloated over every misfortune to befall
Active and he suspected the grudge was why she had not yet brow-
beaten Billy Clarkson into fixing the loose shock absorber on the
Suburban. No doubt she viewed the Nimiuk animal husbandry
case as another opportunity for revenge.

"Here's your travel authorization." She handed him an envelope. "You're all booked on Lienhofer at noon. Bon voyage."

He walked into his office and was just closing his door

when she spoke again: "Hey, Nathan. Makes you want to howl, doesn't it?"

He began to gather what he'd need for the case in Nimiuk, reflecting with something approaching gratitude that it might at least take Grace Palmer off his mind for a few days.

CHAPTER TWENTY-THREE

Two days passed before Active got back to Chukchi, it having proven impossible to wrap up the animal husbandry case before the next day's afternoon flight in from Nimiuk.

He returned with the videotape, with a full account and a signed complaint from Marcus Ashashik, and with a humiliated Willie Piqnaraq, an elderly widower who barely spoke English and whose only statement had been "Better than little girls, like some of these old guys."

After seeing Willie up to the jail on the top floor of the Public Safety Building, Active returned to his office about three-thirty to write up his report on the ridiculous case. He still hoped some fatal defect would present itself, but he was afraid to engineer one because of the Miranda problem in his interview with Grace Palmer in Dutch Harbor. He couldn't afford another screwup any time soon.

His phone rang and he picked it up, grateful for the distraction.

"Guess who's coming up to your office?" Lucy Generous's voice carried an odd charge.

"I don't know, who?"

"Grace Palmer. But she's not wearing lavender." Lucy clicked off before he could say "What?" or anything else.

He rushed into the hall just as Grace topped the stairs, looked the wrong way, then turned and spotted him. The silence stretched on and on.

She was trembling slightly and looked right off Four Street. Dirty jeans, a work shirt mostly covered by a stained, green, waist-length parka. "Hi, Nathan," she said.

She filled the hall with the smell of old cigarette smoke, old booze, old dust, and sweat. One eye was ringed in purple and brown from a two- or three-day-old bruise, and a cut was scabbed over near her right ear. Her face was closed and unreadable, the fox eyes iced over. "Got a minute?"

Wordlessly, he led her past Evelyn O'Brien's wondering eyes to his office and shut the door. He walked behind the desk and motioned for her to sit in one of the chairs in front of it. She remained standing, so he did, too.

"I think I need your help."

"I'm afraid you're beyond my help."

"He's dead, Nathan. The son of a bitch is dead."

"Who's dead," he asked, feeling stupid because he knew already.

"Jason." She crumpled into one of the green chairs and began to sob, the same kind of sob he had heard on the hillside over Captain's Bay.

"How?"

"Shot."

"Are you sure he's dead?"

She nodded. "I think so."

"Where?"

"In his office at the high school."

He picked up his desk phone and punched a button.

"Dispatch." Lucy's tone was cold and professional. She would know from her console who was calling.

"It's Nathan," he said, just in case her console was malfunctioning. "I think Jason Palmer's been shot. Get the EMTs over to his office at the high school right away, and the city cops. And let Jim Silver know."

"Stand by," Lucy said, all business for real, now. She clicked off and the city's hold music, a feed from Kay-Chuck, came on.

She was back in less than two minutes. "Okay, everybody's on their way. Chief Silver asked if we have a suspect."

"Tell him I have one in custody."

"Who? You mean Grace? Grace shot him?"

"Apparently."

"That's terrible." Lucy sounded relieved.

He hung up and looked at Grace Palmer, still crumpled in the chair, but no longer crying, eyes now on her hands. She was toying with the zipper of her parka. Up four inches, down four inches, up again.

"You killed him, huh?"

She raised her eyes to his. "I, I need your help, Nathan."

He returned the gaze for a moment before speaking. "You have the right to remain silent. Anything you say can and will be used against you in a court of law. You have the right to be speak to an attorney, and to have an attorney present during any questioning. If you cannot afford a lawyer, one will be provided for you at government expense."

"Then get me a fucking lawyer, goddammit!" She fished in the big side pockets of the parka, finally pulled out a semiautomatic pistol, pushed his cup of pens and pencils aside, and dropped the gun onto his desk. It bounced onto the paperwork from the Nimiuk case.

• • •

A few days after Jason Palmer's death, Active gave his statement to Silver and Charlie Hughes, the Chukchi district attorney. He told of Grace's arrival in his office with the pistol that the state's Anchorage crime lab had swiftly established as having fired the two bullets that had hit the principal of Chukchi High.

The statement also described Grace's days on Four Street, Active's trip to Dutch Harbor, her seduction attempt, her fantasy of drowning the reflected man, her howl of rage and terror when she learned the orphaned Nita had gone to live with the Palmers, and the call to Active's home from the Junction a few nights before the shooting.

And Active noted that she was the subject of another murder investigation, headed by a Lieutenant Boardman of the Anchorage Police Department's homicide unit, and finished off with a summary of the Angie Ramos case.

"Christ," Silver said after some moments of silence. "What a story."

The chief was tall and paunchy with an acne-cratered face. He had been around Chukchi since before Active was born. Active imagined that Silver would still be there, like the blizzards and mosquitoes, when he, Active, had moved on.

Silver shook his head. "Even for a Chukchi kid, she . . . Jesus."

"No shit," said Charlie Hughes, who sat beside Active across the desk from Silver, blue eyes twinkling above rosy cheeks. Hughes was a reluctant Chukchi resident whose main ambition, Active had gathered from working with him, was to avoid any mistake that might prevent him from being transferred to a warmer jurisdiction as soon as possible.

"Yeah, she's had quite a life." Active shrugged. When he had first told Grace Palmer's story in full, to Lucy Generous, he had been awestruck himself. Now it just depressed him. "So how does this match up with whatever else you've got?"

Silver told him that Jason Palmer had last been seen alive a little after one o'clock on the day he was shot. He had been working in his office at the school, little Nita there with him to give Ida some rest, when Ida had called to remind Nita to go to the store to get some things for dinner. Nita had taken off for Arctic Mercantile and the next thing anybody knew, Grace Palmer was dropping a Colt semiautomatic on Nathan Active's desk. There were no witnesses. With classes out for the summer, the school had been empty, except for some kids playing pickup basketball at the other end of the complex. They hadn't heard a thing.

Hughes rubbed his chin. "It makes me a little uneasy, that it was a call from the mother that got Nita out of his office. I don't know."

Active looked at the prosecutor. "Was that unusual, her sending the girl to the store?"

Hughes shook his head. "Apparently she does it a lot, now that it's hard for her go herself. And the little girl likes it, because she gets to pick the dessert. Routine, according to the people at the store. And Nita, too."

"Then it probably is," Active said. "What does Grace have to say about it?"

"Absolutely nothing," Hughes said. "Her lawyer entered a not guilty plea for her and that's it so far."

Active raised his eyebrows in the white expression for 'go figure.' "Who's her lawyer, anyway?"

"Theresa Procopio," Silver said. "New public defender, Stanford

Law, supposed to be pretty good. I imagine she's out here to keep the big, old evil system from abusing the poor, downtrodden rural Alaskans."

Hughes turned his incongruous, twinkly blue eyes on Active. "I was just wondering why Grace Palmer would surrender to you, Nathan. You have any thoughts on that?" Hughes sucked a little coffee out of a Styrofoam cup, waiting.

"It may be that she thought I would screw up the case." Active said this after some reflection, looking at his knees to avoid Hughes's eyes. "When I interviewed her in Dutch Harbor about the Anchorage homicide, I, um, neglected to Mirandize her. It might have complicated things a little for APD when they took over, but they got it straightened out."

"Yeah, I think we heard something about that," Hughes said.

"Well, she wasn't exactly in custody."

"Still, it's a fine line," Hughes said. "You never hear of a case getting thrown out because a cop did give the warning."

Silver waved a hand, looking sympathetic. "Don't beat him up, Charlie. It happens."

"Not to me." Active shook his head. "Not ever again. Not this time, for sure. When I read her her rights, she threw the gun on my desk, asked for a lawyer, and shut up."

Hughes nodded. "Maybe that's why she came to you, then, hoping she'd get lucky. But there's also some issues with the Colt."

"Did I hear through the grapevine it belonged to her father?"

Hughes nodded again, and pulled some papers from the stack between himself and Silver. "Jason kept it with his hunting gear, which he kept in the basement, according to the mother. Presumably Grace knew from childhood where he kept the gun. So she went to the basement, found it, went over to the school, and shot him."

Active nodded. "Makes sense."

Silver shook his head. "Except Charlie thinks he has a missing bullet."

"The Colt has an eight-round clip," the prosecutor said. "We found five live rounds in it, a slug in Jason, and another one in the wall behind his desk, where it apparently lodged after passing through his hand. And we found the two empty casings on the floor from the two slugs. Five plus two is seven, so where's number eight?"

"Is this a quiz? You tell me."

"We can't tell you, because we can't find it," Hughes said.

"Maybe he only kept seven rounds in the clip."

"We also found a twenty-round box of ammo for the Colt. Eight rounds were missing. So where's number eight?"

"Maybe Jason fired a round," Active said. "To test the Colt or the new box of ammo or something."

Hughes nodded. "Maybe. But why wouldn't he reload the clip before he put the gun away?"

"How important is this?" Active said. "There's always loose ends in a case, right?"

"Right, right, always," Hughes said. "But they worry me, and your juries up here are tough."

"But the gun did kill Jason Palmer and it did have Grace Palmer's fingerprints on it, right?"

"Absolutely," Hughes said. "Right on both counts, and there was residue on her right hand. The lab work is unambiguous." Hughes was nodding, the blue eyes twinkling.

But Hughes's eyes always twinkled, Active had learned, and he still had that look on his face. "But . . . ?"

Hughes shook his head. "But there's no other fingerprints on the gun, just Grace Palmer's. Why aren't Jason's on there?"

Active shrugged. "Good question."

"I don't have the answer either and that worries me, too," Hughes said. "Just like bullet number eight. Missing bullets, missing fingerprints, they all worry me."

Silver flipped a hand in deprecation. "I told him, guns rarely pick up much in the way of fingerprints, too many rough surfaces and too much oil. We were lucky to find Grace Palmer's fingerprints on it."

"I know that, just like everybody else in law enforcement," Hughes said. "But just try to make the jury believe it after Theresa Procopio chews on it for a while."

"Maybe Jason cleaned the gun before he put it away," Active said.

"There you go, Charlie," Silver said. "Didn't I tell you Nathan would come up with something to tell the jury? He's smart, went to the university, the trooper academy." He winked broadly.

"Yeah," Hughes said. "Jason takes it out, fires it once, cleans it so carefully there's not even a smear of a fingerprint left. Then he puts it away without reloading."

"So what are you saying? You don't believe she did it?"

"Oh, I believe she did it, all right. But I got my doubts a jury's gonna believe it with all these little holes. I can just hear Theresa now, telling 'em how Grace found her father dead and did what any conscientious, law-biding, citizen would do, which is to turn the gun over to the cops."

There was a gloomy silence that lasted until the light broke over Active. "We're idiots," he said.

"What?" Hughes and Silver said together.

"The reason we've got these holes is that she put them there," Active said. "She shoots Jason, wipes down the gun to take off his fingerprints, handles it again to leave hers on it, throws away a round of ammunition and presto. Confusion, questions, reasonable doubt."

Hughes puckered his lips and made a sucking sound. "You think she's smart enough to do that, Nathan?"

"Absolutely. Remember the bingo cards and . . . trust me, you never know where the bottom is with her."

Hughes looked depressed. "Shit. We gotta find that other cartridge. Jim?"

Silver threw up his hands and shrugged. "It's not in Jason's office, that's for sure. We went over it with tweezers. She could have pitched it anywhere. In the bay, on the tundra, anywhere."

"I'm fucked," Hughes said. "I know it."

"You think they'll drag in the child-molesting thing to justify her killing Jason?" Active asked.

"They won't need to," Hughes snorted. "I have to drag it in myself. Otherwise, what have I got for a motive? I told you I was fucked."

He looked from Silver to Active, obviously hoping one of them would explain to him why he wasn't fucked. Neither offered any comfort.

Hughes shook his head. "But to answer your question, there's no sign of what they have in mind. Like I said, they ain't sayin' nuttin' yet."

Active flipped through the folders till he found one labeled "Ida Palmer." He scanned it and looked up at Hughes and Silver. "So Grace's mother still insists he never molested her?"

Hughes nodded.

Active shrugged. "Well, there's that. And, Jason was no threat to Grace now, so it wouldn't meet the test for self-defense even if it was true. And her thinking he might molest her cousin someday isn't any kind of justification."

"Legally, no." Hughes's cherubic countenance sagged in depression again. "But the men on the jury are going to see this beauty queen talking about what her father did to her, she'll get tears in those eyes of hers, and they're going to be outraged against Jason Palmer, the ones that aren't jealous of him, and they'll convict him by acquitting her."

Hughes looked more depressed than ever as he continued. "And the women on the jury—how many of them are going to have a daughter or a sister or a girlfriend who went down the same road as Grace Palmer but never came back? Those ladies are going to sit there and tell themselves, 'This is a man's world and it's hard for girls, pretty ones especially, and even if Grace did go too far trying to protect her little cousin Nita, sometimes a woman has to break the rules because it's men that make up these rules.'"

Active studied Hughes with new respect. He was showing unexpected depth.

Hughes looked from Silver to Active and sighed. "What do you think, Nathan? Was she telling you the truth about Jason?"

Active gazed out the office window, not seeing the traffic outside on Church Street or the rain ruffling Heron Lake near the lagoon. Grace Palmer had been convincing in Dutch Harbor, and distraught in the call from the Junction. And something had certainly sent her reeling down Four Street, but there was no way to know what had done it. Perhaps it was nothing more complicated than the susceptibility to alcohol that Eskimos had, or so he believed, because they had first been exposed to it only a few generations before.

"I think she believes it," he said. "Whether it's true, I don't know. She . . . she can be very persuasive."

"That's what I'm afraid of," Hughes said.

Silver cleared his throat. "What was that business her father was talking about? The Electra complex and erotic, ah—"

"Erotomania," Active said. "It's when somebody fantasizes a sexual relationship that doesn't exist. You read about a crazed female fan stalking a male celebrity, that's erotomania."

Hughes nodded. "And the Electra complex has to do with a little girl wanting her mother out of the way so she can have Daddy all to herself. So you put them together and—"

"Daughter gets the hots for dad, never grows out of it, and eventually starts to fantasize the relationship has been consummated?" Carnaby looked at Active, then Hughes.

Both nodded.

"Whew," Carnaby said.

"Uh-huh," Active said.

"You find this Regina Watkins, Charlie? Any hope there? She gonna say it was all in Grace's head?"

Hughes shook his head. "We found her, all right. She works in Kodiak these days, but she's not gonna be much help. She did tell Jason about the Electra complex and the erotomania thing back in the day, but it was pure speculation, because Grace wouldn't talk to her."

"So all she knew was what Jason told her."

"Uh-huh."

"Huh," Silver said.

"Exactly. But let's say I do convince the jury she imagined the whole thing? Where am I then?"

"They let her off for being crazy?"

"Probably. The insanity defense is tough in this state, but maybe."

"So why aren't they asking for a deal?" Active said. "If this Theresa Procopio went to Stanford, she ought to be smart enough to know our side's tied in knots."

"Beats me. Maybe they're shooting for acquittal." Hughes frowned. "Like I said, my motive is her defense, besides which, any juror looking for reasonable doubt has the missing bullet and Jason's missing fingerprints, in addition to whatever else Theresa Procopio can cook up at trial. I'm fucked, I can feel it."

"Aw, cheer up, Charlie." Silver's was jovial, relaxed, the cop who had done his part and handed the case off to the lawyers and the jury and the judge. "You'll feel better when you actually get into court and start examining witnesses and making arguments."

Hughes's blue eyes swung onto Active's. "Why didn't she run? Just get on a plane and find herself another place where people go to disappear like she did after she killed that girl in Anchorage?"

Active stared at Hughes for a moment, thinking over the question. "You talk to her yet?"

Hughes shook his head. "So far, Theresa Procopio has done all the talking, and without saying much of anything."

"She's too tired to run." Active paused and thought it over some more. "It's so deep it doesn't show until you do talk to her for a while, and I'm not sure she sees it herself, but it's there. Something inside her just can't run anymore. I think that's why she came home."

Active stayed out of the case as Grace Palmer was indicted for the murder of her father and the horrible summer dragged on.

The story was big news on Kay-Chuck, but not for long. Grace said nothing, her attorney entered a not-guilty plea and said nothing. Bail was set at a million dollars because of the defendant's vagrant past, and she remained in jail awaiting trial. Eventually, that was not worth saying again, and Kay-Chuck fell silent about the case for lack of developments.

A few days after the arraignment, he heard through the public safety grapevine that Grace Palmer had changed the plea to not guilty by reason of insanity, supposedly over the objections of Theresa Procopio. At least it was an admission of sorts, in case there had been any doubt about who killed Jason Palmer. He pushed it away, grateful again it wasn't his case.

The *Anchorage Daily News* ran a story on the cover of its Metro section, headlined "Bush beauty queen charged in father's murder." But the paper, like Kay-Chuck, didn't mention child molesting, focusing instead on Grace Palmer's days as Miss North World and running the same photograph that was blown up to mural size on the wall at Chukchi High. That, and the mug shot of a gap-toothed Grace Palmer after her prostitution arrest at the Junction. Either the paper had not done enough digging to hear about Grace's charges, Active figured, or it hadn't believed them.

Things went rapidly downhill with Lucy Generous, starting with his loss of interest in sex, simultaneously with his loss of the ability to perform it, as they discovered but never discussed.

What they did discuss, in their final discussion, was clothes.

"Do you have a moment?" It was a Thursday evening and dinner was cooking, but they were no longer doing what they had done earlier in the summer while dinner cooked. Lucy was watching the Alaska news on the state-run Bush satellite feed, while he first paid some bills, then paced, then went to straighten out his closet.

"Lucy? Do you have a moment?" Apparently she hadn't heard the first time.

"Sure, what?" she yelled from the sofa in the tiny living room of the troopers' bachelor cabin.

"Can you come in here for a minute?"

With a bound she was through the bedroom doorway, hope smiling from her face. The smile faded when she saw him standing near the closet and not looking amorous in any way. She stopped and leaned against the door jamb, as if to keep her distance.

"Some of your slacks, your jeans and things, are mixed in with mine again." He pointed into the closet where they both hung their clothes, now that Lucy was staying with him most of the time. Lucy's dresses hung at the left end of the wooden rod, then her blouses, then her slacks and jeans. Then his trousers, then his shirts. At least, that was how it was supposed to work.

"I'm sorry." She shrugged. "I probably wasn't paying attention when I hung them up. I didn't mean to crowd you."

"I'm not saying that. It's just—"

"I said I was sorry."

"I know that. But I don't want you to think I'm an ogre. If you want to dry your bras on the shower rod, you can, or you can leave your curlers in the sink. I don't mind."

"I understand about the slacks, Nathan." She moved to the closet, standing beside him now.

"It's really just a matter of efficiency. If we have to look through each other's clothes to find our own, well, it may take twice as long. You see?"

She looked at him, shook her head, and began rearranging the clothes. "Sure, I see. And I'm sorry I mixed them up. And now I'm putting mine back where they belong."

Finally she pushed her things left a few inches. "There, you see. My clothes aren't even touching yours now."

This last came out through gritted teeth and he knew it was time, past time, to stop this idiotic discussion. He was unable to remember why he had thought it worth starting in the first place.

"I mean, it's small." He said. "Obviously I could live with mixed slacks if I had to, but—"

"It's. All. Right. Nathan." Each word came out like a punch. "I. Under. Stand. It's. Important. To. You."

"No, I shouldn't have mentioned it. I could have moved the slacks myself, like I always did before."

"No, you should bring up things that bother you. How else can we clear the air?"

"It's just that small things accumulate."

She stared at him hands on her hips. "Nathan, it's only clothes. Here, I'll move my slacks and stuff over like this . . ." She lifted the whole section of her slacks from the rod with one hand and with the other slid her blouses over next to his trousers. Then she hung her slacks where the blouses had been. "There, you see. My slacks, my tops, your pants, your shirts. No chance of any more mix-ups. You happy now?"

"Fine, if you're sure you don't mind."

"I don't." She shook her head emphatically. "I promise, I don't care."

"Good, then."

"Good," she said. She paused, studying the clothes. Then she looked at him, eyes squeezed almost shut. "Good nothing!" she shouted. "Goddamn you shit this isn't about clothes and why don't you just say it? Its about her!"

She stumbled out and he heard her doing something under

the sink in the kitchen. He walked to the bedroom doorway just as
she returned with a roll of white trash bags. She peeled one off and
began stuffing it with her clothes, some of them still on hangers.

"Come on, don't do this. What are you doing?"

"Pretty soon me or my clothes won't be mixing up your life."
She had one trash bag full now and peeled another off the roll.

"You don't mix up my life. And when you do I like it."

"Liar! Then why haven't you touched me since that jailbird
beauty queen of yours . . . ah, shit!"

Her end of the closet rod was empty now. She dragged the two
bulging trash bags out to the living room, peeled a new one off the
roll, and stamped into the bathroom. He heard bottles clanking
into the bag as he followed her out of the bedroom, wondering that
they didn't break, wondering that there should be so many. How
far in she had moved!

"Look, I'm sorry about, about . . . you know." He waved a hand
in the direction of the bedroom. "Maybe we could get counseling.
From a minister or something."

"Hah!" She stamped over to the telephone at the end of the sofa.
"You don't want counseling, you want Grace Palmer." She glared
at him. "Don't you?"

He broke the gaze. "I don't know. She's a murderer. Apparently.
Maybe a double murderer."

Lucy picked up the phone and dialed. "Can you send a cab to the
trooper cabin?" She said after a few seconds, "Thanks."

"Don't do that, it's ridiculous. Let me drive you."

"No thanks!" She picked up the three trash bags, dragged them
into the *kunnichuk*, then had to wrestle with the bags to get the
outer door open. "Dammit!" she said before she finally squeezed
through.

She sat on the front stoop in the cold, wind-driven rain that had begun four days earlier and looked as if it might continue until it turned to snow in a few weeks. She was hunched over, head almost between her knees, shoulders shaking.

"At least wait inside till the cab comes. You're getting wet."

Her only answer was to twist around and slam the *kunnichuk* door.

He watched from the living room window, able to see just her right leg from the knee down, and occasionally her right shoulder. Finally an old Ford station wagon pulled up, a sign that said "Arctic E-Z Ride" glowing from the roof. She put her trash bags in the rear seat, got in beside the driver, and the cab pulled away as he marveled again at how much harm it was possible to do with no malice whatever.

He walked into the bedroom and studied the half-empty closet rod, tempted to drink for the first time in his life as he thought of Lucy in the cab, Jason Palmer on Cemetery Bluff, and his daughter in jail on murder charges. What if he had tried harder to bring a child sex-abuse case against the principal? Or to get Grace Palmer arrested for shoving Angie Ramos into the snowplow? Or to love Lucy Generous?

CHAPTER TWENTY-FOUR

Summer drifted on, the rain and west wind becoming almost continuous.

Cowboy Decker came home from the hospital with one leg in a cast from the knee down, a diagonal furrow across his forehead where he had hit something in the Aztec's cockpit, and a distant look in his eyes.

Willie Piqnaraq went to trial and Theresa Procopio packed his jury with elderly Inupiat men. Active watched their disbelief turn to amusement as Hughes played the videotape, and waxed indignant over the depraved acts that Willie, then sitting calmly at the defense table, had committed with Jewel, the fabled lead dog of Marcus Ashashik. Active had been much relieved and not at all surprised when the old hunters and whalers voted to let Willie Piqnaraq go.

Active was sent twice to the village of Ebrulik, once on a bad case, once on a good one.

The bad one was the result of a drunken teenage party on a sandbar on the Isignaq River. A boy, drunk, pushed a girl, also drunk, into the water. She drowned, and there was just enough evidence of intent that it was not possible to avoid charging the boy with manslaughter. He promptly pleaded guilty, against the advice of his attorney.

The good case was a result of the bad case. Two of the party-goers were so depressed by the tragedy that they not only decided to identify the bootlegger who supplied the booze for the party, but agreed to testify as well.

The bootlegger was Donnie Grant, a young Inupiaq just home from a stretch in the Army. Active brought him into Chukchi, put him in jail, and felt reasonably confident he would soon tell how the booze was getting from Chukchi to Ebrulik. Then, the troopers would take down a bootlegging enterprise. True, it would be small and another would spring up in its place, but it would be done without the labor and expense of the troopers mounting an undercover operation of their own.

As for the Grace Palmer case, the grapevine had it that Charlie Hughes and Theresa Procopio were wrangling endlessly over the insanity defense. Would Grace Palmer be sent to Anchorage for psychiatric evaluation, or would a psychiatrist be brought to Chukchi? And was one enough, or would a three-psychiatrist panel be required, as the defense was demanding? And where would the court find the money to finance it all for this virtually indigent defendant? Active stayed as far from it as possible and cultivated numbness. It made the situation at least manageable, which he supposed was the best to be hoped for.

Summer limped into fall. The rain turned into a wet snow that didn't stay on the ground long. Then came a string of ever-shortening sunny days, hard and bright, warm at first, but colder every night until ice glazed the puddles in the mornings and the tundra rusted red-gold along the bluffs back of the lagoon.

Grace Palmer slashed her wrists in jail and was rushed to the

Chukchi hospital. By the time Nathan Active heard about it and, despite himself, went to the nursing station to check on her, she was already patched up, discharged, and back in jail under a suicide watch. Active shrugged it off, resumed numbness, and focused on work.

The village plunged into its fall frenzy, the same as it had each year he had been there, the same, he assumed, as it had each year since the first ancient Inupiaq landed and raised the first tent of caribou hide on the gravel spit that would become known as Chukchi. Hammers pounded until last light, putting up new siding or new roofing. Boats pulled away from the waterfront along Beach Street, headed upriver, came back riding low with loads of arctic char, whitefish, moose or caribou, and gallons of blueberries and salmonberries picked by the women and children as the men hunted or slept. The last cargo barge of the season dropped anchor a few miles offshore, and a fleet of smaller vessels scurried across the shoals, lightering groceries and trucks and snow machines to the Chukchi docks in a wild, excited hurry.

From his office window, Active watched a pair of four-wheelers, their cargo racks loaded with moose meat, sputter past the Public Safety Building towards the back side of town. The lucky hunters pulled up at a house on the next block, and soon the yard was full of women and children and one old man, all admiring the kill and helping unload the meat.

Active turned his attention to the folder open on his blotter, which was the bootlegging case that had grown out of the Ebrulik drowning. It was about time for another chat with Donnie Grant. Time to remind him again that he was sitting in jail while his source in Chukchi walked around scot-free, perhaps loading gear into his boat this moment for a trip upriver to hunt caribou, while

Donnie's girlfriend back in Ebrulik was no doubt doing what girl-friends traditionally did while their men were in jail.

Active's phone chirruped and he picked it up. "Nathan," said the voice of Jim Silver. "You got a minute? I'm up here in my office with Charlie Hughes and we've got a, ah, situation in the Jason Palmer case."

"I'm really not interested. I told you everything I know already."

"Oh, you'll be interested in this. Trust me."

Active sighed, told the police chief "Sure" and headed upstairs, stopping at the machine in the break room to buy a preemptive Diet Pepsi. Silver made the strongest coffee in Chukchi and insisted in serving it in Styrofoam cups in the belief that only petrochemicals could unlock the full flavor of the coffee bean.

Both men stared at him as he entered Silver's office and set the Diet Pepsi on the edge of the chief's battered metal desk.

"You're not gonna believe this, Nathan," Hughes said finally. "I don't know if you heard, but I finally got Theresa Procopio cornered into a put-up-or-shut-up hearing on this damned insanity defense." He looked at his watch. "It's supposed to start in about 45 minutes."

Active nodded, still wondering why he was there.

"You know much about the insanity defense, Nathan?"

Active shook his head.

"That's probably because it's rarely used," Hughes said. "And even more rarely successful, because when it's raised the jury almost invariably comes back with a verdict of 'guilty but mentally ill.'"

"And?"

"And off you go to a home for the bewildered till you get un-crazy," Hughes said. "Then you get to serve your murder sentence. Two stretches for the price of one, sort of."

"Okay," Active said. "But why am I—"

"So all summer I'm wondering, why are they going for insanity? Why risk it?"

"And?"

"And now I know. They weren't risking it. They were stalling. Theresa's filed to withdraw the insanity plea and move for dismissal."

Active started, interested now. "On what grounds?"

"It seems they've got a new perp for us."

"What? Who?"

"Ida Palmer. She's going to confess to killing Jason."

Active was speechless, but only for the moment it took him to realize what was going on. Then he snorted in disgust. "That's bullshit. She's just lying to protect her daughter. How did Grace's fingerprints get on that gun? How did the powder residue get on her hands? Why wasn't there any residue on Ida's hands? You did test Ida, right?"

Hughes nodded.

"Oh, yeah," Silver said. "Her and the kid, too, while we were at it. Both clean."

"So all the evidence points at Grace Palmer. How are they going to explain it away?"

"I don't know." Hughes pulled at his chin and frowned. "But you know, that missing bullet, Jason's fingerprints not being on the gun. I don't like it."

The district attorney sighed. "Maybe Grace Palmer was just decoying us away from her mother till Ida was too sick to try. That would explain why we spent the summer on this insanity nonsense."

"Nonsense is right!"

Both men stared at Active in surprise and it occurred to him that it might be the first time either of them had heard him shout. With an effort, he continued more calmly. "This is nothing more than a dying woman lying to save her daughter. Ida's the decoy, not Grace."

Hughes looked at him with a skeptical expression. "You really think she could be so cold, put her mother up to something like this?"

"Absolutely," Active said. "This is a woman who'll go to bed with anybody for a bottle of Bacardi."

The other two men stared at him through the difficult silence that ensued.

"But what about the suicide attempt in jail," Hughes said. "If she was that unhinged, could she . . ."

"Did she slash her wrists across the veins or up and down?"

"Across," Silver said. "That's why she survived. You have to—"

"—do it longitudinally or the cuts close up again," Active said. "She knew that. She had a friend who tried it and did it wrong and survived. She told me about it in Dutch Harbor. You can't make any assumptions about what she's capable of, or not capable of."

Hughes grunted, scraped his chair backward and stood. "Well, we're not going to figure it out sitting here. Let's go hear what they've got to say." He looked at Active for a moment. "We'd like you to tag along, too, Nathan, give us your reading after Ida's spoken her piece, okay?"

Active felt the case, felt Grace Palmer, sucking at him again and opened his mouth to say no, then felt a surge of fury at the fox-eyed girl who could make him, make any man, believe anything.

"Wouldn't miss it." He rose and headed for the door.

CHAPTER TWENTY-FIVE

The hearing on the motion to dismiss the charges against Grace Palmer took place in the state court building, across Caribou Street from the Lions Club bingo hall and a Korean hamburger joint.

Hughes attempted to have the hearing postponed, on the grounds the dismissal motion was a surprise and there hadn't been time to prepare.

Theresa Procopio, curly haired and intense, said she would agree to a continuance if they would let Ida Palmer give her testimony today. There was some doubt, Procopio advised the court, that Mrs. Palmer's health would permit her to testify at a later date.

"You're saying it's now or never?" asked Judge David Stein, a former legal services lawyer who'd married a local woman and become a true Chukchi-ite, right down to the snow machine, the boat, and the fish camp on his wife's Native allotment up the Katonak River. Stein was clean-shaven, neat-haired, bespectacled and, at the moment, looking highly skeptical and annoyed.

Procopio nodded.

"Then maybe you should have thought of this earlier, counselor," Stein said. "You have consumed inordinate amounts of this court's time over the past few months with your insanity defense, not to mention considerable sums of public money flying expensive psychiatrists back and forth across Alaska. And, now, it's 'Never mind, we didn't mean it'? I have to say, this miraculous last-minute confession raises some ethical questions for me, Ms. Procopio."

"Me, too," Hughes put in. "Your honor, I have to believe that either—"

Stein raised a hand. "I'll take care of this, Mr. Hughes." He swung on the defense attorney. "Ms. Procopio, your insanity defense can hardly have been raised in good faith if you had this alleged confession in your back pocket all the time."

"I knew nothing of it until yesterday, and the insanity defense was never my choice," Procopio said. "Miss Palmer insisted on it, against my advice. As the court is well aware, I twice asked to be excused from representing her because of it. She's a nightmare defendant and this is a nightmare case. Your honor will recall the suicide attempt?"

From his seat behind the railing, Active couldn't see the nightmare's reaction to all this, only the back of her head. Her hair, he noticed, was longer now, almost touching the collar of her blue jail denims. He wondered if they allowed lavender perfume in the Chukchi jail.

Hughes was on his feet. "Alleged suicide attempt, in our opinion, your honor. Trooper Active has told us that Miss Palmer was well aware that a transverse cut to the veins of the wrist wouldn't inflict a life-threatening wound."

"Now, now, Mr. Hughes, that's not the issue before us today," Stein said. "Our issue, one of them at least, is whether Ms. Procopio knew all along that Mrs. Palmer would be coming forward with a confession. If she did . . ."

"If she did, I'm going to object again to Ida Palmer's testimony," Hughes said. "As your honor was suggesting earlier, it clearly indicates the insanity defense was raised in bad faith."

"Your honor, I've made it clear I didn't know about Ida Palmer's role in the murder when I mounted the insanity defense, which, if I may remind you again, the court essentially compelled me to do over my own objections," Procopio said. "I'd be happy to go under oath on that point if the court wishes. So would my client."

Stein shook his head. "That won't be necessary, at least for the moment."

Procopio nodded. "Thank you, your honor. In any event, in light of this development, I felt I had no choice but to bring Mrs. Palmer's evidence forward and move for a dismissal."

"Just how much time have these two been spending together?" Hughes asked. Then he looked at the face of Jim Silver, seated beside him at the prosecution table, and his own face sagged. "Never mind, your honor. I don't think I want to know the answer."

"The court would be interested to know," Stein said.

"I believe Miss Palmer was allowed to visit her mother in the hospital once or twice a week for the past couple of months," Procopio said. "Before that, her mother was well enough to visit the defendant in jail."

Silver sank down in his chair, dodging the glare Hughes shot at him. "It seemed like the human thing to do," Active heard the police chief mutter.

Stein was silent a few moments. Finally he shook his head again, then spoke. "I have to admit, I'm still deeply skeptical of all this, but I think we do have to allow Mrs. Palmer to testify. Her evidence, such as it is, is clearly exculpatory of the present defendant."

"Then let her testify at trial," Hughes said. "That's the time and place—"

Stein held up a hand. "Sorry, Mr. Hughes, but the one thing I am persuaded of here is, as Ms. Procopio claims, that it's likely now or never for Mrs. Palmer's testimony. You'll have to do your best on cross-examination."

"I still see a problem here," Hughes said. "If Ida Palmer is about to confess to murder, does she have representation? Ms. Procopio can hardly represent them both."

"She's waiving her right to an attorney," Procopio said.

"Very well," Stein said. "Will you need some time to bring in your witness, Ms. Procopio?"

"Yes, your honor, about twenty minutes," Procopio said. "Also, with the court's permission, we've arranged for Mrs. Palmer's testimony to be videotaped. As noted, today's proceedings may be her only chance of testifying at her daughter's trial, if it comes to that."

Hughes rose, crying "Your honor!" on the way up.

Stein waved him off. "Save it, Mr. Hughes. You two can argue about admissibility later. We're in recess for thirty minutes."

Fifteen minutes later, Theresa Procopio returned with a young Inupiaq Active didn't know, who set up a video camera and pointed it at the witness box.

Ten minutes after that, a nurse's aide from the hospital pushed a shrunken and frail-looking Ida Palmer into the courtroom. The cameraman fiddled with his equipment, then signaled he was ready. Ida Palmer didn't take the witness stand, but was sworn in below Stein's bench in her wheelchair. Stein verified that she was testifying voluntarily, was waiving her right to counsel, and knew what that meant.

"Whenever you're ready, Ms. Procopio," he said.

Procopio rose and gazed at her witness. Like Charlie Hughes, Procopio was new to Chukchi and still maintained the trappings of urban professionalism. She wore a dark blue business suit with an actual skirt.

"Go ahead, Mrs. Palmer," the public defender said when the formalities were out of the way. The shrunken figure in the wheelchair was silent for a moment, eyes closed. Active noticed the failing liver had now turned her skin yellow. Finally she opened her eyes. The drained face, surrounded by damp strings of silver-streaked black hair, looked incapable of speech, but when she spoke her voice surprised Active with its strength.

"It was me that kill Jason, all right," Ida Palmer began. "I hear him talking to little Nita, my niece, and when I hear what he say I know Gracie always tell me the truth about what he do to her and Jeanie, even if I always never believe it before, and I know he's gonna do same thing to little Nita if I don't stop him." She began to cry, then spoke in Inupiaq, looking at Grace.

"It's okay, *aaka*," Grace said.

"Your honor!" Hughes said.

"Ms. Procopio, your client will refrain from addressing the witness," Stein said.

From behind, Active saw the two dark heads at the defense table nod.

"Mrs. Palmer, do you want Esther here to translate for you?" Procopio pointed at the nurse's aide, who had taken a seat near Active in the front row of the spectator section. "Would you feel more comfortable speaking Inupiaq?"

The woman in the wheelchair shook her head. "No, I know you *naluaqmiuts* will understand me better if I talk in English."

"Okay," Procopio said. "Then why don't you just start from the time when Grace came to see you the day Jason was killed. I think we'll understand it better if you start at the beginning and go up to now, like telling a story."

Ida gave a tired sigh. "Okay, I will." She fell silent as if gathering her energy. For a moment she looked almost dead, except for a subdued fire in the eyes.

"I'm home by myself resting," she began. "Nita's over at the school with Jason, he's catching up on some of his work, when someone knock at the door and it's Gracie. She look terrible, all beat up and smell like a bar, and I tell her to go away because I know what she's going to say about Jason, same old lies as always, that's what I think." She sniffled a little and smiled wanly at her daughter. "But Gracie start crying and she say this one time I have to listen or Nita will end up like her or like Jeanie and something just make me say okay and I finally let her come in."

She closed her eyes for perhaps a minute, then opened them again with the same subdued fire.

Grace, she said, had repeated the old stories about Jason Palmer molesting his two daughters, the same stories Ida Palmer had never wanted to believe and still didn't want to believe.

Finally Gracie had asked where Nita was and when Ida had said she was with Jason at the school, helping him with his paperwork, Gracie had begun to wail, just like Ida herself had wailed when the coffin with Jeanie's ashes was lowered into the ground, and Gracie had said, "That's where he always starts, the school. That's where he always starts." And then Gracie had left, still crying.

After that Ida had tried to rest again, tried to tell herself again that Gracie was just the same crazy, lying daughter as always, but this bad feeling kept growing inside her heart. It was like the cancer that had been growing in her liver all these years since Roy was born and it wouldn't stop growing and she decided she had to go to Jason's office and see for herself.

So she had left the house and crossed the alley to the back door of the school and crept to the door of Jason's office and listened outside. She had heard Jason showing little Nita a biology textbook with pictures that explained about sex. "That's when I know it's true, everything what Gracie always say, because that's what Gracie tell me he say to her when it start, how they could look at the school book to learn about how men and women love each other. Oh, why I never believe her?"

This last came out as a wail and Ida stopped and looked around the courtroom as if someone present could answer the question. When her gaze stopped for a moment on Active, he looked down and waited for her to continue. Finally she started again.

She had dared to take one glance through the window in the office door, and had seen the two sitting side by side looking at the text on little Nita's lap, Jason's one hand resting on her knee as he pointed at the page with the other.

Nita didn't look like she even noticed Jason's hand on her. That was probably because she was so young and trusting and hadn't been around men very much.

But Ida knew she had to get Nita out of there, so she crept down the stairs and went back across the alley to her house and called the office and told Nita to go to the store and Nita said, "Uncle Jason was teaching me biology," not sounding worried or upset at all. Dessert was going to be Nita's favorite that night, Oreo cookies and vanilla ice cream and, yes, Ida had told her, she could eat some

Oreos on the way home, but no more than three, so Nita was happy to go to the store.

After that, Ida had sat in her living room a long time, thinking what to do. And she had decided finally that only one thing was right. She had one daughter that was lost and one that was dead and now there was little Nita who pretty soon might have no one to protect her from Jason.

So she had gone down to the basement and dug Jason's gun out of his hunting gear and gone to the school again and shot him with it, missing his body once and hitting his hand. That had surprised her, because she was pretty good with guns from being around them all her life and from hunting with Jason in his plane before the children came along and he quit flying.

So she had aimed better the second time, hitting him in the chest, the heart, she thought, and she had said, "That's for what you do to my girls."

She had thought he was already dead, sitting there slumped back in his chair with one hand, the hand that was shot, pressed over the spot where all the blood was coming out of his chest. But he had opened his eyes and looked at her and said in a weak, bubbly voice, "Tell her I'm sorry." Then he had slumped forward onto his desk and didn't say anything else or move.

So Ida had returned home, put the gun back in the basement and gone upstairs to think what to do next, maybe call the police and turn herself in because they would probably figure it out anyway, but then what would become of Nita? She had dozed off, awakened, and started thinking about it again when Gracie had come to the door with Jason's gun and asked if she had killed him.

When Ida had told her yes, then Gracie had said she would take care of it, had told her to do some dishes to get the gunpowder off her hands, then lie down and rest until the police came. And Gracie had explained what she should say when the police asked her questions. "After that, I guess you know everything that happen, the police wrote down everything I said when they came to my house."

The courtroom was silent.

Finally Stein spoke. "Any questions, Mr. Hughes?"

Hughes rose and looked at Silver, who shrugged. Then the prosecutor looked at Ida Palmer in her wheelchair, and finally at the defense table. "Mrs. Palmer, we can see you love your daughter very much, is that right?"

Ida nodded.

"And you'd do anything to help her, is that right?"

"Oh, yes," she said. "Like any mother."

"What if you needed to lie for her? Would you do that?"

She seemed surprised by the question. "Of course."

Now it was Hughes's turn to look surprised. He looked at his notes for a moment to recover his composure. "Of course a mother would do that. And are you lying now to save your daughter?"

The tired yellow face smiled. "No, not any more. I was lying before, but now Gracie say it's time to tell the truth, so that's what I'm doing here today."

Hughes opened his mouth, closed it, and looked at the defense table. "Your honor, is our present defendant going to testify here today?"

Procopio nodded. "She is, your honor."

"Then I'd like to reserve any further cross-examination of Mrs. Palmer until we've heard from her daughter."

The judge looked at Ida, then at the nurse's aide who had brought her to the courtroom. "Mrs. Palmer, could you wait in my office a few minutes? We can get you some coffee or tea there, and you can rest on my couch, if you like."

She nodded wearily, and Stein had a bailiff show her and the nurse's aide to his chambers. Then Grace Palmer took the stand and was sworn in.

It was Active's first clear look at her in months. Without thinking about it, he'd been expecting someone who looked crazy, disheveled, wild-eyed—the Grace Palmer who had slammed the pistol down on his desk. But, no, she was the cool, clear-eyed, calculating Grace Palmer of the Triangle lunchroom.

"Miss Palmer, would you tell us what happened after your first visit to your mother's house the day your father died?" Procopio said.

"After mom kicked me out," she began, "I walked around town for a while, then I went over to the old cemetery behind the Arctic Mercantile store and looked at Jeanie's grave. It seemed like all these years had passed and nothing had changed. Nobody believed me and Jason was going to keep . . . hurting little girls."

The quicksilver eyes drifted out of focus, returned. "So I decided to go back to the school and kill him. I couldn't function anymore with him alive and doing what he was doing, so what did it matter if I went to jail again?"

So, she told them, she had gone back home, let herself in quietly, and descended to the basement to see if Jason still kept his pistol there. She had found it, the same old gun as always in its same old holster, the same gun Jason had taught her to shoot when she was only eight or nine, so little the recoil almost knocked her down. She had gone to the school to kill him with his own gun, only to find him already dead, his blood covering the desktop like a red carpet on which, she hoped, he would walk straight through the gates of hell, the son of a bitch.

She stopped and sat back slightly as if recoiling from her own words.

"Anyway," she continued, "I sat in the office and looked at him for a while and I knew it had to be mom, and it made me so happy that she finally believed me and she finally stood up to him after all these years." She fell silent and wiped her eyes with a Kleenex.

"And I just decided the son of a bitch wasn't going to claim another victim if I could help it, so I went and told mom that I'd take care of it, all she had to do was act surprised and say she didn't know anything when the police came and told her I killed Jason."

"Mom didn't want to do it," she continued. "She told me I was still young and she was dying anyway. She was right, but I just couldn't let my mother go to jail for killing that son of a bitch. We had a big fight, and finally I promised, if she didn't get well, if they didn't get a match for a liver donor, then we could tell the truth, like now."

"Then I told her to wash some dishes with a lot of detergent, in case you guys would check her hands for gunpowder, and then I went over to Nathan's office and gave him the gun. I couldn't confess, of course, because of what I promised mom, but I wanted to make sure I was the only suspect for a while." She stopped, with an inward smile and a silver flash from the eyes. Active sensed she was waiting for something, had the old feeling she was ahead of him, ahead of all of them. "And the rest you know."

Hughes was silent, looking over his notes. Then he raised his head. "If you never fired the gun, how did the powder residue end up on your hand?"

"Oh, but I did fire it." Grace's smile widened. "You don't have to watch much television to know about gunshot residue. I went back down into the basement and cleaned the gun and then I fired it into a post down there and I made sure not to wash my hands. You'll find the bullet hole behind an old black snow machine suit hanging from a nail on the post."

Hughes thought for a while before speaking. "And I suppose we'll find the casing in a pocket of the suit?"

Her smile widened even more, her teeth showing now, and she gazed straight into Active's eyes. "No," she said, "I believe you'll find that in a cup of pens and pencils on Trooper Active's desk. I dropped it in there—"

By now, the scene in his office was flashing before Active's eyes, Grace pushing the cup aside as she dropped the Colt on his desk. Had there been a little clink?

"—when I brought him the gun."

She dropped her gaze, so that her smile seemed the reflection of a private joke for a moment. Then she turned her gaze on him again. "You haven't cleaned that cup out lately, have you, Trooper Active?"

"We're fucked." Charlie Hughes glared at Active's desk blotter, where the empty .45-caliber casing they had just extracted from the pen cup lay in a plastic baggie. "Double fucked. Buggered, banged, humped and screwed like Marcus Ashashik's lead dog."

He raised his gaze and fixed it on Active, the twinkle in the blue eyes looking more like a blaze for once. "Nice work, hotshot."

"This doesn't prove anything." Active heard his voice getting high and tight, and tried to calm down. "It's just a stunt to get Grace off the hook. I still can't believe you're buying it."

"Doesn't matter what we're buying," Silver said. "Question is, would a jury buy it? I think they would."

"I agree." Hughes grinned sourly at Active. "You gotta admit,

Grace letting you hold the exculpatory evidence for her was a nice touch. Jury's really gonna love that."

"It's not exculpatory!" Active picked up the baggie with the casing in it and waved it at them. "All it proves is, she shot a post. It doesn't prove she didn't shoot her father."

"So what?" Hughes said. "We're fucked either way. If I bring Grace Palmer to trial and they play that videotape, or worse, have Grace and Ida re-enact it all in court . . . well, the jury won't just acquit Grace, they'll probably convict me of felony time-wasting." He shuddered.

"Which that Procopio woman is well aware of," Silver said.

Hughes shuddered again. "As you know Nathan, we lost your animal husbandry case and there wasn't a soft spot in it, not one. This one's like rotting ice."

Active looked at his knees again, grinning despite himself at the memory of the jury's reaction to Hughes's prosecution of Willie Piqnaraq. "Yeah, that was a bitch, all right."

"No shit," Silver chimed in. "Whole damned system's going to the dogs." He raised a Styrofoam cup to his lips to mask his own smile, but ended up snorting a blast of coffee out his nose, at which point he and Active burst into helpless laughter, all the tension and stress of the day and of the tangled, twisted Grace Palmer case coming out of them in huge, belly-deep guffaws.

"Jesus," Hughes said. "Who did I piss off to get sent up here with you morons? This is serious."

Active finally calmed down and tried to look serious. "All right, so what about Ida, then? Easy conviction, right?"

Hughes grimaced. "Fat chance. No jury's going to convict a dying woman, in the unlikely event she ever gets well enough to stand trial."

"But she just confessed," Active said.

"Trust me on this one," Hughes said. "A jury will be very sympathetic to a woman with terminal cancer in a wheelchair accused of shooting her husband to protect a little girl from being molested. Theresa Procopio will get at least a hung jury."

Active shook his head. "She's representing both of them?"

"If Ida Palmer is charged, yes. That's what she said on the way out today."

"Can she do that?"

Hughes shrugged. "The Chukchi defense bar consists of exactly one attorney: Theresa Procopio. I could raise a little hell about it if we ever get to trial, but we probably aren't going to, and, if we do I probably won't."

"Well, one of them surely did it," Active said. "You have to do something."

Hughes rested his elbows on Active's desk and studied the casing in its baggie. "I think I'll go along with Theresa's motion to drop the charges against Grace, then get an indictment against Ida and suspend proceedings until she's well enough to stand trial, which is obviously going to be never, and release her into the custody of . . . well, the hospital, I guess."

Active shook his head in despair. "Come on, you know Grace did it. She's smarter than God and she's always run circles around me." He grabbed the baggie and shook the casing at them again. "Now she's doing it to you guys, too, and you're letting her."

Hughes shrugged. "I don't know she did it and, like I said, I'm fucked either way. At least this'll clear the books and I won't have another damned acquittal on my record. Kind of a nice package, actually."

Active looked around the office for inspiration and suddenly remembered, "At least check on the Angie Ramos case before you pull the plug here."

"Why?"

"I don't know. Maybe one of you has something the other one can use for leverage. Maybe the Anchorage cops have been talking to the people Grace was with on Four Street before she came up here and one of them heard her say something about going home to kill her father."

"Nah." Hughes grimaced and waved a hand dismissively. "Not worth the time and trouble. Let it go, Nathan."

"Well, then, I'll call them." He reached for his phone, punched the speaker button so they could all hear, then noticed the watch on his wrist. It was now after six, and dark outside except for splotches of orange-white where the street lights hit the sparse falltime snow cover. His shoulders sagged. "Sorry, it'll have to be tomorrow, I guess."

"Yeah, well, call me if you turn up anything," Hughes said. "Just do it before I have to go in front of Stein again at eleven o'clock."

Hughes and Silver stood, scraping their chairs back.

"Don't mind if we take this, do you?" Silver plucked the baggie and casing from the desk blotter.

"Don't worry," Hughes said. "We'll give it back when this is all over. Kind of a souvenir."

CHAPTER TWENTY-SIX

Dennis Johnson didn't answer his desk line the next morning, but Active did catch him on his cell phone.

"So where's the Angie Ramos case?" Active asked after they got the whatcha-been-up-tos out of the way.

"Don't you rem—oh, shit, I forgot to call you, didn't I? I'm sorry."

"What?" Active's throat was so tight the word came out in an adolescent bleat.

"Your beauty queen's off the hook. Cullars came through."

"Cullars? The missing persons guy? No."

"Yep, he found the dispatch logs from the night Angie Ramos was killed. Well, he didn't exactly find 'em. What he did was, he calls up records one day and says, 'When you guys gonna get these archive boxes outta my basement?' "

"You mean—"

"Yep, the logs were there all along. The same boxes that were in the hall when we went to see him."

"Geez, that must have impressed the chief."

"Oh, yeah. The head of records actually got a reprimand in his personnel file. We all thought it was just a rumor till somebody leaked a copy to the *Anchorage Daily News* and it made the Alaska Ear."

"So Grace Palmer's really off the hook? The dispatch log supported her story?"

Dennis chuckled. "Did it ever. Turns out the guy on the cell phone called back about ninety seconds after the first call, said one of the women had left the scene, the bitchy one who said he should give himself a blow job, and was about half a block up Four Street and was going to get clean away if we didn't start acting like cops instead of bureaucrats."

"I guess that pretty much settles it," Active said.

"More than, in Lieutenant Boardman's opinion," Dennis said. "He sends his love to the trooper hotshot and says he's faxing your boss a bill for all the APD time you wasted on this wild goose chase."

"I was just following it all to its logical end."

"Yeah, right. Well, you might wanna break the news to your beauty queen. Homicide might get around to calling her about it or they might not."

"I'll let her know."

"How's that thing up there going, anyway? She really shoot her old man for messing with her when she was a kid?"

Active switched ears with the phone, and was silent so long Dennis said, "Hey, buddy, you there?"

"Yeah, I'm here. Actually, her mother confessed to it yesterday."

"Really? I thought you said she was real sick—lung cancer or something."

"Liver. But she was more or less in remission at the time of the shooting."

Dennis whistled. "That's some tough women you Eskimos raise. I'd grab one if I was you."

"When I need advice—"

"One in particular."

"Yeah."

"Now that she's not a double murderer anymore."

"Yeah."

"So long buddy."

"Yeah, so long."

Active hung up and sat silently at his desk for a long time. Finally he left the office and climbed to the top floor of the Public Safety Building where the city maintained its little jail. An Inupiat matron let him into Grace's cell.

She put down a copy of *Tess of the d'Urbervilles* and smiled. "Sorry about the casing."

He looked away. "The Anchorage police have cleared you in Angie Ramos's death. They finally found the dispatch logs from that night with the cell phone call about you and Angie. Two calls actually. The guy called a second time to report you were leaving the scene and the cops better hurry if they wanted to get both of you."

"Now aren't you ashamed of yourself?"

He turned and stared at her until she looked away to fold down the corner of her page and close the book.

"Look at me," he said.

She turned the fox eyes on him again.

"Who killed your father?"

The eyes were open wide, unblinking, unwavering. "My mother."

He held the gaze a few seconds, then nodded and left.

Back in his office, he dialed Charlie Hughes's number and told the prosecutor Grace Palmer had been cleared in the Anchorage case.

Hughes breathed a relieved-sounding sigh and said he'd also drop his charges against Grace Palmer and get an indictment against Ida Palmer, then seal it and do nothing further unless the widow miraculously regained sufficient health to stand trial.

"So Grace is really in the clear? Under your theory of the case, she obstructed justice to protect her mother, you know."

"Leave the woman alone, Nathan. I've got better things to do with the People's resources than torment Grace Palmer."

"And she committed Oil Dividend fraud in Dutch Harbor."

Hughes sighed again. "I don't want to hear about it. Call the DA in Dutch Harbor."

"Well, you're my official point of contact with the criminal division."

"All right, you did your duty. You reported her. Your conscience is clear."

Time resumed its drift for Nathan Active, the landscape becoming whiter, the days shorter, until the first blizzard of winter blew up from the Bering Sea to the south of Chukchi. For two days and nights the village was locked down as tight as though it were still a huddled cluster of sod and driftwood huts with seal-gut skylights. No jets in or out, the charter fleet grounded, not even the canniest old hunters venturing out by snow machine.

The third day broke to dying winds and clearing skies and a village drowned in white, long fat dunes of perfect titanium white, blue in the shadows, that stretched downwind from the buildings, hundreds of feet downwind in the cases of the high school and the National Guard Armory and the other big buildings. By midmorning he heard a roar from the direction of the airport as the first jet after the blizzard touched down and the pilot hit the thrust revers-ers. By noon the city snowplows had the street in front of his cabin open. After lunch, he dug the Suburban out of its snowdrift and was on his way back to the office when he heard on Kay-Chuck that Ida Palmer had died during the blizzard and would be buried in two days on Cemetery Bluff across the lagoon from Chukchi.

The announcer reminded her audience of Jason Palmer's recent demise, of the charges leveled against his daughter, then dropped, of the mother's rumored indictment on the same charges, now never to be tried.

Active had supposed Grace Palmer would leave town once her mother died, go to Anchorage or Fairbanks—maybe Harvard if she wanted to, with her freakish intellect—to resume her stud-ies, but she stayed on as winter deepened, stayed in the job she had found in the Chukchi administrative headquarters of the Gray Wolf copper mine, which was in the foothills of the Brooks Range a hundred miles north of the village. He heard this through the grapevine, as he avoided contact with Grace Palmer when he saw her on the street or anywhere else.

He also heard that Grace was trying to adopt little Nita, who was gradually recovering from the triple shocks, so close together, of her mother's death in the air crash at Isignaq, of her beloved Uncle Jason's shooting, and of her equally beloved Aunt Ida's death from liver cancer.

One day, he found himself at the dispatch station inviting Lucy Generous to dinner again, hoping she'd say "Where?" so he could say "My place?" just like in the old days. And she almost did, he was pretty sure of that, but then she got a sad smile on her face and said, "I guess not, Nathan. I just hope somebody opens you up someday like you opened me."

He tried to catch her eye, but she was studying her dispatcher's console. "Thank you," he said after a long time. "Thank you for everything."

Not long after that, he started seeing her around town with a young white schoolteacher who hunted a lot and played basketball in the city league. Lucy looked pretty happy, Nathan thought, and he hoped the schoolteacher would be nice to her.

He was thinking this over at his desk one day a couple weeks before Christmas and marveling at how Grace Palmer had upended his life, or perhaps led him to do it himself. It was as incomprehensible as everything else about her.

His phone warbled and when he picked it up, Lucy's voice was carefully neutral. "Grace Palmer's on her way up to see you."

He thought for a moment of hiding in the men's room until she gave up and left, but decided Grace would just come in after him. So he got a fresh cup of coffee from the pot in the main office, returned to his office, and closed the door.

He watched through the window in his door as she came into the outer office and spoke to Evelyn O'Brien. No visible trace of Four Street, no bruises or cuts, no scars except the one on her cheekbone he had seen in Dutch Harbor. Her hair reached almost to her shoulders now, glossy black with just the slightest hint of red-brown when the light hit it right. She was wearing Sorels and jeans and a red knee-length winter parka with a huge fur ruff that looked to be wolf. Her cheeks were slightly flushed from the blizzard wind that, even dying, still rolled across the tundra at perhaps twenty miles an hour.

She was the Grace Palmer of the high school mural again, though grown to full womanhood. And there was one other difference: the old resentment seemed gone, as if it had never burned in the fox eyes. Was such healing possible? With Grace Palmer, perhaps so.

Evelyn O'Brien looked at him questioningly through the window and he nodded. Then he watched as Grace walked to his door, opened it, and took one of his guest chairs, filling the little office with the scent of cold, clean air that usually followed someone in from a winter day. That, and lavender. He thought she would say "Hello" or "Nathan" or something, but she just stared at him.

"Hello," he said finally, and nodded. "How have you been?"

"Not bad, considering I'm an orphan now." The fox eyes twinkled for a moment.

He tried to think of something to say. "Sorry about your mother," he managed, finally.

"Thanks." She nodded. "You've heard I'm trying to adopt Nita?"

He lifted his eyebrows in the Inupiat yes.

"That's what I'm here about," she said. "My history is becoming an issue with the tribal court in Isignaq, to put it mildly. I think it would help if a policeman, particularly an Inupiat policeman, were to vouch for me."

"What could I say that they don't already know?"

"Please?"

It was the first time he had heard her say it, the first time he could remember her asking for anything, except cigarettes.

"If you could just say you believe I'm of good character and I've recovered from the problems that put me on Four Street."

"Have you?"

"Absolutely." The fox eyes flashed as she looked past him, into an indeterminate distance. "When I woke up in a Visqueen lean-to last summer with that guy Jake—"

"I think his name was Jack."

"Was it?" She looked amused that he would remember. "I think you're right. Anyway, I noticed he looked a little like Jason and I thought how they were all a little like Jason somehow. If they didn't look like him, they sounded like him or smelled like him."

She stopped and looked at Active. "I almost feel like we're back at the Triangle. Wouldn't have a Marlboro handy, would you?"

He found himself grinning as he shook his head. "Sorry. This is a smoke-free building."

"Hmm. This is not the Chukchi of my youth. They used to let you smoke in the hospital here." She grinned back. "So I looked at Jake, no, Jack, sleeping it off there in his lean-to and I thought about Cowboy Decker killing my aunt and about Jason up here with Nita and I knew that crash was fate telling me this was never going to be over for me unless I put an end to it or to myself. So I decided to come back home and take care of it, but my mother did it first, God bless her. When I saw Jason slumped over his desk in that office, yes, I absolutely knew that it was over. Like a stone was rolled away from the door of my tomb and I was reborn."

She stopped and thought it over for a few moments. "All of which no doubt strikes you as suiting me perfectly to adoptive motherhood."

"May I see your wrists?"

She bit her lip, then held them out. He reached for them, then decided against touching her and merely bent over them, breathing in lavender. The scars were barely discernible. "That suicide attempt in jail. Another one of your stunts?"

She nodded. "They were going to send me to Anchorage to be evaluated by the shrinks, but I couldn't risk being away from mom. I knew she'd break down and tell the truth. So, a little jailhouse drama and, voila, the shrinks are on their way up here for the evaluation." She shrugged. "I knew it wouldn't kill me, from when Angie tried it."

He lifted his eyebrows. "There's no one in Isignaq to take Nita? No other relatives?"

"Not on my mother's side of the family. I guess Aunt Aggie's husband, my uncle, had a half brother, but they say he never came back to Alaska after he joined the Navy, he must live Outside somewhere." She looked grim for a moment. "Anyway, I'd never turn her over to any man I don't know, not if I could help it. I just . . . I wouldn't."

"What about your brother, Roy?"

"He's overseas and I gather his marriage is falling apart. He's not a candidate."

"Can you support her? I mean, you know how it is with kids. They need braces, the right clothes, CDs—my stepfather says he could afford an airplane if it wasn't for what he spends on basketball shoes for my stepbrother."

She waved a hand as if to fan the problem away like campfire smoke. "Oh, the Gray Wolf pays okay and I have a little savings from Dutch, plus Jason had a few assets, even after mom's medical bills were paid and Roy took his half. Nita and I will get by."

"I'm guessing you already wrote up something for me to sign?"

She smiled and handed him an envelope from her parka. "I did."

He opened it and scanned the letter inside, pulled a pen from the cup on his desk. "I suppose you two will be leaving when the adoption goes through?"

"I suppose," she said. He was surprised by her tentative tone. "I'm not sure about Nita in Anchorage, though. It's been the ruin of many a village girl, you know."

She grinned her fox-eyed grin and he found himself grinning

back, even though she was talking about herself. How could she joke about—.

"You know, you're some kind of freak." Her eyes widened as he went on. "You look like you do, you have that photographic memory, you do that thing with phone numbers, you appear to be physically indestructible, here you are joking about life on Four Street after all that's happened and you, you . . ." The words ran out and he shook his head.

"Amazing Grace, at your service."

"And you—who the hell was Shakespeare's girlfriend, anyway?"

"Emilia Lanier. The Dark Lady of the sonnets."

"I thought she was a big mystery. Didn't he make her up or something?"

She shook her head. "The mystery's been solved for some time now. Emilia was this gorgeous brunette who made quite a career for herself as girlfriend to the high and mighty, not to mention Shakespeare. When she was in her forties and she heard his sonnets were finally going to be published, she rushed into print with her own version of the events recounted in said sonnets." Grace was grinning broadly now. "By that time she was quite churchy and probably not so gorgeous anymore, which may explain why she took such a strong feminist stance against the same activities she had embraced with such enthusiasm as a young dish."

"Such as men defacing the wombs wherein they were bred? Was that the line?"

She nodded with another grin. "Um-hmm."

"How many people in Alaska would know that?"

"At least two, now."

He shook his head. "And you had Charlie Hughes and Jim

Silver chasing their tails on your father's murder. And that stunt with the shell casing in my pencil cup . . ."

"I didn't plan to embarrass you with it, not at first. But when I found it in my parka pocket that day in your office here, I had to do something with it. I was going to ask you to help me keep them away from Ida till she died. But then you assumed right away I did it and gave me that Miranda warning and you were so . . ." She shrugged and smiled. "That's when it dawned on me. I could let you keep them focused on me."

"So you basically winged all of this. Made it up as you went along."

She nodded with a smile. "Mostly. But it worked out well, wouldn't you say?"

He said nothing as she looked into herself for a moment. Then, "What if I don't leave? I could work on my degree through the community college here, I think."

He laid the pen down to cover up his reaction, but she must have seen something in his face.

"What?" she said.

"Nothing. Stay, go, do what you like."

"You don't want me around?"

"It would be very painful to see you every day, considering."

"Considering what?"

He waved his hand in a semicircle to take in all the things too agonizing to enumerate. "It's more than I can explain."

She was silent for a long moment, fiddling with the zipper of her parka. "Nita and I were wondering if you'd like to come to dinner tonight? I mean, for signing the adoption letter and all."

"You cook, too?"

"I can take things out of packages and heat them up, yes. And

I'm sure if it became necessary, I could learn to baste and season and mix and blend and fold and do all those other Martha Stewart things."

He thought it over. It wouldn't hurt to see Grace and Nita together if his name was going to be on a letter of recommendation to the tribal court in Isignaq. "Sure, where are you staying?"

She gave him an odd look. "At our place, of course. My place, now. Roy and I worked it out."

"You're living in Jason's house? Isn't that kind of . . . creepy?"

She shook her head, teeth showing in a wolfish grin. "Nope, I'm enjoying it for the first time since I was twelve years old, now that the son of a bitch is dead."

She looked at the letter, still lying on his desk, and smiled. "Well, you going to sign it or not?"

He looked at it, too. "Who really killed him?"

"I told you. Ida."

He looked down at the letter, then back at her.

"You're never going to know, are you?"

He shook his head. "Never. And I just can't, without knowing. Sorry." He pushed the letter across the desk to her.

"Christ, Nathan, how do you know anything?"

"I see it with my own eyes."

"And if you don't see it with your own eyes?"

"I don't know."

Her face softened and she leaned over the desk and touched his hand. "You poor thing, such a man. Don't you know that belief is all we get? Knowledge is too much to ask."

He was silent.

"Can you think of one thing I ever said to you that turned out to be untrue in any particular?"

Suddenly his eyes were hot with tears and he was blinking rapidly, belief welling up inside him and illuminating the past few months like a sunrise.

"You lied about Nita."

"What?"

"She's not your cousin, is she?"

"No, I—"

"When was she born?"

She lowered her eyes. "Does it matter?"

"Where was she born?"

"Why does that matter?" Her voice was tight.

"She's your daughter isn't she? And Jason's? You had her in Anchorage while you were at the university and somehow you gave her to your aunt to raise and . . . a tribal adoption, right?"

"That's ridiculous."

"Look at me and say that."

Instead she turned away and her shoulders began to shake. "Don't tell anyone. Please?"

"Is this what this was all about, you trying to keep the case out of court because we might find out about Nita somehow?"

She nodded, still facing away, looking out the window of his office. "That, and keeping mom out of jail, yes. I crossed my fingers and stalled the case until she got so sick I didn't think Charlie would be able to try her."

"Wasn't there some chance she'd get well?"

"Not much, but if she did, then I would have pleaded guilty to manslaughter and gone to jail."

"But what about Nita?"

"She'd have stayed with mom till I got out of jail."

"Which could have been a very long time."

She shrugged. "Not that long. Charlie hated this case as much as Theresa did and he was dangling the manslaughter plea right from the start. Theresa thought with credit for time served already, and time off for good behavior, I would have been released to a halfway house in a couple of years. Maybe less."

She turned from the window and studied him, wiping her eyes on the back of her wrist. "Anyway, Charlie and Jim never figured it out about Nita so I was starting to hope it would stay buried with Jason and Aggie and Ida. But now you know and you're so . . . you're such a . . ." She raised her eyebrows in the white expression of inquiry. "Will it? Stay buried? Nita shouldn't have to live with that."

He looked down at the letter until his eyes cleared. Then he coughed, picked up the pen, scrawled his name across the bottom of the page, and handed it to her. "Neither should you."

"Thank you, Nathan." She released a breath he hadn't been aware she was holding, blinked rapidly a few times, folded the letter, and put it back in her parka. "Um, about dinner. Nita's still not sleeping well. I've got her in counseling with the tribal healer, old Nelda Qivits, but she has a ways to go yet."

He nodded, wondering as usual where the conversation was headed and reminding himself as usual that it was pointless to wonder about such things where Grace Palmer was concerned.

She dropped into the chair again. "So the hospital prescribed a sedative, I give it to her after dinner, and she's out like a light till morning."

"Well, I'm sure she needs her rest."

"An earthquake couldn't wake her. Dynamite couldn't."

Suddenly he was remembering again, this time their conversation in the hallway at the Triangle Bunkhouse and what they had told each other on the hillside over Captain's Bay. "What are you, ah, do you mean what, ah . . ."

She nodded and put her hands under her thighs like a nervous schoolgirl. "'Some other time,' that's what we said Dutch Harbor, and I wondered if, now that some time has passed, if you'd like to help me complete my recovery." At his shocked look, she added in a hurried tumble of words, "I told you I don't know how normal people do these things."

"In your father's house?" he croaked through a tight, dry throat.

She looked him squarely in the eye, the most direct gaze he had ever faced. "In his bed, ideally."

"Why me? Of all people?"

"I told you. You came all that way."

"That's no answer."

"Actually, it is." She shrugged. "When I saw you in that lunchroom in Dutch . . . well, I never believed in that sort of thing before, but there it was. One look and I knew."

He cleared his throat and nodded. "And I guess I knew it when your father showed me your picture at Chukchi High. It was stupid, you were either dead or a street drunk, as far as anyone knew, but I, ah, I . . ."

She blinked back tears. "Uh-huh?"

He shook his head. "I'm sorry. I can't talk about these things. I've never been able to."

She nodded and spoke in what struck him as a mother's voice. "With me you can."

He sighed. "I've never been able to trust any woman. Or my feelings about any woman. My, ah, my mother, she, ah, adopted me out. She gave me away and—"

"And another woman took you in."

He nodded. "That's true, I guess."

"And now I'd like to."

He broke their gaze and looked out the window for a moment, then back at her. "I'll be there for dinner, but, about the other, I don't know, I . . ."

The secret, inward smile spread across her face. "Perhaps if you see me with your own eyes," she said. Then she winked at him.

He stared. "You terrify me. You're too large to comprehend."

She smiled again, rose, and turned for the door with a flash from the corner of her eye. She was whistling the little melody she had built on his phone number in Dutch Harbor.

Evelyn O'Brien stared after her as she crossed the outer office and went out the main door into the hall. "What was that song she was whistling? I know it from somewhere."

"It's not a song, it's a piece, and it's called Nathan's Song." He ducked back into his office and closed the door as she hurled a "Thanks, asshole," at his back and returned to her keyboard.

ACKNOWLEDGMENTS

Many people helped bring this story to life, and I thank them all. In particular I salute the assistance of Helen Jung and Jim Paulin, two reporters who told me things about Dutch Harbor I wouldn't otherwise have known, and that of Ron Emmons of the Anchorage Police Department, who told me what happens when an unidentified body turns up in Alaska's largest city. Also, my gratitude to Monette Draper for counsel on the insanity defense, and to Philip M. Hawley and D.P. Lyle for advice on liver disease.

Continue reading for a preview of the next Nathan Active mystery

VILLAGE OF THE GHOST BEARS

CHAPTER ONE

"See why they call it One-Way Lake?"

Cowboy Decker rolled the Super Cub into a slow arc as Alaska state trooper Nathan Active peered over Grace Palmer's shoulder. One-Way Lake was a blue teardrop cupped in the foothills of the Brooks Range, with caribou trails lacing the ridges on either side. The outlet, One-Way Creek, lined with stunted black spruce and a few cottonwoods gone gold, threaded south across the rusting fall tundra toward the Isignaq River. At the lake's head, wavelets licked a fan-shaped talus under a steep slope of gray-brown shale. More caribou trails cut across its face.

Grace was wearing the intercom headset, so Active was obliged to shout at the back of the pilot's head. "Looks pretty tight," he said.

"Yep," Cowboy shouted back. "One way in, one way out. You land toward the cliff and take off going away."

Active lifted one of the headset cups away from Grace's ear. "What do you think?"

She shifted on his lap in the cramped back seat of the Super Cub and turned her head toward him. "I'm game. Anything to get out of this damn airplane."

"Let's do it," Active shouted.

Cowboy leveled the wings and flew a half mile down One-Way Creek in the slanting fall sunlight, then swung back for the approach to the lake. He came in low, floats barely clearing the tree-tops along the creek, chopped the power, and dropped the Super Cub onto the water, throwing up spray that painted a brief rainbow in the air.

Cowboy slowed to taxiing speed and pointed the nose at a spot on the bank that boasted a tiny gravel beach and a stand of spruce on high, dry ground suitable for camping. The floats crunched into the shallows and Cowboy shut off the engine, ushering in a sudden and deafening silence broken only by the slap of their own wake reaching the shore.

Cowboy popped open the Super Cub's clamshell doors, letting in the smell of the Arctic—the wet, fertile rot of tundra vegetation, a hint of resin from the spruce, and something else—something sharp and cool that Active associated with autumn in the mountains near sunset. Winter, perhaps, hovering just over the ridges to the north. It was already a couple of weeks late and couldn't be far off.

Cowboy, wearing jeans and the usual bomber jacket and base-ball cap, pulled up his hip waders and jumped into the shallows. He grabbed the nose of a float, tied on a yellow polypropylene line, and dragged the plane forward a few yards, then walked into the trees and snubbed the Super Cub to a spruce. He returned to the beach and surveyed the lake with an air of great satisfaction. "You get into One-Way this time of year, you got caribou walking by; you got grayling in the creek, maybe some arctic char, maybe some pike in the lake; and you got the best blueber-ries in the Arctic." He raised his eyebrows and grinned. "And you got total privacy. There's only a couple guys can get in here, and you're looking at half of 'em."

Not for the first time, Active marveled at the pilot's intuition, and at his utter lack of discretion in dealing with the insights it brought him. Cowboy might sense that fishing, berry picking, and caribou hunting were the least of their reasons for coming here, but it was none of his business. "We probably oughta get unloaded," Active said.

He helped Grace climb onto a float, then extricated himself from the torture chamber that is the rear seat of a Super Cub and clambered ashore, stamping and stretching to unkink his muscles.

Cowboy walked onto the float and began emptying the cargo pod under the Super Cub's belly and the space behind the back seat: food in cardboard boxes, two cased rifles, two fishing rigs, a bright orange Arctic Oven tent, a Woods Yukon single-double sleeping bag, camp stove and fuel, cooking gear, and all the other impedimenta required to support human life in the Arctic.

Active and Grace ferried gear ashore until finally the plane was empty. Cowboy untied the Super Cub, waded into the shallows, walked the plane back until it floated free, then swung the nose around to point across the lake. "Okay, you two, I'll see you in a week. Enjoy yourselves, huh?" His eyes twinkled behind his steel-frame glasses, and the grin reappeared.

It was not reciprocated.

Cowboy shrugged. "If you run into any trouble, just set off your EPIRB, and somebody'll be along to check on you." They nodded, and he climbed into the plane.

He cranked up and taxied to the foot of the cliff, then turned and put on full power, filling the bowl with the roar of his engine as he accelerated down the lake. They watched as the pilot got onto step, lifted one float clear of the water, then the other, and cleared the trees at the outlet.

As the red-and-white plane shrank to a dot in the sky, Active put his arm around Grace's shoulders, breathing in the scent of lavender. "What do you think?"

She shrugged stiffly. "I don't know yet."

He gave her a squeeze. "Don't sweat it. Good fishin', good huntin', good berry pickin', good weather, good company—who needs the other?"

She looked at him with a quicksilver flash from the corner of her eye. "Every couple does. Otherwise they're just . . ."

"Roommates?"

"Don't say that. I hate that word."

"It's all right if we're roommates for a while," he said. "It'll happen when it happens."

"Feel free to shop elsewhere."

"Thanks, but no thanks."

She turned into his arms and pulled him down for a kiss. "Thank you," she said after a long time.

When they separated, he cleared his throat. "I guess we should do something about getting a camp together."

She nodded. "I'll organize some dinner if you want to set up the tent."

She busied herself putting up a Visqueen awning for the camp kitchen while he stamped about the mossy floor of the spruce grove, looking for the flattest spot big enough for the Arctic Oven. He found one a few yards off, requiring only that he dig out a few rocks and pitch them aside. Then he tugged the tent out of its pouch and spread it on the moss as the sun drifted below the ridge and the basin sank into blue shadow.

Later, in the tent, came the conundrum of the Woods single-double. Each half could be zipped into a bag for one person, or the two halves could be zipped together for a couple.

"One bag or two, madam?" he asked without much optimism.

He studied her face in the buttery light of the propane lantern as she turned it over in her mind. The hunger for normalcy showing as always in her eyes, the desire to please him, and the dread that, if she let him take her, he would be transformed somewhere deep in her wounded psyche into her father, who had been the first man to do so.

"One, I think, kind sir, but no guarantees." Like him, she was playing it light, keeping the escape route open.

"None needed."

He unrolled the bag and zipped it together, stripped down to his shorts and T-shirt, and crawled in. Then he watched her next internal debate: undress with the light on, or off? Put on the long johns, or go for broke in panties and one of his T-shirts?

She looked at him, stuck out her tongue like a twelve-year-old, and closed the valve on the lantern. He listened in a kind of fever dream as clothes whispered off in the darkness and something was pulled on. Long johns, or a T-shirt?

She slid into the bag, and he felt a smooth, hot thigh against his own. She turned toward him for a kiss. Her lips soft and wet, a flicker of her tongue. But when he slid his hand under her T-shirt, she stiffened, quivering. As usual.

He eased his hand off her breast, stroked her hair, and felt her relax. He kissed her cheek and tasted salt.

"Sorry, baby," she said.

"All in good time."

"You know I've started seeing Nelda Qivits again."

"Okay."

She put her hand on his chest, scratched him lightly, sighed, and let the hand trail southward. "Liar."

"Eh?"

"I see things are not altogether all right down there."

"What are you—"

"I think I could—"

"Mmmm, oh, God . . ."

"You should register those hands with the FBI," he said a few minutes later. "They're lethal weapons."

"That would explain why I won the shoot-out," she replied with a giggle.

He laughed out loud, pleased that her joke was dirtier and more original than his own. But how to get into the real issue? "Am I imagining things, or did we just have a breakthrough?"

"Progress, at least." She shifted to put her head on his chest.

He was silent for a time. "What do you think accounts for it?"

"It's just different out here. I don't know."

"Maybe it's being out of that house."

She stiffened again. "Don't overanalyze it. Leave it be."

"I withdraw the remark, your honor."

"Noted." A long moment passed. Then she relaxed again and rolled toward him a bit. The tent was filled with the smells of lavender, sex, and his own sweat, now cooling.

"It was nice, but it does seem a bit one-sided," he ventured at length. "Anything I can do to reciprocate?"

She shrugged. "Someday, maybe. For now, your pleasure is my pleasure."

He flipped back the sleeping bag to cool off and—now that his eyes had adjusted—to admire the curve of her calf thrown across his thigh in the dim light seeping in from the evening sky.

"You know something?" She was serious, suddenly.

"Mmmm?" He was drowsy and hoped this wouldn't get too deep.

"You're so polite."

"Mmmm." He tried to stay drowsy, thinking they could work this out tomorrow, whatever it was. But 'so polite'?

He opened his eyes, resigned to it. "Meaning?"

"I mean, you keep trying, but not too hard. Sometimes I'm not sure how much you want me. With my past, I could understand . . ."

"Well—I mean, my God, look at you. You're the most beautiful . . . what man wouldn't . . ."

She was silent, slightly tense against his side and chest.

"I—are you saying you want to be taken?"

"I don't know. Maybe it's what I need. Some women do."

"By force?"

"Sometimes. If it's someone they trust. They want to be wanted that much."

"Are you one of those women?"

"I don't know. I want to be normal, is all. I just don't know what that is." Her hand drifted south again. "But I see the idea interests you at least a little?"

"Of course." He moved the hand back to his chest. "But I'm not the caveman type. For us, what we have is normal, for now."

"Well, then, have some more of it, on me." She rolled over and kissed him, hard, her hand moving south again. This time, he let it roam.

OTHER TITLES IN THE SOHO CRIME SERIES

Sebastià Alzamora
(Spain)
Blood Crime

Stephanie Barron
(Jane Austen's England)
*Jane and the Twelve Days
of Christmas*
Jane and the Waterloo Map

F.H. Batacan
(Philippines)
Smaller and Smaller Circles

James R. Benn
(World War II Europe)
Billy Boyle
The First Wave
Blood Alone
Evil for Evil
Rag & Bone
A Mortal Terror
Death's Door
A Blind Goddess
The Rest Is Silence
The White Ghost
Blue Madonna
The Devouring

Cara Black
(Paris, France)
Murder in the Marais
Murder in Belleville
Murder in the Sentier
Murder in the Bastille
Murder in Clichy
Murder in Montmartre
*Murder on the
Ile Saint-Louis*
*Murder in the
Rue de Paradis*
Murder in the Latin Quarter
Murder in the Palais Royal
Murder in Passy
*Murder at the
Lanterne Rouge*
*Murder Below
Montparnasse*
Murder in Pigalle

Cara Black cont.
*Murder on the
Champ de Mars*
Murder on the Quai
Murder in Saint-Germain
Murder on the Left Bank

Lisa Brackmann
(China)
Rock Paper Tiger
Hour of the Rat
Dragon Day

Getaway
Go-Between

Henry Chang
(Chinatown)
Chinatown Beat
Year of the Dog
Red Jade
Death Money
Lucky

Barbara Cleverly
(England)
The Last Kashmiri Rose
Strange Images of Death
The Blood Royal
Not My Blood
A Spider in the Cup
Enter Pale Death
Diana's Altar
Fall of Angels

Gary Corby
(Ancient Greece)
The Pericles Commission
The Ionia Sanction
Sacred Games
The Marathon Conspiracy
Death Ex Machina
The Singer from Memphis
Death on Delos

Colin Cotterill
(Laos)
The Coroner's Lunch
Thirty-Three Teeth
Disco for the Departed

Colin Cotterill cont.
Anarchy and Old Dogs
Curse of the Pogo Stick
The Merry Misogynist
*Love Songs from
a Shallow Grave*
Slash and Burn
*The Woman Who
Wouldn't Die*
*The Six and a
Half Deadly Sins*
I Shot the Buddha
The Rat Catchers' Olympics
Don't Eat Me

Garry Disher
(Australia)
The Dragon Man
Kittyhawk Down
Snapshot
Chain of Evidence
Blood Moon
Wyatt
Whispering Death
Port Vila Blues
Fallout
Hell to Pay
Signal Loss

David Downing
(World War II Germany)
Zoo Station
Silesian Station
Stettin Station
Potsdam Station
Lehrter Station
Masaryk Station

(World War I)
Jack of Spies
One Man's Flag
Lenin's Roller Coaster
The Dark Clouds Shining

Agnete Friis
(Denmark)
What My Body Remembers

Leighton Gage
(Brazil)
Blood of the Wicked
Buried Strangers
Dying Gasp
Every Bitter Thing
A Vine in the Blood
Perfect Hatred
The Ways of Evil Men

Michael Genelin
(Slovakia)
Siren of the Waters
Dark Dreams
The Magician's Accomplice
Requiem for a Gypsy

Timothy Hallinan
(Thailand)
The Fear Artist
For the Dead
The Hot Countries
Fools' River

(Los Angeles)
Crashed
Little Elvises
The Fame Thief
Herbie's Game
King Maybe
Fields Where They Lay

Karo Hämäläinen
(Finland)
Cruel Is the Night

Mette Ivie Harrison
(Mormon Utah)
The Bishop's Wife
His Right Hand
For Time and All Eternities

Mick Herron
(England)
Down Cemetery Road
The Last Voice You Hear
Reconstruction
Smoke and Whispers
Why We Die
Slow Horses
Dead Lions

Mick Herron cont.
Nobody Walks
Real Tigers
Spook Street
This Is What Happened
London Rules

**Lene Kaaberbøl &
Agnete Friis**
(Denmark)
The Boy in the Suitcase
Invisible Murder
Death of a Nightingale
The Considerate Killer

Heda Margolius Kovály
(1950s Prague)
Innocence

Martin Limón
(South Korea)
Jade Lady Burning
Slicky Boys
Buddha's Money
The Door to Bitterness
The Wandering Ghost
G.I. Bones
Mr. Kill
The Joy Brigade
Nightmare Range
The Iron Sickle
The Ville Rat
Ping-Pong Heart
The Nine-Tailed Fox

Ed Lin
(Taiwan)
Ghost Month
Incensed

Peter Lovesey
(England)
The Circle
The Headhunters
False Inspector Dew
Rough Cider
On the Edge
The Reaper

(Bath, England)
The Last Detective

Peter Lovesey cont.
Diamond Solitaire
The Summons
Bloodhounds
Upon a Dark Night
The Vault
Diamond Dust
The House Sitter
The Secret Hangman
Skeleton Hill
Stagestruck
Cop to Corpse
The Tooth Tattoo
The Stone Wife
*Down Among
the Dead Men*
Another One Goes Tonight
Beau Death

(London, England)
Wobble to Death
*The Detective Wore
Silk Drawers*
Abracadaver
Mad Hatter's Holiday
The Tick of Death
A Case of Spirits
Swing, Swing Together
Waxwork

Jassy Mackenzie
(South Africa)
Random Violence
Stolen Lives
The Fallen
Pale Horses
Bad Seeds

Sujata Massey
(1920s Bombay)
*The Widows of
Malabar Hill*

Francine Mathews
(Nantucket)
Death in the Off-Season
Death in Rough Water
Death in a Mood Indigo
Death in a Cold Hard Light
Death on Nantucket

Seichō Matsumoto
(Japan)
*Inspector Imanishi
Investigates*

Magdalen Nabb
(Italy)
*Death of an Englishman
Death of a Dutchman
Death in Springtime
Death in Autumn
The Marshal and
the Murderer
The Marshal and
the Madwoman
The Marshal's Own Case
The Marshal Makes
His Report
The Marshal
at the Villa Torrini
Property of Blood
Some Bitter Taste
The Innocent
Vita Nuova
The Monster of Florence*

Fuminori Nakamura
(Japan)
*The Thief
Evil and the Mask
Last Winter, We Parted
The Kingdom
The Boy in the Earth
Cult X*

Stuart Neville
(Northern Ireland)
*The Ghosts of Belfast
Collusion
Stolen Souls
The Final Silence
Those We Left Behind
So Say the Fallen*

(Dublin)
Ratlines

Rebecca Pawel
(1930s Spain)
*Death of a Nationalist
Law of Return
The Watcher in the Pine
The Summer Snow*

Kwei Quartey
(Ghana)
*Murder at Cape
Three Points
Gold of Our Fathers
Death by His Grace*

Qiu Xiaolong
(China)
*Death of a Red Heroine
A Loyal Character Dancer
When Red Is Black*

John Straley
(Sitka, Alaska)

*The Woman Who Married
a Bear
The Curious Eat Themselves
The Music of What Happens
Death and the Language of
Happiness
The Angels Will Not Care
Cold Water Burning
Baby's First Felony*

(Cold Storage, Alaska)
*The Big Both Ways
Cold Storage, Alaska*

Akimitsu Takagi
(Japan)
*The Tattoo Murder Case
Honeymoon to Nowhere
The Informer*

Helene Tursten
(Sweden)
*Detective Inspector Huss
The Torso
The Glass Devil
Night Rounds*

Helene Tursten cont.
*The Golden Calf
The Fire Dance
The Beige Man
The Treacherous Net
Who Watcheth
Protected by the Shadows*

**Janwillem van de
Wetering**
(Holland)
*Outsider in Amsterdam
Tumbleweed
The Corpse on the Dike
Death of a Hawker
The Japanese Corpse
The Blond Baboon
The Maine Massacre
The Mind-Murders
The Streetbird
The Rattle-Rat
Hard Rain
Just a Corpse at Twilight
Hollow-Eyed Angel
The Perfidious Parrot
The Sergeant's Cat:
Collected Stories*

Timothy Williams
(Guadeloupe)
*Another Sun
The Honest Folk
of Guadeloupe*

(Italy)
*Converging Parallels
The Puppeteer
Persona Non Grata
Black August
Big Italy
The Second Day
of the Renaissance*

Jacqueline Winspear
(1920s England)
*Maisie Dobbs
Birds of a Feather*